KISS YOU

"While you were busy being charming and wrecking all my thoughtful plans, I was trying to nail this account." Darcy knew she wasn't being fair but it was easier to fight with him than what she really wanted to do.

"And I wasn't?" He scowled. "I worked my ass off this weekend."

He had. And they'd loved him. "I'll admit you were impressive. But don't let it go to your head. You did what you do every weekend. You played."

"We both worked our asses off, okay?"

"Okay," she conceded. "But I finagled that entire picnic lunch, practically had to promise my first-born child, and didn't get one word of praise from you. Not so much as 'this looks great, Darcy.' All you did was stuff your face."

"You want credit? Fine, I'll give you credit." He leaned over and planted his lips on hers, the move so surprising that Darcy froze.

He rolled over so that he was practically lying on top of her and tucked his hands under her head so he could take the kiss deeper. The pull of his mouth made her forget everything. Her frustration, her disappointment, the fact that they were in her grandmother's house with the door open. She twined her arms around his neck as he explored her mouth with his tongue.

He tasted like beer from the Indian restaurant and desire. So much desire that she lost herself in him. . . .

Books by Stacy Finz

The Nugget Series

GOING HOME
FINDING HOPE
SECOND CHANCES
STARTING OVER
GETTING LUCKY
BORROWING TROUBLE
HEATING UP
RIDING HIGH
FALLING HARD
HOPE FOR CHRISTMAS

The Garner Brothers

NEED YOU
WANT YOU
LOVE YOU

Collections

THE MOST WONDERFUL TIME
(with Fern Michaels, Shirlee McCoy,
and Sarah Title)

SANTA'S ON HIS WAY
(with Lisa Jackson, Maisey Yates,
and Nicole Helm)

Published by Kensington Publishing Corporation

Love You

STACY FINZ

ZEBRA BOOKS
KENSINGTON PUBLISHING CORP.
http://www.kensingtonbooks.com

To my husband, Jaxon.

ZEBRA BOOKS are published by

Kensington Publishing Corp.
119 West 40th Street
New York, NY 10018

All Kensington titles, imprints, and distributed lines are available at special quantity discounts for bulk purchases for sales promotion, premiums, fund-raising, educational, or institutional use.

Special book excerpts or customized printings can also be created to fit specific needs. For details, write or phone the office of the Kensington Sales Manager: Attn.: Sales Department. Kensington Publishing Corp., 119 West 40th Street, New York, NY 10018. Phone: 1-800-221-2647.

Zebra and the Z logo Reg. U.S. Pat. & TM Off.

First Printing: August 2018
ISBN-13: 978-1-4201-4194-8
ISBN-10: 1-4201-4194-5

eISBN-13: 978-1-4201-4195-5
eISBN-10: 1-4201-4195-3

10 9 8 7 6 5 4 3 2 1

Printed in the United States of America

Chapter One

Someone was breathing on Win Garner's neck. Warm puffs of air that felt like dog's breath. Lucy or Ricky? Nah, the two Labrador retrievers lived with his parents. He racked his brain to remember if he'd brought someone home. Maybe that brunette he'd played darts with at Old Glory. Nope. He didn't do that anymore.

He rolled to the other side of the bed and in his half-asleep state, chalked the sensation up to a drafty apartment. Or a dream. Or a ghost. He didn't really care which one because according to his internal clock, he was still on snooze control.

Then it happened again. A soft little tickle across his cheek. He swatted it away and rolled onto his stomach. This time he felt the mattress dip and something brush against his arm. Something warm and distinctly human. The realization startled him awake and he jolted upright.

"What the hell?" He reached for the lamp, thinking once he turned it on he could use it as a weapon. Bad idea because he didn't have a lamp or anything that could be used as a weapon, except a baseball bat, which he kept with his sports gear. And his sports gear was scattered all over his puny apartment, which meant it was probably within arm's reach. Somewhere.

"Shush," someone said in the dark. "It's just me."

He searched his memory for "me" and came up empty. But "me" was definitely female. Soft, round, and very good-smelling. Six months ago, it wouldn't have been too unusual having a strange woman crawl into his bed in the middle of the night. But Win was on the wagon from anything that was bad for him, which included hookups of any variety. Been there, done that, nearly had the shotgun wedding to prove it.

"Who's me?" he asked as the fog began to clear and his brain began to sharpen.

"Darcy."

Darcy? He hadn't met a Darcy that night. The brunette had been an Ida. He remembered because the name was unusual for someone in her thirties. And she'd kicked his ass in eight ball, which was also unusual. The only Darcy he knew was the receptionist at his family's extreme sports company, Garner Adventure.

"Darcy Wallace?" he asked tentatively because if she was here someone he cared about was in the hospital. Darcy and Win's brother, TJ, made the trains run on time at GA. This also entailed notifying the rest of the family whenever an emergency came up. And in the adventure business they came up a lot.

When she didn't answer, he swung his legs off the bed and stumbled in the dark to the light switch.

Holy shit!

Darcy Wallace lay in his bed in a fire-engine red lace teddy, spiked heels, and nothing else. Her breasts were spilling out of the cups of the lingerie and her blond hair curled around her shoulders in a style reminiscent of every high school girl's senior yearbook photo.

Whoa, not the Darcy he knew. Not even close. He shut his eyes, hoping to erase the picture. She was every dude's wet dream and she wasn't supposed to be. She was supposed to be Garner Adventure's office sweetheart, not a freaking centerfold. He opened them just long enough to take two long strides to the bed and flip the covers over her.

"What are you doing here, Darce?" It came out like a growl, not because he was angry, because he was . . . affected. And he didn't want to be.

She wouldn't make eye contact and her face turned as red as the teddy. "I'm . . . uh . . . here for sex."

It was the story of his freaking life. Women loved him. Young, old, single, married, it didn't seem to matter. From the time he was old enough to grow whiskers, they'd been throwing themselves at him. And in the interest of fairness, he'd been throwing himself right back. But not Darcy. She was . . . well . . . a friend. Sort of. The truth was unlike the rest of the female population, Darcy barely gave him the time of day. Until now.

She tossed the blanket off, stretched her arms down at her sides, and lay stiff as a board, like she was waiting for an undertaker to come get her. "Okay, let's get to it then."

He blew out a breath. "Since when am I your type?" he asked, and continued to stand there, a bit shell-shocked, wondering if perhaps this was someone's idea of a practical joke.

Her face got even redder. "You're everyone's type. But apparently, I'm not yours." She jerked the blanket back over her and tugged it up to her chin.

Until six months ago, every woman was his type. He was trying to change that image and Darcy wasn't making it any easier. His gaze flipped to the front door, which he would've sworn he'd locked after coming home from Old Glory.

"How'd you get in?" He checked the clock on his desk, which was cluttered with cups from the Juicery. Jeez, it was two in the morning.

"I have your key, remember?" When he did overnights with GA's tour groups she took care of his cat. Correction: The neighborhood cat that had turned out to be a lousy mouser. Someone had to feed the mangy thing.

He sat in an old, overstuffed chair the last tenant had left behind and ran his fingers through his hair. Pants would probably be good but he didn't know where they were and couldn't seem to focus on anything other than her. "Let me ask you something. How would you react if one of your guy friends showed up in your bedroom in the middle of the night, uninvited? I would hope you'd call the cops."

She sat up and leaned her back against the headboard, clutching the blanket until her fingers looked like they were ready to snap in half. "Is that what you're going to do, call the police?"

Hell no. Win's eldest brother was the police chief. One look at this scenario and Colt would automatically blame Win, accuse him of seducing their shy, little receptionist. Except from where Win was sitting, Darcy wasn't so shy. Or little. From what he'd seen, she was a curvy package, round in all the right places.

And the fact that he was even contemplating Darcy's curves was violating his new policy against casual hookups. But old habits die hard.

"No," he said, and flipped his hand between them. "But I'm still not clear on what you're doing here." Win never would've pegged Darcy as the booty-call type. But it was always the quiet, demure ones who surprised you.

"I told you." She leaned forward and appeared to be summoning her gumption. "Sex. I was in the mood."

"And you just thought you could break into my house, get into my bed, and I'd put out?"

"Exactly." She bobbed her head.

He supposed he had a reputation that was hard to shake. But come on. It was dangerous sneaking around someone's apartment, not to mention disrespectful. On the other hand, Win had never gotten much respect. That's why he was going cold turkey.

"Why do you want sex?" Stupid question. But it was two in the morning and he wasn't firing on all cylinders. "Let me rephrase that. Why do you want sex with me?"

"Because I'm guessing you're good at it and I didn't think you'd make such a big deal out of it. It's not like I'm asking you to marry me."

Not a good enough reason, at least not for Darcy. And not for him to quit his moratorium. "Darcy, you can't just jump into bed with someone for sport."

"Why not? You do it." She had a point.

"Not anymore."

She actually had the audacity to roll her eyes.

"What, you don't believe me?"

She took a strand of hair and curled it around her finger. It was a nervous gesture, not meant to be seductive. Yet, it was sexy as hell. "If I was someone you were attracted to, you would."

He'd been attracted to Ida but he'd come home alone. Proof that he was sticking to the program. "Nope. After Britney I'm a changed man."

Britney, the wack-job blackjack dealer who'd nearly tricked him into marrying her, was now married to someone else. Thank God.

"I would never do what she did to you," Darcy said.

No, she wouldn't dupe him into believing she was

pregnant with his baby when it was really someone else's. "That's not the point, Darce."

"What exactly is the point then, Win?" She gave him a withering glare.

"The point is that you coming here like this in that"—he waved his hand at the teddy that was now concealed under yards of his ugly plaid comforter—"was not a good idea. And it has nothing to do with whether I'm attracted to you. For God's sake, Darcy, we work together."

"So." She shrugged. "It would be a one-night thing. Don't tell me you haven't had flings with some of the tour guides."

Too many to count but Win was taking the Fifth. "What's your sudden interest in sex?" Another asinine question.

Before she turned away, Win caught a new shade of red creep up her cheeks. So, their girl Darcy wasn't getting any. Granted, Glory Junction was a small town but it was so flooded with tourists—hence the reason why an adventure-tour company did so well here—that she should've been spoiled for choice.

"Darce, look at me." When she wouldn't, he walked over to the bed, which was a singularly terrible idea because she looked so vulnerable and sweet huddled under the covers that he was tempted to give her what she wanted. Take one for the team.

"If you'll just turn around, I'll get my stuff and leave," she said, her voice tinged with humiliation.

He looked around the studio apartment, which was roughly the size of his sister-in-law's walk-in closet, and wondered what precisely was Darcy's "stuff." And then he saw the white down puffy coat strewn across his couch. "That yours?" He nudged his chin at the jacket.

"Yes. Could you hand it to me, please?" Darcy clearly didn't want him to get a second look at her in the teddy.

Kind of a disconnect for a woman who five minutes ago wanted to do the nasty.

"It's seventy-five degrees out." June in Glory Junction.

"I know but I don't own a trench coat."

He grabbed the puffy jacket and handed it to her.

"Turn around, please."

Quite frankly, he wanted another look but being a gentleman, he complied. "So how long has it been?"

"Huh?" He could hear the rustling of nylon and a zipper.

"Can I look now." She said "yes" and when he turned back around the Stay Puft Marshmallow Man was taking off her come-fuck-me stilettos. "Since you last got laid?"

"Not that long ago," she said, clearly lying.

"So at two in the morning you got an itch to come over to my place?"

"Something like that. Could you please forget this ever happened?" She looked around his apartment.

It wasn't the best but he didn't need much, mostly just a place to sleep. He put in a fair number of hours guiding everything from extreme skiing expeditions to white-water rafting trips for Garner Adventure. Lately, he'd been thinking about taking on more responsibility at the family business to prove he was more than the Garners' prodigal son. While he and his three brothers owned an equal share of Garner Adventure, everyone but Win had his own calling. Colt, the oldest, was Glory Junction's top cop. TJ, next in line, was GA's CEO and all-around business tycoon. Josh, just a couple of years older than Win, was a former army ranger and war hero.

Other than dropping out of the Olympic team ten years ago, Win's claim to fame was . . . nothing. He was considered the family screw-up. And the Britney shitstorm hadn't helped matters.

"You're not hot in that?" He was sure the puffy coat came in handy during Glory Junction's punishing winters.

But even in his underwear, Win felt the cloying spring night on his skin.

"A little. But I'll be home soon." Darcy lived with her grandmother, Hilde Wallace, on the outskirts of town.

When Win was a kid, the widow Wallace had caught him and his buddies TPing her house. Out of guilt, he'd gone back the next day to clean up the mess and she'd made him cookies and hot cocoa. She'd pretty much been his dream woman ever since.

Darcy had come to live with her about a year ago. That's really all he knew about her background. She hadn't grown up in Glory Junction like the rest of them and they didn't stand around GA, talking about their pasts. Although last winter she'd been the first person he'd confided in about the whole Britney fiasco. It had been the only substantive conversation they'd had since she'd started the job. Darcy was reserved and pretty much kept to herself. That's why her coming here tonight was so out of character.

"Hang on a sec," he told her as she started for the door, then rummaged through his closet. "You can wear this." He tossed her a GA T-shirt that would be long enough to pass for a dress. At least on her.

"Can I change in your bathroom?" She pulled the puffy coat tighter as if she wanted to disappear inside of it and his eyes automatically moved to her breasts.

For a woman who was trying to get him in the sack, she wasn't exactly pulling out all the stops. "Sure."

She vanished inside the john and he took the opportunity to find his jeans and slip them on. When she came out, the T-shirt replaced the jacket, which was slung over her arm.

"You okay?" he asked, feeling like whatever happened here tonight might put a crimp in their work relationship.

"Of course." She stuck out her chin but Win swore her bottom lip quivered.

"No hard feelings, right?"

"Nope. I'm sorry I forced myself on you." And for the second time, those baby blues of hers wouldn't meet his.

"Nah, it wasn't like that. But, Darcy, be careful about whose apartment you break into. It's really not advisable to solicit sex that way."

"You think?" She gave him another classic eye roll. "I only did it with you because I thought you'd appreciate the element of surprise."

Before Britney, before he'd started reevaluating the trajectory of his life, he probably would've appreciated it—and her—way too much. But the times they were a-changing. It was high past the point to show the world that Win Garner had substance, that there was more to him than what everyone chose to see.

"I'll take you home," he said.

"I drove." She dangled her shoes from her finger, found her purse on the floor by the bed, and lifted her face to his chest, blinking a few times.

He went back inside his closet for a shirt. "We'll take your car and I'll jog home." It was only about three miles.

"Don't be ridiculous. It's not like I'm drunk."

He'd sort of wondered, only because this was so uncharacteristic for Darcy.

"I'll at least walk you out." Glory Junction was a safe town but California had its share of kooks, even in rural areas.

"Don't worry about it. I'm good."

He ignored her and found a pair of flip-flops near the couch, grabbed his key ring off the tiny kitchen counter, and put his hand at the small of her back. She led him to her car, which was parked on the street in the front of his complex. Four attached Spanish-style studios that made a square around a grassy courtyard. Not quite the big family home he'd come from just a few miles down the road but centrally located so that he could walk or ride his bike to Garner Adventure on Main Street.

"Careful," he said because she was barefoot and the sidewalk was uneven. "No moon tonight."

She didn't respond, which made things even more awkward than they already were. He searched for something humorous to say that might put her at ease but couldn't think of anything off the top of his head.

When they got to her Volkswagen, she tugged the T-shirt down, even though it already fell to her knees, and gazed up at him. "I don't know what I was thinking coming here like this. You're not going to tell anyone, right?"

He shook his head. "Never."

"Promise?"

"Scout's honor." He held up his right arm and did the three-finger salute. And then for no reason at all he touched her lips with his and kissed her.

Chapter Two

In and out, in and out. Darcy practiced her breathing exercises on the drive home. Exactly the way her therapist had taught her. A year of counseling and she still needed to use the technique to calm herself. And right now, she was one lungful away from a full-blown panic attack.

Of all the boneheaded moves, stuffing herself into a Victoria's Secret scrap of lace, breaking into Win's house, and begging him to do her was right up there with . . . her wedding night. But she didn't want to go there. She'd had enough humiliation in the last hour. No need to reminisce about years past.

She should've known better than to make a fool of herself over a guy who could spend the night with a super-model if he wanted to. But of all the men she knew, Win was perfect for what she had in mind. A one-night or even better, a one-month, stand with her own personal scholar of the Kama Sutra. His reputation as a man who knew his way around a woman's body preceded him.

And while he could charm Darcy's seventy-eight-year-old nana out of her granny panties with just one smile, he wasn't the type of guy someone like her could get serious about, which made him all the more suitable. True, his buff bod, chiseled features, and deep blue eyes were the stuff of underwear commercials, she didn't want to be a nurse maid to a man-child.

But all she'd gotten for her mortifying stunt was a pity kiss, a sort of consolation prize for the weird girl who answered the phones at his family's adventure company and was delusional enough to throw herself at him. How would she ever face him again?

Her cell phone rang and despite Win's rejection, it was hard to be angry with a man who called to make sure her five-minute drive home had gone safely. Who else could it be at this ungodly hour? She pulled into her grandmother's driveway and answered because it would be petty not to.

"Hello."

"Do you know where my red tie with the blue stripes is? I've looked everywhere and can't find it."

"Lewis? Is that you? It's three o'clock in the morning." She kicked herself for not checking caller ID first.

He sighed. "Sorry. You were always a night owl so I thought you wouldn't mind."

Well, she did mind. Divorce meant never having to say find your own goddamned tie. "Last time I saw it"—which was a year ago—"it was in the bottom drawer of the Chippendale highboy in the guest room."

"Walk with me," he said and she rolled her eyes.

Darcy hung on, listening to his breathing as he climbed the stairs and scraped open what sounded like a drawer. "Well, I'll be damned," he said. "You're a peach, Darcy Wallace."

Yes, she was, even if she felt like a failure. "Good night, Lewis." She hung up before he could rope her into something else she didn't want to do.

The sprinklers were on and she zigzagged across the cobblestone walkway, trying to dodge getting wet. Unlike the modern monstrosity Darcy had grown up in or the Reno condo she'd left a year ago, Nana's gardens were filled with flowers. Persian violets, Siberian irises, Oriental poppies, Japanese anemones, and plants Darcy had never heard of.

Her grandfather had built flower boxes for the clapboard cottage before he died and Nana still spent hours every day tending to her aster, English lavender, and meadow rue. What her grandmother couldn't manage, the gardener handled. Darcy's thumb was about as green as a desert summer.

The bursts of color and sweet fragrances from the yard filled her with happiness. And the cozy cottage was more of a home than any place she'd ever resided. Still, she wished her new life held more excitement. Being a telephone operator by day and sleeping alone every night wasn't much different than the existence she'd left behind.

"Darcy, is that you, sweetheart?"

She cringed, wishing she could've snuck in undetected. But Darcy's grandmother slept in a bedroom on the main floor because the stairs to the master suite had become too difficult for her to manage. "It's me, Nana. Sorry I woke you. Go back to bed."

Her gray-haired grandmother padded into the front room in slippers and took Darcy in from head to toe. "Where are your shoes, sweetheart?"

"I left them in the car." It's not like she would be needing them anytime soon. The last time she'd worn them was to her divorce party, a small affair of one at an expensive restaurant where they'd gotten her order wrong and lost her wrap in the coat check.

Her grandmother came around to noticing the T-shirt that hung in folds over Darcy's figure. Lewis's T-shirts had been tight, stretching across her chest like an ACE bandage. "Was it a swim party, dear?"

She let out a breath, hating to lie. But how do you tell

your grandmother you were making a house call for sex? You didn't, even if Hilde was the most progressive seventy-eight-year-old she knew.

"No, Nana, I was working late." Since Darcy put in a lot of hours at Garner Adventure it wasn't too far of a stretch, though three in the morning would've been an all-time record.

"Oh?" Hilde clearly wasn't buying it. But she was good about giving Darcy plenty of personal space so they left it at that. "I made that cake you like if you're hungry."

Chantilly cake. White layer cake with custard filling, whipped cream frosting, and berries from Nana's garden. The cake and all the other good things Nana made in her kitchen were the reason Darcy had gained six pounds since moving to Glory Junction.

"Maybe tomorrow," she said, and dropped a kiss on her grandmother's cheek. "Good night."

Usually up by seven, Darcy slept in until nine. And despite the adage that things would be better in the morning, they weren't. She was still sex-deprived and mortified from the night before. So she showered, went downstairs, and cut herself a huge slice of cake, the breakfast of champions. Through the window, she spied Hilde in a big, floppy hat, holding a pair of flower shears, in the garden.

The house phone rang and when she saw it was Lewis, she let it go. "Why aren't you picking up your cell phone, Darcy?" he asked on the answering machine recording.

"Because I'm no longer married to you, Lewis!" she shouted into thin air, and then kicked herself for not having the balls to pick up the phone and tell him to bugger off. For good.

But Lewis wasn't really a bad guy and the things that

had happened between them were just as much her fault as his. She wanted to stay friends, she really did. But she no longer wanted to be his keeper. Because being Lewis's keeper—and wife—was a full-time job without any benefits. None at all.

She thought about putting in a few hours at GA. But on a Sunday she might run into Win. The spring-summer season was kicking in and Win had back-to-back tours to guide. She knew because she did most of the scheduling at the adventure company when she wasn't fielding phone calls and making doughnut runs. The Garners each had a legendary sweet tooth and an unbelievable metabolism. Probably from all the physical activity they did. Anyway, going to the office today was a bad idea.

She'd have to face Win eventually but today . . . there was cake.

Monday morning, she waited for her number to be called at Tart Me Up, Glory Junction's premier bakery. GA's meeting was at nine, which meant the pastries had to be in the conference room by 8:55, sharp. It was an extremely challenging job. So challenging that an eight-year-old could do it while standing on her head. Six months ago, she'd asked for a promotion. And here she was, still waiting for pastries.

It wasn't that TJ, her boss, was a jerk. In fact, he was the best supervisor she'd ever worked for. High on praise, low on micromanaging. And like all the Garners, he was nice to look at. And taken by the equally adorable Deb Bennett, who also worked at GA. The company, though highly successful, was small and so was its budget. For that reason, things like promotions moved up the family chain at a glacial pace.

In the meantime, she tried to dazzle everyone with her extraordinary organizational skills. And they were extraordinary. It was the reason Lewis had fallen in love with her. At least that's what he'd told her on the day he'd proposed as she drove his Volvo station wagon through the Buggy Bath Car Wash on Jefferson Street. He'd made her take the wheel because car washes gave him claustrophobia. As did movie theaters, nice restaurants, vacations, or any other place she wanted to go. So, for the next two years she ran his office and his home, organizing his life right down to his sock drawer. Then one morning, after one empty bed too many, she decided this was no life. No life at all.

In fact, it mirrored her parents' loveless marriage and the cold, soulless home she'd grown up in. So she filed for divorce, taking only her clothes and severance pay, and moved in with Nana, hoping to start over and find the kind of fulfillment she never did with Lewis.

But she'd been in Glory Junction a year now and hadn't dated once. No one had even asked for her phone number. She'd thought about joining a dating site but one look at the local pool—a sixty-eight-year-old widowed sheep rancher, a twenty-two-year-old avid collector of spherical objects, and a fifty-six-year-old lesbian—and she bagged the idea. The age-appropriate men weren't interested in her, not even a little.

And Win had been downright uninterested, if you didn't count that pity kiss when he'd walked her to her car. She was starting to think she was the problem, not Lewis. Maybe he'd been a cold fish because she lacked any kind of sexual appeal. It wasn't as if she was ugly. She had nice blond hair that was usually clean and tidy, big blue eyes that netted her plenty of compliments, and dimples that made her look younger than her thirty-one years. She might be out of shape and fifteen pounds heavier than a woman five-foot, two-inches tall ought to be, according to the body-mass-index chart at her doctor's office, but no worse off than most women her age.

The kid behind the counter called her number and Darcy gave him her pastry order. Rachel Johnson, the baker and proprietor of Tart Me Up, came out of the kitchen to say hi.

"You must be stocking up for the morning meeting at GA," she said, and threw a few extra cinnamon buns into the box. When women weren't throwing themselves at the Garner brothers, they were giving them free baked goods.

"Yep," Darcy responded, and from the corner of her eye she saw Boden Farmer take a number from the ticket dispenser. The owner of Old Glory, the local watering hole, was gorgeous in a *Sons of Anarchy* kind of way. Tall, ripped, and a little dangerous-looking in his biker boots and chains. And although he was single and roughly the same age as Darcy, he'd never given her a second look.

Rachel handed her the box of goodies over the counter. Darcy thanked her and took her own morning pastry to one of the empty tables. She had fifteen minutes until the meeting started and wanted to eat in peace and quiet. Munching on her cheese Danish, she watched Rachel and the counter kid swiftly serve food and coffee to a growing line of customers. When Boden's number was called he dropped his phone into his back pocket and gave his order. Never once did he acknowledge Darcy, which ordinarily she would've accepted as par for the course. But today it made her feel even more invisible than she usually felt.

She finished eating and was halfway to the door with her pastry box when she worked up the courage to say something. Anything. *Fine morning we're having, Boden.* Or . . . *I've been in your bar a million times to pick up food orders and you can't even greet me? Wave? Nod your head in my direction?*

She spun around, planning to confront him, and smacked into something hard. The impact alone would've smarted enough, except the burn of hot liquid dripping down her sundress distracted her.

"Ah, jeez, I'm sorry." Boden righted her with one strong arm, put down the spilled cup of coffee with the other, and grabbed a wad of napkins from the condiment bar. "Are you okay?"

Darcy plucked the top of her dress away from her chest. "It was my fault. I wasn't watching where I was going . . . I'll pay for your coffee."

"Don't worry about the coffee." He started to pat her down with a towel Rachel had brought from behind the counter and grimaced. "Did it scald you?"

"I have some aloe vera ointment in the first-aid kit. Let me get it," Rachel said, and Darcy wanted to crawl under the nearest table.

"I'm fine. Really. What about you?" The coffee had missed Boden's white T-shirt but had splattered all over his boots. She put down the box, took the towel from him, crouched down, and tried to wipe them dry.

He gently tugged her up. "I've got it."

"But your boots," she argued, "they'll be ruined."

"Darcy, I slosh beer on them all day and night."

Rachel returned with the ointment and began dabbing it on Darcy's chest in the middle of the bakery while the counter kid mopped up the mess. At that moment, she wished she could curl up and die. Then she suddenly remembered the time.

"I've got to go." The meeting. She'd be late.

"You're sure you're okay?" Rachel gave Darcy's dress one final swipe with the towel. The coffee was already starting to dry, leaving a brown stain in the center of her boobs. Great.

"I'm good," she said, and grabbed the pastry carton, jogging the two blocks to Garner Adventure.

By the time she walked in the door she was out of breath and sweaty from the early sunshine beaming down on the newly blacktopped road. Only nine and it was almost eighty degrees. She was on her way to the conference room to leave off the pastries before seeing what she could do about her dress when she bumped into Win, capping off her perfect morning.

He of course looked breathtakingly mussed, like a model in a billboard, advertising a singles gym. A Garner Brothers T-shirt, similar to the one he'd lent her, and a pair of long Adidas shorts, and lots of tan, golden skin.

"What happened to you?" He eyed her breasts and not in a good way.

"Nothing," she said, and tried to walk away.

He caught her arm and flashed his super-white smile. "We still friends?"

"I guess," she said, though she didn't know if she would've ever gone so far as to call them friends. Acquaintances, coworkers, feeder of his cat.

"You guess? What kind of answer is that?" He folded his arms over his mile-wide chest, looking more confused than perturbed.

"I just don't know that we were ever pals, that's all." *Because if you were really my friend you would've done me when I needed it the most.*

"Bullshit! I'm your friend and you're my friend. We're gonna start hanging out."

"No, we're not." She tried to walk away but he wouldn't let her.

"I've got tickets to the Reno Rodeo, box seats one of our clients gave me. Wanna come with me?"

"Uh, A) I hate rodeos, B) why me, you couldn't get

anyone else to go? And C) You don't have to be nice to me just because you kicked me out of your bed." This last part she said in a whisper, not wanting TJ or Deb to hear. Win wasn't as conscientious.

"I didn't kick you out of my bed." He had the audacity to grin, then give her a slow once-over. The rat. "You could've stayed if you wanted but you chose to leave."

"What was the point of staying?" Once he'd turned her down, she'd had the sudden urge to clean and organize his apartment. A habit she was trying to break, even if his place was a disaster.

He shrugged. "We could've talked."

That was the thing about Win, he probably meant it. He was as nice as he was good-looking. Darcy had seen him interact with clients. He was always accommodating with the demanding ones, encouraging with the less-than-athletic ones, and patient with the overeager ones. That's why it hurt so much that he hadn't granted her one small favor. Was she that bad? That unappealing?

"At two in the morning?" she asked, sticking her chin out in challenge.

"Sure, why not?"

She lowered her voice. "But you wouldn't sleep with me?"

"It has nothing to do with you." He gave her another mild once-over. "I just don't do that anymore."

Sure he didn't. Just wait until the next pretty face came along. Win's promiscuity was kind of legendary. His brothers liked to joke about all the various women he went home with. Darcy had hoped that someone with his wealth of experience could teach her some things, primarily how to be more provocative. But he'd made it clear that that wasn't on the table.

"Whatever," she said, wanting desperately to extricate

herself from the conversation and get the coffee stain out of her dress. "You're going to be late for the meeting."

The sunlight streaked through the window, glinting off the gold highlights in his light-brown hair. The stubble on his face looked sexy rather than unkempt. And his T-shirt matched his blue eyes. Why was life so freaking unfair?

"Meet you in there," he said, nudging his head at the conference room. Then he cocked his hip against the wall, blocking her way to the bathroom.

"I need to get by, please."

"Yeah? What's it worth to you?" Again with the obnoxious smile.

"What are you, twelve?" It was too early in the morning for fun and games. Having already made a colossal fool of herself at Tart Me Up, not to mention Saturday night at Win's, she wasn't in the mood.

That was the beauty of Win. Even though he was the type of guy who should've made her stammer and blush, he made her gutsy. With him she felt emboldened to say whatever the hell she wanted and even call him on his presumptuousness. Most of the time she was accused of being mousy.

Her mother "affectionately" called her "the dish towel." Geneva Wallace constantly accused her of being too timid, too complacent, and not outgoing enough. Then again, nothing Darcy did was ever good enough for her mother. Except Lewis. Her parents thought he was the second coming of Christ. And being the pleaser that she was, she'd married him, hoping to finally do something that made her mother proud of her. Big mistake. She supposed she'd become malleable all those years running interference between the war zone that was her parents. But with Win she could say what was on her mind.

"Come on, Darce, go to the rodeo with me tonight. I don't have anyone to take."

"Ah, the truth comes out. Read my lips." She mouthed, *No way in hell*, then managed to squeeze by him, brushing against his front on the way to the bathroom. Everything about him was rock-hard and while their contact only lasted less than a few seconds, a jolt of electricity arced through her. That's how hard up she was.

"Don't kid yourself, Darce, if I wanted to find someone else to go with I could. But I want to go with you."

She eyed him, reconsidering. He was probably up to something but it would be the closest thing she'd had to a date in ages. So why the heck not? It wasn't like there was anything better to do on a Monday night.

As if he knew what she was thinking, he said, "I'll pick you up at six-thirty, then." He pushed off the wall and sauntered into the conference room.

Chapter Three

Win picked through the pastries until he found a cherry turnover. There was no sign of his three brothers yet. Usually, TJ was the first person in the conference room for the Monday morning meeting. Hell, TJ was the first person in the building and the one who turned the lights out at night. Though not so much anymore. Ever since he and Deb had gotten together, TJ had been enjoying life. Which was good, Win supposed, but was going to take some getting used to.

In the last five-and-a-half years since his parents had decided to semi-retire from the company, TJ had been running the show with Josh as his newly appointed wingman. Colt helped out when he could but policing Glory Junction was a full-time job. Besides guiding tours, Win's role in the company was . . . he didn't really have one other than that but was thinking about becoming more active in the day-to-day operation as soon as he figured out what that was.

He heard Darcy in the adjacent kitchenette making coffee. The chick was a head trip. Painfully shy one minute, hopping into his bed the next. But right now, he needed a distraction during his self-imposed female freeze. And the truth was he found her interesting, even if she just wanted to use him for his body. Or maybe that was why. She'd made it clear she wasn't into him in any kind of be-my-boyfriend way—a first and damned refreshing. But her odd behavior the other night piqued Win's curiosity. There was something up with her. And he loved to unravel a good mystery.

"You're here early." TJ came into the conference room, carrying his tablet.

"Where's Deb?" He glanced at his brother's oversize grin and threw up a little in his mouth. Not because TJ had gotten engaged to Win's high school girlfriend—he was cool with that—but because when Garner men fell they looked like drooling idiots. Not Win, though. Even with ample opportunity, he'd never fallen hard and was starting to think there was something wrong with him.

"She had stuff to do," TJ said, and went back to grinning like a loon.

"Let's do this thing." Colt entered in his Glory Junction police uniform and a fresh suntan from his honeymoon. Another drooling idiot. He went over to Win and gave him a noogie. "What's up with you, lover boy?"

"I've got nothing. Where's Josh?"

"Right here." He walked in and immediately started rummaging through the pastry box until he found the other cherry turnover. "No doughnuts today?"

"Darcy went to Tart Me Up," Win said. Usually they got a couple dozen doughnuts from the Morning Glory diner, just down the street.

Darcy brought a carafe of coffee, set it in the center of the table, and took a seat. The front of her dress was wet as if she'd been scrubbing it in the sink and her hair had come loose from its ponytail with frizzy tendrils sticking to the sides of her face. She looked like she'd run a marathon. And lost.

TJ opened his tablet and fired it up, then turned his attention to Win. "How do you know Madison De Wolk?"

Madison De Wolk? Win searched his brain for a connection but the name didn't ring a bell. "I don't. Why, am I supposed to?"

"She's the CEO of FlashTag." When Win gave his brother a blank stare, TJ said, "It's a social media start-up in Silicon Valley. Investors include Elon Musk and Mark Zuckerberg."

"The Facebook dude? Yeah, so?"

TJ exchanged a glance with Colt and shook his head. "She's interested in contracting with Garner Adventure to do corporate team building and she specifically requested you."

"Win?" Josh pretended to choke on his coffee. "Why Win?"

"Isn't that obvious?" Win said blandly. No one could deny he was the king of extreme sports. Before he'd thrown away his chances by quitting the US Olympic freestyle ski team, he'd been a favorite to medal.

"She says she met you on a kayaking trip in Alaska."

Win remembered the trip—seven days at sea, whale-watching in the George Islands—but not De Wolk. He hitched his shoulders. "I don't remember anyone by that name."

TJ tapped the keys on his tablet and turned the screen so Win could have a look. A bio picture of a smoking-hot brunette smiled back at him and a vague recollection of that face tugged at his memory.

"Ah, jeez, you didn't sleep with her, did you?" Colt got up and grabbed a Danish from the box.

"No." He'd taken the trip with Haley, a former GA guide who'd had friends at the Alaska tour company. As a professional courtesy, the company had given them a deal. The trip had been a blast and he and Haley had had a good time together, going their separate ways afterward. Last he'd heard, she'd moved to Costa Rica. "Not that it's any of your business."

"Well it's my business if I'm going to put you on the account, the account we haven't gotten yet," TJ said, and added for emphasis, "The account we could really use to offset the cost of Stanley Royce." Royce, one of their clients, had sued GA after tumbling down a mountainside in a porta-potty. Long story. The short version: GA had settled out of court and instead of having their insurance handle it and watch their premiums skyrocket, they'd dipped into their reserves. The whole fiasco had cost the company plenty and it had happened on Win's watch, putting the blame squarely in his court.

"FlashTag is also looking at another company out of Mammoth. Mountain Adventure. It's between us and them so we need to kill it." TJ turned to Darcy, who as usual never said a word during these meetings. Despite being a closet sex fiend, she was an introvert around his brothers. "I want you on this too."

"Me?" She shrunk back.

Win had to admit it was odd casting. Darcy's knowledge of adventure sports was right up there with Win's experience giving birth.

TJ drummed his fingers on the table. "You still want that promotion? If so, I need both of you to get this account. Win, you dazzle them with the sports stuff and Darcy . . . you keep things organized."

Okay, Win was willing to concede that he wasn't the most systematized. But if someone told him when and where to show up, he brought his A game. He glanced over at Darcy but couldn't get a read on her. Other than doing that twirling thing with her finger and hair, her face remained neutral. Sometimes, he'd catch her at the front desk, talking on the phone, smiling, and those dimples of hers would deepen. It lit him up, those dimples.

"You down with this?" he asked her because sometimes TJ was overzealous and tried to bend people in ways they didn't want to bend.

"I want a promotion." She stared down at her lap.

Win took that as a yes. "Okay," he said. "We're on."

TJ mapped out the plan, which entailed a lot of wining and dining. Not really Win's thing. Give him a kayak, a raft, skis, rock-climbing gear and he was good to go. Otherwise, he was a bit out of his element. And he doubted bashful Darcy was any better at buttering up slick Silicon Valley suits. She was the quiet, studious type. That is when she wasn't breaking into men's homes and jumping their bones.

"Where do we come in?" Josh asked, motioning between him and Colt.

"Anything Win or Darcy wants you to do to make this deal happen," TJ said. "It's Win's contact so he takes the lead."

"So we're resting the future of GA on Win's delicate shoulders?"

Win responded by giving Josh a middle-finger salute.

"Scary, but we aim to deliver and Madison De Wolk wants Win. What can I say? There's no accounting for taste." TJ pretended to shudder.

Win, being the youngest, was often the butt of his family's jokes (though no one was immune from being razzed in the Garner family). Admittedly, part of the teasing he'd brought on himself. Between the carousing and the women, he wasn't taken too seriously. But he was working to rectify his reputation. And if he could help turn around the company . . . Royce had not only cost them a good chunk of change, he'd hurt GA's reputation. In the age of social media, it didn't take much to derail a business. Since the porta-potty incident, GA had seen a drop-off in clients.

He and his brothers would fight with all they had to save their parents' legacy. Gray and Mary Garner founded the company in the 1970s and had weathered recessions, bad investments, and the expense of four college tuitions. But after the Royce setback they couldn't afford to give Darcy a raise with her promotion. Or buy new gear. As far as Win's shoulders being delicate, ha, he wasn't even going to dignify that with a comeback. But more than anything he'd like to prove himself, show the family he was just as important to Garner Adventure as the rest of them.

"Meeting adjourned, then?" Colt fiddled with his cell phone. He didn't like to leave the police station for too long. Jack, his assistant chief, had his back but Colt was a control freak.

All Win's brothers were, making him wonder how that particular trait had skipped him.

After the meeting, he went in search of Darcy, who'd disappeared. Maybe she'd ducked into the john again to work on that stain. It was too early for lunch and Win didn't have a tour until that afternoon. A couple who wanted to go parasailing for their thirtieth anniversary. He couldn't think of a better way of celebrating.

To kill time, he left the building, thinking Darcy might've stepped out too. It occurred to him that he didn't know how she spent her time out of the office and didn't have the first clue where to look for her. So he headed in the direction of Paddle and Pedal on the boardwalk. The company did a killer business in summer, renting everything from kayaks and canoes to bikes and surreys to the tourists. Surrounded by a lake, a river, and five major ski resorts, Glory Junction was an outdoor adventurer's paradise. And Paddle and Pedal was a good spot to connect with prospective clients. Plus, he liked shooting the breeze with the two guys who owned the shop.

Halfway down Main Street a beat-up Chevrolet pickup drew up next to him.

"Where you off to?" Rita Tucker, the town's mayor, asked in her gravelly smoker's voice, and gave him a thorough up and down. "I have some new ideas for the calendar."

"I think I'm out this year, Rita."

She pulled to the shoulder and turned off her engine. Ah, hell, Win didn't want to spend his morning facing off with the mayor over her pervy calendar, even if it did raise tons of cash for the volunteer fire department. But posing, oiled up in nothing but a Santa hat and a holly wreath, was precisely the image he was fighting against.

She pushed open the door and stomped out of the cab. "Since when?"

He tried for diplomacy, instead of telling her the calendar was cheesy as hell. "I think it's time to give someone else a chance. What about Boden?"

"I have him penciled in for March. You've always been December, the Christmas gift that keeps on giving." She cackled while leering lasciviously at his crotch. It made him feel dirty. The woman was almost old enough to be his grandmother.

"What about Chip, then? He hasn't been in the calendar for a while."

"Never again!" Rita's expression went sour.

Back when Chip had been drinking, there'd been an incident. No one knew for sure exactly what had transpired between Rita and the Fish and Wildlife warden. But it had something to do with a bottle of Jim Beam, a bear rug, and a lewd proposition.

He could see they weren't getting anywhere and he didn't want to waste an hour arguing with Rita so he humored her. "All right, let me think about. We've got time."

"Not much."

The calendar came out in January. It was only June. "You can afford a day." Or a week or month. It's not like the calendar was high art or that Annie Leibovitz was taking the photos. Just Rita with her ancient Nikon. He and eleven other local guys, including his brothers, had been volunteer models for the last three years. But Win got the most ribbing for it, including some of the female shopkeepers tacking December up all year long. While he liked the idea of raising money for the GJVF it was, well, embarrassing— and undignified to have his junk on display across town.

"You better make up your mind while I'm still young." She harrumphed, got back in her truck, and drove away. It was hard to believe they let someone like that be mayor.

He continued to the rental shop, wending his way through throngs of tourists who strolled along Main Street and the boardwalk, taking in the sights. There was a line outside of Oh Fudge! And the Morning Glory appeared to still be doing a brisk breakfast business, even though it was past ten. He waved across the street to his sister-in-law, Hannah, who was creating new window displays in her store, Glorious Gifts.

"Looking good," he called, giving her a thumbs-up, and she waved back.

He credited Hannah with saving Josh. After his brother nearly lost his leg in a roadside bombing in Afghanistan, Josh had returned home in a deep funk. The kind of depression you didn't easily come out of. But Hannah had whipped his ass into shape by helping him get through physical therapy and generally not letting him feel sorry for himself. Thanks to good doctors and a succession of successful surgeries, Josh barely walked with a limp anymore. He'd been able to come back to the family business, guiding tours, though Win took the more challenging ones.

When he got to Paddle and Pedal, Sawyer and Ethan were busy assisting two families with bikes. A couple of teenage girls were waiting to rent paddleboards so Win jumped in to give the shop owners a hand. It was a good town that way; everyone helped one another.

When Sawyer and Ethan came up for air, Win shot the breeze with them for a while. He told them about Flash-Tag's interest in Garner Adventure and Glory Junction. Corporate accounts like that were a boon to the entire town. Hotels, restaurants, and shops all benefited from the business. Win tried to remember what he could of Madison De Wolk but nothing was standing out. He'd spent most of his time on that humpback whale–watching trip with Haley.

On his way back to the office, he popped into the Morning Glory, hoping to find Darcy. She wasn't there so he grabbed a tuna melt and ate it at his desk. He didn't like spending time in the office, or indoors for that matter, but part of his plan to become more involved in the day-to-day business at GA was to put in more face time.

Darcy passed his office on the way to the bathroom and he called her in.

"I've been looking for you. What do think of us working together?" He cleared off a chair for her to sit in but she remained standing.

"It'll be weird."

He cocked a brow. "Because you tried to have your way with me in my sleep?" When her face turned fifty shades of red, he said, "For Christ's sake, I'm teasing, Darcy."

"No you're not. You're never going to let me live it down, are you?"

It wasn't as if she were fragile, at least not where he was concerned. She gave as good as she got, so much so that he'd started thinking of her as an honorary Garner. Still, he was pretty sure Saturday night had been an aberration. Darcy didn't strike him as the type who made sex calls in the middle of the night. He started to visualize her in that teeny teddy, got a little hot, and made himself shut it down.

"We've all got weird shit."

"Really?" She sat in the chair and folded her arms over her chest. "What's yours?"

No way was he telling her all his baggage so he stuck with what she already knew. "Britney."

"Britney was a witch. You have nothing to be embarrassed about where she's concerned."

Yet he was. She'd duped him and made him look like a fool to his entire family. Not to mention that the debacle had confirmed their opinion of him as a reckless, irresponsible womanizer. "Let's just say it was an unfortunate situation. The point is we all have them, so get over it."

She let out a breath and gave him a long, hard look that made him hot again. It was just the moratorium, he told himself. It had been a long time since he'd been with a woman. His eyes darted to her breasts.

"You never did tell me what happened." He nudged his head at the stain that had now faded to a discolored, brown-edged kidney shape on the floral fabric of her dress.

"I spilled coffee." She deliberately turned sideways in the chair as if she knew he was checking out her rack. For a small woman . . . He stopped and forced himself to level his eyes at hers. Cornflower blue. And those fucking dimples.

"I guess we should start strategizing." The truth was he'd never had to work for an account. He'd attracted clients to

GA like wasps to a Sunday picnic without much effort. Certainly not because of any sales job he'd done. He just chatted people up, made the less experienced outdoor-sports enthusiasts feel comfortable and the hot dogs know Win would up their game.

"All right. But I have to help TJ with payroll right now."

"We'll come up with a game plan at the rodeo tonight."

She let out an exasperated sigh. "You really think beer-swilling, cheering crowds are a conducive work environment?" Clearly, it was a rhetorical question.

"Yup, I work better in chaos. Jeez, lighten up, Francis."

She looked at him as if he was one electroshock shy of the loony bin. Apparently, she didn't know the movie *Stripes*, his and his brothers' favorite.

"It's Darcy," she said.

"Miss Wallace if you're nasty." Win winked and when nothing registered in that sweet-as-apple-pie face of hers, he blew out a long breath. "Don't tell me you don't know who Janet Jackson is, either?"

She shook her head, got up, and started to leave.

"Don't forget to wear your shit kickers," he called to her back.

Darcy didn't have a pair of cowboy boots; she couldn't get the shaft over her calves. But at six-thirty, Win showed up, wearing a pair of brown suede ones with pointy toes, faded Levis that fit him better than any jeans she owned fit her, and a straw cowboy hat that said HURLEY across the front. He looked more surfer than wrangler with his shaggy locks and golden tan. Actually, he looked like a model in a Guess jeans ad. All he needed was Claudia Schiffer and a motorcycle.

It was a little sickening.

He'd brought Hilde a bouquet of flowers that looked like something he'd picked up outside a gas station. But her grandmother cooed over the carnations like they were the most exotic posies known to mankind. Then she fixed him a sandwich and a glass of milk. He sat at the breakfast bar wolfing down the food, flirting with Nana until she blushed. The man was a serious ho. How had Darcy even managed to repel the sluttiest guy in Glory Junction? It didn't say much for her skills at seduction.

"You ready to go?" she asked impatiently.

"What's your hurry, you got a date with a bull?"

"The only part of the rodeo I like is when the flag girls ride out on horseback for the national anthem and we're going to miss it."

"Yeah, I like that part too." He waggled his brows and she considered smacking him upside the head, except her grandmother wouldn't like it. "Let's go, then."

He took his dishes to the sink, which surprised her. After seeing his studio apartment the other night, she'd gotten the impression that he didn't know what a sink was. On the occasions she'd fed his cat it had taken all her willpower not to clean the place.

They got in his Jeep and made the thirty-five-minute trip to Reno with his radio blaring awful rap music, him drumming the steering wheel, singing at the top of his lungs. A couple of times when they'd stopped at signal lights a car would draw up alongside them and the female driver or passenger would gape at Win like he was a movie star. It was nauseating.

He found a parking spot in the VIP section of a dusty dirt lot that had been marked with chalk lines. A bunch of kids, wearing neon vests, directed traffic. The minute she got out of the Jeep, the smell of manure and hay hit her.

Win grabbed a blanket from the back. Although it was close to eighty degrees out, it got cool in the desert at night.

He looked at his watch. "Shit, if we don't hurry we'll miss the mutton busting."

She snorted. As far as she was concerned mutton busting was sanctioned child abuse. Win guided her across the uneven lot, through the rodeo grounds to their box seats. Oh goody, they were right up front.

Win shielded his eyes and checked out the unobstructed view of the bucking chutes. "These are righteous. You want a beer, some funnel cake?"

She wondered if that last request was a gibe about her weight. "I'm good."

"Are you? You seemed a little sex-starved to me the other night." His lips quirked.

She elbowed him in the ribs. "You promised not to bring that up again."

"No, I didn't. I promised not to tell anyone, which I haven't."

"Wow, such a gentleman. Someone ought to give you a Nobel Prize."

He made a clicking noise with his tongue and made a pair of guns with his fingers. "That's me, gentleman extraordinaire. I'm getting a beer. You sure you don't want one?"

"I'm good," she said, though she wouldn't mind funnel cake.

He must've read her mind because he returned with not only the funnel cake but nachos and a tri-tip sandwich. A beer for him and a soda for her. "I'll start my diet tomorrow," he said, and put the food between them to share.

He was sort of a health nut, she'd noticed, living on green smoothies, acai bowls, and trail mix. It was nice to know that even he had moments of weakness. When she didn't make a move to eat any of his offerings, he fed her a mouthful of funnel cake.

"Come on, Darce, live a little."

"So good," she said in between bites. Deep-fried stuff was her soft spot, though she had a healthy appetite for anything sweet. And fattening. And she sort of liked the idea of him feeding her, even though they were probably making spectacles of themselves.

Win stuffed a few nacho chips in his mouth and washed them down with beer and she was loath to admit that she liked watching him eat. There was something unabashedly masculine about it.

"Shit," she said as a flash of something familiar crossed her periphery vision, then made his way across an adjacent box to get to her.

"Darcy, is that you?" Lewis stood over her in a pair of pressed jeans, a pearl-snap shirt that looked straight off the rack, and a string tie. Who wore a string tie to the rodeo, for Chrissake? He took in their array of junk food and sneered.

"Hi, Lewis. What brings you here?" The dust and animals had to be wreaking havoc on his asthma.

He pointed across the arena at one of the bucking chutes that held a large banner with the Snyder Real Estate logo on it. "I'm a sponsor," Lewis said proudly, and suddenly seemed to notice Win.

Win rose, stuck out his hand, and introduced himself, only to be interrupted by the opening chords of "God Bless the USA." Darcy hoped it would be Lewis's cue to leave but he stood there, looking ridiculous in his Woody from *Toy Story* getup.

When the song was over Lewis turned his attention back to Darcy. "Why haven't you returned my calls and messages?"

"Things have been busy at work."

Win looked from Darcy to Lewis, clearly curious. There

was a long, awkward pause and the announcer heralded that the bronco-bucking event was about to start. Darcy craned her neck past Lewis's shoulder at the ring, feigning huge interest in the hopes he would take a hint and skedaddle.

He didn't.

"How do you two know each other?" Lewis waved his hand between Win and Darcy.

Darcy started to say they worked together but Win cut her off at the pass.

"We're engaged," he said, and she watched Lewis jerk his head so fast that she thought it would snap off. Win draped his arm over her shoulder. "Yep, we're living the dream."

She tried to kick him in the shin but he inched his leg away. Win had good reflexes, she'd give him that.

"You didn't tell me you were engaged." Lewis actually looked hurt, which made Darcy want to tell him the truth, though being Win's fiancée, even if it was only for a few seconds, made her feel vindicated for all the nights she'd slept alone.

"It just happened," Win said. "Saturday night she surprised me by coming over in the middle of the night and—"

This time she managed to land the toe of her tennis shoe in the middle of Win's calf. His boot had probably protected him from the brunt of it but he got the message loud and clear.

He winked at Lewis and said, "Well, you know how it is."

No, Lewis didn't. He was as dense as he was frigid.

"When's the wedding?" he asked, his expression glum.

"Uh . . ." Darcy stammered, and Win deftly came to the rescue.

"Winter," he said. "A destination ski wedding for two hundred in St. Anton, Austria." Whoa, scary how that had just slipped off his tongue. Who knew Win Garner was such an accomplished BSer? Either that or he'd given a great deal of thought to his dream wedding. Doubtful.

"But you don't ski," Lewis said pointedly to Darcy, who

felt her cheeks heat. The farce was getting out of control and it would be Darcy who wound up with egg on her face. No one like Win married someone like Darcy. Of all people, Lewis had to know that, had to know he was being played by a guy who played for a living.

"I gave her lessons last winter," Win said, and Darcy shot him a death glare. Enough was enough.

"Huh." Lewis tilted his head. "Coordination has never been one of Darcy's strong points, has it, Snookums?"

Win's brows shot up and his lips curved in the corners as if to say, *Snookums? Really?*

"Well, it's been great seeing you again, Lewis. But they're getting ready for calf roping and it's Win's favorite event. Isn't it, hot buns?"

Win choked on his own laughter. "Yep. Love me some calf roping."

Lewis wasn't the best at reading social cues but even he realized she'd just told him to get lost. In the nicest way possible, of course. But if he stuck around much longer, Win was liable to tell him more outrageous lies that would wind up humiliating Darcy in the long run.

"I'll be on my way, then." Lewis stood there for a beat. "You'll still help me transfer my records to that new software program, right?"

She'd promised, despite being bogusly engaged to another man. "Of course, Lewis. I'll call you as soon as my workload at Garner Adventure lightens up." He wouldn't wait. Even though it had been more than a year since their split-up, Lewis hadn't been able to let go. At least not of her managerial skills.

Win watched Lewis climb the bleachers to his own seat, then turned to her. "How do you know Howdy Doody?"

"We were married for two years," she said.

Chapter Four

"How come you got divorced?" Win asked on the ride home. It had taken the rest of the rodeo for the fact that she'd been married to sink in. Shy, quiet, horny little Darcy. He never would've guessed it. Not in a million years. Then again, he didn't know much about her personal life. All their conversations had either been work-related or about him.

"It didn't work out," was all she said, signaling that it was none of his business.

Bullshit! If they were going to be engaged he deserved to know.

"Why not?" he asked.

"It just didn't and I'd appreciate it if we didn't talk about it anymore."

"That doesn't seem fair, since I told you about Britney. Jeez, Darce, learn to share." He got into the left lane so he could pass the slowpoke doing forty-five in a seventy-mile-an-hour zone.

"Britney was just another one of your side pieces. Lewis was my husband." She grabbed the oh-shit handle on the roof of his Jeep. "Could you please slow down. This isn't the Indy 500."

He switched back to the slow lane. At least he was in

front of Snail Car. "Britney was almost the mother of my child." She'd been pregnant but as it turned out the father was some dude named Cortland. Britney had waited to give him that little piece of information until after Win had put the Rock of Gibraltar on her finger. "We were engaged."

"For fifteen minutes, which I suppose is fourteen minutes longer than our engagement." She grabbed the bar again. "Watch out for the guy on the left, he's weaving like he's drunk."

"Stop side-seat driving. I've got this." He passed the weaver and took the turnoff for Glory Junction. "We were engaged for nearly a month." The longest month of his life.

"Why'd you tell Lewis we were getting married? For all you knew he was a guy I wanted to date."

He slid her a sideways glance. "That dweeb?" Lewis's jeans actually looked pressed, like he'd put a crease down the middle. And that string tie, WTF?

"Win, I was married to that dweeb."

"We both know you can do better."

She sneered. "Like you?"

"Don't start that again." He got into the slow lane to let some asshole in a Jaguar pass. "You know, Darcy, you used to be sweet." When she'd first started working at GA she was afraid of her own shadow; now she had a smart mouth and a bad attitude. And truth be told he kind of liked it. "For the first time in my life, I'm trying to take responsibility, be a better person. You could be more supportive, you know. So what does Little Lord Fauntleroy do for a living?"

"Don't call him that. He owns a very successful real estate company in Reno. They sell ranchettes, farms, and large parcels."

He turned to look at her and she admonished him to watch the road. "Why, is it doing tricks? Did you used to work at the real estate agency when you lived in Reno?"

"I was Lewis's assistant," she said, and continued to squeeze the grab handle as if he was going to veer off the mountainous road and kill them both.

"You didn't want to stay on after you two broke up?" He was interested. Darcy had always seemed so . . . staid. This new side of her intrigued him.

"I moved here, so how could I?" Reno was only a thirty-minute drive. Twenty if you drove it like he did.

"Why'd you leave Reno?"

"Who are you, Inspector Clouseau?" she said, and glanced at his speedometer. "My grandmother needed me."

Hilde appeared pretty spry to him. She'd lived in that cottage alone since Win was a kid. "If you're not working for Lewis anymore how come you're helping him transfer records?" He didn't know what that entailed but Darcy already had a full-time job.

"Because I said I would." The question appeared to irritate her.

Win got the impression the entire conversation did. Darcy looked cute when she was irritated so he kept up his rapid-fire questioning until they were parked in front of Hilde's house.

"You want to grab dinner at Old Glory?" he asked, not quite ready to end the evening, even if it was a school night. He looked at the clock on his console. Shit, it was past eleven.

"We just stuffed our faces—and clogged our arteries— with fake cheese and grease. You're still hungry?"

"I just thought we could talk about the FlashTag account. We never got around to it at the rodeo."

"Is Old Glory even still open?" She gazed out the window at Hilde's house. There were a few lights on, besides the one on the porch. "My grandmother's up. I better go inside."

"All right," he said. It was late and he had a white-water rafting tour at ten. "Thanks for going with me."

"Thanks for taking me. It was . . . fun."

Did it kill her to have to say that? In the past, he'd gotten very few complaints from women about his company. Right off the top of his head, he could think of quite a few women who would've been happy to spend the evening with him at the rodeo, or anywhere for that matter. And after meeting Lewis, Win had to think he was a better date.

"Yep," he said, and helped her out of the passenger seat only because her Lilliputian legs might not find the ground on their own. And since he was already out of the Jeep he walked her to the door. "I'd kiss you good night, but I'd hate to get you all hot and bothered and have you break into my apartment again."

She threw it right back at him. "As long as we're engaged I wouldn't want you to break your vow of chastity. It's good that you're saving yourself for our wedding night."

Unassuming Darcy had become a real smartass.

"See you tomorrow." He jogged down the cobblestone walkway and got back in his Jeep.

The neighborhood cat was on his front porch when he got home so he let it in the house and gave it a bowl of milk. The thing was probably full of fleas. He put his phone on the charger stand and noticed he had a few missed calls and checked his voice mail to see if anyone had left a message.

The first one was from Deb. She and TJ were having a family dinner at their house on Wednesday and wanted to know if Win could come. The next three were from women who all held various levels of interest in hooking up with him. He quickly erased their messages and got ready for bed.

He was still trying to wrap his head around the fact that Darcy had been married when he drifted off to sleep and forgot to set his alarm. By the time he dragged his ass into work the next day, he had less than an hour to load the gear for the rafting trip and meet his group at the river.

"You look like a sack of shit." TJ passed him in the hallway with his standard greeting. "Darcy made a pot of coffee in the kitchenette. Madison De Wolk called to say she's sending three of her underlings here this weekend for a tour of the town. I expect you and Darcy to cover that so don't make any plans. Make sure they love the place before they leave. Deb will load you up with GA swag to give them to take back to FlashTag."

"Yeah, we'll woo 'em with baseball caps and water bottles." He started for the kitchen, needing that coffee. "By the way, where's Darcy? She wasn't at the front desk when I walked in."

"Dunno." TJ shrugged and disappeared behind his office door.

As Win filled a mug, Delaney, Colt's wife came in, looking like a fashion model. "Hey, good-looking." He kissed her on the cheek. "What brings you by the office?" Her design company, Colt and Delaney, was on the outskirts of town in an old John Deere warehouse.

"I'm meeting with Deb about our fall line for the store."

Fall? It wasn't even July yet. But Win supposed that that's what *fashion-forward* meant. It had been TJ's brilliant idea—at the time he'd proposed it no one had thought it was that brilliant—to sell adventure wear and gear from an online store on their website. Deb ran the store and Delaney, a world-famous clothing designer, did an exclusive line for GA. Business on the retail end had been slowly picking up.

"Nice." Win poured her a cup of coffee and handed her the mug. "How's things going over at Colt and Delaney?"

"Excellent. No complaints at all, though I have a lot of catching up to do." She and Colt had recently gotten back from a three-week honeymoon. "How about you? I hear you and Darcy are trying to lure a big social media company to sign on with Garner Adventure for corporate team building."

Win nodded. "FlashTag." Where did people come up with these names?

"Exciting," Delaney said.

"We could use the cash."

Deb joined them and she and Delaney started talking cargo pants and ski jackets. Definitely his cue to leave. He finished his coffee, kissed the ladies good-bye, and headed to the gear room to load up.

As he bent over, gathering up what he needed for the white-water trip, someone cleared her throat behind him. He knew it was a she because of the shoes. Elfin flats attached to a short, albeit shapely, pair of legs. He straightened up to find Darcy hovering.

"What up?" He gave her an efficient once-over and grinned. Maybe it was his imagination but she seemed to have dressed up today. White pants that came to her ankles and a tight short-sleeved sweater that showed off her assets. Instead of her signature ponytail, she'd left her hair loose in bouncy curls around her shoulders. "That your picking-out-our-wedding-centerpieces outfit?"

She responded by giving him the finger. Nice. "TJ says VIPs from FlashTag are coming this weekend and we're supposed to show them around. I thought I should line up some outings."

He liked to be more chill about these things, go wherever the mood led them. "Uh, yeah, sure. But save room for spontaneity."

"What does that mean?"

He pulled his phone out of his back pocket and fiddled with Google until he found *Merriam-Webster*. "'The condition of being spontaneous; spontaneous behavior or action.'"

She gave him a stony glare. "I know the definition, Win. I'll go ahead and plan stuff." She started to walk away and he called her back.

"You want to hang out tonight? Maybe go to Old Glory."

She stared at him as if he'd lost his mind. "Am I like your sponsor now? You know, as long as I'm with you, you won't fall off the wagon and have sex."

He chuckled, giving her sweater another look-see. "Works for me. We can walk over after work." Without giving her a chance to turn him down, he filled his arms with personal floatation devices and made his way to the back door.

She was better company than his boring self, which was all he had these days now that his brothers had shacked up with the loves of their lives. Normally, he would've taken off, gone camping or traveling. The surf was good this time of year in the Mentawai Islands. But it was GA's second busiest season next to winter when the extreme skiers arrived. And with this FlashTag deal looming over them, he had to stick around.

He'd promised himself he wouldn't screw this up. In the past, his follow-through hadn't been the greatest. TJ liked to say that everything came too easy to Win but that's not the way he saw it. Sure, superficial opportunities, like women who wanted sex and arm candy, presented themselves more often than they did for a lot of other guys. But that shit wasn't real life. Real life had actually been harder for Win than most people knew, including his brothers. A learning disability had made the scholastic part of school intolerable so Win had tried to make up for it by being good at sports. And being the "popular kid" had helped get around the embarrassment of barely being able to read.

And then making the Olympic team happened. But the rigorous training schedule didn't work well with Win's chill schedule and he dropped out, which he'd never stopped hearing the end of. The truth was he hadn't felt right about getting the spot after TJ scored too low to make the team. The Olympics had been his brother's dream, not his. Win had despised the cutthroat competitive nature of being on the circuit. It sucked the joy out of skiing, a pastime that in a lot of ways had saved Win. You didn't have to read or write to perform a perfect aerial.

At seven o'clock he met Darcy at Old Glory. She'd snagged two places at the bar and was still wearing her white pixie pants so he figured she'd stayed at GA late as she often did. He had gone home after rafting to shower the river off him and change into jeans. The place, covered from ceiling to floor in American flags, wasn't especially crowded since it was a Tuesday night. He filled a basket with peanuts from one of the oak barrels scattered around the restaurant before taking his place next to Darcy.

Boden gave him a head nod, then ambled over to take his drink order. "You want a dinner menu?"

Win slid the menu down to Darcy. "You interested in eating?"

Boden looked between them. "Sorry, I didn't realize you two were here together."

"It's a work thing," Darcy said.

Win couldn't tell whether she was embarrassed to be seen with him or if Boden had assumed Win was there alone. Or not with Darcy.

"We'll share an order of chicken wings and sliders," Win said. "And a Sierra Nevada for me and whatever Darcy wants."

She got a Coke and when Boden left to put in their

orders she said, "I thought you were starting your diet today."

"You think I need one?" He ran his hands down his chest in a cheesy porn flick way and she choked on her soda.

"You know you don't. How does it feel to be a perfect specimen of manhood?"

He huffed out a breath. "The truth, it's getting tiresome. What do you got there?" He nudged his head at the tablet sitting next to her on the bar.

"I thought we could make a few lists for this weekend."

He groaned. The last thing he wanted to do after a long day of work was more work. "Don't you just ever have fun? Come on, I'll teach you how to make a perfect bank shot." He hopped off the stool and tugged her arm.

"Our food's coming. And I'm not good at pool."

"How do you know if you don't try?" That's what the tutor used to tell him when he'd struggled with words and letters moving on the page and didn't want to learn to read.

"I just know," she said. "Why all of sudden am I your new playmate? It's not like we have anything in common, oh, except for the fact that you've sworn off sex and I'm clearly unappealing to you."

"Stop with that already, would you? If I didn't know better I'd think you had bad self-esteem." He snapped a peanut shell in half and popped the nuts in his mouth. "Ever since I told you about Britney, you've intrigued me."

Her eyebrows winged up. "Intrigued?"

"Yeah." He watched her for a second. "You were nice to talk to, a good sounding board. And I seem to be the only person on earth who doesn't make you nervous. What's up with that?"

She thought about it for a while. He could see the wheels spinning in her head, probably looking for a pithy insult.

"Oddly, I feel supremely comfortable with you. Even

though you're Brad Pitt on steroids there's something about you that puts me at ease. Call it a gift." Judging by the red rash creeping up her neck, the confession had embarrassed her.

But the words made him feel good. "Thanks. I guess." He should've left it alone but he couldn't. "What about Lewis? He make you feel comfortable?"

She stared at the bottles on the back bar, getting lost in them for a moment, then said, "Lewis is Lewis."

Before he could quiz her on what that meant, Boden brought their food. "Bon appétit." He refilled their glasses. "I hear you all are in the running for a big corporate account."

It didn't take long for word to travel in Glory Junction. Some of the old busybodies had never recovered from Ma Bell getting rid of the party line so they'd taken on the chore of spreading news and gossip themselves.

"Maybe we'll bring them in this weekend for lunch or dinner," Win said. "We're supposed to be showing some of the bigwigs the sights."

Boden leaned across the bar. "There's this dude in Nugget, a pro bull rider, who gives lessons. Why don't you take them there?"

Nugget was about thirty minutes up the road. "What's the guy's name?"

"Lucky Rodriguez. He used to ride in the PBR. A world champion."

Win looked at Darcy, who was already typing it into her tablet.

"Thanks. It's a good idea," she said.

Plus, Win had always wanted to ride a bull.

Rita Tucker came in the bar. Stevie Nicks's "Stand Back" came on the jukebox and unfortunately, Rita did anything but. She came right up to Win and breathed ashtray breath all over him.

"Well? Have you made your decision about the calendar?"

"It's been a day, Rita." Jeez, the woman was higher strung than a racehorse.

"You're our biggest draw. If you don't do it I'll have to go outside and get some real talent."

Darcy snorted up her cola. "What about that new guy on search and rescue? He's hot."

Win shot her a look. "I'm not out yet. I'm just thinking about it, you know, in case I want to run for office someday. How do you think me standing with my junk on display would look to my constituents?"

Boden threw his head back and laughed. "Politics, huh? Yeah, I don't see it."

Why not? Win could shake hands and kiss babies with the best of them.

"Take it from me," Rita said, "you don't want to become a public servant. All anyone ever does is bitch. What do you think drove Pond Scum to steal?"

Before Rita, Carter Pond—not-so-affectionately known as Pond Scum—had been the mayor of Glory Junction. Then he was arrested on corruption and embezzlement charges.

"You should hold a contest," Darcy told Rita. "Get some fresh blood in that calendar. I bet lots of men would compete to be Mr. December."

"Hey!" Win poked his finger in the air at Darcy. "I haven't said I won't do it yet."

She hitched her shoulders. "You could compete too." And then her lips curved up in an evil smile. She was taunting him, that's what she was doing.

Chapter Five

When Darcy got home that night there was a Mercedes-Maybach convertible in Nana's driveway and that could only mean one thing. She girded herself and walked to the front door as if she were walking the plank.

Inside, the eleven o'clock news played on the television. Nana liked to watch it before going to bed. There were hushed voices and Darcy could smell the remnants of dinner permeating the air.

"Is that you, dear?"

She seriously thought about turning tail, jumping in her Volkswagen, and getting the Fahrvergnügen out of there. But her grandmother's voice came again.

"Darcy?"

She headed for the staircase, hoping to make it to her bedroom sight unseen. Then she could call down that she was bushed and turning in for the night.

Too late.

Except for the lift and tuck around the lids, a pair of blue eyes so much like her own stared back at her.

"Hello, Mother."

Geneva gave her a swift examination and went in for a hug. Darcy stiffly returned the embrace.

"You've put on a few pounds," her mother said, and backed up to give her a more thorough appraisal.

"You're here to visit?" Darcy asked hesitantly. Geneva rarely came to Glory Junction, even if Nana was her mother-in-law and getting on in years. Darcy's father was no better but at least he called Nana once a week.

"Just for a day. I needed fresh air." Geneva tried for a smile but it never quite met her eyes. More than likely she and Dad were fighting again and Geneva thought she could manipulate Nana into teaming up with her against Max. It wouldn't happen but Darcy's mother had delusions of grandeur. Always had.

"Well then, I'll see you in the morning." She climbed the stairs, knowing that her mother was watching and banking flaws to criticize later.

Don't wear capris, darling, they're for tall women. Let me get you in to my stylist, Laurent; you could benefit from a good cut and some decent highlights. She'd heard the jibes so often they no longer hurt. Not much, anyway. Not like when Darcy was a kid and Geneva used to buy her clothes a size or two too small in the hopes it would compel her to lose her baby fat. Or when she forced a painfully shy Darcy to perform piano recitals in a crowded auditorium. Or insisted that As were for ordinary students. Extraordinary students got A-pluses. Geneva's obsession with perfection rivaled that of the worst tiger mother. Darcy had the claw marks to prove it.

Before going to bed, she checked her phone for messages. Ridiculous because the only person who ever contacted her was Lewis. As she suspected there was nothing so she brushed her teeth and applied a night mask to her face so her mother couldn't find anything wrong with her complexion.

The next morning, she went downstairs to find Nana making coffee.

"Mother's not awake yet?" If Darcy skipped breakfast she could hopefully avoid her all together.

"Not yet, dear. I'm making French toast."

"I've got to run, Nana. Big day at the office."

Her grandmother sported a placid smile. But her words were anything but. "Chickenshit."

Darcy couldn't help but laugh, then whispered, "What is she doing here?"

"According to her, she's angry that you didn't tell her about your engagement." Nana arched a snowy brow. "So you and Win Garner, huh?" Hilde's eyes danced with merriment. "I couldn't be more pleased, though I've always wanted the man for myself." She opened the pantry door to show off her Glory Junction calendar, perpetually pinned to the month of December. Darcy had begged her to take it down so many times she'd lost track.

"It was a joke, Nana. We saw Lewis at the rodeo and Win blurted it out."

Her parents owned a mortgage brokerage in Reno and did a lot of business with Snyder Real Estate. That's how she'd met Lewis in the first place.

"And you didn't try to correct him?" Nana laughed. There was no love lost between Hilde and Lewis. Nana thought he pushed Darcy too hard to do his work for him.

Darcy shrugged. "To be truthful I sort of liked seeing the shock on Lewis's face." Not to mention being engaged to someone as good-looking as Win. In real life, though, he'd be the last person suitable for her. Too pretty, too laid-back, too . . . Let's face it, the Darcy Wallaces of the world didn't wind up with the Win Garners.

Hilde exchanged a conspiratorial glance with Darcy before saying, "What do we tell your mother?"

Darcy sighed and decided to stay for French toast after all.

"The truth, of course." One look at Win and her mother would instantly know their engagement was a farce anyway.

As it turned out Darcy got a stay of execution. By the time she'd finished eating breakfast, Geneva still hadn't risen from her crypt yet.

"Don't worry, I'll deal with her later," Darcy told Nana on her way out.

"Have a good day at work and kiss your fiancé for me." Nana waggled her eyebrows, making Darcy laugh.

When she got to GA she immediately brewed coffee. She was the only one in the office who made a decent pot. TJ came by her desk and stood over her while she checked messages.

"Yes?" After a year of working at Garner Adventure she'd finally become accustomed to TJ's abrupt style. In the beginning, he'd intimidated the heck out of her. Now, she was discovering that she could talk back. In fact, he even liked it when she did. "What can I do for you?"

TJ sat on the edge of her desk, his long denim-encased legs stretched out in front of him. "How are plans coming along for this weekend?" TJ didn't leave things to chance like his younger brother. If you looked up *Type A* in the dictionary, you'd find TJ Garner's name in the definition.

"Good," she said, even though they didn't have any concrete plans. Win couldn't sit long enough to strategize, which would leave Darcy to do it all. Same song, different station. Working for Lewis, she knew exactly how this went. She'd done all the work, Lewis had taken all the glory. She didn't need, or even want, to be the star of the show. All she'd ever asked for was to be valued and not ignored. Or in her mother's case, not endlessly criticized.

Off the top of her head she threw out, "There's a professional bull rider in Nugget who we're thinking of taking the group to meet. Apparently, he gives lessons."

"Lucky Rodriguez," TJ said, repeating the same name Boden had given them at the bar. "I like it. But keep in mind he owns a dude ranch that offers corporate team building too. We wouldn't want FlashTag to ditch us for him."

"Should we not go, then?" This is where it would've been handy to have Win add his two cents. But she hadn't seen him all morning. As far as adventure sports and team building went, she was completely out of her depth.

"Go. I think it's a great idea. Just keep in mind that we're competitors, though Lucky's outfit focuses on rodeoing. Calf roping, steer wrestling, bull riding, barrel racing, that kind of thing. But there's no reason we can't join forces to give our clients a full adventure experience." TJ checked his watch as if he had somewhere to be. "What else do you have planned?"

"Uh, we're working on it."

"It's Wednesday, Darce, work faster." With that he headed out the door.

It looked like Darcy was on her own to line up the weekend, starting with lodging. She got on the phone to the Four Seasons where GA had an account, then made a reservation at the Indian place for dinner. The restaurant was formally Zaika but everyone within a fifty-mile radius simply called it the Indian place. It had become a destination restaurant in the Sierra Nevada, that's how good it was. She called the Morning Glory and Old Glory and reserved tables for breakfast and lunch.

When she finished planning their meals and making reservations, she Googled Lucky Rodriguez, kicking herself for not simply asking TJ for the number to the dude ranch. She found him easy enough, though. There were at least a dozen or more news articles about him, including a *Sports Illustrated* piece about his champion bull-riding days and how he was hanging it up to found a cowboy camp and be with his family. She plugged in the terms *Nugget*, *cowboy camp* and *Lucky Rodriguez* in the search engine and voilà. A beautiful website, almost as nice as Garner Adventure's, popped up. Darcy dialed the number on the camp's home page and in no time at all she was setting up their visit.

When noon rolled around she had mastered a pretty tight itinerary and strolled over to Tart Me Up to reward herself with a sandwich. And maybe one of those fruit tarts Rachel made that were to die for. Then she remembered disapproving Mommie Dearest was in town and the thought of consuming anything worth eating soured in her stomach.

Today, she'd been extra careful with her wardrobe choices, selecting pants that fit snugly through the thighs and flared at the bottom, a top with vertical stripes, and heels with a low-cut vamp. According to *Cosmo*, this was supposed to trick the eye into making her appear tall and willowy. According to Darcy's mirror, nothing had changed. But at least Geneva couldn't fault her for her selections.

There was a line to take a number at the bakery, making Darcy consider her options. They were in the thick of tourist season so any of Glory Junction's eating establishments would likely be busy. Carrie Jo Morgan, Colt's receptionist at the police department, was ahead of her. Darcy didn't know her well but she'd always seemed nice and funny, saying anything that popped into her head, even to Colt, who scared the crap out of Darcy. He'd never been anything but nice but he had a gruff, hard-as-cement exterior that made Darcy stumble over her words every time he talked to her. Once she nearly choked on a doughnut while he was in the room.

Carrie Jo took a number, saw Darcy, and came over to wait with her in line. "This is nuts, isn't it? I told Rachel she should franchise."

It was pretty crazy. But then again Oprah had recommended

the bakery and now people drove up from San Francisco, more than three hours away, to get a piece of strudel. Darcy didn't think Oprah had ever been to Glory Junction but somehow she knew about Tart Me Up.

"Someone should open one of those little food carts on Main Street, sell hot dogs, pretzels, and falafel," Darcy said.

"In winter, chestnuts. They'd make a fortune." Carrie Jo checked the board to see what number they were on. "At this rate, I'm going to have to get back to the office before it's my turn."

"How much time do you get for lunch?"

Carrie Jo hitched her shoulders. "Technically, thirty minutes but His Royal Pain in the Ass doesn't keep tabs." Darcy assumed she was talking about Colt. "What's going on at GA? I hear Snapchat's coming to town."

"FlashTag. They're considering using us for corporate team building." It was the first time Darcy had ever used "us," which worried her. She used to think Snyder Real Estate was an "us" until she found out it was just a Lewis.

"Cool. I hope it works out."

Carrie Jo's number got called and she went up to the counter to put in her order. Not long after, Darcy's flashed on the board. With her half sandwich and fruit salad, she went back to the office and ate at her desk.

Around three, Win walked in the door. Despite hours on the lake or river or mountainside or wherever he'd been, he still managed to look like a Ralph Lauren ad. Windswept but not stirred. The man was so good-looking it was nauseating.

"What's cooking, good-looking?"

She would've been flattered except he used that line on everyone. "Thanks to your lie, my mother's in town."

"Huh?" He cocked his hip against the counter and stared down at her. "What're you talking about?"

"Lewis told my mother we were engaged. She came to

help plan the wedding." She expected him to freak out a little but he just laughed. Because the joke was on her.

"You tell her the truth?"

"Not yet. I've been too busy setting up our weekend."

For a minute, he looked confused, like he'd forgotten that they were supposed to entertain the very people who could make or break her promotion. "I told you we were going to be spontaneous, let Mother Nature and the vibe I get from our prospective clients dictate our schedule. It's good to get a read on the mood, then make a plan."

"Well, TJ wanted us to be more structured."

"My brother has a stick up his ass."

His brother ran a successful company with that stick up his ass. Darcy handed Win a stack of printed material.

"Our itinerary, including pictures, bios, and cell phone numbers on the FlashTag veeps so you can be familiar with their faces, names, and positions."

He studied the pages for a few minutes. "Looks good. Want to come to TJ and Deb's for dinner tonight? They're grilling steaks with the fam and we may go out on TJ's boat."

It took a moment for her to grasp that he was inviting her to a family dinner. She was an employee, not family, and she certainly wouldn't be Win's date. So what was he up to?

The skepticism must have shown on her face because Win quickly amended, "We could use the time to go over this." He held up the itinerary she'd just handed him. That made sense, though Win doing after-hours homework was a surprise. He typically flew by the seat of his pants. She knew because she was constantly trying to hunt him down and keep him on course to ensure the schedule didn't get screwed up.

She'd never been to TJ's house but had heard it was spectacular. Right on the lake with its own dock. But as much as she'd like to see it, there was her mother to consider. This was Geneva's last night in Glory Junction. Although her parents only lived in Reno her mother would take it as a personal slight if she didn't have dinner with her.

"I can't," she said, already regretting not being able to go. Even though the Garners en masse turned her into a timid bird, she much preferred their company to Geneva's. Especially after Win's whopper of a lie about their engagement.

Her parents adored Lewis and she'd deeply disappointed them when she'd filed for divorce. Geneva had all but said she didn't think Darcy could do better. And judging by her social life, Geneva was right. But if Darcy had to do it all over again she would. Not the marriage part, just the divorce. Because it was easier to be unhappy by herself than with a controlling husband who reinforced all her insecurities and expected her to be his full-time caretaker with none of the rewards.

And even though her life lacked the kind of adventure she'd hoped for by moving to Glory Junction, it was still better than living in Reno with people who made her feel bad about herself.

"Why not?" Win continued to stand there, looking supremely surprised that anyone would turn him down. Darcy didn't think that happened to him too often.

"I have to hang out with my mother."

"Don't you think your fiancé should come first?" he said, and his mouth quirked. Everything was a joke to him.

"Earth to Win, we're not engaged."

"Don't make me go to this alone." He perched on the corner of her desk as much as a two-hundred-pound man could perch.

"It's your family," she said, baffled. "Not a wedding." There was nothing worse than going to a wedding alone.

"Everyone is coupled up, I'll be odd man out."

"So? It's not like you couldn't have a date if you wanted one."

"Damned straight but you're better than a date." He grinned.

She didn't know what that meant exactly but suspected it was offensive. Instead of going head-to-head with him, she let the comment slide. "Sorry, no can do."

Win didn't know what the big deal was. It was just dinner at his brother's house and probably a few turns around the lake in TJ's boat. It would've been nice for him to have a plus one for a change. The last woman he'd brought to a gathering with his family had been Britney and that hadn't gone too well. Before that, Deb. But that was back in high school. Deb was with TJ now.

When TJ had been single, Hannah and Delaney had tried to set him up with all their girlfriends. But no one did that for Win. He supposed they thought he could find his own dates, unlike TJ, who'd been too busy working twelve-hour days to meet women.

Besides wanting a companion to accompany him, Darcy had sort have become his El Capitan. Painfully shy one minute, ballsy smart-mouthed the next, she'd become as challenging as scaling Yosemite's three-thousand vertical-foot sheer rock granite.

Five days ago, she wanted him to have sex with her. And now he had to beg her just to go to the rodeo with him. She was exasperating, that's for sure.

He was getting ready to walk away when a statuesque blonde came through the door into the lobby and flipped her designer sunglasses to the top of her head. It took a while for Win to realize she was middle-aged, probably in her late fifties. But she hid it well. Just enough makeup to highlight her Nordic features without showcasing the subtle lines near her eyes and mouth and a tailored dress that hugged a toned, tanned body. She wasn't from Glory Junction, Win could tell that right off the bat. San Francisco, LA, maybe Sacramento, or some other big city.

He started to ask if he could help her when it struck him that her face had an uncanny likeness to someone else he knew. Same blue eyes, same blond hair, same bone structure.

"Mother, what are you doing here?" A glowering Darcy nearly hurled herself over the burl-wood counter to get to her. Win got the impression she wasn't too thrilled to see her mom, which made him want to stick around, watch some fireworks.

"Is that a way to greet me?" The tall blonde gave Darcy one of those European cheek-kisses, and then quickly pulled away like she might get rumpled. She took one look at Darcy's appearance and sniffed. "Suck in your stomach, dear."

Darcy smoothed the wrinkles from her shirt and nervously tugged on her pants that had probably stuck to her from the heat and sitting in a chair all day. "I wasn't expecting you."

"I wanted to see where you work." Darcy's mother darted a glance around the reception area, regarding it with interest.

The old log lodge was awesome. Win's parents had purchased it during the recession because they wanted the walk-in traffic from Main Street and had updated the building with a gym and rock-climbing wall, using the old bedrooms as offices. There was an enormous stone fireplace in the lobby and a seating arrangement where they often held orientations for group tours.

After taking her fill, her gaze fell on Win. She looked him up and down, sizing him up like a boot camp sergeant. It was a little unnerving and his arms stiffened at his side. He was just about to introduce himself when she beat him to the punch.

"I'm Geneva Wallace, Darcy's mother." She drilled Darcy with a look, silently rebuking her for not doing the honors.

Win watched Darcy shrink before his very eyes and something protective stirred inside him. Moving closer, he draped his arm over her shoulders. "Now I know where Darcy gets her beauty from."

Usually mothers lapped that up like puppies with a bowl of milk.

"She doesn't look anything like me," Geneva said, her face puckering up like she'd just been sprayed by a skunk. "She takes after her father."

The truth was Darcy was soft and round and small, nothing like Geneva's tall angular frame. And not to make snap judgments but Geneva gave off a sour vibe. Darcy, when she wasn't constantly giving him a hard time, was the personification of sweet.

"I was hoping to meet your fiancé," Geneva said, and brushed past Darcy to peer down the hall as if he might be hiding behind the Xerox machine.

It was the way she said "fiancé," almost with a sneer in her voice, that pushed Win over the edge. It took a lot to make him dislike a person but he was pretty sure he disliked Geneva Wallace. She seemed cold and disapproving. Win's own mother was a hugger. Even though her grown sons were three times her size, she still would've rocked them to sleep at night if she could. Win remembered her soothing him, kissing away his tears, after a bad report card, before anyone had figured out he had dyslexia.

"Where is he, Darcy? Lewis said he worked with you."

It was so many kinds of wrong but Win couldn't help himself. "At your service," he said, and bowed. It was unctuous as hell but he was going for shock and awe.

He looked up expecting to find gratitude shining in Darcy's cornflower blue eyes. Instead, they were blazing with something akin to anger. Well, shit! He wasn't used to that reaction from women and it just made him want to dig in his heels.

"You're Darcy's fiancé?" Geneva gave him a closer inspection as if she were searching for flaws.

Darcy cleared her throat and stared daggers at him. "He's not."

Geneva straightened. "I didn't think so. Where is he? I'd like to meet my future son-in-law."

Darcy seemed to be weighing her options. Go with a lie or come clean.

Win was too busy gleaning the meaning of "I didn't think so." The dismissal stuck in his craw. Was he to interpret it as Darcy wasn't good enough for him or that he wasn't good enough for Darcy? He could deal with the latter. In a mother's eyes, no man was ever good enough for her daughter. But ever since Geneva had walked in the door he'd sensed a mother-daughter hostility that was palpable.

"I'm not her fiancé," he said. "I'm Darcy's husband."

Chapter Six

Geneva's eyes grew so large Darcy was sure her pupils would burst. "You're married? Lewis said you were engaged. When did this happen?" she asked skeptically as if she knew she was being duped.

"We're not—"

"Telling anyone." Win wouldn't let her talk and was clearly making it up as he went along. "We wanted it to be a surprise."

"Well, I'm definitely surprised." Geneva sank into one of the couches. "The ink isn't even dry on your divorce."

"I was divorced a year ago, Mother."

Win went to the cooler and poured her mother a glass of water.

"We were hoping you and Lewis would reconcile," Geneva said, and Darcy felt a hot flash of anger spark through her.

First, the statement was offensive to Win, her fake husband. But more important, how could her parents want her to get back with a man who'd made her so unhappy? "Mother, that's never going to happen."

"Lewis is seeing someone," Win said, and handed Geneva the cup he'd just filled. "We hear it's serious."

Who knew Win was a pathological liar? Darcy would've kicked him if he was standing closer. He kept digging them in deeper and deeper.

"Lewis never said anything about a girlfriend," Geneva said.

Win coughed, then gave a small shrug. "She's a stripper. People can be touchy about that sort of thing."

Darcy shot him a death glare. *Shut up!* Something was seriously wrong with him.

Geneva sipped her water, gripping the glass as if it was a lifeline. "When were you married?"

"Saturday night," Win said. "Darcy came over to my place and surprised me."

Darcy's mother gazed at both of them, skepticism in her eyes. Of course she was skeptical. None of anything Win said made sense. The man was deranged. A complete lying lunatic.

Just then TJ came out of his office and found them sitting next to the fireplace. He and Win exchanged glances, TJ clearly curious about what was going on.

"This is Darcy's mom, Geneva," Win announced.

"Oh, hey, so nice to meet you." TJ came around the corner and extended his hand, then turned to Darcy. "You should've told us your mom was coming."

"We just broke the news to her about the wedding," Win told TJ, who looked as unconvinced as Geneva.

"Never mind." Darcy wanted to stop this train wreck. It was bad enough she'd have to explain to her mother why she worked with a pathological liar, she didn't want TJ involved too.

"What wedding?" TJ asked.

Win's mouth curved up. The psycho was truly enjoying himself. "We didn't tell my brother, either. See . . . big surprise." He turned to TJ. "You owe us a gift."

"There was no wedding!" Darcy wanted this to stop. Now.

TJ ignored her, going along with Win. The whole family was nuts. "You and Darcy?" he asked his brother, then dropped a kiss on her forehead. "Welcome to the family." The rat bastard knew it was a ruse and was playing along.

"Mother, we're not married." How did Darcy explain that this is the way the Garner brothers got their jollies? "It's all a big misunderstanding."

"How do you misunderstand someone saying he's your husband?" Geneva wasn't finding any of this funny. "Either you are or you aren't."

"I give up." Darcy threw her hands in the air. "We're not married but believe what you want."

Geneva looked from Darcy to Win, who flashed her one of his killer, I'm-sexy-and-I-know-it smiles, the one that said believe me, not her. He tucked Darcy under his arm and let his hand slowly brush down her side in a way that would've made her purr if not for the fact that Geneva was watching. Then he took it a step too far by squeezing her ass. Oh, heavens, it felt good.

She tried to step on his foot to make him stop but those phenomenal reflexes of Win's kicked in again and he moved just in time.

TJ broke the silence, saying "I've got to take off," and then staring longingly at the door. Away from Crazy Town. "Mrs. Wallace." He bobbed his head.

She got to her feet. "It's been a pleasure." Her expression said just the opposite. "I was hoping we could have dinner together, Darcy. Hilde has a garden club function."

"Of course." Darcy would use the time to explain to her mother that Win was psycho and that they weren't married, engaged, or even dating. "I just have to finish up here. Why don't you browse along the shops on Main Street and I'll text you when I'm ready to go?"

"That sounds perfect." She gave Win a sly sideways glance that said she knew. The jig was up. Darcy was surprised Geneva hadn't called him on his lie from the beginning, knowing full well that her daughter would never run off and get married without telling anyone.

As far as her and Win together . . . Ha! Her mother could go back to dreaming that she and Lewis would reunite. Darcy was sure she'd get an earful about it at dinner.

Geneva set off for her stroll in downtown Glory Junction and Darcy buttonholed Win in his office. "What the hell was that about?"

Win sprawled out in his beanbag chair and one corner of his mouth tipped up. His obnoxious half grin did something to her insides. Something she didn't want to explore too closely because Win's smiles set women's panties aflame across the Sierra Nevada. Probably across the Continental Divide. And she didn't want to be one of them.

"I didn't like how she told you to suck in your stomach," he said. "It bugged the crap out of me."

She lowered herself into one of the chairs and reached under her to toss away a pair of athletic socks. The place needed to be cleaned and organized. Not my job, she reminded herself. She'd done enough cleaning and organizing to last her a lifetime.

"We've got a complicated relationship," she said. "Still, that wasn't a reason to lie."

"Sorry," he said, but he didn't look the least bit sorry. "Is it that bad being married to me?"

She laughed because it was difficult not to get caught up in Win's charm. For a man who had the world by a string, he was pretty self-deprecating at times. "So far, you're better than Lewis but the jury's still out."

"What's up with your mother's obsession with him? The dude struck me as a geek, just saying."

A geek like her. They should've been the perfect match but they weren't.

"He has his good points."

Win twisted around in the beanbag chair. For someone over six feet tall, he was extremely agile. All that outdoors sports, she supposed.

"Yeah, what are they?"

"He wouldn't hurt a fly and he's a good businessman." They'd lived in a gorgeous condo, drove new cars, and could travel whenever they wanted, though they rarely did.

"Selling real estate? Sounds boring."

She'd always thought so but she hadn't done the actual selling. Perhaps if Lewis had let her meet with clients and show property she would've enjoyed the job more. But he'd said she was more valuable to him in the office, doing the drudge work. The work he took for granted and forgot to ever give her credit for.

"Not everyone can play for a living," she said, and he frowned. Must've touched a nerve. "You're good at it, though, I'll give you that."

He nodded while scanning her outfit. "Your stomach looks okay in that. I wouldn't worry about it."

She self-consciously sucked it in, not sure if he was trying to get back at her for the "playing" comment.

"So I guess you're really going to dinner with her," Win said.

"She's my mother. And thanks to you I'm going to get an earful about the stunt you pulled."

"Ditch her and come with me to TJ's."

A part of her was more tempted than he would ever know. She rose, needing to return a few e-mails and power down her computer before she left for the evening. "See you tomorrow, Win."

She dashed off a text to her mother and met her at Old Glory, where Geneva had already secured a table.

"Cute place," Geneva said, doing a visual lap around the room.

"It's known for its microbrews. The owner is really into craft beer." Darcy had never acquired a taste for it herself and preferred wine or margaritas but she knew it was a huge draw for tourists and locals alike.

"Hmm." Geneva peered at the menu. "Is there anything that isn't fried?"

Darcy wanted to say it wouldn't kill her to eat something with flavor for a change but what was the point? "I'm sure they can rustle up some lettuce or kale for you."

"Was that supposed to be sarcastic?"

"I was just kidding," Darcy said sheepishly. "They do have good salads."

Geneva closed her menu and pushed it to the side. "Your husband didn't want to join us?"

Now who was being sarcastic?

"He was just playing around, Mother." In his own warped way, Win was trying to defend her. And despite the fallout—because her mother would surely ride her about it—Darcy had been touched by his championing of her.

"There's something wrong with that man," Geneva huffed.

Win was no saint—his womanizing was a major topic in Glory Junction—but for the most part, Darcy thought he was misunderstood. Notwithstanding his faults, he was the kindest person she knew. And completely nonjudgmental. Hence, the reason she felt so comfortable around him.

"There's nothing wrong with him, Mother. And technically, he's one of my bosses." She never actually thought of him that way but it would hopefully get Geneva off his back. The one thing her mother understood was chain of command.

Geneva arched a brow. "He's not for you."

No, he wasn't but Darcy still resented her mother pointing it out. "He's better than Lewis." It was childish to make the comparison but she was feeling defensive. That in and of itself was new. Usually, she let her mother run roughshod over her because it was easier than fighting.

"He may be better-looking but I doubt he's half as reliable." Now how would Geneva know that? She'd met Win for all of ten minutes.

"I don't want to talk about Lewis, Mother."

"You're the one who brought him up." Geneva gazed across the table. "Sit up straight, dear. That slouch isn't doing anything for your tummy."

A server came to take their order and even though Darcy wanted chicken wings, she got the chopped salad. Geneva of course got hers without dressing.

When the server left, Geneva launched into the same old, same old about how she was throwing her life away, working in a dead-end job. "You'd be better off working for Snyder Real Estate."

"I like this job better, Mother." TJ, unlike Lewis, listened to her and often took her advice. And if she got her promotion there would be a raise and a title. "I meet interesting people and the Garners are wonderful."

"I just can't imagine answering a phone all day long. And do you want to live with Hilde the rest of your life?"

Living with Hilde was not the problem. "I do more than answer the phone, not that there is anything wrong with that." Her mother was such a damned snob. "In fact, I've been put in charge of getting a huge account for Garner Adventure." A bit of an exaggeration, since Win was really in charge but TJ believed in her.

Her mother shrugged. "I don't see you as a salesperson but if this is what you want . . ." She trailed off and Darcy didn't bother to ask what the sales quip was supposed to mean. Whatever it was, it couldn't be good. Geneva liked to nitpick.

"This is what I want," she said as forcefully as she could without coming off as defensive, which she was sure she sounded anyway. Geneva had a knack for making Darcy doubt herself. She could do it with just one glance.

Their salads came and they ate in blessed silence, the tension so thick she could cut it with a machete. For once she wished she and Geneva could just have a nice meal together, talk about things normal mother-daughters did, be kind to each other.

"How's Dad?" Darcy asked to break the awkwardness and try for a neutral topic.

"He's fine." The answer was terse and quick. Too quick.

"Everything with the business is okay?"

"Of course." Geneva took a sip of the wine she'd ordered before Darcy had arrived. It was obvious she didn't want to talk about whatever was eating her.

Or, it was more fun to carp on Darcy. Geneva hadn't gotten to Darcy's hair, her nails, or even her outfit yet. Darcy was sure it was coming.

"Lewis mentioned that you were going to help him with some data entry," Geneva said between delicate bites of her salad.

Everything always came back to Lewis. Darcy gritted her teeth. "Maybe. I have to see how it goes with our clients. I may be too busy."

"I wish you could see your way back to him."

Darcy wished she could see her way back to the Garners' barbecue where she could've eaten something besides lettuce and spent her evening talking about someone other than Lewis. And Win would've been there. And even though he wouldn't have sex with her, he surprisingly made her feel good about herself.

Chapter Seven

Colt was manning the grill when Win got to TJ's place. His brother had turned the once fixer-upper into a rocking lakeside pad, complete with man cave and private dock. Now that Deb had moved in, she'd put her touch on things. But she was so much like TJ everything meshed pretty well, including the outdoor entertaining spaces where she'd added a bar and a fire pit.

On his way to the backyard, he passed TJ and Deb in the kitchen making guacamole. These days those two were connected at the hip, which made Win smile. He loved the shit out of all his family, even if they were monster pains in the ass.

Hannah, Delaney, and Josh were drinking beer around the fire pit with a big fire going. Win noted that his parents hadn't shown up yet.

"Hey, dipshit." Josh threw a tortilla chip at him. "Grab a cold one and pull up a seat."

Win got a beer from the cooler, strolled over to see what Colt was massacring on the barbecue, then found an empty chair next to Delaney.

"TJ says you're married now." Josh let out a laugh. "Poor Darcy."

He should've known that TJ would blab. The guy, like the rest of his brothers, couldn't keep his mouth shut. At least their significant others were more discreet. "She's damned lucky to have me. I'm a loyal hound."

"You're a hound all right," Colt called from the grill. "But loyal isn't the first thing that comes to mind."

Right, he was a player, a ne'er-do-well, a miscreant. He'd heard it all before.

"Seriously, what are you guys talking about?" Hannah asked.

Win told her the whole story, starting with Geneva's poor treatment of Darcy. "It pissed me off. Darcy's sensitive enough as it is." Though lately she'd been a real ballbuster, at least where he was concerned.

"That was so sweet of you to lie to her mother," Delaney said. Now that she was married to Colt she'd become too damned sarcastic. And cynical.

"I'm really disappointed in the way you've let Colt turn you into a sour, bitter person," Win said. "You're better than that, Delaney."

Another corn chip beaned him in the head. This time from Colt.

"Watch how you talk to my wife."

TJ and Deb came out with their big-ass bowl of guacamole. Deb set it on the edge of the fire pit, grabbed a beer, and made herself comfortable on the bench next to Hannah.

"I hear you've been telling stories again," she said to Win, then turned to the others and made the cuckoo sign with her finger.

"What kind of shit was that?" TJ wanted to know. "You really put me on the spot there."

Win took a long drag of his beer and eyed his brother over the bottle. "You seemed to catch on quick enough."

"Next time a little heads-up would be good. WTF, Win, you don't mess with people's parents that way. I didn't know if Darcy wanted me to play along or beat the crap out of you."

"She definitely wanted to be married to me." Not exactly, but she wanted to sleep with him. Or at least she did a few days ago. "As for beating the crap out of me, in your dreams, Thomas Jefferson."

TJ flipped him the bird, grabbed a handful of chips, and stuffed them in his mouth. Win gazed out over the lake as the late afternoon sun shimmered off the water. Except for a few boats and a couple of paddleboarders it was quiet. Come the weekend, it would be Grand Central Station. Between the townies, the tourists, and the weekenders, the lake was a mob scene, though Win would take it in a heartbeat. Homes right on the waterfront were highly coveted, despite the crowds.

TJ, like with most of his dealings, had finagled his way into this one and made it a dream home. Thanks to their wives, both Colt and Josh had great houses, too. Only Win lived in a one-room rental. It used to be more than sufficient, just a place to sleep and keep his sports gear. Lately, though, he'd been thinking about buying a place, putting down roots.

"Burgers are ready," Colt shouted.

"What's taking Mom and Dad so long?" Josh asked.

TJ reached over, grabbed a stack of plates from the picnic table, and handed them out. "They're probably having a nooner."

"Ew." Win punched him. "Seriously?"

"Yeah," Josh said. "I could've done without that visual. Besides, it's a little late for a nooner."

A few minutes later, Mary and Gray Garner showed up with Lucy and Ricky. The labs were getting up there in age but his parents still took them everywhere. The dogs ran to the edge of the lake and stuck their noses in the water. Win found a stick and tossed it across the lawn and watched as the dogs streaked across the grass to fetch it. Lucy brought it back to him covered in slobber. He did it a few more times before going inside to wash up.

While he was in there, he checked his phone in case Darcy had changed her mind or had gotten done early with Geneva and wanted to swing by. Nothing from Darcy but a woman he'd met kayaking over the weekend left a message, inviting him to join her for drinks at Old Glory.

He hit the delete button and returned to the party, filling his plate. TJ sidled up to him.

"You and Darcy hammer out this weekend?" TJ couldn't enjoy himself unless he was talking shop. Win knew it was that kind of drive that made his brother so successful but it was annoying as hell. The guy could never just let go.

"Yep. Rather, she did. I had that bouldering group today, so she came up with a plan." As he'd told her repeatedly, he wanted to get a feel for the group before he decided on what activities to throw at them. But like TJ, she was anal.

"Good. We could really use the business."

Win gave him a long look. "I know. I fucked up with Royce . . . shouldn't have let him use the porta-potty."

TJ shook his head. "There's not much you could've done, Win. It was Royce who ignored the danger tape and used a condemned outhouse. But we took a hit, no question about it."

"I'll get us FlashTag," Win said. "Can I have a bonus if I do?"

TJ leaned back, surprised. "You need money?"

Win lived a pretty inexpensive life. He owned his Jeep free and clear, his apartment's rent was nothing, and all his recreation was paid for. The last time he'd asked TJ for a raise it was because he thought he was going to be a father and needed to support a family. He could tell that his brother's mind had automatically gone there.

"I might want to buy a place."

"Really?" TJ gave Win a hard look as if he was hiding something. "Is there something I ought to know about?"

"Jeez, can't a guy want to buy a house? You did."

"I thought you were too busy running around, having a good time, to settle down."

Win didn't blame TJ for his assumption. Until recently it had been true. Mostly. He wouldn't necessarily call buying a home settling down, but he'd like to at least get out of his studio apartment, which was fine for someone in his early twenties. Not someone approaching thirty-two. Why pay rent when he could be putting that money towards a mortgage? California real estate was a good investment. "I was planning to buy something when I thought Britney and I were getting married. Just because she's out of the picture doesn't mean the plan has changed."

Back when he thought he was bringing a kid into the world his parents had offered to help with a down payment. Win wouldn't take the money now. He was a grown man and could stand on his own two feet. GA paid him well and he had managed to sock some money away but California real estate didn't come cheap and Glory Junction with its five ski resorts had become prohibitively expensive in the last five years.

"Sure," TJ said. "You get the account and I'll give you a bonus. I'll even help you look for a place."

"All right." Win would take his help. TJ had a good eye for diamonds in the rough. His lake house was a perfect example. "Hey, did you know that Darcy's divorced?"

"Yeah, she mentioned it once or twice. Why?"

Win hitched his shoulders. "I hadn't known, that's all."

And it bugged him that maybe she'd told him and he hadn't been paying attention. She'd been good to him during the Britney situation, taking the time to listen while he went into panic mode.

TJ grabbed a couple of pickle chips off Win's plate and popped them in his mouth. "I don't think she goes around talking about it much."

"I met him the other day . . . Lewis."

TJ stopped chewing, his interest piqued. "Yeah, what's he like?" Of everyone at GA, TJ worked the closest with Darcy. He'd been the one to hire her.

As far as Win was concerned she was the best hire they'd ever made. Though she didn't know dick about extreme sports, Darcy was punctual, reliable, and . . . she got shit done. Her multitasking skills were off the hook.

"He seemed decent enough," Win answered, *though a bit overdressed*.

"Huh," TJ said as if he was expecting Win to describe an ogre. To everyone but Win, Darcy came off a bit on the timid side, so it wouldn't be out of the realm of possibilities that her ex was a pumped-up dickhead. "I guess it just didn't work out."

"Guess not."

Gray wandered over and put both his sons in a headlock. "Heard we have a big Silicon Valley company on the hook." Even though Gray was semiretired from the company, he still guided tours and kept his eye on the back office.

Gray and TJ became involved in a business conversation that bored the crap out of Win so he strolled off, looking for something entertaining. As the night air grew chilly, they moved the party inside and ditched the idea of taking the boat out. By the time Win got home, it was late and the neighborhood cat needed to be fed.

When he got into the office the next morning Darcy had

her headset on and was talking to someone. He loitered by her desk, waiting for her to end the call.

"You get things straightened out with your mother?"

"Yes, no thanks to you."

He sat on the corner of the desk, checking out her legs. Today she had a short dress on and a pair of high heels, similar to the ones she'd worn yesterday. "Does that mean we're no longer married?"

"Yep," she said, distracted by the message slip she was filling out. "The love is gone."

"So we're not even engaged?"

"Nope. You're free to roam." She didn't even look up.

Her brusque way of treating him was starting to get on his nerves. "Want to go to lunch later?"

She picked up a brown paper bag on her desk, held it in the air, and continued to write on her damn pink slip. "I brought."

Win took the bag and opened it, sniffing. "Bologna?"

"Don't be gross. Nana made it." She swiped the bag out of his hand, looked inside, and made a face. "You might be right."

"No worries. I'll swing by your desk at noon." He took the bag from her and on his way to his office, tossed it in the staff refrigerator. Without a tour until three, he was at loose ends. He popped his head into TJ's office but his brother wasn't there. More and more, TJ was guiding short trips. Mountain biking, kayaking, mountain climbing, nothing that kept him from his CEO duties for too long but enough to quench his need for speed.

He sifted through the itinerary Darcy had given him. Not surprising, she'd even taken care of restaurant reservations for the entire weekend. There was a burger joint in Nugget he was hoping to stop in at during their trip to the bull rider's ranch. Great curly fries. In high school, when their respective teams had played each other in sports, he and his buddies used to go there after games to get burgers and shakes. But Darcy had the group back in Glory Junction for lunchtime. He might have to change that, depending on the group. The place had no indoor seating and if the suits were fancy pants they might not like that. Usually he felt things out first, then tailored the tour accordingly. The scary groups had members who thought they were Sir Edmond Hillary. Then there were the folks who just needed a little encouragement. Maybe they weren't the toughest or had the most stamina but the looks on their faces when they made it to the top of the mountain was the best. Just the best.

His cell rang and he checked the caller ID. It wasn't a number he recognized but he answered anyway.

"Win Garner."

"Hey, Win, this is Stephanie." The name didn't register and Win didn't say anything, trying to figure out who she was. "Uh, we met kayaking the other day."

"Oh, hey, Steph. Sorry about last night. I had a family thing and couldn't make it to Old Glory." He probably should've messaged her back but figured she was just trying to kill time while passing through. Ordinarily, he would've been down with a one-nighter, but he was trying to kick the habit.

"You interested in getting together tonight? I'm here for a couple more days and thought . . . you know, why not?"

Unfortunately, yes, he knew. He hated to offend her but . . . "I'm gonna have to pass, Stephanie. But it was really great meeting you the other day."

"Um, okay." There was a long, silent pause. Just her breathing on the other end of the phone.

Ah, jeez, he'd embarrassed her. "I'm seeing someone," he blurted, hoping to soothe the sting.

"It didn't seem like you were the other day." There was a bite to her voice.

"It sort of just happened," he lied, feeling a wee bit guilty that he was so good at it. But it was a white lie. He didn't want to flat-out reject her. "I'd like to get to know her without a lot of distractions if you know what I mean."

"I do," she said, sounding somewhat mollified. "But it's not serious?"

"Not yet but you never know."

"Good for you," she said like she meant it. "I hope it works out."

"You're a good person, Steph. You take care now." He hung up.

"Who was that?" Colt walked in his door, uninvited. Hopefully, he'd only caught the tail end of the conversation.

"A friend," he said, and cleared off a chair for his brother to sit. His office could use a deep cleaning. Mostly, he used it as an extra closet but as often as he was coming into the office these days it wouldn't kill him to tidy up the place. "Things slow at the cop shop?'

"Not really. I just came over here hoping there were doughnuts."

Win thought it was supposed to be the other way around. "I've got a protein bar if you're hungry."

Colt scrunched up his nose. "Nah, I'll pass. Where's TJ?" Everyone was always looking for TJ.

"I have no idea. Probably making a merger somewhere."

Colt laughed. "What's this about you buying a house?" News traveled fast in the Garner clan.

"I'm not buying anything yet. Eventually, though. It'll depend on what I can afford." Which would depend on what kind of bonus he got.

"There's a place near us that just went on the market. It's open Sunday if you want to take a look at it."

The houses near Colt and Delaney's were probably out of his price range. The neighborhood was walking distance from town and most of the homes there had been supersized by city folk who wanted a country address near the ski slopes on the weekends.

"I've got FlashTag duties but maybe." If the VIPs headed back to the city early enough there might be time to check out the house.

"Jenny Meyers has the listing."

Shit! Win had slept with her a few times last summer. She'd just gone through a divorce and was looking to get back on the horse so to speak. He'd done his civic duty to help her with that. Then she started getting needy and he . . . did what he always did. Got the hell out of Dodge.

"On second thought, I'm looking for something near the lake."

Colt raised his brows. "Good luck with that. Let me know when you win the lottery."

"TJ found something there."

"That was a couple of years ago. Prices have soared since then." Colt stood up. "You sure there's no doughnuts?"

"Ask Darcy but I didn't see any."

Colt went back to the station, leaving Win alone to keep his own company, which was too bad because these days he was so over himself. He started a game of Candy Crush on his computer and halfway through thought about TJ. This wasn't the way his older brother would be spending his day. So Win stopped his game, picked up the phone, called an old corporate client, and cajoled him into booking a weekend of team building. Not bad for an hour's work. At noon, he went to fetch Darcy.

"You ready?"

She put on her shoes, which she'd kicked under her

desk. Her toenails were a bright pink that matched her dress. "If I must."

"You know it wouldn't kill you to pretend you like me. I do own an equal share of the company you work for."

Her response was to look at him and roll her eyes. He opened the door for her and they walked up Main Street to the Morning Glory. The restaurant, popular with locals, was a fifties-style diner. Black-and-white-check floors, red pleather upholstery, and enough chrome to open an auto body shop. Felix, the owner, was a champion snow boarder, who'd crashed so many times he could no longer compete. But he made a damned good tuna melt. Apparently, Felix wasn't the easiest to work for because he bled staff faster than anyone Win knew.

"Look what the wind blew in." Ricki, the waitress, grabbed two menus and showed them to a booth toward the back of the restaurant. She wasn't his number-one fan. Ricki was friends with Deb. Back before TJ, Win and Deb had had some unresolved feelings for each other—she was another woman he'd let down. But that was water under the bridge and he and Deb had patched up their differences. Ricki apparently hadn't gotten the memo.

"Don't spit in my food, okay?"

"I'll try not to." She pulled a pad from her apron pocket and a pencil from behind her ear. "What'll you have to drink?"

They both got waters and ordered meals without cracking the menus, since they knew it by heart. The place started to fill up and Ricki ran off to seat a couple of city council members.

"I guess you haven't won Ricki's heart the way you have the rest of Glory Junction's female population." Darcy pulled the paper off her straw.

"I bet she wouldn't throw me out of bed." He winked,

then gave her a slow, pointed look. "Some women just want me for my body."

"If you're talking about Saturday night, would you get over it already?"

"Why should I?"

"Because it's humiliating." She played with her fork, unwilling to look him in the eye. "I really would appreciate it if we never spoke of it again. Especially now that we're forced to work together."

"Forced? I think we're a great team," he lied for the second time that day. Darcy was way out of her league when it came to outdoor adventure sports. He was pretty sure she didn't even own a pair of hiking boots. And their styles clashed. She was anal-retentive and he was . . . well, the opposite.

"I hope so because I want my promotion." This time, she held his gaze, squinting her eyes at him. "Don't screw this up for me."

"Why does everyone automatically assume I'm a screw-up?" Granted, he had a more laid-back way of approaching things. It didn't make him a screw-up. "I've got a bonus riding on us getting this account. So as long as you have my back, I'll have yours."

"Did you go through my itinerary?"

"Yep. Looks fantastic. But I may have to change things up a bit."

She gave him the stink eye. "Don't mess with my itinerary, Win."

"Trust me. You'll be happy you did."

Darcy raised her brows and shook her head. "Only because you know way more about adventure sports than I do."

That he did. But Darcy's multitasking skills put him to shame, no question about that. The lodging and food planning alone was a headache and she'd booked it all without breaking a sweat. Impressive.

"So what's the deal with Geneva?" Win didn't want to just come out and say, "Your mom seems like a bitch."

Darcy let out a long breath. "She showed up without notice, saying it was because Lewis told her I had gotten engaged but I don't believe it. For that she would've just picked up the phone."

"Doesn't she come occasionally to visit Hilde?"

"Rarely. Only when she's fighting with my dad and wants to recruit my grandmother to her side against her own son."

"Does Hilde take the bait?"

"Hilde's Switzerland, even though her son is no prize either."

"I remember you once told me they have a loveless marriage." At least Win had retained a modicum of Darcy's personal life. From now on he was going to try harder to pay attention.

She nodded, took a sip of water and said, "I don't know why they got married in the first place, except that my mother loves money and my father makes a lot of it."

Just when it was getting interesting Ricki interrupted with their order. "Hope you don't choke on it," she told Win as she shoved a tri-tip sandwich in front of him, then gingerly placed Darcy's bowl on the table. "Careful, hon, it's hot."

He glanced over at her soup. "It looks good but not in eighty-degree weather."

"I feel a cold coming on."

Darcy seemed fine to him. "What does your father do?"

"He owns a mortgage brokerage. My mother works there too but mostly in an ambassador role."

"What does that mean?" Win took a bite of his sandwich. It tasted good, despite whatever hex Ricki put on it.

"She glad-hands a lot and passes out business cards at parties and functions between shopping sprees."

"You like her a lot, don't you?"

Darcy dipped a spoon in her soup. "I love her, she's my mother."

He arched a brow. "You know what they say, 'you can pick your friends but you can't pick your family.'"

"They're not the Garners, let's put it that way. But they're all I've got besides Nana. And she makes up for them. She's the best grandmother a person could ask for."

He had to admit Hilde Wallace had it going on. Brains and beauty, even at seventy-eight. And she could bake, which earned her major points in Win's book. But it was sad that Darcy felt the way she did about her parents. He hadn't missed the way she folded into herself when she talked about them.

"Your parents keep in touch with Lewis?" To hear it from Geneva she wanted her daughter to go back to the dude. There was a lot not being said here and Win wanted to explore it. Mostly because he was bored with his new life of celibacy and responsibility. At least that's what he told himself.

"They do a lot of business together, him being in real estate and all." She tore off a piece of her bread and popped it in her mouth.

"So they liked him, huh?"

"Yes." The terse, one-word answer wasn't good enough. Win was on a fishing expedition and he planned to catch something.

"Why?" He tilted his head and held her gaze.

"I suppose because he's successful and reliable."

Neither of those things could be said about Win, but he'd never wanted to be husband material. Still didn't, especially after his catastrophic near marriage to nutjob Britney.

"Then why did you dump him?" he asked.

"What makes you think I dumped him and not the other way around?"

Good question. But something intrinsic told him it had been her choice to leave the marriage, not Lewis's. Perhaps it was the way Lewis had hovered over her at the rodeo.

"Just a gut instinct," he said. "It was those string ties he wears. They drove you nuts."

She laughed, even though Win could tell she didn't want to. "How about we talk about something else?"

"How about we don't?" The more she resisted, the more tempted he was to dig in.

Maybe Lewis was a compulsive gambler. Nah, too interesting. The man had come off dull as dirt. Then again it was always the unassuming ones who turned out to be cross dressers or serial killers.

She stared at him over the rim of her water glass. "Why all the sudden interest in my love life?"

"If we're going to work together there should be no secrets between us," he said, and grinned.

The little witch shook her head. "It's private . . . and painful."

Painful.

That stopped him in his tracks. "I'm sorry. I didn't mean to pick at scabs."

Yet, he still wanted to know.

Chapter Eight

The FlashTag group came Friday night and Darcy met them at the small airport outside of town. In recent years, the airfield had grown to accommodate the influx of wealthy part-time residents who flew up in their private jets from the Bay Area and Los Angeles to enjoy a weekend on the slopes or a summer at the lake.

FlashTag had chartered a puddle jumper out of San Jose. Darcy was going to shuttle the three VIPs—Remy, Sue, and Russell—to the Four Seasons, let them get a good night's sleep, and pick them up the next morning for breakfast and a tour of GA and Glory Junction. Win was supposed to be with her on pickup duty to meet and greet their prospective clients but had run late on his white-water rafting excursion. No surprise there. As long as she'd known him he had trouble keeping to a schedule.

She had no intention of letting him screw this up for her. If need be she'd handle the orientation on her own, which would be no easy feat because she knew nothing about adventure sports. Win's unreliability was infuriating.

Worse, she'd begun dreaming about him in her sleep. Erotic dreams that felt so real she'd wake up in a sweat, panting. She knew she wasn't the first woman to fantasize about him. Win was the kind of man who could stir any female, even a dead one. But no one could accuse her of being delusional. That's why she refused to be part of his adoring fan club.

"It's really pretty here," Sue said, staring out of the passenger-side window of the minivan as they climbed higher up the mountain. The pink-streaked sky was fading from dusk to dark and soon it would be too hard to see much of anything.

"It's even more beautiful in the daytime." Darcy had always loved it here. Even as a young girl, visiting her grand-parents, she'd known that Glory Junction was a special place. "I think you'll like your accommodations. It's a beautiful hotel. There's a full gym and spa and indoor and outdoor pools if you're interested in taking a dip before you go to bed or tomorrow morning."

She hoped she wasn't babbling. Small talk and being charming was Win's bag, not hers. Her skills had always been behind the scenes. She silently cursed him for missing this. First impressions were important and she worried that she wasn't making a good one. The whole drive had been full of long stretches of silence.

"Anyone interested in getting a drink in the bar?" Remy asked, and she fervently hoped the invitation didn't include her. Remy, Sue, and Russell seemed perfectly nice but she'd never been comfortable in a group of strangers.

Her phone beeped with an incoming text as she drove through the gates of the Four Seasons. She waited to pull up to the front of the hotel before taking a quick glance. Not Win, Lewis. Darcy shoved the phone back in her purse.

"Here we are," she said too brightly, and jumped out to help with the luggage. A bellhop beat her to it.

She went inside to get her guests checked in and to make

sure that everything was covered on Garner Adventure's account.

"I know you probably want to get situated in your rooms." Darcy scribbled her cell phone number on a stack of Win's business cards—she didn't have any of her own—and handed them to the trio. "Feel free to call if anything comes up. We'll pick you up at the valet stand at nine o'clock tomorrow."

They said good-bye and she sprinted out of the lobby, breathing a sigh of relief. That had gone off without a hitch. At least for now. What she'd like to do was stop by Win's apartment and threaten to break his legs if he pulled a disappearing act in the morning. Instead, she took the minivan home and nearly took out a row of Nana's azalea bushes, trying to back the damn thing up to the garage.

The first thing she wanted to do was take off her shoes, which had pinched her toes all day, and take a hot bath. Then she planned to raid the refrigerator as she'd never had dinner. Before she could get in the house her phone rang. Finally.

"I can't believe you hung me out to dry," she blurted by way of a formal greeting. Okay, it wasn't exactly Win's fault that his tour had taken longer than expected. But more than likely he'd dawdled, which he had a habit of doing. Or had spent so much time flirting with his all-female group that they'd gone into overtime. Darcy had seen the women before they'd left for the river. Four blondes in teeny-weeny bikini tops. He was probably at Old Glory with them now or . . . she didn't even want to think about it.

"Darcy, it's me, Lewis."

Shit, shit, shit! Why hadn't she checked caller ID before answering her damn phone? Because she'd been sure it was Win, that's why.

"Oh, hi, Lewis. I thought you were someone else."

"Your fiancé?"

For God's sake, Win wasn't her fiancé. "A coworker. It's not important. What's up?"

"I was hoping you could help me transfer those files this weekend." Help? What he meant was he wanted her to do it for him. As in all by herself.

"I can't this weekend, Lewis. We have clients here from out of town and I'm spending the weekend showing them around." Not that it was any of his business but she felt guilty. After all, she'd promised to do it for him.

"I see," he said. "Isn't there anyone else who can show them around?"

She wanted to say, *Isn't there anyone else who can transfer your data for you?* But what was the point? "No, Lewis. We're trying to score a big account and I'm part of the sales team. It's actually a big deal and could mean a promotion for me." Why she was even bothering to tell him about her career plans was beyond comprehension.

He was silent for a while and she considered hanging up when he finally said, "Since you're working the weekend for your employer is there a way you could take time off during the week to do it for me?"

Since she was working the weekend she had hoped to take time off on Wednesday to go shopping with her grandmother in Reno. Not to work for Lewis. "I'll think about it. I've got to go now." She clicked off and hobbled to the house in her torturous shoes. They were a post-divorce purchase that had set her back almost two hundred dollars. Now she was ready to donate them to the Goodwill.

The TV was playing when she got inside and something smelled delicious. Her grandmother loved to cook and Darcy was the beneficiary of all her tasty dishes.

"Nana?" She wasn't in her usual chair, watching one of her programs.

Darcy checked the kitchen and finally found her in her bedroom, sitting on the side of her bed, fully dressed.

"Nana, are you okay?" Her grandmother looked pale and out of breath.

"I'm fine, dear. I came in to use the bathroom and got a little dizzy. Too much time in the sun today."

Darcy went into the kitchen and got her a glass of water. "Maybe we should go and get you checked out." Tonight, her usually hale grandmother looked every one of her years and it scared Darcy. Without Nana, she didn't know what she would do.

"I just overdid it, is all. Give me a few minutes and I'll be right as rain."

Darcy sat on the edge of the bed next to her grandmother. "Are you sure? It would only take a few minutes to drive to urgent care."

"Don't be silly." Nana took Darcy's hand. "Let's have a slumber party. We could watch *The Late Show* together in bed."

She wondered if she should insist on taking her to the hospital. But her grandmother's face had gotten some of its color back and her voice sounded strong. "You promise you're okay?"

"To prove it, I'll make the popcorn."

"I'll make it, Nana. You stay here and relax. Just give me thirty minutes to bathe and change."

"You're on," Nana said.

Darcy took a fast shower and put on her PJs. Before heading downstairs to the kitchen, she shot Win a text. I'll pick you up in the morning. Be ready!

Just as she placed her phone on the charger, her phone dinged with an incoming message: an emoji of an okay sign and *Anyone ever tell you you're bossy?*

Win's quick response told her he probably hadn't gone

home with one of the blondes from his tour. Though it shouldn't have, the knowledge that he wasn't with anyone made her ridiculously happy.

Halfway to the bottom of the stairs, she heard her grandmother humming in the kitchen and called, "I'm coming, Nana."

Win was waiting on the sidewalk outside his apartment when Darcy pulled up in the minivan. It should've been illegal to look that good this early in the morning, she wanted to tell him. But he already had too healthy an opinion of himself. He was dressed in Delaney's custom-designed cargo shorts and a GA T-shirt that stretched across his broad shoulders and washboard abs. His hair was slightly damp and finger combed. He hadn't bothered to shave, sporting a fashionable layer of stubble.

"Chic dishevelment" is what Darcy liked to call it. And no one wore it better than Win.

He opened the passenger door, dropped his backpack on the floor, and bobbed his chin in greeting. "Want me to drive?"

"Nope. I want to get there in one piece."

"Whatever." He buckled himself in. "Hit it."

Before pulling back onto the road, she turned sideways in her seat and sniffed him. "Cologne?"

"Just soap, babe."

She should've known better. Cologne would've ruined the whole I-just-rolled-out-of-bed-naturally-gorgeous thing he had going on.

He eyed her up and down. "Where are your hiking shorts and boots?"

She didn't own any. "Why? We're not hiking."

"Yes, we are."

"Check your itinerary, Win. There's nothing on there about hiking. After breakfast, we're giving them a tour of the town . . . from the van." He didn't say anything, which worried her. "I worked hard on the schedule, we're not changing it."

Silence.

"Win?" She gripped the steering wheel as they took the road to the Four Seasons.

"Just a quick stroll up the Miwok Trail on Sawtooth for that breathtaking view, then we'll return to your regularly scheduled program."

"A quick stroll?" She took the turn a little too fast and Win planted his feet on the dashboard to stabilize himself.

"Jeez, take it easy, Mario."

"That's a three-mile climb." Straight up. She knew that because it was one of the tours they offered. It was guided by a retired naturalist who could talk about the plants and wildlife in the area.

"It'll be nice . . . get the blood flowing."

In a minute, his blood was going to be flowing all over the minivan. And when Colt came to investigate she would tell him it was justifiable homicide.

"It wasn't on the itinerary. Remy, Sue, and Russell won't be dressed appropriately for a hike because they don't know anything about it," she said, hoping to put an end to his asinine plan for once and for all.

"They know about it now," he said, and she shot him a look. "What?" He smiled a little too brightly. "I texted them a few minutes before you picked me up. They're excited about it."

"I'm not excited about it," she spat. Her feet were still killing her from the horrible shoes she'd worn the day before.

"Just drop us, then, and say you have somewhere else to go."

He would like that, wouldn't he? Instead of being his equal partner, she'd be a glorified chauffeur. "You're crazy if you think you're taking that hike without me."

"That's good, too." He glanced down at her tennis shoes. "Those will work."

She would've called him some choice names but they'd arrived at their destination and their crew was waiting at the valet stand, bright-eyed and bushy-tailed. Before she even stopped the van, Win jumped out. She watched him shake everyone's hand with a big grin on his face. Even from the driver's seat, she saw Sue's eyes pop out of her head.

Could the man be any more affable? She wished he would give it a rest already.

"Good morning," Remy said as he climbed into the back seat of the van.

"Morning." She plastered on a smile. "I hope you're all okay with the change in plans."

"A hike sounds great," he said. God, she hated millennials, even if she was one herself. They were so damned chipper.

"Are you sure? What about your shoes?" She turned around and . . . great . . . he had on a pair of Merrells.

"We were expecting to be out in the wild so we all packed accordingly," he said, making room for Sue and Russell, who'd torn themselves away from Win long enough to get inside.

"You guys hungry?" Win hopped in the front. "Or should we wait until after the hike to grab a bite?"

Goddamn him, she'd made a reservation at the Morning Glory.

"I had a cup of coffee at the hotel, so I'm good to go," Sue said, and the other two agreed.

Darcy gritted her teeth. Not only had she forgone her first cup of coffee of the day to pick Win up on time but she was starved.

"Felix is going to kill us," she muttered. There were lines to get a table at the restaurant on a Saturday morning this time of year. Actually, any time of year.

"I'll take care of it," he said. And the infuriating part was Felix would forgive him. A halfhearted apology from Mr. Charm and all sins would be absolved.

At the trailhead, one look at the uphill course and Darcy wanted to throw up. In the best of times, she wasn't the most athletic. After a year of sitting on her ass, eating Nana's baked goods, she would be lucky to make it a quarter of a mile without dropping dead. What kind of impression would that leave on the FlashTag VIPs? She could guarantee not a good one. But no way was she leaving Win to his own devices. She wanted that promotion, which meant keeping him in line. And more important, she wasn't going to let TJ down. He'd given her this job and by God she was going to make him proud, even if it killed her.

"I'll take the back," she volunteered. At least if she collapsed, no one would notice.

Win cocked his head to one side. "Okay," he said, and led the way, climbing the mountain as if he were a goat.

While Remy, Sue, and Russell held their own, it was abundantly clear that they didn't have Win's stamina, stopping every so often along the trail to sip from the bottled waters Win had doled out from the back of the van.

"Would you look at that view?" Darcy turned her back to the group, pretending to scan the horizon so she could catch her breath and not die. As a stall tactic, she fished her cell phone from her pocket and took her time snapping pictures.

Unfortunately, they hadn't even passed the one-mile marker yet. And the rest of the climb was even steeper than the beginning. The only thing that kept her hanging on was the knowledge that what went up must come down.

"You okay back there?" Win called down.

"Great," she croaked, and silently cursed him. Besides the fact that she was practically doubled over, she felt a blister raging on the bottom of her right foot.

He came down the mountain to join her. "You done looking at the view, Darce? I'm getting hungry."

If she could've shoved him into a ravine she would've. But for all the obvious reasons she didn't, though the temptation was so strong that when no one was looking she pinched his arm. He had the nerve to pat her bottom.

"If you want, I'll carry you the rest of the way," he whispered.

She responded by muttering an obscenity under her breath and followed it with "you." He responded by laughing.

By the time she trudged to the next plateau, the sole of her foot was on fire. She hid her grimace under the bucket hat Win had shoved on the top of her head before the hike. Even with it, she felt the morning sun scorch her arms and neck. Thank goodness, she'd worn jeans.

One look at her, and Win came down the trail again. He fetched a tube of sunblock from his pack and rubbed it all over her bare skin, including the top of her chest, which made her tingle. Or maybe that was sun poisoning.

"Anyone else?" He held up the tube.

"I could use some," Sue said, and Darcy got the distinct impression that she hoped Win rubbed the lotion on her the same way he had Darcy.

To his credit, he tossed her the bottle. "We ready to go?"

"Let's do it," Russell said enthusiastically, making Darcy feel like a wuss.

When they finally got to the top, Darcy thought she was going to stroke out. Taking large gulps of air, she started to cough. Win rushed over.

"I swallowed my water wrong." As proof, she showed him her empty bottle, the one she'd drained half a mile ago.

"It's all downhill from here," he consoled.

If it wasn't for the fact that her feet were bloody from blisters she would've kicked him. At least Sue and Remy were also hunched over, trying to catch their breath as if they might pass out. Russell, on the other hand, stared out over the vista, a big gooey smile on his face. He was crazy like Win, who hadn't even broken a sweat and could carry on a conversation as easily as if he was riding in a car.

It had taken them ninety minutes to go up—more than a twenty-minute mile, that was for sure—and only thirty to make it back to where they started. It would've been faster if Darcy hadn't come down part of the way on her butt. Win had offered to carry her again. She in turn had quietly told him to do something anatomically impossible. Win's comeback was to plant a big sloppy kiss on her cheek.

"That, my friends, is team building," he said as they climbed back into the van.

She had to admit that they had bonded during the hike. Even she was chatting amiably with the group as if they were old friends.

"I'm starved," Sue said. "We probably burned a thousand calories."

And now it was closer to lunchtime than breakfast and all they'd had was the protein bars Win had handed out with the waters. Their lunch reservation wasn't until noon.

"Would you like to go back to the hotel and shower before we eat?" she asked, hoping the time it would take would get them back on track.

"Nah," Win said. "We'll just get sweaty again."

No, they wouldn't. She had them down for a tour of Garner Adventure where one of their summer guides was going to demonstrate a climb on the rock wall.

"Hang a right on Main," he told her just as she was about to take the turnoff for the Four Seasons. "There's a great diner we want you all to try. The place has a Belgium waffle that's off the hook and steak and eggs that'll melt in your mouth."

"I could go for that," Russell said.

Win was screwing up her schedule. If they ate breakfast now no one would be hungry for lunch. She'd reserved a back table at Old Glory where Remy, Sue, and Russell could get plenty of the rustic gastro pub's ambience without the noise. She was going to make Win call Boden and cancel, since it was his fault they would miss the reservation.

Darcy found a parking space close to the Morning Glory and even though it was just a diner and this was the Sierra Nevada, where outdoor recreation was a way of life, she felt self-conscious going inside all grubby. Win had no such compunction and pushed ahead of the group to find Felix. Then again, he bore no trace of their hike. No pit stains on his T-shirt, no dirt on the seat of his shorts, and if Darcy was to guess, his feet weren't blistered. And unlike the rest of them, he probably smelled like the clean outdoors.

She watched him chat up the grouchy restaurant owner, even saw Felix smile—a rarity. But after all that Win came back frowning.

"Felix doesn't have a table," he said. "We'll have to go to Tart Me Up, I guess."

While Darcy loved the bakery, it wasn't a restaurant. Ordering croissant breakfast sandwiches at the counter and cramming around a bistro table was too low rent for entertaining Silicon Valley clients.

"What do you mean he doesn't have a table?" Darcy pointed to a large, circular booth that would easily fit the five of them. Out of earshot of the others, she hissed, "Felix is getting back at you for blowing our reservation."

Darcy marched toward the restaurant owner and pulled him out of sight, into the kitchen. She was so angry at Win she threw nonconfrontational out the window. Her job was to make everything perfect, starting with their meals.

"Come on, Felix. GA gives you a ton of business. Their doughnut orders alone probably keep your lights on. What's wrong with the large booth?"

Felix stepped back, a little stunned. "You know in the entire time you've been coming here to pick up said doughnuts I don't think you've said two words to me."

"I'm shy." She folded her arms over her chest.

His brows shot up. "Could've fooled me. I've got a large group coming in at noon. There won't be time to turn the table."

Probably not, since that was only thirty minutes away. "Can't you figure out a way to make it work? It's important to Garner Adventure." She knew the name held weight despite Felix's cavalier attitude. "We're sorry we missed our reservation. It was an accident."

"I held the table for nearly an hour and had to turn business away. You know what this place is like on a Saturday, especially during tourism season. You couldn't bother to call?"

That should've been Win's job since he'd been the one to change the plan in the first place.

"Win and I got our wires crossed," she said. "It's not an excuse and it won't happen again. You have my promise on that." Darcy looked at him imploringly. "If we get this account it'll be good for you, too. Everyone in Glory Junction will get more business."

"Look around," he said, gesturing to the dining room. "I don't need more business."

"Please, Felix. We have three extremely hungry clients. Don't make us go somewhere else."

He puffed out a breath and stood there long enough that Darcy thought his answer was going to be an emphatic "No." But then he surprised her by grabbing five menus and begrudgingly leading her to the circular booth she'd wanted.

"GA owes me. And the next time you come in here, don't pull that shy crap with me, you hear?"

"Thank you, Felix."

Win slid in next to her like it was no big deal that Felix had relented and given them a table.

"What are you getting?" he asked, his lips hovering less than an inch from her ear. "I want pancakes and an omelet, so let's share."

She drilled him with a look but the truth was she was hungry enough to eat both meals all by herself but didn't want to make a pig out of herself in front of everyone. "Fine, but I want the waffle instead of the pancakes."

"Done!" Under the table he touched her knee. "You did great this morning."

She turned sideways in her seat to see if he was joking. *Great*? Not only had she complained the entire way, she'd held up the group with her constant breaks. Even Remy and Sue had more stamina than she did. But she saw no sign of sarcasm in his expression, only animation as he gave an extensive background lesson on the area. His audience sat rapt as he described Glory Junction's first settlers and told stories of the Gold Rush. Who knew Win was a history buff?

What he wasn't was a man who could keep to a schedule. By the time they left the Morning Glory they were supposed to be finishing up their tour of GA. That was why they were here in the first place—to sell the company.

But nooooo, Win decided they should go on a bike ride. No way in hell was she suffering through that. Both her ass and feet rebelled at the same time. She was considering how to bow out tactfully when Win told everyone that she'd planned a picnic at the end of the ride, near the lake. No, she hadn't. And there was no time to set up something like that now. She glared at him as they pulled the van into GA's back lot to collect the bikes.

"Are you purposely trying to sabotage me?" she asked when she got him alone. TJ had come out to meet the group and was taking them on a tour of the building.

"What are you talking about? Just go call Rachel at Tart Me Up and have her deliver a spread to TJ's house. We'll do it there."

She knew his home was less than ten minutes from a public bike trail that ran alongside the water.

Teeth clenched, she hissed, "If you haven't noticed Rachel runs a thriving business. She needs notice to pull off something like this. I had us booked at Old Glory but you screwed that up."

"Fine, I'll handle it. You load the bikes." He started inside.

"Oh, no you don't." She raced in front of him. "This bike ride is your idea, you load the bikes."

He turned around. "Try not to be so difficult."

"I don't understand why you have to change everything. I planned this down to the minute so that we'd look professional . . . organized."

He tugged her into a corner and pinned her against the wall. "Did you even take the time to read Remy's, Sue's, and Russell's bios?"

Of course she had. She'd been the one to provide him the damn things. So what was his point? "What about them?"

"These people make high achievers look like slackers. They spend most of their time behind a computer, trying to outdo one another. Their sole goal in life is to be the best.

The smartest. The most successful. A tour of GA isn't going to cut it, Darcy. Folks like Remy, Sue, and Russell need to be challenged to the breaking point. That's what they thrive on. That's why I changed things up. It wasn't to mess with you and your schedule, it was to get the account. Because believe it or not, I know what I'm doing. And I actually have a strategy." He walked away, leaving her feeling stupid because he was right. Win had read their prospective clients better than she had.

Despite her pride, she had to fall in line and work with him.

After ten minutes of Darcy begging and finally promising to pay twice what Tart Me Up normally charged, Rachel agreed to set up a picnic at TJ's. Even if it would be way past lunchtime when they finished Win's bike ride.

After meeting Remy, Sue, and Russell and schmoozing with them while Win loaded the bikes, TJ came to the front desk to find her. "I thought we were doing a rock-climbing demonstration."

"Win thinks we need to spend more time outdoors, doing activities." She shrugged. "They seem to enjoy it so Win's decided to take them on a bike ride."

"Okay. Whatever makes them happy because if they sign I'm happy." A not so discreet reminder that they better seal the deal. TJ was a great many things, but subtle wasn't one of them.

"Gotcha," she said.

"How do you think it's going so far?"

"Good." At least she thought so. They'd survived the hike and seemed to have enjoyed breakfast—or brunch. And who wouldn't like three nights at the Four Seasons?

"Where are they now?" She felt like she should be with them, networking or whatever you were supposed to do. This was the first time she'd ever had this much contact with clients. Working with Lewis, she'd always been the silent partner, though the word *partner* was overstating it. And at GA she talked to people on the phone all day but rarely met them in person as they typically met their guides off site.

"Using the bathroom and taking advantage of the locker rooms to clean up. Deb gave them all Garner Adventure cycling jerseys."

Smart, which reminded her about the swag bags. "I planned to give them the gift baskets Deb made up on the last day."

"Sounds good." He gave her wilted appearance a once-over. "You want a jersey?"

Hell, no. The clingy fabric would accentuate her muffin top. "That's okay."

"What about some shorts? You're going to melt in jeans."

Then her legs would burn. Even with sunblock, her pale skin was no match for a Glory Junction summer. "I'm fine."

She limped outside to find the bikes had been fully loaded. Apparently, there was no way she was getting out of this. At least she knew the trail was flat from having ridden it when she'd first moved to Glory Junction with big plans to get fit . . . and find a man who could make her feel like a woman. Unfortunately, both goals remained on her to-do list and she hadn't moved any closer to getting them done.

"Ready to move out?" Win had also changed into a bike jersey. No muffin top on him. Not even love handles.

"Let's do it," Russell said. He was way too into this.

She'd give Remy credit. He was a little overweight, a lot out of shape, but unlike her, a good sport. Sue, on the other hand, was lean and looked as if she worked out regularly but probably in a gym. The hike had winded her too much for someone who routinely climbed.

Darcy took the wheel and drove to a small lot near the public beach. In no time at all, Win had the bikes unloaded and ready to go. He handed out helmets, waters, and more sunblock.

"How you holding up, hot stuff?" He adjusted her chin strap, lingering a little longer than he should've, especially in front of an audience.

"I'll live."

He winked. "That's the old spirt."

Twenty minutes into the ride and her bottom and legs screamed. How was it that she remembered the trail being flat? There was a restroom up ahead and she used it as an excuse to stop. The others, even Remy, were pedaling at a steady clip so she told them she'd catch up. Ha!

She took off her helmet and stuck her entire head under the faucet in the sink and pressed a wet paper towel to her face. When she came out of the bathroom she found Win waiting for her.

"Where are the others?"

"Up ahead. You okay?"

No. If she had less pride she would've sat on the ground and cried. "My ass is on fire."

His mouth curved up in a sympathetic smile. "It's almost over and I think it's going pretty well, don't you?"

She did. The group seemed to be enjoying themselves. "As long as I don't wind up in the emergency room."

"Come here." He crooked his finger at her but she wouldn't budge. "Come on, Darce." He reached for her, brushed her hair behind her ears, and put the helmet on her head. "We're almost done. When we get to TJ's I'll ride back and bring the van."

She nodded, feeling like a big baby. Getting on her bike, she made a resolution to work out more, or at all, and tried not to wince from saddle soreness. When they arrived at

TJ's she nearly threw herself off the bike and kissed the ground. Instead, she got a second wind and raced around the house to the backyard to make sure the food had been delivered.

Rachel had outdone herself. A red-checkered cloth covered a round table, set with real dishes, not paper. The plates were blue ceramic with bright red anchors in the middle and had matching cobalt glasses. The centerpiece: a pail of white hydrangeas and a circle of votive candles. Darcy didn't know if Rachel had brought the tableware or whether it had come from Deb and TJ's kitchen. Wherever it had come from it was beautiful and so perfect for the lakeside setting.

A long table facing the water sagged with platters of sandwiches, bowls of salads—potato, coleslaw, fruit—baskets of chips, and pitchers of ice tea and lemonade. On a smaller table, Rachel had laid out a dessert spread. Brownies, cookies, and miniature cupcakes with the GA logo. Whoa, when had she had time to do that? As soon as they got back to town, Darcy planned to personally thank her. Rachel had gone above and beyond and as much as she hated to accept it, Win had been right about the picnic. It was impressive while seeming casual and intimate. Better than a restaurant, more creative.

Darcy stretched her sore muscles and took the time to really look around. TJ and Deb's place was gorgeous. The yard backed right up to the lake with expansive lawns, a dock, and a boathouse. The main house was a rustic three-story with light brown shingles and chocolate brown trim and scads of windows to take advantage of the lake views.

Win had unlocked the front door so Remy, Sue, and Russell could use the bathroom and wash up before lunch. Darcy had every intention of going inside and snooping through the rooms. It just didn't get much better than this, she thought as she peered out over the water. And better yet, she was off that stupid bike, even if she was walking bowlegged.

Win came outside, scanned the spread as if it was no big deal, poured himself a glass of lemonade, and gulped it down in one drink. Not one word. She supposed she should be used to it after working for Lewis for two years.

Darcy figured it was a good time to go inside, freshen up, and take a tour of the house. She pushed past him and pretended not to hear him when he called after her.

She went around to the front, not sure if the back door was unlocked, and let herself in. Jeez Louise, the place was awesome. Not stuffy like her parents' mausoleum but not quite as lived-in as Nana's country cottage. A perfect in between. Touches of comfort everywhere, including color-ful toss pillows, kilim rugs, and tons of family pictures.

She took a quick whirl around the kitchen, and peeked around the main floor where she used the powder room. Then she dashed upstairs and poked her head into a couple of bedrooms because she was nosy that way. Back on the main floor, she locked the front door, fearful that Win would forget. Glory Junction was a safe town but there had been a slew of break-ins the previous summer. She went in search of the back door to the yard and found it on the bottom level of the house, which had been tricked out with a big-screen TV, pool table, and a big comfy seating area.

The house was as different from Win's studio apartment as the two brothers were. TJ was methodical while Win was haphazard. TJ bordered on intense while Win was more chill than an easy chair. At least she'd thought he was. Today, he'd proven that he wasn't as laid-back or as haphazard as everyone thought.

Believe it or not, I know what I'm doing. And I actually have a strategy.

Outside, she found the group sitting at Rachel's prettily set table, eating. Win was telling a story that had everyone laughing and as usual was the center of attention.

"I saved you a chair," he said, and patted the seat next to his.

"Thanks." She looked down at the heaping plate of food and the tall glass of ice tea he'd fetched for her. Yep, Win Garner was just full of surprises.

Chapter Nine

Win rode back to the trailhead to get the van. Without the others in tow, it took half the time as the ride to TJ's. Even though the trek was quick, he enjoyed the solitude. It wasn't easy being on 24/7 but that's what people expected from him. Win Garner, the charming one. Instead of being the brightest or the most heroic, he was the brother who made people laugh or smile. It was a role he'd learned to play as a little boy who'd been dubbed "slow."

Laugh with him, instead of at him.

The other thing he'd learned was to do everything else fast. Riding a bike, throwing a ball, skiing down a mountain, getting a woman into bed. Skills that had earned him a strange amount of admiration, despite his learning disability. After lots of educational specialists and therapists he could read now. But once you've been labeled "the life of the party" it was difficult to lose the tag. He should know, not that he was complaining. It was better than being a wet blanket, like a certain blond sprite.

Granted, he'd blown up her detailed schedule but there was a method to his madness. To get the account, GA had to stand out from its competitors. He'd been in the adventure business a long time—his whole life if you counted coming to the office as a little tyke with his parents—and everyone made their pitch Darcy's way. A basic orientation that highlighted the area and its attractions with a really good spiel of why the . . . fill in the blank . . . company would best serve the client's needs. Effective but definitely not a slam dunk, especially because it was the cookie-cutter approach. Safe but not ballsy.

His method was the same as Nike's. "Just Do It." If they spent the weekend actually team building, instead of talking about it, Garner Adventure would have the edge. Of course, there was the risk that everyone would have a miserable experience and go home mad at each other. Then Win would wind up with egg on his face. But he was willing to chance it. And so far, it was going pretty well, he thought. The only one who appeared to be having a bad time was Darcy.

But when this was all over and GA had the FlashTag account, Darcy would get her promotion. Win would make sure of it.

By the time he returned to TJ's with the van, Darcy had cleaned up from lunch. The woman was efficient. And cute, even if she wanted to cut off his balls right now. Sometimes he wondered what it would've been like if he'd slept with her. A few times this last week he'd even considered asking her if sex was still on the table but at the last minute had stopped himself.

He loaded up the bikes while the others dipped their feet in the lake. If he'd been thinking ahead, he would've asked TJ for use of his boat to take everyone out on the water.

"What now?" he asked Darcy as they piled back in the van.

She threw up her hands. "Who knows, the schedule's so screwed up."

"You're adorable when you're mad, you know that, right?" He said it in her ear so no one else would hear.

She held up three fingers. "Read between the lines."

"I think TJ's bad attitude is rubbing off on you." He had taken the driver's seat to give Darcy a break from shuttle duties and started the engine. "I'll take them back to the hotel so they can have a little downtime before we do the cave tour. We can end the night at Old Glory."

"A cave tour was never on the itinerary," she huffed. The others were too busy carrying on a conversation in the back to hear.

"It is now." He nosed the van toward the road to the Four Seasons.

The next day was better between them because this time he stuck to her timetable. For the most part, anyway.

At nine they picked up their crew at the hotel, stopped at the Morning Glory for breakfast, and made the thirty-minute drive to Nugget. Compared to Glory Junction, Nugget looked a little worn around the edges. Not shabby exactly but devoid of the frills that came with a ski-resort town. Instead of wealthy tourists, Nugget catered to the area's cattle ranchers and the Union Pacific Railroad. No fancy shops, no sidewalk cafés, no more than one hotel, which Win admitted was impressive. An old Victorian, dripping with gingerbread, that took up roughly a quarter of the town's commercial square and looked pretty as a postcard with its inviting front porch and pleasing color scheme. According to TJ, some big San Francisco hotelier and his sister had purchased the mansion and brought it back from the dead.

The Ponderosa, also on the square, was the town's only sit-down restaurant and doubled as a bar and bowling alley. As a kid, Win and his brothers had spent many Friday nights at the old-timey Western saloon. In recent years that too had gotten a facelift. Two women from the city had rescued the falling-down place and now ran it.

Darcy leaned over the console and told Win, "I've never been here before."

"You grew up in Reno and never came to Nugget?" How was that possible? The two towns were less than an hour away from each other.

"I don't know what to tell you. Maybe we just don't get around that much in Nevada. It's cute, sort of."

"We used to kick their ass in football, though they always made it into the National High School Rodeo Finals. Glory Junction didn't have a team."

"Do you know where you're going?"

"Of course I do." He didn't have a clue but how hard could it be to find a dude ranch owned by a celebrity bull rider?

Twenty minutes later, on a dirt back road, he admitted he was lost. Their guests were too enthralled with the breathtaking landscape to notice. Win rolled down his window as he approached three men on horseback. On closer inspection, it was a man and two teenage boys.

"Hey there." He stopped, careful not to spook the horses, and stuck his head out. "We're looking for Lucky Rodriguez's Cowboy Camp. Any chance you know where it is?"

The man rode closer and peered inside the van's windows. "He expecting you?"

"Yes, sir. We have an appointment."

The cowboy looked at Darcy and tipped his hat. She smiled back at him.

"You want to keep going straight," he said, and pointed to a bank of mailboxes up ahead. "See that stretch of fence? Hang a right at the last post and head up the hill about a mile. That's when you'll see the big entrance to the camp."

"Thanks." Win waited for John Wayne to ride back to his posse and followed his directions, sliding Darcy a glance. "That your boyfriend?"

"I wish."

Sue giggled. "Don't we all."

"You ladies like them old, huh? Daddy issues?"

Russell howled with laughter and Remy gave Win a high five.

"Hey, both hands on the wheel." That was Nervous Nelly Darcy for you.

Sure enough, a big wrought-iron gate with lots of scrollwork in what looked to Win like a cattle brand announced that they had arrived. Win followed the signs to a small lot, next to a tidy wooden building, which he suspected was the office. Everyone hopped out of the van and a man wearing a Stetson and a silver belt buckle the size of a dinner plate came out to greet them.

"You Darcy Wallace?"

"I am." She blushed.

What the hell was it with Darcy and cowboys? He wanted to tell her to get a grip before she embarrassed herself.

Darcy made the introductions and the guy turned out to be Lucky Rodriguez himself. He stood back for a second, examining the group.

"Who's gonna ride first?" Rodriguez looked directly at Darcy and grinned. "How 'bout you? You look tough."

Win thought she was going to faint, even though it was obvious the dude was joking.

"I'll go first," Win volunteered, and Rodriguez took a minute to size him up, lingering on his hiking boots.

"Those aren't going to work but I'll hook you up. Before we do anything, there's a short safety orientation I need to go over and there's the tour."

"Definitely the tour." Darcy shielded her eyes with her hands and gazed around the property.

Win got the impression that Darcy had never been to a working ranch before, which was weird since she'd said her ex-husband sold them. Win had been to many. Growing up in the Sierra it was unavoidable. Half the kids he'd gone to school with lived on one.

Lucky showed them around, cracking jokes as he took them down rows of animal pens.

The corrals were clean and the livestock looked well cared for. They stopped occasionally along the way so Lucky could scratch one of the bulls behind its head. Lucky bred and raised bucking stock for rodeos and Pro Bull Riders events, he explained. From here they looked docile and even a little sweet, but Win suspected that wasn't the case once you got on one of their backs.

It was a nice piece of property. Most of it was flat with rolling hills in the foreground and a spectacular view of the Sierra mountain range. There were a series of outbuildings, including several barns and a massive stack-stone and timber-log lodge that served as the camp's mess hall and cantina. The whole setup was imposing and Remy, Sue, and Russell didn't know where to look first. This was the real deal.

Win couldn't help but think that they should be doing more business together. A day trip with some of GA's family reunions and corporate groups and vice versa with guests of the cowboy camp. They could trade expertise, cross promote, and make a fortune together.

The business end of Garner Adventure was TJ's bag but there was nothing to say that Win couldn't be more assertive in that regard. It was time for him to take on more. To be more.

"This is impressive," he told Lucky. "Tell us what goes into being a world champion bull rider."

"A lot of concussions and busted teeth," Lucky said, and spent the next twenty minutes describing life on the bull-riding circuit.

He was a compelling storyteller and Remy, Sue, and Russell drank it up. Win figured the trio had never been to a rodeo, let alone a PBR event. He wouldn't call them tech nerds exactly but they probably spent a lot of time playing video games, going to Coldplay concerts, and watching sci-fi flicks. Or maybe he was just stereotyping.

Darcy seemed entranced too and she wasn't even a rodeo buff. Just apparently a fan of cowboys, which was starting to piss him off.

Lucky's daughter, a cute tween with pigtails, joined them and followed Win around wherever he went, which wasn't unusual. Kids liked him.

"Katie, you want to do a barrel racing demonstration for our friends, here?" Lucky ruffled her hair.

The girl trotted off and came back a short time later on the back of a horse. They followed her to a large ring where three barrels were already set up and took seats in the metal bleachers to watch. Win made sure to sit next to Darcy so he could give her a hard time about her cowboy fetish.

"You're crazy," she said as he poked at her. "I'm just trying to be friendly."

He whistled the theme music to *Bonanza*. "That make you hot?"

She shook her head. "I think you must've hit your head on our bike ride yesterday and got permanent brain damage."

He squeezed her leg because he couldn't resist razzing her. Win hitched his head at the others, who stood leaning on the rails of the arena, watching Katie take turns around the barrels at breakneck speed. "I think it's going pretty well, how about you?"

"Now that you're sticking with the program, I think it's going great." The corners of her mouth kicked up.

She gave as good as she got, he'd give her that. But not with everyone. Colt barely looked at her and she shrank ten inches. Josh's voice gave her the fidgets. TJ didn't intimidate her as much as he used to and a few times Win had even heard her talk back to his brother. But she was her bravest with him. Hell, she was downright feisty. And Win liked it. A lot. He liked their banter, even when she was sticking it to him.

"You ready to do some bull riding?" Lucky asked, and everyone hooted and hollered.

He called to a couple of ranch hands and told them something in Spanish. Win picked up enough to know that he wanted them to load the chutes with some *toros*. "Mean as hell" might've been mentioned too but Win's grasp of the language wasn't good enough to know for sure.

"What size boots you wear?" Lucky asked Win, and sent Katie off to fetch a pair.

He had them follow him to one of the outbuildings, which turned out to be a small auditorium and did a slide presentation on safety and bull riding. An oxymoron if Win ever heard one. He suspected it wasn't half as easy as the PowerPoint made it out to be but he assumed the bulls they'd be using were for beginners. Gentle giants.

There was a mechanical bull in the room and Lucky asked for a volunteer. Russell, God love him, jumped on it.

Lucky winked at Darcy. "You next."

She turned beet red and Win had to keep from rolling his eyes.

Russell got on the bull and didn't make it anywhere close to the eight-second bell, the time he needed to stay on to qualify for a score. Yep, harder than it looked and the thing wasn't even real. Lucky gave him a second try and turned down the bucking settings. Russell lasted three seconds longer than his first time but was still short of the bell, which equaled disqualification.

"You ready?" Lucky asked Darcy. She responded by backing away.

"I'll pass," she said, and clung to Win.

"How about Remy or Sue?" Win said, and protectively wrapped his arm around Darcy. She didn't have to do anything she didn't feel comfortable doing. "One of you want to try it?"

"I do," Sue said.

Lucky helped her get on the back of the bull and pulled the switch. Her time was better than Russell's but only slightly. Remy was next to give it a try and didn't even last three seconds. He laid on the rubber mat, laughing his ass off. At least everyone was having a good time.

Lucky nudged his head at Win. "You want to try this or go straight to the real thing?"

"Real thing." He was pumped. "You don't know how long I've wanted to do this."

Lucky's mouth twitched. "It's pretty addictive."

Katie had brought him a pair of boots to change into and Lucky had him buckle himself into a pair of chaps and a helmet with a hockey mask. He also gave Win a glove to put on his rope hand.

They went to the bucking chutes where Win climbed up and the ranch hands told him to straddle the bull.

"This isn't Bushwacker, is it?" Win asked.

The men threw their heads back and laughed. Bushwacker was a three-time world champion PBR bull. He'd thrown off the greatest bull riders in the world.

"Just making sure," Win said, trying to find his center balance and imitate the technique he'd seen in the presentation by slipping his hand under the rope handle and wrapping the tail once around his grip.

Darcy handed up her phone to the cowboy helping Win get settled. "Would you take a picture of him for me?"

He snapped a few shots of Win grinning his ass off and handed the phone back to Darcy.

"You feeling good?" Lucky asked him.

As good as a guy could feel on top of fifteen hundred pounds of bull. "Yep. I'm supposed to keep my free arm in front and not touch the bull with it, right?"

Lucky chuckled. "Just concentrate on staying on."

"Roger that." He couldn't stop smiling.

After scooting up on the bull's shoulders he gave the nod to let the chute operator know he was ready to go.

The gate opened and the bull shot out into the arena, bucking hard enough to give Win a jolt. He held on for dear life, forgetting everything he'd learned in the PowerPoint. Somewhere at the back of his mind, he knew this was amateur night, that the bull was probably Katie's pet. But it sure didn't feel like it.

"Five seconds to go," he heard someone yell in the distance, and thanked God he had good core muscles. Because right now that was the only thing keeping him from the cold, hard dirt or worse, a pair of sharp horns up his ass.

He started to get the hang of it when Lucky shouted, "Hot dog, you made it."

Win assumed that meant he'd conquered the requisite eight seconds. The question now was how to get off the dang thing. Ah, the hell with it, he was just going to jump and hope for the best. He'd taken worse tumbles down a ski slope so how bad could this be? Scoping out a good landing spot, he pulled his hand from the rope wrap, swung one leg over the beast, and dove off, landing on his feet. What he hadn't calculated was the bull coming after him.

The first thing he heard was Darcy scream and from the side of his eye he saw a blur of black run toward him. He rocketed to the fence, grabbed it with both hands, and hoisted himself up. Damn. When he looked over his shoulder to see if it was safe, two of the hands were shooing the bull away. A few new guys had joined Lucky, who stood with one foot resting on the first rung of the fence and his arms draped over the top, watching the action and laughing his head off.

"You're a natural," Lucky called to him, and Win had a sneaking suspicion he was messing with him.

But he'd made it. He'd made it to the bell and he was still in one piece. He snuck a peek at Darcy, who looked as if she was recovering from a heart attack. The others from their group looked damned impressed.

"That was seriously righteous, dude." Russell came toward him and gave him a high five. "Check it out." He shoved his phone in Win's face and played a video of him on the bull. "You mind if I post this on FlashTag?"

"Knock yourself out," Win said.

"Be sure to tag Garner Adventure," Darcy added.

"And the cowboy camp," Lucky said. "Now who wants to go next?"

Silence. Not one person made a sound.

What happened to Russell? He was usually game for anything.

Win glanced his way. "You don't want to try?" When Russell gave him a sheepish shrug, Win said, "No pressure."

"I'm out," Remy said. "The mechanical bull was one thing, it didn't have horns."

"I'm too chicken to do it too." Sue scraped her upper

lip with her teeth. "But how lame would it be for one of you to take a picture of me sitting on the back of a bull in the chute?"

Win's lips curved up. "Not lame at all, totally cool. Can we do that, Lucky?"

"Absolutely." Lucky looked at the others. "You guys want pictures too?"

"Hells to the yeah." Remy pumped his fist in the air.

Sue was the first to climb up over the chute and straddle a bull named Crème Bulle. Where they came up with these names, Win would never know. Lucky popped his cowboy hat on her head and one of the chute guys took a few snapshots with her phone. Remy and Russell followed suit. The three of them stood in a huddle posting their pictures from their phones to FlashTag and various other social-media platforms.

"What about you, Darcy Lou?" Lucky had certainly taken a shine to Darcy, which annoyed the crap out of Win. It shouldn't have but it did. He told himself he was just being protective. Like a big brother. But no big brother he knew had seen his sister in a red teddy and imagined her in it. Often.

"Not on your life," she said. "I'm good right down here."

"Then come meet my wife."

A wife? Okay, that lightened Win's mood. Lucky led them up a treelined path with a flagstone walkway to a small house, which turned out to be a boot shop and studio. Win had never seen so many cowboy boots. Exotic skins, distressed leather, round toe, pointy toe, fancy stitchwork, rhinestones, you name it.

Win put his hand under Darcy's chin. "Close your mouth, you're drooling."

Lucky chuckled. "My wife, Tawny, designs them." He

pointed to a pair with a San Francisco Giants logo. "Those are for Bruce Bochy. That pair over there, Harrison Ford."

"You're not supposed to tell anyone that." An attractive brunette came out of one of the back rooms. "Cordovan-client privilege."

"She's too ethical." Lucky draped an arm over her shoulder and Win could see pride bursting from every pore in the cowboy's body and wondered what it would be like to be that consumed by a woman. That in love.

He sure hadn't felt it with Britney or even Deb, who'd been the closest thing he'd ever had to a serious girlfriend. But it was nothing like what he was witnessing now. The air around Lucky and his wife crackled with electricity. No one could miss it.

Lucky made the introductions and they chatted for a while before everyone went off in different directions, looking at the boots. Even Win, who wasn't much of a shopper, found himself trying on a pair. Tawny had said the ones in her shop were either samples, seconds, or custom orders that the client had never paid for. They were expensive but well worth the price, given the workmanship.

He spied Darcy in the corner, modeling a red pair for Tawny, the two looking slightly conspiratorial. Win planned to ask her about it later. Right now, he just enjoyed watching her. Funny, how they had worked together for almost a year and it wasn't until recently that he'd noticed how appealing she was. Smart, pretty, bullheaded. Okay, he could do without that last part but at the same time it sort of cracked him up. She was a third of his size but that didn't stop her from telling him what to do.

And knowing that she toed the line with everyone else made him feel special. With him, she felt comfortable enough in her own skin to push back.

And thirty minutes later she was pushing back all right.

To say she was livid was an understatement. Once again, he'd blown up "the plan" to eat at the Bun Boy, the burger drive-through he liked so much. They were supposed to have lunch at the Indian place in Glory Junction. But they were here now and all the time they'd spent on Lucky's cattle ranch had made him hungry for beef.

The Bun Boy didn't have indoor seating and only a pickup window where a pimply-faced kid called your name when the food was up. Way more casual than Darcy wanted for their VIP clients. But Remy, Sue, and Russell seemed more than happy to sit outside at a picnic table, under a leafy oak tree and munch on curly fries while tourists on their way to the Feather River walked their dogs in the tall grass.

They had brand-new cowboy boots in the van, pictures of themselves pretending to ride bulls on their camera phones, and food in their bellies. Free food that Garner Adventure had picked up the tab for. What more could anyone want?

But Darcy continued to shoot him death glares throughout lunch. He had an overwhelming urge to kiss the scowl off her face in front of their VIPs, God, and everyone just to see what she would do. The woman needed to relax. He had this.

He went back to the window, waited in line, and ordered her dessert. Maybe a soft serve ice cream cone would sweeten her disposition. He brought it back to her and he could swear she wanted to shove it in his face.

"It's all good, Darce," he whispered. "They're having fun."

"I went to a lot of trouble to make reservations and plan everything out to the minute. And you . . . eating at a drive-through has nothing to do with team building. It just looks lame."

"It's authentic and rustic and something different than

they're probably used to." There was nothing wrong with being spontaneous if it got the job done. She on the other hand needed to get laid or do something to make her loosen up. Ordinarily, he would've helped her with that but he was still on the abstinence train. Though it—and he—was getting harder every day.

"It's my promotion on the line," she continued but he suspected that it was more than a raise and a title. She wanted to be acknowledged for her hard work. He got that. He really did.

"You did a fantastic job organizing this, Darcy. The bull riding was the highlight of the weekend so far and it was your doing, not mine. But there's no *I* in team." He'd played enough sports to know that firsthand.

"You're starting to get on my nerves," she said.

She was starting to get on his nerves—the ones in his dick. With her hands on a pair of shapely hips, her breasts heaving in frustration, and her plump bottom lip protruding in agitation, he wanted to put them both out of their misery.

She looked up at the sky, impatiently, let out a breath, and stomped off to the van. The whole ride back to Glory Junction, she made amiable conversation with Remy, Sue, and Russell but wouldn't spare him so much as a glance. All over a stupid lunch.

To make it up to her, they spent their last dinner with the FlashTag group at the Indian place. Darcy had sweet-talked the owner into making space for them, even though the place was booked and they'd flaked on their lunch reservation.

They'd already been to GA to hand out the goody bags, which Deb had filled with an assortment of gear they sold from their online store. TJ, being the control freak that he was, showed up—on a Sunday no less—and tried to close the deal. But their VIPs made it clear that Madison De Wolk had the final say. They'd done all they could do. At least for now.

Remy, Sue, and Russell had been a fun bunch and Win hoped they could continue to work together. He also wanted the bonus TJ had promised for his house and for Darcy to get her promotion. Most important, though, getting the FlashTag account would go a long way to putting GA in the black after Royce's lawsuit. Keeping his parents' legacy profitable was important to him, though he'd always taken it for granted before.

But his priorities were changing. And unfortunately, so was his taste in women, he thought as he glanced at Darcy, who was in a lively conversation with Sue. Since when was he turned on by anal-retentive women who thought he was good enough for sex but not worth much of anything else? Never, that's when.

Chapter Ten

Darcy was exhausted. She didn't think she'd talked her entire life as much as she had this weekend. All she wanted was a hot bath and a soft mattress. As soon as Win paid their restaurant bill, they'd drop off the FlashTag crew at the Four Seasons and she could go home.

Home away from Win, who was starting to make her feel pent up with an uncomfortable sort of energy she couldn't identify.

"Ready to go?" He returned to the table from the men's room with his hands jammed in the pockets of his jeans. The same ones he'd worn while riding that bull, which had nearly given her a heart attack.

She'd actually wanted to smack Lucky for letting Win go through with it. Other than the short presentation, Win had no training riding bulls. He'd pulled it off, though, like he did everything else. With a big toothy grin and a truck-load of swagger. One of these days that swagger was going to get him killed.

"What about the bill?" she asked, since Win was the one with the GA credit card.

"Took care of it."

As they walked through the restaurant she saw a few

female glances turn Win's way. A blonde, who looked as if she'd spent a good part of the day in the sun, drank him up like a tall glass of lemonade. Either Win didn't notice or she wasn't his type. To Darcy the blonde looked like every man's type. Big, brown-sugar eyes, big boobs, and big, glossy lips.

They piled into the van and Win drove up the mountainous road to the hotel, slipping her occasional glances. She wondered what he was thinking. That come Monday he would be free of her? She was loath to admit it but despite all their arguing they'd made a pretty good team.

By the time they reached the hotel, she was too tired to think. But not too exhausted to hop out of the van and hug Remy, Sue, and Russell good-bye. Darcy was going to miss them. During the two days they'd had together, she'd bonded with the FlashTag trio, which wasn't easy for her to do. She'd never been good at making friends. Although she wouldn't be conducting any team building exercises, she hoped TJ would let her somehow be involved with the group if GA got the account.

On the way home, she must've nodded off because at some point she was awakened by a rush of warm air and a strong pair of arms that lifted her from the van's passenger seat. All too aware that it was Win, she kept her eyes squeezed shut and pretended to still be asleep, nuzzling her head under his chin. He made a sound deep in his throat and suddenly warm lips touched her forehead. They lingered as if he was breathing her in. Darcy shifted, snuggling deeper into his chest, worried that he would figure out she was awake and put her down. She liked being in his arms, feeling the warmth of his body and the breadth of his chest surround her. It made her feel delicate and feminine, and deliciously safe. Even the slow beating of his heart felt oddly comforting. And his smell—Indian spices, sweat, and man—enveloped her like a hug.

And then they moved or rather he did, taking long strides that ate up the cobblestone walkway, his feet crunching as they went. The fact that he could lift her at all said something about how strong he was. But being able to carry her the distance from the driveway to her nana's front door was impressive.

She heard whispering, then felt Win cross into the house, walk through the foyer, and climb the stairs. At the top of the hallway, a door swooshed open, a light flickered on, and then he unceremoniously dumped her in the middle of her bed.

"You can quit playing possum because I know you're awake."

Uh-oh. Feigning sleep seemed like a wasted effort but at least he might go away and save her from the embarrassment of faking it. That's what a gentleman would do.

But Win wasn't a gentleman. The bed dipped and she felt him stretch out next to her. What the hell was he thinking? Her grandmother was just one flight below them.

He turned on his side and was looking at her. She couldn't see him because her eyes were closed but she knew. She could feel his breath on her face. He was only maybe an inch or two away. It was a meager double bed, barely enough room for both of them and his feet were probably hanging over the end.

"If you were thinking of becoming an actor I'd keep my day job if I were you," he said.

She flipped onto her back and propped her arms under her head. "You suck."

He laughed.

"You could've just left me on the couch if I was too heavy for you."

"You're not heavy." He flexed his bicep like a ninth grader. "Were you testing my strength?"

"No, I was too tired to walk." And just for once she wanted someone to carry her. Not literally but figuratively. "Because while you were busy being charming and wrecking all my thoughtful plans, I was trying to nail this account." She knew she wasn't being fair but it was easier to fight with him than what she really wanted to do.

"And I wasn't?" He scowled. "I worked my ass off this weekend."

He had. And they'd loved him. "I'll admit you were impressive. But don't let it go to your head. You did what you do every weekend. You played."

"That's bullshit, Darcy. We both worked our asses off, okay?"

"Okay," she conceded. "But I finagled that entire picnic lunch, practically had to promise my first-born child, and didn't get one word of praise from you. Not so much as 'this looks great, Darcy.' All you did was stuff your face."

"You want credit? Fine, I'll give you credit." He leaned over and planted his lips on hers, the move so surprising that Darcy froze.

He rolled over so that he was practically lying on top of her and tucked his hands under her head so he could take the kiss deeper. The pull of his mouth made her forget everything. Her frustration, her disappointment, the fact that they were in her grandmother's house with the door open. She twined her arms around his neck as he explored her mouth with his tongue.

He tasted like beer from the Indian restaurant and desire. So much desire that she lost herself in him. In the hard planes of his chest, pressing her into the bed, the warmth of his mouth, plying her with pleasure, and the sensation of his fingers, tangling in her hair.

She arched up, wanting to feel all of him and he obliged by grinding against her, the evidence of his arousal pushed between her legs. She heard a moan of pleasure. Maybe it was hers, maybe it was Win's. She was too caught up to know or to care. His hands moved down her arms and inched their way under the hem of her T-shirt. She sucked in a breath as he touched the bare skin of her stomach and moved up to her breasts, feeling the weight of them through her bra. Never once breaking the kiss.

Darcy might not be the most experienced lover but there was no doubt Win was an expert. The things he was doing with his body, lips, and tongue were out of this world.

Her hands moved to the waistband of his jeans. She wanted to hold him . . . stroke him, make him feel as good as he was making her. He shuddered as her fingers scraped his rock-hard abs and he glided his lips over the side of her face, landing on her neck and sucking.

She worked his belt, desperate to feel him between her legs before she exploded. He kissed her breasts, laving them with his tongue, leaving wet spots on her shirt. And this time the moan definitely came from her. If he felt this amazing with clothes on she could only imagine what it would be like naked.

Struggling with his buckle, she decided it would be faster to get his shirt off instead, and began rucking it up over his chest and head. He shoved up her top and continued to kiss his way down her body, his breath tickling her belly.

Oh God, he was killing her . . . taking her to heaven. He rubbed his erection against the part of her that was dying for attention, making her feel so good. At this rate, she wasn't going to make it to nakedness, that's for sure.

In the distance, something clattered. It was loud, reminding them they weren't alone, and they jerked apart. Win scrubbed his hand through his hair, looking slightly bewildered. Then he rolled to the edge of the bed and sat up.

"Shit." He pushed off the mattress and walked out.

Darcy went into the office the next morning, not knowing what to expect. She'd gone over the kiss all night, replaying every detail of it in her head. About three in the morning she finally fell asleep, deciding that it was nothing. Just the two of them blowing off steam. Win had kissed Glory Junction's entire female population, or at least the single ladies, and none of them had meant anything to him. That's the way he operated. Love 'em and leave 'em. But now she was even more frustrated than the night she'd crawled into bed with him.

"What are you doing here?" TJ asked as he passed her desk on his way in.

"Working." And in five seconds, getting the doughnuts at the Morning Glory, like she always did for the Monday meeting.

"All right." He shrugged. "But make sure to take two days off during the week."

She planned to look at the schedule later to make sure she took different days than Win. As it was, he had a tour later and would probably be in soon to attend the meeting, which meant she couldn't avoid him.

"I want you and Win to brief us on how everything went with FlashTag and what we can do to follow up," TJ said, and headed to his office.

Great, she thought, her face heating from the memory of the kiss, then told herself she could remain professional.

On the way to the diner, Darcy bumped into Deb. Either Deb had driven in separately from TJ or she'd been over at

Glorious Gifts, gabbing with Hannah while she opened the store. The two were best friends and soon would be sisters-in-law. Darcy would be the only one in the office who wasn't family, which sometimes could make things awkward. Then again, she'd been married to Lewis and had still felt like an outsider at Snyder Real Estate, even though her husband owned the business. She'd basically been everyone's secretary and Lewis's mother. At GA, the slot of mother had already been filled by Mary Garner.

Felix was working the cash register when she came in and she made sure to give him a big hello.

He grunted something unintelligible that sounded a little like "good morning," then "Your doughnut order will be up in a second."

She sat at the counter on one of the red leather swivel stools and waited. Ricki waved from the back of the dining room where she took orders from a family of five. A woman Darcy didn't recognize asked after Nana. Darcy promised to pass along her salutations.

The restaurant wasn't as crowded as it had been Saturday but it was hopping just the same. Lewis would've called the diner a license to make money. Like her parents, that's all he cared about. It wasn't that Darcy had anything against wealth but there was more to life than buying shiny things and showing up the neighbors. Happiness, for one, something she knew her parents didn't have much of. At least not together. She'd always felt that they had taken out their misery on her by nitpicking everything she did.

"Darcy, don't wear horizontal stripes, dear." "You'll never make anything of yourself if you don't join the right clubs. Learn to network, dear." "Lewis loves you so much, how can you leave him?"

How could she not?

"Here you go." Felix handed her a white pastry box and she walked back to the office. It was cooler than it had been the last two days. With June, you could never tell. By noon, the cloud layer could burn off, sending temperatures into the nineties.

As soon as she walked in the door Colt grabbed the box from her and started rummaging around for a bear claw. The Garner men were partial to them, though they'd settle for an apple fritter in a pinch.

She went to the kitchenette and started the coffee, which she should've done the moment she'd stepped in the door. But she was feeling a bit discombobulated. She chalked it up to working eight days straight and not to the kiss. Because the kiss had meant nothing. Nothing at all. And she felt even more confident that Win felt the same, since he handed them out like a penny slot machine.

"We ready to start?" TJ stuck his head around the corner.

"Yep, just getting the coffee started. I'll meet you in the conference room."

She joined everyone, set the carafe in the center of the long table, and quickly darted her eyes at the chair Win usually occupied. Empty. Her stomach dipped. She told herself it was from relief. Eventually she'd have to face him but she'd rather do it after a strong cup of coffee. Or never. That would be good, too.

No such luck. About ten minutes into the meeting, he drifted into the room with his hair wet and his face covered in stubble. He picked through the pastry box, grabbed a powdered sugar doughnut that Darcy had had her eye on, and stuffed half of it in his mouth.

"Glad you finally decided to join us," TJ said.

"Sorry I'm late." Win poured himself a cup of coffee and took a seat.

She tried to avoid eye contact but it was difficult given

that she was sitting right across from him. A few times she caught him glancing straight at her.

"How do you guys think it went?" TJ looked from her to Win.

Before she could answer, Win said, "Slam dunk. They loved us."

Darcy agreed that it had gone well but wasn't cocky—or brash—enough to call it a slam dunk. In her experience, it didn't pay to be over confident. But confidence was Win's second name.

"Darce?" TJ bobbed his head at her.

"I think it went well. But it's not up to Remy, Sue, and Russell and for all we know it'll go just as well with the other company." Sue had let it slip that they were headed to Mammoth this coming weekend.

"So why didn't this De Wolk woman come if she's the one making the decision?" Josh filched a bear claw off Colt's napkin. When Colt went to grab it back, Josh said, "That was your second one. Get something else."

Colt pawed through the box and found a fritter. "That's the way these big companies do it. The CEO sends her minions, then makes all the decisions. Just like the police department." He grinned.

"Seems like a big waste of time," Josh said.

"Yeah, I'm sure it was a lot different in the army." Colt licked his fingers.

"I don't mean to interrupt but I have a telephonic meeting in five minutes with one of our vendors," Deb said. "You guys don't care if I leave to deal with that, right?"

There was a chorus of "Nos."

"We still doing lunch?" TJ's eyes followed Deb to the door. Darcy got the distinct impression that "lunch" was code for something else entirely.

"Uh-huh. See you later."

TJ continued to watch her until Deb disappeared down the hallway. Win cleared his throat.

"You think we can get back to business here and save you and Deb's sexy time for later?"

"Sure." TJ threw his pen at Win. "I wouldn't want to keep you from anything important, like updating your Tinder account."

"I've got a tour in an hour and I'd like to get organized." Win directed the last part of that statement at Darcy. She stared at her hands and picked at her nail polish.

Colt glanced at his watch. "I've got to get back to the station. So let's move this along."

Darcy tuned out the conversation, wondering why Win had looked at her like that. She really didn't want to discuss the kiss. There was no reason to dwell on it. She'd prefer to just move on as if nothing had happened. And if he expected her to help him prepare for his group, he could forget about it. She had her own work to do.

"Is there anything more you two can do with FlashTag?" TJ asked, snapping Darcy out of her thoughts.

"You mean like ask them to marry us on the jumbotron at the Giants game?" Win said and Colt and Josh laughed. TJ wasn't amused.

"I'll send them thank-you cards today," Darcy volunteered.

"Maybe we should send a box of Colt and Delaney ski jackets." TJ made a note on his tablet.

"Dude, you're trying too hard. They'll think we're desperate."

TJ ignored Win and looked at Darcy.

She had to agree with Win. "Uh . . . yeah . . . it might be over the top."

"Fine, we'll wait until next Monday and follow up."

"In the meantime, why aren't we doing more business with Lucky Rodriguez and his cowboy camp?" Win asked.

Everyone turned to stare at him like he'd grown two heads. Darcy couldn't remember him getting too involved on the business end of GA.

"I'm serious," he said. "He has a great spread and thanks to Darcy booking time with him, it was probably the highlight of the weekend. Seems to me we could be cross-promoting."

It was nice of Win to give her credit. She'd been conditioned to not expect it so the acknowledgment was surprising. And generous. Something she stowed away to think about later. More important, Win was right, GA should be doing more stuff with Lucky Rodriguez.

"He does a lot of corporate team building, too," TJ said. "We're competitors."

"Our operations are totally different. People come to us for adventure sports, they go to Lucky to feel like a cowboy for a week. There's no reason why we can't give our clients a brief taste of that lifestyle and vice versa. Seems like a missed opportunity to me."

The room got quiet.

"Winifred may be right." Josh broke the silence. "Shocking as it might be."

Everyone laughed. The Garners liked to poke fun at one another and especially at Win. This time, though, Darcy thought they should be taking him more seriously. His suggestion could turn out to be a good moneymaker and after Stanley Royce they could use the revenue.

"Okay," TJ relented. "I'll look into it."

"I could do it," Win said and Darcy saw Colt do a double take.

"Something in your Wheaties we don't know about, boy?"

Win leaned his chair back on two legs and flipped Colt

the bird. "Lucky and I have a rapport and none of you have ridden a bull."

"I don't know about riding a bull," Josh said. "But you're certainly full of bullshit."

TJ put up his hand as if to say *enough*. "If you want to feel him out, go ahead. Let me know what he says." He then changed the topic to the pressing matters of schedules, payroll, and ways to cut down on overtime.

Darcy went for a doughnut as she listened to TJ drone on about how much they were over budget and accidentally grabbed Win's hand as he reached for the same buttermilk bar she had her eye set on. They both froze and Darcy pulled her hand back. Win put the bar on her plate and took a jelly doughnut instead.

She managed to get through the meeting without making eye contact with him. Afterward, she rushed out and hid in the bathroom. If she could stay there until his tour started she wouldn't have to face him. Except she had work to do and someone might need to use the toilet. She stalled for as long as she could and returned to her desk.

After fielding a couple of phone calls, she booted up her computer to send out informational e-mails to some of their clients. All of them got a list of what and what not to wear for the various tours GA offered as well as what essentials to pack for their trips. She wouldn't call the work drudgery but she preferred talking to clients directly. Most of them were so enthusiastic about their upcoming trips that it was a little contagious. A promotion would enable her to do more of it as well as use more of her organizational skills. At Snyder Real Estate she'd pretty much run the whole show. Keeping the books, posting new listings on the website, setting up appointments with clients, ordering signs, supplies, and business cards—her responsibilities were numerous.

Even though the work was more stimulating, she liked it better at GA. TJ was always complimentary and appreciative of the job she did and although most of the Garner brothers intimidated her, they were never boring. The idea that they would make a great reality TV show had crossed her mind numerous times. *The Amazing Race* meets *The Bachelor.* She didn't quite know how they would pull that off but she had no doubt that women across the country would tune in weekly to watch.

"There you are." Win tugged her out of her chair. "Step into my office for a second."

"I can't . . . I'm . . . um . . . waiting for a call."

His lips grazed her ear. "No, you don't." He grabbed her cell phone off the desk and shoved it at her. "You can just as easily take it in my office."

She was about to argue that it was a GA call but she could access the switchboard from his office too. Which meant she was stuck. It was either go with him or admit she was a chicken.

"Five minutes, Win, that's all I have."

He kicked the door closed behind her and for good measure locked it. "You're trying to make me fall off the wagon."

"You're the one who got into my bed and kissed me first. Don't blame me. And what wagon?"

"I told you, I no longer do casual hookups."

"Right." She screwed up her face in disbelief.

He sat on the edge of his desk and folded his arms over his chest. "I'm holding out for something real."

She wasn't sure whether to buy it or not but it might explain his sudden interest in her. A lack of sex had driven him to desperation. She quirked a brow. "Something real?"

"Yeah . . . maybe." He hunched his shoulders forward

in a halfhearted shrug. "And that little stunt you pulled, pretending to be asleep, put me on the road to perdition."

"The road to perdition?"

"Exactly. And would you quit repeating everything I say?"

"Seriously, you're blaming me for the kiss? I'll admit that I faked being asleep because I was too tired to walk and because it's your fault that I have blisters all over my feet. But you kissed me all on your own, bucko. So get off your high horse."

He got to his feet and paced. "What are we going to do about it?"

"Nothing," though if not for Nana rattling pots in the kitchen it would've been something. She felt a twinge of disappointment. "Haven't you kissed a million women and walked away?"

He didn't respond, which was answer enough. "In case you're interested, there hasn't been anyone since Britney."

"Yeah, not that interested." Except she sort of was. And surprised, if he was actually telling the truth. "Is it okay if I get back to earning a living now?"

"Yep. One more thing before you go." He walked up to her and put his face an inch away from hers. "I know you liked it so why are you pretending that it was nothing?"

"I told you, I've been going through a dry spell. It really doesn't take much these days." She backed away, afraid that if she stood there any longer she'd do the unthinkable and kiss him again.

"Keep telling yourself that," he called to her as she walked out the door.

Chapter Eleven

Win needed to get out of the office to think and find a way to curb his lust. Darcy wasn't his type but she sure as hell did something to him. It was probably her acid tongue. He liked a woman who called him on his crap.

He walked to the Juicery and got a green smoothie. Doughnuts were his vice but he liked to stay healthy. Main Street swarmed with people, even for a Monday. Paddle and Pedal had a good line of people waiting to rent bikes and inner tubes for the river. It was turning out to be a warm day, perfect for the water.

Good thing because he was taking a group white-water rafting. A family. He usually did the more advanced tours but one of their rafting guides was on vacation. It would be a nice break. Families with kids were the bomb. He loved watching their expressions as they discovered the joy of a great adventure. When they were kids, he and his brothers had lived for getting out on the river, the lake, a black diamond trail, anything outdoors.

He strolled back to the office where his group, the Blake family, waited. The kids were playing on the rock wall while Josh gave them a few pointers. It was high time he and Hannah started pumping out a few children of their own and take the burden off the rest of them, since it was all Mary ever talked about. She wanted to be a grandmother while she was still young enough to chase her grandkids around. Colt and Delaney would probably spit out a baby before too long. And who knows, maybe TJ and Deb wouldn't even wait until their winter wedding. From the way they'd been looking at each other, Win wouldn't be surprised if Deb walked down the aisle in a maternity dress.

He gathered the Blakes and gave them a safety spiel. It was their first time out so he planned to stick with Class I rapids. He loaded the gear into one of the shuttle vans and they headed out. Most of the time he met his groups at the river but this worked just as well.

By the time they got back everyone had taken off for the day, including Darcy. He saw the Blakes off and went home to shower off the river. There was a locker room at GA but he wanted to feed the cat. Afterward, he walked the short distance from his apartment to downtown Glory Junction for a pint and a game of darts at Old Glory. Mondays were usually relatively quiet at the bar, filled mostly with locals. On Wednesdays, all the Garner brothers came to take advantage of Boden's hump day specials.

"Hey, Win." Candace Kelly gave him a finger wave from the table where she sat with two other women.

They'd gone to high school together and now she was Delaney's receptionist. Last he'd heard, she and her husband had split up. Despite not having talked to her in a while, everyone's life in a small town is an open book.

He waved back and took a seat at the bar.

"What'll you have?" Boden asked.

"Sierra Nevada and a burger. Side salad, instead of the fries." He'd eaten a sandwich out on the river but was starved.

Boden put in his order and drew him a beer. Win scanned the dining room through the back-bar mirror. He didn't see any of his regular dart or pool buddies, like Chip. Even though he was a recovering alcoholic, he came to Old Glory after work in the evenings a lot and nursed a cola.

Boden brought his Sierra Nevada. "Don't look now but Candace is checking you out."

Win took a surreptitious glance. "Not interested."

"She's hot."

"Then why don't you date her?" Boden was a lady's man. Chicks went in for his whole grunge biker look. The flannel shirts, the biker boots, the tattoos, the chains.

"Nah, not my thing. Your brother got the one I wanted."

"Which one?" Hannah, Delaney, Deb—they were all gorgeous, smart, funny, the whole package.

"TJ." Boden gave him a hard look.

Everyone in town knew Win and Deb's history. No secrets in Glory Junction. But there was no bad blood between him and TJ. He loved all his brothers like crazy, even if they liked to micromanage his life.

"TJ has good taste and so does Deb."

"What about you?" The kitchen bell rang and Boden grabbed Win's burger and set it down in front of him. "Who you seeing these days?"

"No one. I'm focusing on work and buying a house."

"Yeah? Where you looking?"

Win leaned over the bar, snatched the oil and vinegar from a condiment basket, and poured a little of both on his salad. "I'd like the lake but don't know if I can swing the prices over there."

"Reggie Brown is trying to sell his place on the river. He wants to leave Glory Junction for one of those senior communities. The place needs work but it's got good bones and the views . . ." Boden let out a whistle.

"Really? What kind of place is it?" Reggie was an old-timer, whose wife died a few years ago. Win only knew him through his parents and had no idea where he lived.

"Log cabin. Reggie built it himself."

"No kidding. How much does he want for it?" Win wouldn't mind living on the river, though some of the houses with water access weren't on county roads. You either needed a plow or a snow mobile in the winter.

"Don't know but you should talk to him. Maybe you can swing a deal before he lists it."

"I might just do that." Win took a bite of his burger and Boden moved on to help another customer.

Win was halfway through his dinner when Candace sidled up to him and cocked her hip against the bar. "So how have you been, stranger?"

"I'm doing okay, Candace. How 'bout you?"

"I'm single now." She slid closer so that her hip brushed against him.

"That's what I heard. I'm sorry about you and Dale."

"I'm not," she said, and he was flummoxed on how to respond.

"Well, I'm glad it hasn't been too tough for you. Divorces can get hairy." At least they didn't have kids. Win tried to make eye contact with Boden, hoping the barkeep would rescue his ass because he knew what was coming.

She took the stool next to his, which confirmed his fears. "What are you drinking? It looks good."

It was beer, for Christ's sake. "Sierra Nevada." He supposed that was a hint to order her one but he didn't want to encourage her. He just wanted to finish his dinner in peace.

He was just about to casually mention that he was seeing someone when Dale came into the bar. Craning his neck around the room, he spotted Candace and stomped over, looking mean as a grizzly bear.

Shit.

"Well, that didn't take long. You're screwing Garner now?" Dale said it loud enough that people as far away as Reno could hear him.

"Shut up, Dale, you're making a scene." Candace scooted even closer to Win. He got the impression that she was enjoying Dale's "scene."

"She was just saying hi, Dale."

Dale was a big-ass dude, who used to be an offensive tackle on Glory Junction High's football team. Since then, most of his muscle had gone to fat but he was still a beast.

"I wasn't talking to you, Garner. I was talking to my wife."

"I'm not your wife anymore. And I'm free to see whomever I want." Candace rested her hand on Win's leg.

Why me?

"We're not seeing each other, Dale. I was here having dinner and a beer and Candace came over to say hi. That's all."

They had an audience for sure but no one stepped in to confirm Win's story. And Boden had freaking disappeared.

"Is he telling the truth, Candace?"

"It's none of your business."

Dale moved closer. He smelled like a distillery and gripped Candace's arm, hard. "We're leaving."

"Dale," Win said, "take your hands off her!"

"Who the hell do you think you are telling me what to do?" Dale got in Win's face. His breath alone could've killed a herd of elephants. "Come on, Candace. Don't make me tell you again. We're leaving."

"I'm not going anywhere." She yanked away and Win could see a nasty red mark on her arm.

Win stood up and got between them. "Look what you did, Dale. You're drunk and you're acting like a dick. Go home and sober up, dude."

He should've seen it coming but by the time Dale's fist landed in his face it was too late and he staggered back. Someone screamed, maybe Candace, and then it was pandemonium. Fists flying, glasses breaking, and Boden yelling above the fray. Out of nowhere, a few bargoers had come to lend Win a hand or just brawl. It was hard to tell what their objective was.

Whatever it was, Win didn't want any part of it. All he wanted was to finish his fucking dinner and play a goddamn game of darts. But there was so much pushing, shoving, and shouting that Win was pretty sure that people were just fighting for the sake of fighting.

"Are you happy, Dale?" Candace screamed. Win couldn't be sure because his left eye was throbbing and starting to swell but he thought she looked supremely proud of herself.

"This is your fault, Candace. You're the one who divorced me." Dale lunged at her and Win intercepted by grabbing Dale by the shirt.

He managed to land a punch to Dale's prodigious gut and the dumb clod doubled over. Win rammed him up against the nearest table and pushed him into a chair. "Sit."

In the distance he heard sirens, which was weird because the police department was only a block away. Then again, his left ear was in agony so perhaps it was tinnitus.

He let out a loud whistle and felt the room still.

"The cops are on their way." Boden's voice reverberated off the wood-paneled walls. "And you people owe me for the damages."

Win let out a breath and looked around. It wasn't as bad as it felt when he'd been in the thick of things. A puddle of beer on the floor. His Sierra Nevada. Some broken glass, a smashed plate, and a barstool knocked to the ground.

A family, the Tompkinses, moved toward the door. Mrs. Tompkins was shielding her youngest child's eyes. Win checked his watch. It was only eight o'clock, yet it felt so much later.

Boden bobbed his head at them. "Sorry, folks. Dinner is on the house." He scowled at Dale. "Which you're paying for, asshole."

Dale was slowly recovering and he'd turned his gaze on Candace. The big ox had tears in his eyes and a total look of desolation on his face. He and Candace had been married close to ten years, Win calculated.

It wasn't any of Win's business but he couldn't help himself. "Maybe you two ought to get counseling."

"We tried that," Dale said, and turned his attention to Win. "Are you sleeping with her?"

"No! Dale, we'd barely begun talking when you came in. But, dude, you can't go beating up every guy she has a conversation with."

Colt walked in the door with Bobby George, one of his officers, and he didn't look happy. He was out of uniform so Win assumed he'd gotten called away from home.

He took one look at Win and said, "I should've known."

Win threw up his arms. That was his brothers, always giving him the benefit of doubt.

"Stand over there." Colt pointed. "Bobby's going to take your statement."

Great, he'd been relegated to the corner, which in his mind was equivalent to a time-out.

Bobby did the interview, which took all of eight minutes.

"Am I free to go?" Win asked. He'd lost his appetite for

food, beer, and darts and should probably get some ice on his eye, which he could only partially see out of.

"Yup," Bobby said, and slapped him on the back. The officer had known him since he was a boy.

"Don't go anywhere yet," Colt called to him from where he was standing with Boden. Win should've known his brother would want to get in his face. Colt probably wanted to lecture him about dealing with drunken, jealous husbands.

He continued his conversation with Boden and took his sweet-ass time moseying over to Win. "Whoa, Dale messed up that pretty face of yours. Want me to take you to urgent care, get that looked at?"

"You're kidding me, right?" Win had had worse falling off his bike. "I'll ice it and it'll be fine."

Colt poked at the skin around Win's eye.

"Knock it off, that hurts." And his ear was still ringing. Dale had a mean right hook.

"You want to come over to our place? I've got a pack of peas somewhere in the freezer."

"Nah, I'm just gonna head home," Win said. "Did Dale agree to pay for the damage?" Win sure as hell wasn't. He hadn't done anything wrong. Come to think of it, Dale should pay for Win's goddamn dinner.

"Yeah. Boden's got it worked out with Dale and the other yahoos who got involved. You're off the hook."

"Fuck you, Colt. My only crime was taking a fist to the face for Candace."

Colt locked eyes with him. "That's what Boden said. Still, stay away from Candace."

"You need Boden to back up your own brother's story?" He turned away from Colt and started for the door. "I'm out of here."

Halfway home, he felt a twinge of guilt. Colt was the

police chief and was honorable enough to treat his family members like everyone else. But that warning about staying away from Candace pissed him off. Why was it that Colt just assumed that he was making a play for her? Dale was—or at least had been—his friend and he wasn't remotely interested in Candace. But everyone always expected him to be on the wrong side of whatever the trouble was.

He started to unlock his front door, decided screw it, and made a straight line for his Jeep instead. It was stupid to drive when he could only see out of one eye but he followed the road to Hilde Wallace's house. He parked behind Darcy's Volkswagen, took the cobblestone walkway, and rang the bell.

Hilde answered in her nightgown. Ah crap, it was a little late for a house call.

"Oh my." She put her hand over her mouth. "What happened to you?"

His lips tipped up. "Damsel in distress. Is Darcy here?" He didn't know why but he wanted her to hear the story from him before it turned into a tall tale about how he'd been fooling around with his friend's ex-wife.

"Come in. Let me put something on that and you can tell us all about it."

Darcy came down the stairs, cringed at the sight of him, and suddenly his eye stopped pulsing and his ear stopped ringing and he felt . . . better. Like salve to a wound.

"White water rafting?"

"Nope. Bar brawl."

"You're kidding, right?" She tilted his chin down to get a better look.

"'Fraid not."

"Wow, that's some shiner."

Hilde disappeared and returned with an ice pack wrapped

in a kitchen towel covered in yellow daisies. "Let's go in the kitchen."

They followed and Win took a seat at the breakfast bar and applied the pack to his eye. The cold stung and he waited for blessed numbness.

"You think you should have someone look at it?" Darcy sat next to him.

"Nope. The ice is good. Thanks, Mrs. Wallace."

"You're welcome, my dear boy." She got a pie from the refrigerator, cut three generous slices, topped each one with a scoop of vanilla ice cream, and passed them out. God, he loved her. "We want details." Hilde leaned against the counter and dipped her spoon into the pie.

He told them what happened, glossing over Candace's role in the melee. She could've told Dale that there was nothing going on between her and Win but she'd been intentionally nebulous. Win didn't like being used that way.

"I always adored Dale Kelly," Hilde said. "He put new hinges on my cabinets when I couldn't find a handyman to do it and didn't charge me a dime." Dale's parents owned the local hardware store.

"He sounds psycho to me." Darcy took the ice from Win so he could finish his pie. "If I were that Candace woman I'd get a restraining order."

"Nah, he's just going through a hard time . . . they both are." Win didn't know what had happened to their marriage but there was a time when Candace thought Dale hung the moon.

"Did Colt arrest him?" Darcy ate her ice cream but Win noticed she hadn't touched the pie. And it was freaking delicious, almost as good as Hannah's late aunt's pecan pie.

"Nope, but he has to pay Boden for the stuff he broke at Old Glory." The whole thing had been a shit show.

"Well, I'm going to leave you young people alone,"

Hilde said, and stuck her plate in the dishwasher. "I'll leave the pie out in case you want seconds."

"Thanks, Mrs. Wallace." He got up, went around the island, and gave her a peck on the cheek. "Sorry I came over so late. I sort of lost track of the time."

"You're always welcome." She waved him off and left him alone with Darcy.

"You think she would marry me?"

"Not if she has half a brain." Darcy played with her pie.

"Give me that." He took the plate away from her and dug in. "Man, this is good. What kind of berries does she use?"

"Blackberries." Darcy watched him scrape up the extra filling on the plate. "They're from her garden."

He pointed in the direction Hilde had left. "That right there is the next Mrs. Garner."

Darcy raised her brows. "There are others?"

"My mom, Hannah, Delaney, and pretty soon Deb."

"Delaney is Scott," she said dryly.

"You know what I mean." He finished the pie and put the ice pack back on his eye. Even with half his vision gone, he noted she didn't have a bra on under her sweats, which reminded him of her breasts. She had really good breasts.

Darcy gave him a long assessment. "No ice at home?" When he didn't respond because he knew what she was getting at, she said, "Why'd you come over?"

He lifted his shoulders. "I wanted you to hear the story from me, not town gossip."

"Why?"

Jeez, wasn't it obvious? "Because of the kiss." He figured that was enough but she wouldn't let it go.

"And that matters why? As we've already noted, kissing is your middle name."

God, he was so tired of being stereotyped. "I came to

tell you that I hadn't run from your bedroom to Candace's. That's all."

She started to say something and he stopped her. "Leave it alone, Darcy."

"Fine, but—"

"No more." He got up and recovered the pie with the plastic wrap Hilde had left on the counter and put it in the fridge. "I mean it, not another word."

A cell phone charging next to the landline vibrated. Darcy glanced over at it and exhaled.

"That yours?" he asked.

She didn't say anything and ignored it, which made him curious. He walked over and read the display. Lewis.

"Your ex." He would've arched a brow but his face hurt too much. What the hell was he calling so late for? "Aren't you going to answer it?"

"Nope." She got to her feet and took over the cleanup. "Sit and ice your eye."

"How come?"

"Because it's getting big as a balloon."

That's not what he meant but he went to the freezer and found a fresh pack, since the one he had was melting. Hilde certainly came prepared. "How come you don't want to talk to Lewis?"

She let out another breath. "Because he wants me to do work for him and I don't want to."

"So just say no."

"It's not that easy."

Yes, it was. He did it all the time, especially to TJ, who'd work him like a dog if Win allowed it. "Does it have to do with your divorce settlement?" Maybe she owned a share of the company.

"No, but I left him in the lurch when . . ." She sighed. "Sometimes I have trouble speaking up for myself."

He laughed. "Could've fooled me by the way you were biting my head off over the weekend. Just because you dumped him doesn't mean you owe him free labor."

"There you go again, assuming that I dumped him."

"You did, didn't you?" He was as certain of it as he was that tomorrow was Tuesday.

She sat at the breakfast bar again. "I was the one to physically leave but he dumped me first." When he looked confused she shook her head. "The Win Garners of the world would never understand."

"Then enlighten me." He moved the ice pack to his ear so he could see her better. "And don't pigeonhole me, it pisses me off."

"Okay then, tell me the last time you were dumped."

He thought about it for a few seconds and she let out a snort.

"See, it's never happened to you."

"Bullshit. I've been dumped. Of course I have."

"When and by whom?" She made the give me gesture with her hand.

"Deb. Last winter."

"That doesn't count. Deb wasn't even your girlfriend when she and TJ started dating. In fact, you were engaged to Britney."

"There you go, Britney dumped me."

Darcy shook her head. "No, Britney tricked you. You didn't even want to marry her in the first place."

Damn right he didn't. "Well, there have been other women. I just can't think of them right now." He pointed at his face. "Not after what I've been through."

She laughed, the sound so sexy that it aroused him.

"I should get going," he said, hoping she would ask him to stay. But no invitation was forthcoming.

Chapter Twelve

Darcy didn't see Win on Tuesday, though she thought about him often and even considered stopping by his place on her way home to see how his face was faring. Even puffy and black-and-blue, the man was gorgeous.

The fight at Old Glory was all anyone was talking about. When she went to Tart Me Up to pick up a sandwich for lunch and thank Rachel for providing the fantastic picnic spread for the FlashTag extravaganza, at least four people in line were gossiping about the dustup. One of them was Foster, owner of Sweet Stems flower shop and Deb's and Hannah's BFF.

"What's the mood like at GA?" he asked, making Saturday's shenanigans seem more dramatic than the way Win had described it.

"Quiet," she said, not wanting to get sucked in. Despite the fact that she and Win had forged a sort of friendship—the truth was she didn't know what to call what they had—it probably wasn't a good idea to engage in spreading information about one of her employers. Although Win wasn't technically her boss, he did own an equal share of GA.

"Is it true that Win sent Dale to the hospital? Deb's not picking up her phone."

From what Darcy had seen last night Win was the one who should've gone to the hospital. "Not from what I heard."

Foster moved closer and whispered, "Who's your source?"

"Just stuff I overheard at the office. But Deb would know more, or even Hannah."

The person behind the counter called Foster's number. Before putting in his order, he said, "See you at book club tomorrow night?"

She didn't know what he was talking about because as far as she knew she hadn't been invited to anyone's book club. But to save them both from embarrassment she nodded.

By midday, she was jonesing for chocolate and ran over to Oh Fudge! The candy shop, an old Victorian storefront, was near the boardwalk on Main Street. In summer, the ornate screen door swung open and closed all day long by customers. Black and white stripes painted the walls and a harlequin pattern in the same color scheme covered the floor. Little lace curtains on the windows fluttered in the breeze. The jewel box of a place reminded Darcy of a doll-house.

The homemade chocolates, truffles, and fudge were just as pretty. And they were more addictive than heroin. Darcy tried to avoid the place the same way she did all other things that were bad for her but sometimes she needed a fix.

The two customers ahead of her were deep in conversation about the brawl at Old Glory.

"I hear it was over a love triangle," said a woman who was a dead ringer for Magda in the movie *There's Something About Mary*. Tan and leathery.

"The EMTs took one of them away in an ambulance," her sidekick added, sounding a little too delighted.

Darcy kept a low profile behind the nuts and chews, not wanting to be pulled into the discussion. That was the thing about living in a small town, it was very inclusive.

When her turn came, she got a half pound of fudge and bumped into Hannah on her way back to the office.

"You coming to book club at my house tomorrow?"

"Uh, I didn't know I was invited."

"You didn't get the e-mail? Huh, that's odd. I sent it to your GA address."

Hannah had always been friendly to Darcy but this was the first time she'd ever invited her to anything. It made her feel like she belonged. She'd grown up in Reno and even though she'd been in Glory Junction for a year, she still felt like an outsider.

"It might've gone to spam." Or Darcy might've missed it; she'd look again.

"Well, anyway, it's at my house at seven."

"Uh, okay. But I doubt I've read the book." Her current reading material was *How to Get Ahead at Your Job*.

Hannah laughed. "No worries, we never get around to talking about it anyway. But in case you're interested it's Trevor Noah's *Born a Crime*."

"Should I bring something?" Darcy didn't even know where Hannah lived but she'd get the address from Josh.

"Just yourself and your appetite. Foster's making enchiladas."

"Thanks for the invite," Darcy said. Nana was always telling her to be more outgoing, so here was her chance.

She brought the chocolate back to GA and left it in the kitchenette to share. While the Garners were fond of their doughnuts, it turned out chocolate not so much. So she nibbled on it herself, making the afternoon pass much more quickly thanks to her sugar rush. When the big hand landed on six she began to gather up her stuff. A million times during the day, she went back and forth on whether she should stop by Win's. Half the time she told herself it was the neighborly thing to do—check to make sure he had everything he needed. The rest of the time she reminded herself that Win wasn't the type to lack for sympathetic company. Besides, she didn't trust their newfound friendship, or whatever it was. A little voice in her head told her there was something fishy about it. And the last time she ignored her gut, she'd wound up married to Lewis.

She did enjoy Win a hell of a lot more than Lewis, though. She enjoyed their sparring. And she had definitely enjoyed their makeup session. And as perfect as Win was he didn't seem to judge her for being . . . a lot less than perfect. Which except for Nana was a first.

She'd made up her mind to make a pit stop at his apartment. Just five minutes, she told herself, and wrapped the leftover fudge in plastic to bring as a get-well offering. Normally, she wouldn't bring someone used chocolate but Win didn't strike her as too picky.

Darcy was just preparing to leave when she got a call from Nana, which completely blew up her plans.

Darcy's father was waiting when she got to her grandmother's cottage. He looked funny on Nana's chintz couch, his masculine Gary Cooper looks at odds with the tiny cabbage rose fabric and his long legs jammed against the antique coffee table. Both her parents were tall. It was a mystery how she'd topped out at only five-two.

"Hi, Dad."

Deep in thought, he hadn't heard her come in and jumped at the sound of her voice. He took her in without saying a word, then patted the spot next to him. "Come sit next to your old man."

She hesitantly made her way around the sofa, mentally preparing herself for a lecture about Lewis. *This has gone on long enough, Darcy. It's been a year, it's time to go home to your husband.*

It didn't matter that Lewis was her ex-husband. In her parents' minds, she was simply on hiatus from her marriage, a short vacation from real life.

She sat, girding herself for the speech that was sure to come. Instead, he took her hand and sandwiched it between his much larger ones. Neither of her parents were particularly demonstrative so even that small gesture of affection surprised her. Darcy's initial thought was the unthinkable. *He's dying and he's come to say his final farewell.*

Her heart stopped. "Dad?"

He didn't say anything, letting the silence envelop them. Her imagination ran wild with all the terrible possibilities. What if it wasn't her father but Geneva? What if she had cancer? What if it was Nana? No, Darcy would know if it was Nana.

"Your mother and I have filed for legal separation."

She tried to grasp what he was saying. Of all the things it could've been, divorce hadn't been one of them. Legal separation wasn't necessarily divorce, she reminded herself.

"Why?" was all she could seem to manage.

He cleared his throat and maybe Darcy was seeing things but his eyes seemed to water. "Because we don't love each other."

As far as she knew they never had. Or it had been a strange love, filled with icy indifference. Their relationship had been nothing like Nana's and Grandpa's. Sweet, passionate, and enduring. Sometimes it was hard to believe Max Wallace was their son.

A thousand questions swirled in her head. She assumed because Max was here to deliver the news, the breakup was his idea. "Are you moving out?" That would kill her mother, to whom appearances were everything.

"I'm renting a condo. We'll eventually sell the house."

Another thing that would kill Geneva. As sterile and vulgar as it was, she loved that house.

"What does Mother say about this?" It explained her impromptu visit to Reno. Darcy had suspected that it had nothing to do with her alleged engagement to Win.

Max picked a piece of lint off his slacks. "She's not happy about it."

Because she didn't want the divorce or because divorces were sad?

"Where will she live?" It was an inane question but Darcy was still parsing her father's words. Her relationship with Max and Geneva was strained but they were still her parents. The idea of their being apart, separate units, was hard for her to wrap her head around.

"Ah, honey, we haven't worked out those details."

Honey? She couldn't remember the last time her father had called her by an endearment. Possibly never until now. She looked around the house and it suddenly dawned on her that her grandmother wasn't here.

"Where's Nana?"

"She went to the store," he said. "She wanted us to have time alone together."

"Are you staying the night?"

"No." He took a long pause. "I have to head back but I wanted to tell you in person."

"What about Mother?" she asked, and he looked at her

like he didn't understand the question. "Why didn't she tell me? She was here, you know?"

"I didn't." He wouldn't meet her eyes and she wondered why. What was that about? "It was sudden and I suppose she's still trying to collect herself."

How sudden could it be if he already had a condo?

"Was it your idea?" Even though she suspected it was, she wanted to know for sure.

She could feel him squirm under her inspection, then he let out a breath.

"The separation was a mutual decision," he finally said. "Perhaps tomorrow you could call your mother and lend her your support."

She nodded, though she didn't know what she could say that would make it better. She and Geneva weren't exactly tight. And when Darcy had gone through her own divorce, her mother had pretended that it was a "phase." That was the ridiculous word she'd used for it. A "phase." God forbid she tell her friends that her daughter was no longer married to Lewis Snyder, the best a girl like her could hope for.

"Is there any chance you might reconcile?" Darcy asked. The question had been a recurring theme of her breakup with Lewis. At the time, she'd resented it but now she understood why people asked.

"I don't think so, honey."

She sucked in a breath, lost for what to say next. This felt worse than leaving Lewis. It felt like a part of her world was crumbling. Granted it wasn't a world with lots of happy childhood memories, but it was her world nonetheless.

"What did Nana say?"

He shook his head and scrubbed his hand through his hair. "She's disappointed, I guess."

Nana had never been a fan of Geneva's, though she'd

never come out and said it. But in those dark teenage years when Darcy had struggled with everything from her weight to incredible shyness, Nana had been her protector against Geneva's constant put-downs. She'd also blamed Max for not stepping in to stop Geneva's relentless bullying.

But what was done was done. There was no use looking backward. All Darcy felt now was a jumble of emotions and a melancholy that hollowed her from the inside out.

Max stood up. "I'd like to get back before nightfall."

Darcy joined him. "You sure you don't want to stay?"

He pulled her in for a hug, another novelty. "I have an early morning. But let's get together soon."

"Of course," she said but it sounded empty even to her own ears. When had they ever gotten together besides holidays? Never. "I'll walk you out."

Nana pulled up the driveway just as Max was leaving and he rolled down his window to say good-bye. Hilde got out of her car and together they watched him disappear down the driveway.

"How are you doing, dear girl?" Nana wrapped her in a hug and Darcy began to cry.

"I don't know why I'm getting so emotional," she said, swiping at the tears running down her face. "It's not like they were happy together. This might be good for them."

"I think it will be," Nana said, and held Darcy's cheeks in her hands. "You too. Maybe they'll get to know you better."

Darcy thought that ship had sailed but she didn't want to dash Nana's hopes. It was bad enough that her only son and granddaughter had failed at love.

After dinner and a long talk with Nana, Darcy found herself sitting in front of Win's apartment. She told herself she was just checking on his well-being but the truth was hers could use a little TLC. And despite the fact that he was prettier than her, he made her laugh. At least this time when she breached his door, she'd be fully clothed. With pie. She had the rest of Nana's berry pie.

A TV was on inside his studio; she could see the reflection of a baseball game in the window. Relieved that she wouldn't be interrupting something important, Darcy took the path to his unit. The smell of fresh-cut grass and a hint of jasmine filled the still night air. And the stray cat that Win wouldn't admit he'd adopted lay on the sill of an open window, swishing its tail.

Darcy called through the screen door, "Anyone home?"

"Uh, yeah, hang on a sec."

He came to the door bare-chested and unhooked the latch. "Hey."

"Hey," she said back.

His eye had turned several shades of black and blue and green and was the size of a Ping-Pong ball. It gave her something to stare at besides his chest, which was something of a work of art in and of itself. Broad and muscled and lightly furred with a happy trail that disappeared behind the waistband of a pair of low-slung jeans.

He hung his hands from the top of the doorframe and stretched and she nearly lost her mind.

"Here." She handed him the dish. "The rest of the berry pie. I had some fudge too but I ate it on the way over."

He took the pie to the kitchenette. She couldn't help herself and started picking up various articles of clothing that had been flung here and there.

"You come over to clean or to eat pie?" He got down two plates and some forks from a drawer. "How big a piece you want?"

"I'm good," she said, and folded a pair of shorts and put them on top of a pile by his bed. "I ate before I came over."

His hair was mussed and he ate standing up and even with his Cyclops face he was breathtaking. Just looking at him made her sigh.

He stabbed his fork at her. "What's wrong with you?"

"You look god-awful."

He tried to catch a reflection of himself in the microwave glass.

"Don't look," she said. "I'm serious, you might throw up."

"That bad, huh?" His mouth slanted up in an obnoxious grin. "How was work? Anything from FlashTag yet?"

"Nope. The day was pretty uneventful." Until she'd gotten home—then it had blown up. "What about you?"

"Just hung out here." He started to rewrap the pie. "You need the dish back right away?"

"You can return it when you're done." She made room on the couch by pushing more of his crap to the side and sat down.

He looked around as if he was seeing the apartment through her eyes. "I'm gonna buy something soon."

"So you said." She wanted to mention that a new place, just like the old, wouldn't clean itself. "According to town legend, you, Candace, and Dale are involved in a ménage à trois and they had to take Dale away from Old Glory in a stretcher."

"Oh yeah." He cocked a hip against the counter. "Glad to know it wasn't me on that stretcher."

"How are you feeling?" She examined his eye again from across the room and let her gaze drop to his chest. No injuries there.

"The doctors say I have two weeks to live." He bent over the fridge to put the pie away and came around the kitchen to sit next to her, tossing all the debris on the floor.

"Did you come over to fool around again? Since I'm dying, I might break with my twelve-step program."

"Don't get any ideas. The last time, you didn't live up to the hype."

He snorted because he was as conceited as he was good-looking. "Could've fooled me. But if that's true a do-over is in order."

She laughed because how wonderful to be that damned confident in yourself. "My parents are splitting up. My dad just left after breaking the news."

"Ah, jeez, Darcy, I'm sorry." He put his hand on her shoulder. "Was this unexpected?"

"Sort of," she said, and gazed off into the distance. "They weren't much of a couple but they'd lived that way for so long I'd just assumed that's how happiness looked to them."

"You talk to Geneva?"

"Not yet. I will tomorrow. Anyway, that's not why I came over."

He gave her a long, slow perusal and she waited for a wisecrack about her not wearing the teddy or some other sexual innuendo.

"You can talk about it if you want," he said. "It's gotta suck to have your parents break up, even as an adult. I know I'd be pretty upset."

Yes, but his parents were the real deal. His mother still had all her children over to the house on Sundays for dinner. And Gray and Mary Garner loved each other. Anyone who looked at them could tell. Hell, Darcy had seen them holding hands while walking down Main Street like a couple of teenagers. If they suddenly announced that their divorce was imminent, planet Earth would stop spinning on its axis.

"It's not like that with us. The Wallaces are a stoic lot."

He held her face in his two hands and her gaze with his blue eyes. "You can leave that stoic shit behind when you're with me. I won't tell anyone."

And that's when a few mortifying tears dripped down her cheeks. He wiped them away with his thumbs. But it was when he took her in his arms that she broke down, crying into that massive chest of his. Big, ugly, racking sobs. His hands moved over her back, rubbing circles, and he rocked her. And it felt so good that she just wanted to stay there, even if it was just for a little while.

It was the last thing she expected of him. Wild, happy-go-lucky playboy Win to give comfort. He was actually good at it, better than anyone she'd ever known, even Nana, who was her best friend.

"I think I'm getting snot on you." She inched away.

He chuckled and pushed her face back against his chest. "I'm good with bodily fluids. Ah, Darce, I'm so sorry."

"It's okay. Maybe it'll be better for everyone concerned, right?"

"Could be." He brushed his lips over the top of her head.

"I don't want to talk about it anymore." She closed her eyes.

"Then we'll talk about something else." But he didn't say anything, leaving the door wide open for her. The best part was that he kept rocking her.

She breathed him in. For a shirtless guy who'd been lying around all day, he smelled pretty good. Salty with a hint of that soap he used. He reached over for the remote control and she heard the TV go off.

"You were watching the game."

"Don't worry about it, the Giants are having a bad season anyway."

A long silence stretched between them and it started to feel awkward, especially because Darcy's face was still buried in Win's most excellent chest. But she didn't exactly want to leave his chest, his arms . . . his apartment. So she just sat there, cuddled against him, thinking of a less depressing topic than her parents' looming divorce.

"You coming to work tomorrow?"

"Yeah, I've got a rock climbing tour first thing in the morning."

"You're going to scare off the clients with that eye of yours," she said.

"I doubt it. It'll just make me look tough."

"You're sort of delusional, you know that, right?" She twisted around to look at him. "You can't find someone else to guide it?" His eye, if not his whole face, had to hurt.

"Nah. We're short-staffed as it is. The fresh air will do me good. How about you? Will you be taking your days off?"

She hadn't really thought about it but it was TJ's edict that she use her comp days this week and Lewis continued to hound her over doing his data entry. "Probably."

"Don't tell me you're going to do your asshole ex's bidding? Besides being a champion of children of divorce, Win was also, apparently, a mind reader.

"Okay, I won't tell you."

He got up and she instantly missed the contact. Worse, he found a shirt in one of the many piles cluttering his apartment and put it on.

"Seriously, you're going to use one of your days off to do more work? That's just crazy town."

She laughed because the statement was so quintessentially Win. Why work when you can play?

"It's my time to do what I like with it," she said.

"You told me yourself that you're doing it out of some bizarre sense of duty . . . or guilt." He combed his fingers through his hair. "Why? Especially if he's the one who left you."

"I left him."

"That's not what you said."

"It's complicated."

"Try me out," Win said. "I'm smarter than I look."

No way was she handing him the single most humiliating scrap of her life on a platter. Not going to happen. Women threw themselves at Win Garner. How would he ever understand that Darcy's own husband wouldn't touch her? That most of the time, Lewis had chosen the guest room over their marital bed. And when he did deign to lie next to her, he treated her like a dead fish.

"There's nothing to explain. He fell out of love with me." Or never had been in the first place. "And I left him. End of story."

"Okay." Win sat at one of the mismatched barstools at his kitchen counter. "Then why work for him?"

"Because we're still friends. And friends help each other."

"Not buying it. I saw you with him at the rodeo. I wasn't getting a strong friend vibe off of you. Just the opposite, in fact."

"I don't know what to tell you."

"The truth." The side of his mouth slanted up in a wry half grin. "It'll set you free."

"It's boring, Win." She started to get up and in two long strides he was back at the couch, pushing her down onto the lumpy cushion.

"Forget I asked. Take a look at this house I'm thinking of buying." He returned to the counter, got his laptop, and brought it over.

She watched as he booted it up, wondering why he was so desperate for her company. He plugged in an address and after a few clicks a picture of a log cabin came up on Google.

"What do you think?"

It was hard to tell from a photograph of only the home's front façade. "Is that the river in the background?" She squinted at the picture.

"Yeah. The house is on River View."

"Wow. Good location. The house looks decent but it's not the clearest picture."

"Reggie Brown owns it. He eats at the Morning Glory all the time. You know him?"

She shook her head. "Why does he want to sell?"

He placed the laptop on the coffee table, next to a Juicery cup and a dirty plate. "His wife died a few years ago and according to Boden, he wants to move into a retirement community. Probably somewhere warmer."

She got that. Glory Junction's snowy winters weren't for everyone. "Can you afford it?" She didn't want to come right out and ask how much the house was. It seemed crass.

He hitched his shoulders. "Dunno. It's not officially on the market yet. I'll have to talk to Reggie about it. You want to look at it with me if he's willing to give me a preview?"

She loved looking at houses, so yeah. But she thought it was strange that he was asking her. TJ would be a better choice. He was a champion negotiator and like with everything else probably had a good head for real estate.

"If you think I picked up a lot of real estate knowledge working for Lewis, you'd be mistaken," she said. "I did the books."

Though a lot of times, Lewis had her run the comps on one of his listings. She'd gotten a pretty good feel for what a place was worth. But that was in Reno, not Glory Junction. In recent years, the prices here had gone through the roof. Nana's little cottage was probably worth a small fortune. And TJ's lake house . . . she could only imagine.

"I can handle that part of it," Win said. "I just want a woman's opinion."

"For your new wife?" All the single women in town wished.

"Wives. Plural. I'm into that."

She tried not to roll her eyes. "I'll go. When are you thinking this is going to happen?"

"I'll call him now." Win started to go for his phone but Darcy tugged on his arm.

"It's getting late, Win. Call him tomorrow."

"All right. You'll go tomorrow?" He quirked one brow. It was a challenge to keep her from working for Lewis. She couldn't figure out why Win would even care.

"Sure. But I'm planning to work at GA tomorrow and take Thursday and Friday off." That way she'd get a four-day weekend, though Lord knew what she'd do with herself all that time. "So make the appointment for after work. Oh wait, I'm going to book club at Hannah's. She invited me." *Duh*. Why she'd needed to add that, she didn't know.

"Oh yeah? That's nice, although I've been to one of her book shindigs and no one talks about the book. It's mostly a drunken gossip session."

"Really? You go?" She couldn't see Win at a book club gathering. It didn't seem like he could sit still that long.

"Not for the book club but to hang out with Josh and play video games. How about lunchtime if Reggie is okay with that?"

"Sounds good but I can't be away from the phones too long."

"Right." Win pulled a face. "TJ will take you around back and shoot you."

He wouldn't even look askance at her taking a little extra

time for lunch. That's not the way TJ rolled, though he expected everyone to do their jobs. But she had a work ethic to uphold. No one could ever accuse her of slacking off. It was the one thing she prided herself on. It was the reason people liked her.

"Well, I better get home." She stood up and Win walked her out to her car.

She started getting in the driver's seat when he took her by the arm. "Call me if you need someone to talk to . . . or if you just want to have phone sex."

He walked back to his apartment in his bare feet, snatched the cat off the sill, and took it inside.

Chapter Thirteen

Win finished with his group, five semi-intermediate-level climbers, at eleven. It had been an awesome morning, just cool enough to keep from melting in the sun. He parked his Jeep in GA's lot and came in the back door with a plan to call Reggie and then shower.

That's when he met with the long arm of the law.

"You look like shit," Colt said.

"Right back at ya."

Colt tilted Win's face to the side to get a better look at his eye. "If I were you I'd have that looked at."

"Good thing you're not me," he said, and Colt socked him in the arm. "We hear anything from FlashTag yet?"

"Not that I'm aware of but I just popped in a few minutes ago. I had to get out of the station because Carrie Jo and Jack are driving me nuts." Colt's receptionist and the assistant police chief were having a passionate affair without the sex. As a result, they fought incessantly.

"Why don't those two just do it already? Jeez, they're both single and clearly have the hots for each other."

"Don't ask me. In the beginning, I was against an office romance but if it'll shut them up they have my bloody blessing." Colt eyed Win's gear. "You've been climbing?"

Win held up his harness. "What gave it away, Sherlock?"

Colt tried to punch him again but he moved out of the way. "Wanna have lunch?"

"No can do. I'm trying to get inside Reggie Brown's log cabin. Boden says he's getting ready to sell it and I might be interested."

"In what?" TJ joined them in the hallway.

"In Reggie Brown's log cabin," Win said.

"You're really serious about buying a house, huh?" Colt cocked a hip against the wall and peered at Win dubiously.

Hell yeah, he was serious. His studio apartment had started closing in on him, making him feel like an over-grown frat boy. "Everyone else in this family owns a house, why shouldn't I?"

"No reason you shouldn't," Colt said. "I just never saw you as a homeowner. You thinking of trading the Jeep in for a station wagon?"

Win flipped him the bird.

"Reggie Brown is selling his log cabin?" For once, TJ didn't join Colt in "let's razz Win." He was too busy sniffing a deal.

"That's what Boden says. I'm taking Darcy to look at it if Reggie will let us in."

"Darcy? Why aren't you taking me?" TJ asked.

"I don't want you to scare Reggie off. Anyway, this is premature until I get my bonus." He pointedly looked at his brother. "Right, TJ."

Colt folded his arms over his chest and watched with interest. If it had been Josh he would've bitched and moaned that he wasn't getting a bonus. Mostly, it was just to mess with Win. The four of them definitely had their sibling rivalries but it was never over money.

"You better hope we get the FlashTag account, then," TJ said.

"No word yet, huh?"

"I doubt we'll hear anything until after their weekend with that Mammoth operation." TJ glanced down at his always-present phone as they were talking. "I've gotta roll. We going to Old Glory tonight for hump day?"

"I'm in," Win said. "Hannah's having her book deal tonight so Josh will want in too."

Colt pushed himself off the wall. "I've got to check with Delaney but probably."

Win stopped in his office on the way to the locker room, called Reggie, who said they could swing by at noon. After a quick shower, he went to fetch Darcy.

"You ready to go?"

She looked up from her computer monitor, gave the one-minute sign, and pointed to her headset. To kill time, he sat on the sectional and thumbed through a GA pamphlet listing their fall tours.

"Okay," she said. "Did he say you can see it?"

"Yup. He wants to give us the grand tour."

They got in his Jeep and Win took a moment to admire Darcy's legs in her sundress.

"What are you doing?" she snapped.

"Nothing. Jeez, why's your mind always in the gutter?" He winked and she kicked him. "And you're violent, too."

She gave him a cursory once-over. "Your eye looks worse than it did yesterday and I didn't think that was possible. Perhaps you should see a doctor."

He started the car, turned on the music, and put on his shades. "That better?" Before she could answer he stepped on the gas and the Jeep lurched, knocking her forward. He would've burned rubber but that was just juvenile.

"I think you missed the turn," she said a mile out of town.

"I've lived here all my life, Darcy, I think I know where

River View is." Two miles later he turned around. Shit, she was right, he had missed the turn.

They took the long, narrow road, rutted from the winter's snow, until it dead-ended at two driveways. Neither of which had a house number.

"Eeny, meeny, miny, moe . . ." He took the one on the right and was greeted by a chainsaw bear, holding a large sign that read THE HAPPIEST PLACE ON EARTH, which clearly the owner had stolen from Disneyland.

"You think this is the right place?" Darcy craned her neck out of the passenger window.

It was a log cabin, though they were plentiful in these parts. A dog came running out of nowhere, barking its crazy fat head off. A grizzled dude with dreadlocks, a beard, and a tie-dyed shirt trailed the hound.

"Yep. We're in the right place." Win hung out the window. "Hey, Reggie."

"Don't mind Oscar. His bark is bigger than his bite."

They got out of the Jeep and Oscar stuck his snout in Win's crotch.

"Oscar," Reggie called, and the dog trotted to the side of its owner.

Win introduced Darcy, then glanced around, trying to get his bearings. The property was off the hook with an amazing view of the river. A copse of tall pines offered plenty of shade and the grounds boasted every kind of plant under the sun. Reggie must be a gardener. You could drop a fishing line right into the water from the wraparound porch.

"Wow," Darcy whispered.

So far, Win was impressed and also thinking he couldn't afford a place like this. But it didn't hurt to look.

"You find it okay?" Reggie asked. "We're a little off the grid back here."

"Not a problem," Win said, and Darcy smirked. "You've got quite a spread. How big is this parcel?" Up here in cattle country that was considered a rude question, sort of like asking someone how much money he had in the bank. But Win figured they weren't talking ranch size and if he was going to make an offer on the place he needed to know what he was looking at.

"It's just under two acres." Reggie shielded his eyes with his hands and turned to the house. "Elsie and I built the cabin with our own two hands."

It was a large two-story and as far as Win knew Reggie didn't have any kids. "It's amazing."

"Let me give you the tour." Reggie started with the property, including a huge vegetable garden near the road where the property got the most sun. There was a nice shed where he kept supplies and an elaborate sprinkler system. Win would kill every plant sure as shit. His thumb was as green as his bank account.

"You take care of all of this?" Win asked.

"I do." Reggie bent over to pull a blade of grass from a row of leafy greens. Lettuce or cabbage, Win couldn't be sure.

He took off his sunglasses and hooked them in the collar of his T-shirt to get a better look. Reggie did a double take.

"Ooh-wee, that's some shiner." He motioned at Win's black eye. "This the young lady you were fighting over?"

Win let out a chuckle because the story had taken on a life of its own. "Nah. Don't believe everything you hear in town, Reggie. This"—he pointed at his eye—"was just a small misunderstanding."

"If you say so." Reggie winked at Darcy and continued the tour, which ended at a dock with a gazebo.

Some of the wood looked rotted and a few of the boards were warped but it wasn't anything a hammer and nails and elbow grease couldn't fix. Win liked the feel of it and could visualize himself sitting out here in the evening, skipping rocks and watching the end of the day go by. He'd build a rack to store inner tubes and a boat, maybe put in a rope swing for jumping into the water.

"I'll warn you now that the house is on the messy side," Reggie said. "I didn't have time to tidy up."

Messy was an understatement. It turned out that Reggie was a bit of a hoarder. Stacks of newspapers, books, and magazines were piled everywhere Win looked. The house had plenty of space but Reggie had managed to fill every nook and cranny with stuff.

"You have a lot of books," Darcy said, staring at the rows and rows of shelves crammed full of hardbound tomes that reminded Win of a reference library. "Are you a botanist?"

It took Win reading a few of the book titles to figure out why Darcy would ask such a question. Most of them were about plant life and science, which explained Reggie's extensive gardens.

"I'm a plant geneticist," he said. "My claim to fame is discovering how to make a tomato taste good again. Not mushy and bland, like most of the supermarket varieties."

"Seriously?" Darcy seemed impressed. "Do people know about this discovery?"

Reggie grinned. "The entire world of biochemists, botanists, and academia. Exciting stuff."

"My grandmother, Hilde Wallace, would find it very exciting."

"I know Hilde," Reggie said. "We're in the Glory Junction Master Gardeners Club together."

While the two of them chatted, Win poked around. The kitchen was just as cluttered as the rest of the house but it had one of those big, stainless-steel professional stoves and a refrigerator as large as a restaurant's. The cabinets were a honey-colored pine that looked top of the line and the countertops—at least what Win could see of them between the piled-up periodicals—were soapstone. There were so many windows that despite all the trees, the room was bright and the views endless. And the vaulted ceilings made everything feel airy.

There was also a lot of disrepair.

Wood floors that needed to be refinished. Windows that needed to be sealed. Bathroom fixtures that needed to be replaced because they leaked. And from what Win had seen of the roof, the house needed a new one. These were all things he found from a brief walk-through. Who knew what a bona fide inspector would discover?

All these fixes would cost money. Lots of it. But the good news was Win, with the help of his dad and brothers, could handle the labor.

"Hey, Reggie," Win called downstairs. "What happens with the road in winter? Who plows?"

"River View is a county-maintained road. They cover it."

That was at least something. Darcy climbed the stairs and checked out the rooms. He couldn't get a read on what she thought of the place but he supposed it didn't matter. He'd be the one living here.

"You see the kitchen?" she asked.

"Yup. You?"

"I did." That was it? That was all she was going to say? Really?

"What do you think?" Reggie called up.

"I think it's amazing. I can't believe you built this place."

"We hired out some of the work but for the most part it was Elsie and me. We did it with our own two hands."

Win suspected it would be tough for Reggie to part with the place, given all the memories it held of his late wife.

It needed a good steward, someone who would preserve the place. Keep it happy. Win jogged down the mammoth pine staircase. He could've spent all day here but he knew Darcy had to get back to GA.

"What kind of price are you thinking, Reggie?" Win probably should've done some research before coming but it had all been pretty spur of the moment. If the deal with FlashTag didn't happen this could be pie in the sky.

"Well"—Reggie rubbed his hands down the legs of his jeans—"I don't really know. I guess I need to sit down with someone and find that out. Why don't I get back to you with a number?"

"Sounds good." Win took another visual spin around the great room, took in the big stone fireplace that reminded him of the one at GA, and got a business card out of his wallet. "My cell's on that."

Reggie walked them to the door and called Oscar inside.

"Thanks for letting us see it. You've got a hell of place here." Win put his hand at the small of Darcy's back and they got in the Jeep.

"Tell Hilde I said hi," Reggie called.

They drove up the long driveway, past the chainsaw bear. Upon reaching River View, he said, "Well?"

"Well, what?"

"You're killing me here, Darcy. Jeez, why do you think I brought you? So, what did you think of it?"

"It's nice. I was trying to be noncommittal . . . you know, in case you want to dicker with him."

"But you liked it, right?" Win got onto the main road and headed back to downtown Glory Junction.

"It needs a lot of work but yeah."

"Wow, I wouldn't want you to go out on a limb or anything."

"Oh, for God's sake, I loved it. If I could afford it I'd buy it myself. I just don't want to get your hopes up because even I know that place is worth a mint. Watch out for that guy in front of you. He keeps braking."

Win shot her a look. "Did you used to side-seat drive with Lewis?"

"Why do you have to bring him into the picture?"

"Because I like bugging you." He put his Ray-Bans back on because the glare from the sun was making it hard to see, especially out of one eye. "You talk to Geneva today?"

"Not yet. I don't want to do it at work."

"You didn't call me," he said.

"Was I supposed to?" She tilted her head, confused.

"For phone sex, remember?" He couldn't help himself.

"What I remember is you kicking me out of your bed." She feigned interest in the highway, which wasn't the least bit interesting.

"That's because I'm saving myself for marriage. But phone sex is fine. You and I"—he waved his hand between them—"could do that." This was payback for her not saying anything about his house. Christ, he was already calling it his house.

She twisted in the passenger seat to face him. "What do you think would've happened if we'd been alone the other night when you and I . . . you know?"

"Who can say? We got pretty carried away. I may have made a promise to God and country to keep it in my pants but a man can only take so much."

"Are you ever serious?" she snapped.

"Are you ever not serious?"

"Let me ask you something." She paused, taking time to consider her question. "Do you find me attractive?"

He answered without hesitation. "Yes. But only when you're not side-seat driving."

"I mean physically attractive."

He didn't know what other kind there was but no one could ever accuse him of not being shallow. "Yes."

She huffed out a breath. "But you find every woman attractive."

"Hell no, I don't. Rita Tucker, not attractive. That chick at the Shell station . . . what's her name? . . . the one with the mustache. Not attractive. I can list some more but I'd rather get lunch."

"I don't have time to eat."

"Yes, you do."

He told Siri or whatever her name was to call TJ on the Bluetooth and got voice mail. "Why aren't you eating at your desk? The house was freaking awesome. Darcy's with me, we're getting lunch. See ya later."

"You can't do that." Darcy pointed at his phone.

"I just did." He pulled into a diagonal parking space in front of the Morning Glory. "This okay?"

"Since when do I get a say?"

"You're right," he said. "Never."

He started to get out of the Jeep when she said, "You don't think I'm fat?"

Where was all this shit coming from? Frankly, the women he consorted with didn't ask bizarre questions like this.

"No," he said. "But to be totally sure I'd need to see you naked." He didn't wait for her to slap him, just walked to the diner and held open the door.

Ricki, another woman he didn't find attractive—not because she wasn't but because she hated his guts—sat them in a corner booth.

"This isn't my section," she said, and looked directly at Win. "You're welcome."

"I think she's the only female on the planet who isn't in love with you." Darcy opened her menu.

"What about you?" Win stuck his between the salt-and-pepper shakers.

She looked up. "That would be suicide."

"That's kind of a crappy thing to say." He'd heard it enough times before but it still stung. Basically, women didn't think he was a good bet. Given his history, they were right. "Then why'd you want to know if I thought you were attractive?"

Her face went pomegranate red like it used to when he'd first met her. She stammered, "Uh, I just wondered how the opposite sex viewed me is all."

He stared her down because that sounded like a load of hooey to him. Win figured under his cool hard gaze he could squirm her into telling the truth.

She cracked. "Since my split with Lewis . . . well, uh, I haven't been asked out on any dates."

He started to tell her that's because she didn't put herself out there but decided why should he help her snag a man? It's not like she'd helped him snag a house. *It needs a lot of work.* Besides, he didn't want her to snag a man. Because . . . ah, fuck.

"You're hot so that's not the problem," he said. "So maybe we have to look at your personality."

"I'm hot?" She asked it as if he was trying to play her, which pissed him off because the one thing he wasn't was a liar. Or at least not in this case.

"Don't believe me?" he said. "Look in a goddamn mirror."

Chapter Fourteen

Darcy didn't know what made her do it but right after work, she grabbed her purse and drove to Win's apartment. He'd said he was coming home after lunch so she assumed he was here. She scanned the street for his Jeep but didn't see it.

That doesn't mean anything, she told herself. Maybe he'd walked home from GA or parked his car in one of the junky garages in his apartment complex, though she doubted either of those possibilities. She forced herself to get out of the car and knock on his door anyway.

When there was no answer she waited. No sense trying again. It's not like he wouldn't have heard her in his sprawling seven-hundred-square-foot studio. She had just started to give up and walk away when he came to the door, his hair smooshed as if he'd been sleeping on it.

"Did you bring me more pie?"

"No." She brushed by him, went inside, and sank down on his ugly corduroy couch. At least the only thing on it today was a crocheted afghan.

He'd actually cleaned. The apartment was spotless. No piles of clothing, no dirty dishes in the sink, no sports gear lying around. There wasn't even a cobweb in sight.

"Come on in, make yourself comfortable." He followed her to the sitting area and sprawled out on the chair opposite the couch.

"My husband never had sex with me."

That seemed to wake him up. "Never? Or not as much as you wanted? Because that's been a problem for me in the past."

She stood up. This had been a colossally bad idea. To think someone like him would understand or be sympathetic . . . well, she was just compounding the problem.

"Whoa, whoa, whoa." He latched on to her arm and pushed her back onto the couch. "Start from the beginning."

"That was the beginning . . . and the middle . . . and the end."

"Never?" He rested his elbows on his knees and leaned toward her.

"Exactly twice. The night of our wedding and six months later after I got him drunk and . . . well, you don't want to know the details."

"Was he gay?"

She shook her head. "I don't think so."

"Well, did you ask him?"

"No. But there weren't men as far as I know, he just wasn't interested in me."

"Then why the hell did he marry you?"

"I don't know." Because she took care of him and all his needs and she was cheap. "The only reason I'm telling you this is to explain the other night and the weird questions."

"It's him, not you," Win said with absolute authority.

"How do you know?"

He looked at her. First her face, then he lingered on her breasts, and his eyes did a slow slide down the rest of her body to her legs, which she'd caught him staring at on the ride to Reggie's. After he got his fill, he looked again, his gaze so heated it made her toes curl. He reached for her hand and placed it on his lap. "Feel that? That's how I know."

She felt a hard ridge pressed against the fly of his shorts and swallowed. He looked into her eyes and lifted a brow.

"For the last couple of weeks, ever since you showed up in my bed, all I've thought about was you. Naked. Under me, on top of me, in front of me, any way I could get you. I want you, Darcy. Any man would be crazy not to. So Lewis is definitely crazy—or asexual."

She swallowed again because she could feel him growing even harder under her hand. "Then why did you turn me away?"

"Because I'm trying to change, become a better person." His gaze took a turn around the studio and the corner of his mouth tipped up. "I even cleaned." He crooked his finger. "Come here."

He brushed her lips with his, kissing her soft as a feather. She wanted more but the sensation of his mouth moving over her like a whisper was hypnotic.

"Are you just being nice to me so I won't feel bad?" she said, leaning into the kiss so that she was nestled against his chest. She loved the feel of him. Strong and solid.

He got up, closed the shades, and tugged her off the couch. "I'm doing this because if I don't I'll probably die."

She highly doubted that. But she wanted to believe he wanted her and didn't think he could fake his physical reaction, which felt as real as it got as he pressed into her. And there was no question she wanted him. The yearning was so bad she could feel it in every fiber of her body.

He pulled her halfway to the bed and whispered in her ear, "Take off your dress."

The command both shocked and thrilled her. "You sure? I don't want to—"

"Shush. Just take it off."

She started to unzip the back as he watched her and then became self-conscious. "Turn off the light."

He closed in on her and took over, letting the dress slither down her legs. "I don't want to turn off the light, I want to see you."

His mouth was on her neck, kissing and sucking. It felt so erotic, standing there in nothing but her bra and panties with the hot pull of his mouth on her skin. He stopped kissing her long enough to survey her body, from the swells of her breasts to the curve of her hips. And she suddenly felt nervous and covered herself with her hands.

He gently pried them away. "This is even better than the red teddy and that was a freaking fantasy."

She started to relax a little. "I'm not very good at this."

"Nah, you're just out of practice. I hear it's like riding a bike." He continued to nuzzle her throat. "What you don't remember, I'll teach you."

"Okay," she said in a voice so breathy she hardly recognized it.

"It'll be good, I promise." He stuck his face in her cleavage. "You smell good." Then he kissed the swells of her breasts and traveled upward, letting his lips graze her ear, sending a shiver up her spine. His hands made a slow journey down her sides and then pulled her hard against him, pressing his erection against the vee of her legs.

He walked her backward until she hit the bed and buckled. Somewhere a window was open and a cool breeze licked over her. But nothing could stop the heat from spreading. She was on fire.

Win straddled her knees and played with the lace on her bra. "Take it off."

Her shaky fingers reached for the front clasp but couldn't seem to unlatch it. Impatient with her fumbling, he did it himself in one smooth move. He held both her breasts in his hands and kissed them, his tongue making slow circles around her nipples.

Her head fell back and she moaned as hot shards of pleasure passed before her eyes. "Oh God."

"Good?" But he wasn't done.

Win made fast work of her panties, leaving her in nothing but her high-heeled sandals. He kneeled and his head disappeared between her legs.

"Win." She tried to jerk him up because no one had ever done what he was doing before and it embarrassed her. "You don't have to . . ."

"Shush. I want to taste you." His eyes flicked up at her, silently begging permission. "Come on, I've been dreaming about this."

She leaned back on the bed and let her legs fall open. He licked and she trembled. And when his mouth covered her she almost died. Nothing had ever felt this good and any shred of self-consciousness she had left vanished in the pleasure he was giving her.

"Oh God . . . Don't stop." She moaned.

His hands were everywhere, fondling, touching, and rubbing. Nothing about him was gentle. He took what he wanted and she reveled in it, her entire body hummed.

"Good?" He slipped a finger inside of her and she saw colors. Reds and blues and oranges and greens.

"So good . . . I can't take any more." Her voice came out like a croak.

"Then let go," he whispered, never stopping all the wonderful, naughty things he was doing.

He slipped a second finger in and she was gone. Her muscles convulsed around him, her body quaked, and she yelled out his name. She fell back on the bed, trying to catch her breath while staring up at the ceiling. So that's what she'd been missing all this time. There was no way to describe the sheer intensity of it but she knew she wanted more. She wanted him inside of her.

Win hovered over her, his lips traveling across her tummy, over her breasts, up to her throat until he latched onto her mouth. She could taste herself on him.

"You ready for more?" he murmured against her lips. "Please say yes."

"Yes," she stammered because she could barely talk. But she didn't want this to end. She didn't want him to stop.

He stood up and she immediately missed the contact of his body. Darcy propped up on two elbows and watched him shuck off his shirt and cargo shorts. She couldn't take her eyes off his abs. They were flat and muscled with ripples like a washboard. Seriously, he had the kind of stomach you only saw on men in exercise magazines after a great deal of airbrushing and photoshopping. How a person could be that fit was a mystery, especially given his doughnut intake. But she'd seen him in action. There was no physical activity Win didn't do and didn't do well. Including of course what they were doing now. She wasn't the most experienced in the bedroom but she didn't think it was farfetched to call him a masterful lover. He'd certainly rocked her world and she was getting the feeling that that had just been a preview of what he was capable of.

When he slipped off his underwear she sucked in a breath. *Oh my!* Even though he'd pressed his erection against her, seeing it now . . . well, it was thick and long and hard, and very impressive.

"Lay the other way," he said because she was crossways and if she stayed that way his legs would hang off the edge of the bed.

She quickly scooted longways and he joined her, picking up where they'd left off. Except this time, they were both naked and the skin-to-skin contact was like a whole new aphrodisiac.

"I'm, uh, not on anything," she said as he played with her breasts.

One hand slipped between her legs. "I've got you covered."

Of course he did. The man probably had a closet full of condoms, which was good, she told herself. Exactly what she needed. A Don Juan to make her feel desirable and teach her the ropes. And with Win she was finding that she could let go of her inhibitions. Instead of judging, all he seemed to care about was making them both feel good. Cherished, even. It was liberating to be able to drop her guard, instead of feeling like someone was cataloging her every shortcoming. In fact, he emboldened her to be more outspoken, braver, even brazen. And . . .

She could no longer think because he was doing things to her that should've been indecent, except they were . . . wonderful. She whimpered as he rubbed his length against her.

A drawer scraped open, and he suited up and entered her a little harder and faster than she was expecting. She flinched.

"Shit." He pulled out.

"No, no." She tried to guide him back in. "Just go slow."

He kissed the side of her throat and inch by inch slid in. "Better? I don't want to hurt you."

"It's good." She ran her hands over his back and felt his muscles bunch. "You can move a little more."

"You sure?"

"Uh-huh."

He picked up the pace, pistoning his hips. It felt so

amazing she thought she might spontaneously combust. She tried to find a rhythm that would match his strokes and when she wrapped her legs around his waist he moaned. It made her feel sexy and just a little bit powerful.

He picked up speed, pumping harder. "Ah, jeez, that's good. So good."

"More," she said because the fullness of him and the friction was driving her mad. This exceeded anything she could've imagined. And her hands began to slowly explore, touching all those hard-as-granite muscles and stroking all the parts of him that had intrigued her for so long.

"That's . . . ah . . . keep going," Win called out, giving her the courage to take the full tour of his body, feeling and weighing and kissing until they were both so worked up she thought they would detonate. "You're killing me, woman," he said, his voice trembling as if he were on the brink.

It made her heart smile. All those pent-up years of sex-less nights had turned her into a wanton. And Win . . . Win was perfect. He made her feel perfect and sexy—and free.

He reached under her bottom and went deeper and harder, pulling out and pushing in over and over again. The tempo made her wild and she started thrashing her head from side to side, scraping her nails down his back and squeezing his firm, muscled ass until he was grunting. His caresses only heightened the pleasure, leaving her breathless.

And just like that she began to shatter. It was even more potent than the first time, her whole body shuddering while white stars exploded in her head. She couldn't be sure but she thought she heard herself calling out his name.

A few seconds later, he threw his head back, his face taut with strain, and let himself go, collapsing on top of her in a heap. He was heavy but his weight felt good, like a warm blanket. And despite his climax, he was still hard inside of her. Summoning the last of his energy, he pumped a few more times, then slowly withdrew.

"You okay?" he said into her neck.

"Yes." She was beyond okay. *Fulfilled*, *sated*, *euphoric* were just a few of the words that came to mind. And she was proud of herself for finally getting what she wanted, even if it was just for one night. "How about you?"

He lifted up on two hands, looked down at her, and curved his lips up into that signature heartbreaker smile of his. "Good. Really, really good, though you made me relapse."

"Sorry about that." But she wasn't, not even one tiny drop. She actually wanted to howl at the moon, she was so happy.

"No worries. It was totally worth it. I'll get back on the program tomorrow." He winked. "Let me get rid of this." He motioned to the condom and disappeared inside the bathroom.

She got up, collected her clothes, and started getting dressed. Her head was still muzzy and her body still thrummed and she never felt so satisfied in her life. Yes, it was good to be alive. And tomorrow she'd deal with the ramifications. But for now, she just wanted to revel in the afterglow of incredible sex.

"What are you doing?" Win came out of the bathroom, seemingly oblivious to the fact that he was stark naked. Either that or he had zero inhibitions, which was more likely the case. And why should he when he had the body of a Greek god? And the stamina of a bull.

"Getting dressed."

"Why?" He swiped his shorts off the floor and put them on.

"So I can go." She turned away from him for a modicum of privacy. Silly, since he'd gotten more up close and personal with her than any man ever. And he'd truly been turned on by her. No way could he be that good of an actor.

"Go? You don't want to cuddle?"

She couldn't tell if he was being facetious. That was the thing about Win, you never knew when he was joking or being serious. In this case, she strongly suspected sarcasm.

"Book club." Darcy checked her watch. She was definitely going to be late.

"Jeez." Win ran his hand through his bed hair and finished getting dressed. "You're running off for that? I thought you'd at least buy me dinner."

"Maybe next time." She took one last longing look at his chest. It was simply cruel to put a man that beautiful on God's green earth and set him free to destroy hearts wherever he went. At least she was made of stronger stuff.

She grabbed her purse off the ratty couch and took one more look at his newly cleaned apartment. Win followed her out to her Volkswagen. She started to get in her car, then did an abrupt about-face.

"Hey," she said, catching up with him as he returned to his apartment, barefoot.

He turned and his lips curved up. "Already back for more?"

That arrogant smile, so quintessentially Win, tugged at her heart and she tried to tamp down a rush of tenderness that claimed her. On tiptoe, she stretched up and kissed him. "Thank you for rocking my world."

She was surprised when he didn't fire back with his usual bravado or make a wisecrack. Instead, he stood there, his hands shoved in his pockets, at a loss for words. If she didn't know better she would've sworn there was a bit of rawness in his eyes. Finally, he said, "The pleasure was all mine," and just like that he was back to being Win.

She drove off without even so much as a backward

glance. He'd been everything she could've dreamed of and more. And not for one minute would she regret what they had done together, but she'd never been a woman prone to getting caught up in fantasies. So it was time to leave la-la land and get back to real life.

"Do you people talk about anything other than dieting and sex?" Rita stabbed a tomato and popped it in her mouth.

"This from the woman whose life's work is a sex calendar," Foster muttered into his wineglass.

Rita hadn't missed the insult and got huffy. "It is not a sex calendar. It's a fund-raising calendar. And what does my calendar have to do with dieting?"

Darcy thought she made a valid point, though she would argue that the calendar was indeed racy. And out of focus. Rita needed a better photographer. The models were good, though. Especially Win.

Hannah had been right, so far no one had said one word about the book everyone was supposed to have read. Instead, they'd gathered around the coffee table in Hannah's living room, eating enchiladas, salad, chips and salsa, and drinking wine.

Carrie Jo had spent much of the night giving a blow by blow of her new gluten-free lifestyle and how it made her hair glossier. Darcy had never heard that before. And Deb gave a summary on why it was better to get married in the winter than the summer.

Then the conversation switched to the bar fight.

"Boden banned Dale from Old Glory." Hannah took a second helping of enchiladas. "Apparently, he's been going in there night after night, looking for Candace and making all kinds of scenes."

"After the brawl?" Deb asked.

"Yep."

"So, are Candace and Win an item?" Foster asked. "Or was she just his flavor of the night when Dale walked in on them?"

Darcy feigned great interest in the label on the Chardonnay bottle before pouring herself a glass. She considered telling everyone the truth, since she knew firsthand that Win had no interest in Candace and that he'd been randomly caught in the middle of her marital problems. But Darcy didn't know if Win would appreciate her interfering.

"God, I hope not." Carrie Jo let out a dramatic sigh. "Candace is batshit. Even back in high school there were major signs that she wasn't right in the head. And poor Dale is a wreck. I don't know what he ever saw in her but she completely broke his heart."

"That's not what I heard." Deb dredged a chip through a bowl of guacamole. "According to sources close to the case, Dale was stepping out on her."

"Would sources close to the case be Delaney?" Foster and everyone else turned their heads to stare directly at Delaney.

"Don't look at me," she said. "I stay out of my employees' love lives."

"I don't think Dale was having an affair." Hannah topped off Rita's glass. "I think they were going through the seven-year itch. Candace got bored and filed for divorce, which is her business. And according to Josh, she was trying to hit on Win at Old Glory and he was the innocent party."

Deb snorted. "Does anyone believe that?"

Darcy cleared her throat. "I do." Everyone turned to her, waiting for clarification. Maybe she should've kept her mouth shut but she was sick of people thinking the worst of Win. It wasn't fair but more importantly it wasn't true. "He came over to my place the night it happened and told me everything. I don't know about Dale having an affair but Win isn't having one with Candace. That I know for sure. He was just being chivalrous by sticking up for her and got decked in the face for his troubles."

Foster tossed his book at her and laughed. "You've been holding out on us, girl. That day I saw you at Tart Me Up . . . You knew all along what went down."

Everyone's eyes were pinned on her and she felt her face start to flush. "Yes, I did. But it was Win's story to tell, not mine. But tonight I wanted to set the record straight."

"Good for you," Hannah said, and drilled Foster with a look. "It's Win's business, no one else's."

Foster snorted. "Aren't you Miss Goody Two Shoes."

Carrie Jo sniffed one of the corn chips and put it back in the basket. "Okay, now that we're done with Candace, Dale, and Win, who else can we talk about?"

For the rest of the evening they gossiped, drank, and ate Hannah's peach cobbler, which was delicious. Carrie Jo of course abstained because . . . gluten.

Darcy, who'd never been to Josh and Hannah's house before, was given the grand tour. It was a darling Victorian with all the original millwork intact. Even the kitchen, which had been updated over the years, retained much of its 1800s charm. It was hard to see rough-and-tumble Josh Garner living here but Darcy supposed that his love for Hannah trumped living in a life-size dollhouse. And anyone could see that he adored his wife. All the Garner men loved their women with the exception of Win, who loved all women.

The memory of her and Win writhing in bed together surfaced and she pushed it out of her mind, focusing on the gathering instead. She'd hoped that living in Glory Junction would improve her social life and it appeared that things were looking up. This was the third event she'd been invited to. In February, there'd been Deb's thirtieth birthday party. And last month, Colt and Delaney's wedding. When she'd been married to Lewis her social life consisted of hanging on his arm at various business functions where she was mostly ignored.

The book club meeting—if you could call it that—had begun to break up. Darcy helped Deb and Delaney with the dishes and grabbed her purse.

"You don't have to leave, Darcy," Hannah said. "Josh probably won't be home for a while. This is his regular night to meet his brothers at Old Glory. The three of us usually hang out together afterward and you're welcome to join us."

Darcy wondered if Win had gone to the bar with them and if he was there now. Hopefully, he wasn't getting himself beat up again. "Thanks for the invite but I'm going to Reno tomorrow and want to get an early start." After everything that had happened today she was feeling especially bold and asked, "So am I officially in the book club now?"

Deb laughed. "Such as it is. Yes, you're an official member, which means next time you either bring the wine or make the dinner."

"I'm happy to do either." She was just thrilled to have friends. "How often do we meet?"

"When all the stars align, once a month," Hannah said. "We usually do it here but sometimes we do it at Delaney's house and once we did it at Deb's."

"I like the way you said that." Deb beamed. "I always just think of the house as TJ's but it's mine, too."

"And it's beautiful," Darcy said. "The house, the lake,

your backyard are just gorgeous. The FlashTag folks were certainly impressed."

"Thank you and I'm glad. I hope we get the account." Deb filled Hannah's dishwasher with soap and turned it on.

"Any news on that?" Delaney asked.

"Not yet. They have another company they're meeting with this weekend so we'll see." She slung her purse strap over her shoulder.

"If anyone can get them it's the aptly named Win, as TJ likes to call him." Deb hopped up on the counter. "Leave it to the charmmeister. I'm sure he's already knocked their socks off."

He had indeed been charming and knocked their socks off. Though she hated to admit it, his improvisation had cemented the weekend as an indisputable success. But it would've been nice if Deb had acknowledged Darcy's hard work too. She'd done just as much as Win to bag the deal and still had the blisters on her feet to prove it. Win might be the athlete and the charismatic one but she was the one who'd organized the entire weekend, booked the hotel and the restaurants, and shuttled everyone around.

Ordinarily, Darcy would've kept her mouth shut. Win was Deb's family and Darcy was an outsider. But she was sick of always standing on the outside, looking in. Even in her own home—her parents' and Lewis's—she'd felt like a second-class citizen. Just once she wanted to be acknowledged.

"He was amazing," she stammered. "You should've seen him ride the bull. Everyone was in awe. But I like to think I was just as instrumental as Win in showing them a good time." There, she'd said it. She'd spoken up for herself and it felt damned good, even though she probably should've kept a leash on her tongue.

"Hell yeah, you were." Deb got off the counter and

topped off her wineglass. "TJ thinks you hung the moon. We all do. And you and Win are the perfect team. He's good with the schmoozing and the physical stuff, you're good with strategizing and coordinating."

"You think so?"

"Uh, yeah. Everyone does." Deb stated it so definitively that Darcy felt giddy.

"Thanks," she said, her chest still swelling from Deb's praise. "I guess I better get going."

On the way home, she rolled down all her windows and set her radio at full blast.

Chapter Fifteen

Darcy awoke to voices in the kitchen. They were muffled but she could make them out just the same. The first one belonged to Nana, the second was the voice of doom, which made her smother her face in a pillow to drown out the sound. She practiced her breathing. In and out, in and out.

It was her day off so she could spend as long as she wanted in bed, just inhaling and exhaling. Except she had plans, ones that she sensed were about to be broken. She inched to the edge of the bed, felt for her phone, and checked her messages under the tent of her blanket, hoping that TJ wanted her to come in. Nope, she was screwed. Why couldn't someone need her when she needed to be needed?

She lazed as long as she could, stretching her legs as far as they would go. Win barely fit on her full-size bed but she couldn't even touch the footboard with her toes. Britney's toes would've touched. Darcy had seen Win's ex-fiancée only once but she'd been tall and slender.

Britney was Win's usual MO, at least in the looks department. And why not? Beautiful people tended to gravitate toward other beautiful people, leaving the lesser mortals to settle for the leftovers. But just for once, Darcy hadn't had to settle. And even though she and Win had been a onetime deal, she'd always have their liaison to remember and to give her a lift in desperate times. Like now.

She forced herself out of bed and dragged herself to the shower, taking extra long to wash her hair because . . . procrastination. Then she took a while to go through her closet and pick each article of clothing to wear with the same care as she would've planning her own funeral. This wasn't procrastination, this was sheer survival. The occasion called for putting on heavy-duty Spanx and going monochromatic from head to toe. She even broke out her kitten heels and put on a full face of makeup.

Her mirror said she was as good as it gets and she strode down the staircase, trying to hold her head up high and not to die from her undergarments cutting off her oxygen flow.

"Mother!" She acted surprised to see Geneva sitting at the dining room table. "I didn't know you were coming."

Geneva gave her a swift examination and the fact that she didn't utter one criticism should've been the tip-off that things were even worse than Max had let on. That's when Geneva burst into tears, leaving Darcy at a loss of what to do. She realized she had absolutely no idea how to comfort her mother. The truth was after thirty-one years they were detached, almost like strangers.

"Max said he told you about the divorce," she said, wiping her nose on one of Nana's linen napkins. "Did he tell you he was leaving me for someone else?"

He hadn't but in the back of Darcy's mind she'd thought it was a possibility. A slight one, but one nonetheless. She hadn't asked because frankly she hadn't wanted to know. "No. I'm sorry, Mother." "I'm sorry" seemed woefully insufficient but she didn't know what to say and a part of her was angry that they were putting this at her door.

When she'd left Lewis, both her parents had been the opposite of supportive. Her mother had made it clear that Darcy would never do better and her father had treated the divorce like a childish phase.

"I can't believe he's doing this to me." Geneva wailed. "He wants to sell the house, probably so he can buy something better for his slut. I worked my ass off to make that house . . . everything. It was the envy of all our friends."

She sounded more upset about losing the house than she did about losing her husband, Darcy noted. And her "working my ass off" consisted of hiring people. But Darcy could understand her disappointment. Her life was being turned upside down. That part of it Darcy understood firsthand.

"You can start over, Mother, get a new house. And you can make it any way you want. I'm sure it will be as gorgeous as yours and Dad's." Darcy sat at the table across from Geneva and glanced at Nana, who seemed as uncomfortable as she was. Max was Nana's son after all and Geneva was clearly here to claim them to her side.

Geneva stared back. "Get your head out of the clouds, Darcy. When your father's through with me I'll be lucky to afford a double-wide. If you don't believe me, look around." To punctuate her insult, she literally turned her nose up as she glanced around Nana's cozy house. "Did you get your own place with your large divorce settlement from Lewis?"

Darcy hadn't wanted anything from Lewis, only her freedom. They'd been married a mere two years; it's not like he owed her anything, though it would've been nice to have been recognized for helping him grow his real estate firm. Her parents, on the other hand, had been married for more than three decades and her mother had helped Max build their mortgage company from the ground up.

"Nevada is a community property state, Mother. You'll

get your due." She rarely spoke to Geneva with such bite but she'd be damned if she'd let her denigrate Nana's house. More love abounded from the fifteen-hundred-square-foot cottage than all of Max and Geneva's four-thousand-square-foot castle. Besides, Darcy lived here by choice.

"Are you really that naïve? Between his tramp and his accountant, I'll be lucky to get a quarter of our financial worth."

Darcy didn't know how the "tramp" fit into this. She and Nana exchanged glances before Hilde got up to refill Geneva's coffee and bring Darcy her own cup.

"Have you hired a lawyer?" Darcy asked, even though the obvious question felt like she was taking sides.

"Of course I have, though your father has already retained the best divorce attorney in Reno."

Darcy assumed there was more than one good lawyer in Nevada but clearly her mother needed to vent. "I'm sure you'll find a good one too." And because Darcy couldn't help giving her mother a taste of her own awful medicine she said, "If you're that worried about it you should try to get Dad back. Clearly, he's a wonderful catch."

At that Geneva burst into a second round of tears, which made Darcy feel like an absolute bitch.

"I'm sorry, Mom. I didn't mean that."

"Yes, you did. You think I don't know how much you resent me for Lewis. I only say the things I do because you're my daughter and I love you. I want you to have a good life, Darcy. I want you to be happy and have what I had all those years, before your father left me."

Geneva did not make a habit of telling Darcy that she loved her. In fact, Darcy couldn't remember her ever saying it before and the words took her by surprise and made her lungs constrict. Perhaps all her mother's sniping was never intended to be hateful. Maybe she really did have Darcy's best interest at heart. But it was still sad. Sad that her mother equated having a good life with having lots of expensive things. Sad that a loveless marriage was better than no marriage at all. And sad that she knew so little about what made Darcy happy. It certainly hadn't been Lewis.

She wanted to go to her mother, hold her, but she didn't know how. They'd never been a touchy-feely family. The table between them may as well have been a chasm the size of the Grand Canyon.

"She's not even beautiful," Geneva said, this time blowing her noise into the napkin. When Darcy looked at her quizzically because she had no idea what her mother was talking about, Geneva said, "Your father's receptionist, the one he dumped me for. She's short, mousy, and chubby. Hardly what one expects *the other woman* to look like."

Darcy was struck by the portrayal. It sounded vaguely familiar because it was all the things Geneva had accused her of being. Darcy the fat dish towel.

And Nana knew it too because she looked Mother straight in the eye and said, "Max obviously doesn't see it that way because he loves her."

Geneva began to wail all over again. Darcy's phone buzzed and she surreptitiously reached for it in her purse and glanced at the screen. She never thought she'd be thankful for a text from Lewis but at that very moment she felt beyond beholden to her ex-husband.

"I promised Lewis I'd spend the day doing data entry for him," she said, quickly shoving the cell back inside her bag. Nana gave her a panicked look. *Please don't leave me alone with your mother*. Darcy hurriedly added, "And Nana has a doctor's appointment. So we need to get going soon."

"You're welcome to stay, Geneva," Nana said. "Perhaps a little time in the garden would do you good."

Mother nodded, her eyes red-rimmed and puffy and

Darcy felt instantly ashamed. "If you want, you can come with us. We could go to that mall you like for some shopping therapy."

"No, I'll stay here. Hilde's right, a little time outdoors might be restorative."

Since when? Geneva hated the sun, was scared to death that it would age her. But it was better than the alternative: Geneva coming with them to Reno.

"When we get back we can all go out for a nice dinner," Darcy said. "There's that gastropub, Old Glory, that you liked so much the last time. Or if you'd prefer we could go to the Indian—"

"Anything is fine." Geneva waved her off. "You go. I'm glad you're spending time with Lewis, maybe there's still hope for the two of you."

Darcy didn't bother arguing. Her mother had enough to contend with. The last thing she needed was to deal with her constant disappointment of a daughter.

After work Win decided to stop off at Colt and Delaney's because it beat going home to his empty apartment. He'd tried to call Darcy a few times from the lake where he was giving a paddleboard lesson to four surly teenagers whose parents wanted to keep them busy. Paddleboard lessons weren't usually his bag but the guide who was scheduled to do it had to fly to Texas because of a death in her family. He'd had an open slot, which this time of year—or any for that matter—was a rarity.

Darcy didn't answer and he wondered whether she was intentionally ignoring him because they'd had sex. Really good sex. What Darcy lacked in experience she made up for in enthusiasm. Or maybe it had been his six-month moratorium. In any event, it bugged him that she seemed totally unaffected by the whole thing, just running off to book club like nothing had happened between them. Women typically wanted more from him after he'd slept with them. And while it was a relief that Darcy was so chill, it also sort of pissed him off. There was something about her that got to him. Her snarky mouth for one. Her curves for another. And those baby blues of hers slayed him. But really, he just liked being with her. He didn't have to pull out the exhausting Win bag of tricks of constant charm and humor with her. He could just be himself.

He pulled up to his brother's house and tried her again. Voice mail. "Darce, did aliens abduct you? Seriously, call me." He didn't give a shit if he sounded needy.

He closed his Jeep door with a thud, his mood growing darker. Colt was sitting on the deck, strumming his guitar, staring at his new carport with a self-satisfied look on his face. Before he'd moved in with Delaney he'd lived next door and parking had been a bone of contention between the two of them. Now they had enough for both their cars and a guest.

"You come to eat my cereal?" Colt put his guitar down.

"That or whatever you're making for dinner. Is Jack on night duty?"

"Yep. Now that we have the new guy I actually get a regular weekend when TJ isn't calling me in to take over someone's tour."

"I got stuck today with giving paddleboard lessons to four kids who couldn't put down their phones for even five seconds," Win said. "Danielle's aunt died."

"I heard. That's too bad. But better you than me." Win definitely had more patience than Colt.

"Where's Delaney?" Win peered through the window.

"Working late. She's getting ready for fashion week."

"Isn't that in the fall?" Win didn't know a lot about the

world of couture but he'd picked up a few things having a
sister-in-law who was a famous fashion designer.

"Yep. But it takes months to prepare." He pinched Win's
cheek. "Something you wouldn't know about, Winifred."

This was the kind of bullshit he'd had to put up with his
whole life. *Winifred*. It was a hell of a lot better than being
named after malt liquor or a gun.

"What've you got to eat?"

"I could grill us some burgers." Colt eyed his big-ass
stainless-steel built-in barbecue, a last-minute add-on to the
carport job.

"Sounds good. You got salad fixings?"

"Probably. You gonna put it in a blender and make one
of your disgusting green drinks?"

Win ignored the crack. So what if he tried to eat healthy?
He went inside Colt and Delaney's house and rummaged
through the fridge. The house was one of those modern
numbers everyone was building in Glory Junction. High on
architectural doodads, low on personality and no yard to
speak of. He much preferred Reggie's log cabin.

He pulled out one of those bagged salads, found a bowl,
and dumped the baby greens in. There was a bottle of ranch
in the door. Colt came in and grabbed a few frozen patties
and soaked some oak chips in the sink.

"What's going on with that house you looked at?" Colt
added hamburger buns to his pile.

"I'm waiting for Reggie to work up a price. I doubt I can
afford it. The place needs work but it's awesome. Right on
the river with a dock and gazebo. Gardens like you wouldn't
believe."

"Mom and Dad might help you."

Colt and TJ had bought their own places without their
parents' help. Hannah had inherited her and Josh's house
from her aunt Sabine. But even so, Josh could stand on his

own two feet. There was no way Win would let himself be the only son who got a leg up.

"Nah, I want to do it myself," he said.

"You were willing before . . . with Britney."

"That was different. I had a baby to think about." At the time, he'd been in a panic to do everything right, even if it meant taking money from his parents. Thank God it had been a false alarm.

Colt nodded in understanding. "Even if this one doesn't work out, you'll find one that does. It's just good that you want to buy a place."

Win got the context of Colt's words loud and clear: It's good that Win was finally growing up. He didn't take offense at it because it was simply the truth. At almost thirty-two it had been a long time in coming and had actually taken the unfortunate situation with Britney to kick him in the ass.

"Now, if you could just stay out of bar fights we'd be getting somewhere," Colt said, and Win gave him the finger.

During the course of making dinner, Delaney showed up and Colt threw another burger on the grill. They ate out on the deck, enjoying the balmy Sierra evening, listening to the katydids, while the sweet smell of jasmine filled the air. Win loved spring in Glory Junction when all the flowers were blooming and the sunsets were the things of old Western landscape paintings with their brushstrokes of bright oranges, blues, and purples.

He helped with the cleanup and headed out but was too restless to go home. Without thinking about it, he took the road to Hilde Wallace's cottage. There was an expensive-looking Mercedes parked in front of Hilde's garage and he wondered what that was about. Darcy had a Volkswagen and Hilde . . . well, she didn't have a Mercedes like that. It was the kind of car he would've remembered her driving.

He parked next to it and checked the time. It was eight o'clock and in his mind not too late to come calling.

He rang the bell and Darcy opened the door, dressed like she was going to a Junior League tea.

He bobbed his chin at her in a half greeting. "What's up with the clothes?"

She looked over her shoulder and whispered, "My mother's here."

"Let me say hi." He started to push his way in but she grabbed his arm.

"Now's not a good time."

"For you or for her?" Darcy was acting weird and he didn't like it.

She came outside and shut the door. "My father's been having an affair."

"Ah, jeez." He scrubbed his hand through his hair at a loss for what to say because it sucked. "Is that what the divorce is about?"

"According to Mom, it is." She shrugged.

"Is that why you haven't been returning my calls?" *Yeah, because it's all about you, asshole.*

Darcy huffed out a breath. "She showed up this morning, hysterical. We just got back from dinner."

Win noticed that she'd sidestepped the question but it sounded like she'd had her hands full. "You okay?"

"To tell you the truth I've been better."

He pulled her in for a hug. Even though she was bantam-sized, she fit and he held on, running his lips over her hair. "Want to go for a drive?"

She looked up at him. "Is that a euphemism for something else?"

"Seriously? Just for once, can you drag your mind out of the gutter?" He grinned. "Nah, I thought we should talk."

He nudged his head at the house. "And it seems like you could use a break."

"Can I change first?"

"Please do." The suit she had on looked constrictive and . . . ugly. He preferred her in the floral sundresses she wore or jeans. "I'll wait in the Jeep."

"I'd invite you in but my mother already thinks you're crazy. And the last thing I need is for you to make up a story that we're expecting." As soon as the words left her mouth, Win could tell she wished she hadn't said it. "Oh gosh, Win, I'm sorry."

"Don't worry about it. I shouldn't have told your mom we were married just like Britney shouldn't have told me she was pregnant with my child."

"It's different," she said. "You didn't hurt anyone, you were just goofing around. Give me five minutes."

He waited in the Jeep, playing Scrabble on his cell phone. Oddly enough, it was one of the board games he and his therapist used to play to help with his dyslexia. Being naturally competitive, it had been a good way to engage him. To this day, it was still difficult for him to make sense of certain words or stay focused on a task. That's why it had always been easier for him to be out in the field, instead of doing the administrative work, like TJ.

"I can't be gone too long." Darcy hopped in the passenger seat.

"All right. Where do you want to go?"

"I don't know. It was your idea to go for a drive."

He took off with no destination in mind, winding up not far from Reggie's cabin, on the river. He pulled into a viewpoint and shut off the engine. It was dark but there was a full moon and he could see light coming off the water. He had the Jeep's top down and could hear an owl in the distance and smell pine from the surrounding forest.

"Is this where you take girls to make out?" Darcy pulled her sweater tighter.

"Why? You didn't get enough of me yesterday and want more?" He put the top back up. "You want me to turn on the heat, too?"

"This is fine."

The women he usually hung out with liked the top down, the doors off, and the music loud. Darcy wasn't anything like them, yet he preferred her company. Lord knew why with that smart mouth of hers.

"Your mom okay with you leaving?" It seemed like a silly question to ask a grown woman but under the circumstances maybe Geneva needed Darcy around.

"She was in bed when I left."

"It's not even nine."

"I think she took sleeping pills. Either that or she could no longer stand Nana's and my company."

"Shocking," Win said, and Darcy socked him in the arm. "Who's the other woman, do you know her?"

"Apparently, his receptionist. There have been so many, I've lost track."

"Of receptionists or women with whom he's had affairs?"

"Receptionists," Darcy said. "As far as I know this is his first affair but the daughter is always the last to know. According to my mother, she's short, fat, and not terribly attractive."

"Maybe she's a nice person."

She looked at him strangely. "Are you saying my mother isn't?" And then she laughed.

"I didn't like the way she talked to you. But I met her for all of what, fifteen minutes? I'm sure she's got her strengths."

"She's beautiful," Darcy said wistfully.

"You look a lot like her." He held her gaze.

"We have the same blue eyes and that's about it."

He didn't say anything because frankly it was a little creepy comparing a woman you'd slept with to her mother. Sort of a Mrs. Robinson situation. "You think maybe we should talk about yesterday?"

"What about it?"

So she was going to play coy. He didn't respond, leaving her dangling in silence. Win could wait her out.

She rested her forehead against the dashboard. "Is it going to be weird at work?"

"It doesn't have to be."

"No, why not?"

"Because we're adults, Darcy."

"I agree," she said. "I've also been thinking that we should continue having sex. Nothing serious, mind you. Just a short-term affair where we each get what we want. My body for yours."

It was about the last thing he expected her to say and just thinking about being inside her again made him hard. "No can do."

She swallowed and her face turned fifty shades of red. "Was I a gigantic disappointment?"

"Hell no. You were beyond fantastic. But I don't do casual anymore. I told you that."

"Then I was a pity screw?"

"A pity screw?" He lifted his brows. "It's pity fuck. And no, because I don't feel sorry for you. You married a lemon and you did what any sane person would do, you returned him. And from what I got a taste of last night, Lewis definitely needed returning. He's an idiot."

"You're contradicting yourself." She folded her arms over her chest, no longer embarrassed, just angry as all get-out.

"No, I'm not. Last night . . . well, it just happened. It

doesn't mean it's going to happen again. Find someone else to use."

"It would be mutually beneficial," she argued.

"Yeah, how's that?" An hour ago, she wasn't even returning his calls. She'd left his bed without so much as a good-bye kiss to go to a freaking book club meeting, no less. Mutually beneficial, his ass. There were women who would pay his mortgage just to sleep with him.

He'd stumped her because she had no pithy comeback. No smart-aleck remark. Nothing. She didn't even propose them trying their hand at a real relationship, not that he would've gone for it.

"So the answer is still no?" she said.

"Yep. Find some other stud." He knew there was zero chance of that.

"Fine. Maybe I will."

Jeez, how had they been reduced to children? This whole thing was bullshit. He wasn't putting up with it anymore. He was trying to be a better person, get his life together, stop having meaningless hookups with women he barely knew. And Darcy wanted to pull him right back in again.

"Go ahead," he said.

"What if I only want you?"

That got him a little in the gut. "Just a minute ago you were ready to try it with someone else."

She let out a puff of air. "That was a bluff. I only want to do this with you."

He turned in his seat. "So, we'd like be exclusive?" What the hell was he asking? He didn't do exclusive. Not even a little.

"If you want."

Jeez, could she sound any less enthusiastic over the prospect?

"I might," he said, and pulled her over the console into his lap and started kissing her. "I'll have to think about it."

Obviously shocked by his sudden change of heart, she slowly regained her equilibrium and kissed him back with the same frenzied fervor he'd initiated. His windows began to fog up and the Jeep was cramped but neither of them seemed to care.

He dragged her T-shirt over her head and popped open the clasp of her bra, palming her breasts in his hands. She whimpered and her nipples puckered, begging for his mouth, which he gladly obliged. She tasted so good, sweet like ripened apricots, and he strained against the fly of his jeans.

She muttered something nonsensical and straddled him, her perfect heart-shaped ass pressed against the windshield. Then she worked open his belt buckle.

They were moving faster than he wanted to but he was so hot for her he couldn't seem to slow things down.

He unsnapped her jeans and scraped down her zipper. But when he tried to slide down her pants there wasn't room to move.

"Shit." He tried to move his seat back but it was as far as it would go. "Outside!"

She stopped kissing him. "What?"

He opened the door, jumped out, and pulled her with him. Tugging her around to the passenger side where his Jeep would block them from the road, he pushed her against the door.

"Win, I'm topless." Yep, and the cool air was doing amazing things to her nipples.

He covered her mouth before she could protest again

and licked his way inside, exploring. She stuck her hand down the waistband of his jeans and stroked him. At this rate, he'd go off like a fire hydrant so he pushed her hand away.

"I want you," she said. "Please."

Win had a mind to make her beg but he didn't have the willpower to wait any longer. Desperate, he pushed her pants and underwear down her legs, leaving them in a heap in the dirt, and lifted her onto the hood of his Jeep. Fumbling through his glove box, he searched for a condom and cursed. He remembered his backpack and emptied it on the back seat. Eureka!

He slid down his zipper, rolled the condom down his length, and dragged her to the edge of the hood. Her head fell back and he tested her with his fingers. She was unbelievably wet.

"Hurry." Her voice came out breathless.

He spread her legs and slid in home. "Hold on."

She clutched his shoulders and wrapped her legs around his hips as he drove deep inside of her. He gripped her ass, squeezing it, pulling her closer.

She kissed him, twining her arms around his neck. In the background, he could hear the river rushing, a soft breeze rustling through the trees, and their heavy breathing. He whispered endearments in her ear as he pounded into her.

"Oh, Win," she cried out, and he felt her body tremble.

She wasn't quite there but he didn't know how much longer he could hold on. He quickened his strokes and worked her with his fingers until he felt her climax. Then he took his own release, holding on to her under the moonlit sky, both of them trying to catch their breath.

When he finally came up for air, he looked into her

heated blue eyes and said, "I guess we could try it." He couldn't bring himself to say *exclusive*.

"I guess so" was her only response.

And without another word they got dressed and got back in the car.

Chapter Sixteen

Geneva went home on Friday and Darcy had a glorious drama-free three-day weekend with just Nana and Win. He dropped by every evening after showering from his day's tour. Sometimes they'd go for a drive and other times back to his studio apartment.

She tried hard to think of their nights together as nothing more than sexual adventure but it was getting increasingly difficult, even though wishing for anything more was the kiss of death. Win wasn't built to last and she wasn't looking for a full-time player.

She figured she'd let their time together run its course and pick up the pieces after it was over. But for now, the sex was too good to pass up and Win was turning out to be a tremendous listener when she needed one most.

She hit him over the head with a pillow. "You better get up. The meeting's in ninety minutes."

He gazed at his bedside clock. "I only need thirty. You showering here?"

"Uh-uh, I'm going home first, then to make the doughnut run. See you at work."

"Come here." He pulled her down on top of him and kissed her. "We have time—"

She wrestled against him to get off the bed. "No time. Unless I go to the office like this." She waved her hand over yesterday's cutoff shorts and tank top.

"Works for me," he said, and tried to pull her back down.

"Not in your wildest dreams," she said, though she was sorely tempted. He looked so good lying there naked with his hair rumpled and a day's worth of stubble. All those muscles and golden-brown skin. She still couldn't believe she was sleeping with Win Garner, heartthrob of Glory Junction. "See you in the city, slicker."

He flipped onto his side and threw a leg over the side of the bed. "At least take a shower with me."

She collected her purse and slid her feet into her flip-flops. "Can't." He was insatiable, which she was still getting used to. After Lewis it was amazing but she didn't delude herself into thinking his sexual appetite was solely for her. Win was just a randy son of a gun.

She took one last delicious peek at him as he stretched, completely uninhibited in his nakedness, before leaving. "Try not to be obvious at the meeting about us sleeping together." Not that she thought he would because no one would believe it anyway. But it was better for all involved if they kept this little arrangement on the down-low.

"You embarrassed of me?"

"Right." She rolled her eyes and walked out the door.

By the time she made it to the Morning Glory diner she was cutting it close to meeting time. Felix greeted her with his usual gruff "Hello," then yelled back to the kitchen, "Garner life preservers."

She made it to GA with just enough minutes left to make the coffee and set the conference table with napkins, plates, and cups, and looked forward to the day when this was someone else's chore. It's not that she minded organizing the Monday morning meeting but she wanted to manage accounts, make deals, have a title and a good salary. The song "Passionate Kisses" flitted through her head. Yes, she should have it all, even Win Garner if only for a short time.

"Hey," TJ said as he came in and sat at his usual spot, the head of the table. "You have a good four days off?"

"I did. How 'bout you? How was your weekend?" Until TJ and Deb had gotten together, he'd worked the weekends and put in twelve-hour days during the week. Now he was spreading more of the responsibility to Josh and spending time with Deb and even guiding a few tours.

"Good. We took the boat out. Thanks for asking." He gazed around the empty room and let out a sigh. "I see everyone is late as usual."

"Not me," she said even though she sounded like a suck-up. One thing she noticed about men, they were shameless self-promoters. Women could learn a thing or two from that.

"Nope, you're never late. Truthfully, you and Deb are the only employees here who are worth a damn, besides me of course. If we get FlashTag I'll get you off the front desk, I promise."

"Who's worth a damn?" Josh came in and went straight for the coffee.

"Not you, that's for sure." TJ grabbed a bear claw before the other brothers could hog them. Felix never made enough.

"Good. Then you won't mind if I take a week off in August."

Both TJ and Darcy spun around to look at him. Darcy speculated they were thinking the same thing. Another surgery on Josh's leg, the one he'd nearly lost in an IED explosion in Afghanistan. Every time Josh went under the knife, the Garners rallied. But it was hard on them to see Josh suffer.

"Why?" TJ asked.

"It's called a vacation, big brother. You should try it sometime."

TJ's relief was palpable. To an outsider, the Garner brothers' constant ribbing of one another seemed like sibling rivalry on steroids. But Darcy knew better. They teased as hard as they played but their love for one another was unconditional. She'd never known a family who had one another's backs as much as the Garners.

"Why August? It's our busiest time before winter."

"I know." Josh picked through the doughnuts until he found one he liked. "But Hannah found an all-inclusive deal to go to Cabo San Lucas. She wants to spread Sabine's ashes."

All Darcy knew was that Sabine was Hannah's late aunt and that she'd inherited Glorious Gifts from her.

"We'll work it out," TJ said. "What time of August? I would hate for you to miss the End of Summer festival."

The Garners lived for the annual weekend event, which included a kayak race that GA won every year.

"We're good," Josh said. "It'll be early August."

Win came in, his hair damp, curling around his collar, and Darcy's breath caught. The man did that to her, made her gulp for oxygen. And when he turned his smile on her she nearly melted in a puddle on the hardwood floor. She still couldn't believe she got to sleep with him every night. Then she reminded herself for the second time today—and it was only nine—that it was temporary. He was just on loan from the public sex library.

"We ready to get this party started?" Colt brushed in wearing his police uniform. "I've only got a few minutes so try your best not to be too long-winded." He looked directly at TJ, winked at Darcy, and filled a paper plate with a couple of doughnuts.

Deb was the last person in and she sat next to Darcy. The senior Garners rarely made appearances at the meetings anymore. She supposed Gray and Mary were enjoying their semiretirement.

"Can I do my report first?" Deb asked. "I've got a thing."

"What kind of thing?" Josh wasn't letting her off the hook that easy.

"Yeah," Colt chimed in. "Share with the rest of the class."

She shot them both looks and let out an exasperated sound. "If you must know Delaney's taking my measurements for my wedding gown."

Darcy didn't even realize she was doing it but she let out a sigh. Four pairs of eyes turned on her. "What? It's exciting. Leave her alone."

Colt threw his head back and laughed. "Four months ago, you couldn't say boo in a crowded room. Now you're a tiger." He and his brothers stood up and high-fived. "You're an official Garner now."

She blew her new tough-girl image by blushing.

"Remember the time you choked on a doughnut because TJ embarrassed you?" Josh said.

It was something she'd hoped to forget and gave him her three-finger salute for reminding her of the humiliating experience. "Read between the lines."

That sent everyone into a second fit of laughter, even Win, who reached out and stroked her hair. And not in a "you're an honorary Garner" way. No, he did it with the sensual familiarity of a lover. Everyone in the room went silent and she could feel the weirdness crackle in the air.

Win tried to cover by making a joke but Darcy sensed no

one was buying the snow job he was selling. She didn't know what they thought they saw but whatever they'd divined from Win's small, intimate gesture was now out in the universe.

Ultimately, it was Deb who saved the moment by distracting everyone with her report. She stood up, cleared her throat, and gave a synopsis of their weekly sales.

"The egg carriers are a major fail," she said. "Who the hell brings eggs backpacking? I believe those were your idea, Colt."

"Bullshit. I said it as a joke. I didn't actually think you would order them."

"Well, I did and they've been thoroughly mocked in the comment section of the online store. So you suck! On the other hand, TJ's brilliant suggestion to carry microfiber packable camp towels has been a huge win. We've sold twenty in three days."

"You're just giving TJ credit because you're sleeping with him." Colt stabbed his coffee stirrer at her.

"Yes, I am sleeping with him but zero"—she made a circle with her thumb and index finger—"for you and twenty for him."

Josh and TJ laughed. Deb grabbed a doughnut and headed for the door.

"I'm out of here, people."

"Bye, little Debbie," Colt said, using the nickname she hated.

"Next line of business is FlashTag." Everyone turned their attention to TJ and Darcy held her breath. He'd held out on her earlier by keeping the news a secret until now. "They want a second round with us. This time Madison De Wolk is coming."

"When?" Win asked.

"This weekend. I want you and Darcy back on it."

"We're down with that, right, Darce?"

"You bet." The fact that Madison De Wolk was coming herself meant they'd passed the first test. All they had to do was get her to sign on the bottom line and the account was theirs.

"I swear to God, Win, leave Darcy alone. I don't know what that was about in the conference room but I do know you're playing with fire, flirting with her like that. She's not one of your party girls and she's going to wind up getting hurt."

Win knew the minute TJ stepped foot in his office and shut the door that his brother was going to make a federal case over the way he'd touched Darcy. TJ didn't know what he was talking about but Win sure as hell wasn't going to enlighten him.

"It's none of your business." He was sick of his brothers' meddling. He was entitled to a private life and what he and Darcy did in their off-hours wasn't any concern of TJ's.

"The hell it isn't. Darcy works for me, she works for Garner Adventure. Last I looked, you were an equal share-holder of this company. Do I need to draw you a picture?"

"There's nothing to worry about." Because Darcy wanted this. He was helping a friend, that's all. "I don't know what you thought you saw but it was nothing. We're buddies."

TJ just sat there, staring at him. "Am I making a mistake having you two work together on this account? This is too important to screw up, Win. So if there's something going on with you two, you need to speak up now. For once in your freaking life be responsible."

Be responsible.

Win had been hearing those words his entire life. His

family stuck by him throughout the Britney ordeal but he'd
known all along what they'd been thinking. He could see it
written across their faces. Good ol' Win, the womanizing
screwup. The guy who dropped out of the US Olympic
team because he couldn't get serious about anything. The
lesser brother who was easily distracted and struggled in
school. The one who barely made it through college.

He'd been typecast for so long, he wouldn't even know
how to play another role. So he did what he did best. He
walked away.

He was halfway down Main Street when he remembered
he had a mountain biking group at eleven. Time enough for
a green shake at the Juicery and to clear his head. TJ was
just dead wrong. This thing between him and Darcy . . . he
didn't know what it was. He only knew that she made him
laugh and she made him feel things he'd never felt before.
And when she was done using him for his body, he'd probably feel like shit. Karma was a mean bitch.

He got his protein drink and was on his way back to GA
to load up when he bumped into Boden.

"You look like someone stole your lunch."

Boden frowned. "That Rachel Johnson is one of the
most difficult people I've ever dealt with."

Win jerked his head in surprise. "We talking about
the same Rachel Johnson? Tart Me Up Rachel?" Because
she was one of the nicest women in town. She always put
in a good word for GA with the tourists who stopped in at
her bakery. She was always the first to donate food to one
of Glory Junction's charity events. She taught a free baking
class at the women's shelter. She'd even caught the attention
of Oprah Winfrey, who'd publicly raved about Tart Me Up.
Before Delaney had moved to town, everyone had held out

hope that Colt would get his head out of his ass and date Rachel.

"That would be her. She's got a real dark side."

Dark side. Since when? "Oh yeah, how's that?"

"First off, she's a control freak. Ask Foster. The three of us get hired to do a lot of events. It's easy money and I'm saving to buy a brewery. The woman wants to tell me where to set my bar up, what to serve, and how the hell to dress. Like this is my first freaking rodeo. I don't even think her buns are that good."

Win's brows winged up. "Which buns would those be?"

"Her sweet buns, you asshole."

Win laughed. "As much as I'd love to hear more, I've got a date with a group of mountain bikers. I'm sure you and Rachel will work out your differences."

"Doubtful," he said, and continued up Main Street. Win had never seen the affable Boden so worked up, at least not since Dale busted up his bar and Win's face.

He loaded his bike in his Jeep and took off for Royal Slope. In winter, the resort boasted some of the most challenging designated ski courses in California. In spring and summer, cyclists bombed down the mountain at breakneck speed.

His group consisted of four experienced mountain bikers from Oregon who wanted to learn the trails. To borrow the cliché: It was a tough job but someone had to do it. Because of assignments like this one you couldn't pay him a bazillion dollars to ride a desk full-time.

Six hours later, he was breathing hard and feeling good. All he'd had to do was get his cyclists up the mountain, point them in the right direction, and they'd ridden until they'd run out of steam. Starved, the five of them grabbed dinner and a beer afterward, then Win went home to soak off the grime.

He found TJ sitting on his doorstep.

"Are the rest of them coming so you can triple-team me?"

"Nah, just me. How'd the ride go?"

Win unlocked his door and waved his hand across the threshold to let TJ in first. "I know you didn't come here to check up on my tour so you can cut the shit."

"Let's go look at Reggie's house."

Win dragged his shirt over his head and ducked into the bathroom. Whatever TJ really came for could wait until Win showered.

"You got anything to eat?" TJ called through the door.

"Check the refrigerator." Shit, Win remembered that Hilde's pie plate was still in there. Since it wasn't monogrammed it could've come from any number of people.

He turned the water as hot as he could take it and got in the tub. It didn't last long. The old complex didn't have those tankless water heaters like GA, TJ, and Colt had. When he got his new place he was going to get one too. He dried off, checked his phone to see if Darcy had called, and turned it off just in case she rang him while TJ was here. Sneaking around sucked but Darcy didn't want anyone to know and whatever they were doing was so new and tentative that he had to agree with her.

He came out to find TJ eating dry granola.

"Your food sucks."

"If you want good food go to a restaurant or Josh's house. Here, I'll show you to the door."

TJ continued to chomp on Win's cereal and appeared in no hurry to leave. Win found clean clothes, put them on, and joined his brother at the breakfast counter.

TJ scanned the apartment. "You cleaned."

"Yep." Win stole a handful of granola.

"You ready to go?"

"You're serious? I'm not asking Reggie to let me in again. He hasn't even given me a price yet. For all I know he's having second thoughts. He built the place with his late wife. There's gotta be a lot of memories in it for him."

"Doesn't mean we can't do a drive-by, check out the neighborhood."

It was hardly a neighborhood. But if TJ wanted to see the cabin Win was game.

"All right."

"I'll drive." TJ fished his keys out of his pocket and Win put on his shoes.

It took less than fifteen minutes to get there. The sun was setting but there was still plenty of light.

"I don't think we should pull through the driveway," Win said. "If he's home he'll see us and it'll be weird, don't you think?"

"You'll look overanxious, that's for sure. But I can't see dick from here." TJ had pulled to the side where the two private roads forked. "Let's hike in, incognito."

Win rolled his eyes. "Should we wear camo and paint our faces?"

"You have a better suggestion?"

"Yeah, let's go to Old Glory and have a beer."

"I want to see the place." TJ shut off the engine and hopped out of his Range Rover.

Win threw up his hands and joined him. "I guess we're doing this. Reggie has a dog, be prepared."

Instead of walking down the driveway like normal people, they went through a copse of pines, using the trees as cover, and wove their way through dense thickets on the property. Win kept waiting for Oscar to bark or an alarm to sound. In backcountry people were prickly about trespassers. Mostly everyone had a shotgun for hunting or to shoo away varmints. Reggie seemed a little too chill to pull a gun on someone and Oscar too old and fat to catch them if they ran. But sneaking around like this would take some explanation if Reggie caught them. It seemed like a bad way to start a business relationship.

"This is stupid," he whispered to TJ.

"Isn't stupid your middle name?"

"Usually, but this was your idea."

TJ broke into a huge grin. It reminded Win of when they used to be kids. Back when TJ was fun and not a sanctimonious workaholic.

"Whatever Deb put in your Metamucil, I like it."

They came up on the back of the house and walked along the river's edge to circle around. If Reggie had been looking out of one of the cabin's huge windows he would've seen them sure as shit. But it didn't appear that he was home or if he was, he was hibernating somewhere.

"This place is awesome," TJ said, looking up at the big wraparound porch.

"Right? It needs a good amount of work, though. And Reggie's a packrat."

"I want to peek in the window."

Win grabbed his arm. "Are you crazy? Don't press your luck."

But TJ was already headed for the porch. Win hit his forehead with the heel of his hand and muttered an expletive. TJ jumped over the railing where the corner of the porch was windowless and crouched along the edge. Win watched from the river's edge as his brother made it to a living room window, shielded his eyes, and peered inside. He crept around the entire porch and popped up where he started.

"The coast is clear." He beckoned Win over.

"Are you sure?" Reggie could be napping in his bedroom. But it was odd that the dog hadn't shown its face.

"Pretty sure. But if he comes out now we can just pretend we were about to knock on the door."

"All right." Win vaulted himself over the railing like TJ had and they walked around checking out the view from various vantage points.

"I'll go in partners with you," TJ said.

"You already have a house and I don't want a partner." Win pressed his face against the glass to get a better look at the kitchen.

"I don't think you can afford it otherwise. Hell, this place is right on the river. The land alone is worth bucks. The cabin may need work but it's got amazing bones. You're looking at a big chunk of change here just to afford the mortgage payments."

"I might have to settle for something else then." Win wasn't going to take money from TJ, just like he wouldn't from his parents. He wanted to do this on his own.

TJ gazed out over the property, at the gardens and the grove of trees, and let out a whistle. "I'd sure like to have this in the Garner family. When Reggie gives you a price let's see what we can work out. Maybe there's a way to swing it. You've got savings, right?"

"Some." Not as much as he probably should have in the bank, given his not unsubstantial salary and his low over-head. His studio apartment cost next to nothing. But over the years he'd frittered away a lot of cash on fancy outdoor gear and equipment, his Jeep, and some pretty extravagant vacations.

"With that and the bonus you get from bagging the FlashTag account—if you get it—we might be able to figure out a loan that would keep your monthly pay-ments down."

If anyone could pull it off, TJ could. He had a master's degree in business from UC Berkeley and was the best wheeler-dealer Win knew.

"It's a sweet property." TJ went down the porch stairs, stepped back from the house so he could appraise it from a distance. "Needs a new roof. But it's a hell of a cabin, really nice design. Solid."

"Yep. Can we go now before someone thinks we're breaking into the place?"

"Uh-huh." TJ was distracted. Win could see the wheels in his head spinning. He was already figuring out a way to turn the place into Camp Garner.

"Come on." Win kicked him in the ass. "Let's go back the way we came."

Ten minutes later, they were headed for the main road back to town.

"Where's Deb?" Win asked to break the silence.

"Doing something with Hannah and Delaney. Probably wedding crap. You want to talk about what's going on with you and Darcy?"

Win figured the question was the real reason TJ had come and he'd used the house as an excuse. "Nope."

The cab of the truck filled with silence until TJ finally spoke. "I was a dick before."

"You? Never."

TJ slid him a sideways glance and his lips quirked. "You've gotta admit that your track record isn't so hot and Darcy . . . well, I'm pretty damned fond of her, not to mention that she's become an integral part of this company. Whatever that shit was you pulled with her mother . . ." He let out a breath. "It wasn't like you. I guess what I'm trying to say is I hope you know what you're doing."

He didn't have a fucking clue. "We're friends, TJ." Which was mostly true but there was more, too. He was a little bit crazy about her. Damned if he understood it but it was there, this desperate need to see her every morning and sleep with her every night.

"That's the thing, Win. What you think is friendship, some women think is more."

Win knew TJ was talking about his whole unfortunate situation with Deb. But it was Darcy who initiated the sexual part of their relationship, not him. "You've got to trust me on this."

TJ turned down Main Street and instead of taking Win home, parked in one of the diagonal spots in front of Old Glory. "It's not that I don't trust you, because I know you don't intentionally set out to hurt anyone. It's not who you are but let's just say you're prone to a lot of misunderstandings and I just don't want Darcy to get hurt."

"You ever think I might be the one to get hurt?" Win didn't wait for TJ to answer, just swung open his door and got out.

Chapter Seventeen

Darcy found Nana in her bedroom, looking peaked again. Her skin was ashy, her breathing shallow, and her bony hands were clutching the side of the dresser to hold her up.

She helped maneuver her to the bed to sit down. "What's wrong, Nana?"

"I think your mother wore me out." Nana wore a weary smile.

She was upset about Geneva and Max's breakup, they both were. But Darcy's mother had been gone for three days and until now Nana had been doing just fine.

"When was the last time you had a checkup?" Darcy shouldn't have fabricated that doctor's appointment to her mother. It was as if the universe was paying her back for being a liar.

"Not too long ago. I'm fine dear, just old and tired."

Clearly, it was more than that. Her grandmother was having trouble breathing. "We have to go in, Nana. This isn't normal."

"All right but give me a few minutes to rest." Hilde reached for the nightstand for leverage and seemed much frailer than she'd been when Darcy had left for work that morning. The fact that she wasn't putting up a fuss about going to urgent care was also a red flag.

Seeing her like this scared Darcy to death. She wondered if she should call one of her parents. They'd never been much for helping in situations that didn't involve them directly. But just this once she wished she had someone to turn to.

She found a pair of sneakers in Nana's closet and socks in the drawer and sat on the floor to put them on her grandmother. Hilde was dressed but she liked to pad around the house in her slippers. Her skin felt clammy but it was a hot day.

"You want a glass of water, Nana?"

"That would be nice." Her voice was thready and Darcy wondered whether she should call nine-one-one.

Darcy went to get her a drink and decided that she could get her grandmother to the emergency room at Sierra General faster than waiting for an ambulance to come.

"Have some of this." She handed Nana the glass. "And then we'll go, okay?"

Nana nodded and Darcy had a moment of panic, worried about how she'd even get her grandmother to the car. It wasn't far and Nana wasn't much larger than herself but she didn't know if she had the strength to lift her if it came to that.

For a second she contemplated calling Win but she didn't need to drag him into her problems. They were sleeping together, they weren't a couple. And frankly she didn't want him to think that she'd come to rely on him. It would just scare him off. Besides, she had this. She'd been taking care of herself for a long time.

She found Nana's purse and grabbed her own. "You think you're able to walk?"

Her grandmother gave another nod and Darcy helped her up off the bed. They walked slowly to the front door, stopping every few seconds so Hilde could rest. Darcy prayed she wasn't making a mistake by not calling for emergency response. It was hard to know what to do in a situation like this.

They finally made it to her car and Darcy helped Nana get in the front passenger seat and buckled her in.

"How you doing, Nana?"

"I'm hanging in there." She patted Darcy's arm. "I don't know what I'd do without you."

Darcy's throat clogged. The truth was she didn't know what she'd do without Nana.

"I'm planning to break some traffic laws," she joked because it was better than being consumed by fear.

Nana forced a weak smile and Darcy drove with the wind, making it to the hospital in record time. She pulled up to the entrance and waved down a security guard.

"We need help. My grandmother's sick and I don't think I can get her inside by myself." During the ride, Hilde had complained of dizziness and Darcy didn't want to risk having her fall.

The guard returned with a wheelchair and helped Darcy transfer her grandmother and get her inside. Luckily, despite a waiting room full of sick people, they took Hilde right away. Darcy assumed it was because of her age. She went to park the car and when she returned the nurse took her to her grandmother's room, a tiny area partitioned by curtains with an exam table, to wait for the doctor.

"You're doing great, Nana," she said as one of the attendants assisted Darcy in getting her grandmother into a hospital gown and onto the table.

Another nurse came in to take Hilde's vitals, typing Nana's symptoms into a computer screen. Darcy had never been here before but for a country hospital, Sierra General seemed to have all the modern amenities. It even had decent paintings on the wall. Landscapes of the Sierra Nevada and a couple of Ansel Adams's John Muir Trail reproductions. She tried to get lost in them but she was too preoccupied with her grandmother's health and all the troubling possibilities.

A woman in a white coat and a stethoscope came in the room and introduced herself as Dr. Lee. A nurse followed and the small room grew tighter. Dr. Lee asked Darcy if she would mind waiting outside while she conducted her exam and told her that someone would call her back as soon as she finished.

To keep busy, Darcy went in search of coffee and wound up in a tidy cafeteria with more Ansel Adams reproductions on the wall. She fixed her coffee the way she liked it and went back to the waiting room where she fiddled with her phone to pass the time. There wasn't anything from Win and she wondered if he was still on his mountain biking tour, though it was getting dark outside. Again, she contemplated contacting her parents but decided to wait for Nana's prognosis.

A short time later, she heard her phone ding with a text. Hoping it was Win, she checked the messages. Nope, not Win, Lewis.

There seems to be a glitch with the files you moved to the new program. Any way you can take a look at it? I'm unable to access them.

Despite her better judgment, she'd stopped by the office Thursday while she'd been in Reno, shopping with Nana, and had transferred the data Lewis had asked her to move from one program to another. He really was an idiot when it came to anything technical. *Glitch*. Ha. He just didn't know how to properly use the software.

She didn't need a psychologist to tell her she was a facilitator. Part of the reason she'd left Lewis was because she no longer wanted to be his handmaiden. And here she was divorced and still at his beck and call. It needed to end. She just didn't know how to stop being needed. That was the crux of the problem. She measured her self-worth by how much someone relied on her.

Slipping the phone back into her purse, she watched the clock and waited. At nearly eight o'clock a nurse came to the waiting room to get her.

"Dr. Lee will talk to you now."

When she got to the examination room, Hilde seemed to have some of her color back, which Darcy took as a good sign.

"I've adjusted your grandmother's blood-pressure medication and prescribed a diuretic I think will do the trick," Dr. Lee said. "Otherwise, Mrs. Wallace's tests came back normal. There are a few results we're still waiting on from the lab but those will take a couple of days. By then we should know if she's feeling better from the changes in her meds."

"She was having trouble breathing." As relieved as Darcy was she wanted to make sure they weren't missing anything.

Dr. Lee nodded and smiled at Hilde. "Mrs. Wallace told me. That as well as the lightheadedness and fatigue could be from the hypertension. It's a bit of a balancing act in someone your grandmother's age. We want to get her systolic pressure down without driving her diastolic pressure too low."

She'd lost Darcy. "And the adjustment in her medication will do that?"

"That's what we're hoping. I want her to see her regular physician but in the meantime the medication should give her some relief. She should watch her diet and exercise, even if it's just walking around in her garden." Dr. Lee glanced at Hilde. "Right, Mrs. Wallace?"

Hilde nodded and gave Darcy a reassuring wink.

"We can go home?" Darcy asked the doctor.

"You can go home. Make sure she gets plenty of fluids, especially in this heat."

Darcy helped her grandmother button her blouse and pull the elastic waist of her khakis up and they made the twenty-minute drive home.

"Are you hungry, Nana?"

"I think we should skip dinner and have banana splits. What do you say?"

"Probably not the best idea. Remember what the doctor said about diet." Darcy helped her grandmother out of the car. "How about soup?"

"You're no fun."

"Maybe not." She laughed and together they walked into the house. Nana was sprier than when they'd come out and Darcy said a little prayer of thanks for the swift turnaround. "But if it'll keep you healthy I'm willing to be a frightful bore."

Hilde stopped in the kitchen and turned to Darcy. "You know, dear, I won't live forever."

"Don't say that, Nana." Because the thought of her grandmother leaving this earth was too much to take.

* * *

"Hey, I cruised by Hilde's house last night to see if you wanted to go park somewhere and make out but the both of you were gone," Win said, leaning against GA's front counter.

"Shush." Darcy darted a look around the hallway to make sure no one was lurking in a corner. It was early but TJ usually beat everyone in in the morning and he had big ears. "We had a small emergency and I had to take Nana to the hospital."

Win went still. "Is she okay?"

"It was her blood pressure. But the doctor adjusted her medication and she's doing a lot better." Hilde had been in the kitchen making coffee before Darcy left for work, looking her old self again.

"I'm glad to hear it. Why didn't you call me?"

She lifted her shoulders, trying to appear nonchalant. "I had it under control."

Win leaned over the counter and held her gaze. "I'm sure you did but you still should've called me."

"Why?"

The question seemed to stump him, but then suddenly a smile tugged at the corner of his mouth. "Because you don't need to do everything yourself. Learn to lean a little." With that he strolled away.

She shuffled the papers in her hand, put them aside, and tried to focus on entering time cards into the database. After entering the same card three times she gave up and stomped down the hall to Win's office. He was leaned back in his chair, throwing a Nerf ball through a toy basketball hoop. TJ had one too.

"I don't do everything myself. And I lean plenty." She rested her back against the doorjamb with her arms folded across her chest.

He stopped pitching the ball and looked at her. "Whatever

you say. But you could've called me. That's what boyfriends are for."

She squinted her eyes at him because she didn't trust him. Not one bit. Win didn't do boyfriend. Still, a part of her dared to hope. Why was a whole other story. Maybe just for once she wanted the popular guy to like her. Or maybe, just maybe, she was crazy about him and had been from the day she walked into Garner Adventure and he showed her where the supply cabinet was.

It wasn't worth analyzing too closely. Win was probably suffering from a sugar high from too many doughnuts. Or he was just trying to add her to the list of women he'd slept with and dumped because the whole town knew there were legions of them.

"Get real, Win. We both know you're not my boyfriend," she said. "And after we snag this account we're done sleeping together." It was better that she made the rules before he dumped her and made her feel like a delusional fool.

"Why wait?" He lifted his brows and folded his arms over his chest. He was challenging her. "Because you like sleeping with me. You like me, Darcy, admit it. You want to be my girlfriend."

She wanted to wipe that smug grin off his face. "Arrogant much?" But he'd nailed it, she did like sleeping with him. Too much. What she didn't like was being made to feel like an idiot. Or a charity case. There was a part of her who believed Win was playing the boyfriend act because he felt sorry for her, like if he sprinkled enough attention on her she'd grow up to be big and strong. And he could pat himself on the back for giving her confidence and sending her out into the world a new woman. Maybe she was his project.

"I like it," she admitted. "Anyone would after the drought

I've been through. But don't get too high and mighty. You and I"—she wagged her hand between them—"are strictly temporary. After FlashTag we go back to being friends and you can return to being the lothario of the Sierra Nevada."

He snorted. "With that winning personality of yours I can't imagine why you went through a drought."

She noticed that he didn't argue with her about being temporary. Good, as long as they were on the same page.

"We have to come up with an itinerary for this weekend," she said.

"All right. I've got a rafting trip in thirty. Why don't we do it tonight over dinner?"

She scrutinized him for a second, trying to figure out his game. He was being way too agreeable. "So you can change everything at the last minute?"

"Possibly. It'll depend on my mood and the weather. But it's always good to have a plan as a jumping-off point." He winked like he was joking but she knew he wasn't. He'd turn everything upside down if it suited him. The man couldn't be bothered to follow a simple plan.

She gritted her teeth and turned back to go to her desk. "Whatever."

"Hey," he called. "Come back here."

She would come back all right, to take a swing at him. She circled around. He waited for her to come inside and kicked the door shut with his foot.

"What?"

"This." He moved toward her mouth and kissed her long and slow. His hands slid down her back, grabbed her butt, and pushed her tight up against the hard bulge in his pants. When they finally came up for air she was out of breath.

"You're nuts, you know that?" she said.

He let his eyes drift over her. "See you tonight."

She walked away shaking her head. Whatever his game was she wasn't playing, though the memory of that kiss stayed with her through the rest of the day. And his words "I'm your boyfriend" played in her head over and over again.

At six she started to pack up when the main number rang on the switchboard. She was about to let it go to voice mail but her anal-retentiveness kicked in.

"Garner Adventure, can I help you?"

"Darcy, it's Lewis. You didn't call me back."

She held the phone away from her mouth and silently yelled, *Shit*. She'd been ducking him since yesterday and he'd finally caught up with her.

"How did you get this number?" She had never given it to him. He had her cell and Nana's number, which were already too many.

"What do you mean? It's listed."

"You shouldn't call me at work, Lewis."

"I wouldn't have but you weren't returning my messages and I got worried."

Bullshit. He wanted her to deal with his computer "glitch."

"I've been busy. I do have a full-time job, you know?"

"I realize that, Darcy. And I wouldn't ask if I wasn't in such a jam . . . and you weren't so good with computers. But the new software is giving us all kinds of problems and the woman I hired to replace you"—he let out a long, beleaguered sigh—"honestly, she doesn't know what she's doing."

She held the phone away again, stared up at the ceiling, and counted to five.

"Everything okay?" TJ asked, and she jerked. "Sorry, didn't mean to sneak up on you like that."

"Hang on a second," she told Lewis, and put the call on hold. "Everything's fine. Are you out of here?" she asked TJ, surprised. He rarely left the office before seven.

"Yep. Deb and I are going to Tahoe to see a show. You should get out of here too. It's summer, enjoy it."

"You didn't get hit in the head with a rock or something, did you?"

He tried to stifle a grin. "I'd like to say I miss the old Darcy but unfortunately I like the smart-ass one better. Congratulations, Darce, you've finally grown a set." He reached over the counter and gave her a hug. "Lock up, okay?"

"Will do." She took Lewis off hold. "That was my boss."

"Oh, sorry. Can you come tonight?"

He had to be kidding. "No, I can't. I have a full-time job and a . . . fiancé. I'm sorry but you'll have to deal with your computer issues yourself. I suggest hiring a good IT person. And, Lewis, I don't mean to sound bitchy but you have to stop relying on me. We're divorced now and I work somewhere else." She hung up before he could protest and before she lost her nerve.

She was definitely growing a set and boy did it feel good.

Chapter Eighteen

On Thursday morning Reggie called with a price on the cabin. Win was at the Juicery and had to get out of line to take the call.

Reggie named an amount that was a lot less than he expected but more than he had in the bank.

"That sounds very fair, Reggie. I've got to sit down and crunch some numbers and I'll get back to you." Win knew it was futile unless the FlashTag deal came through and he got a substantial bonus.

"All right," Reggie said. "But don't take too long. That agent, Jenny Meyers, has been hounding me for the listing. She says summer is prime time for selling real estate and I don't want to miss my window of opportunity."

Win knew the minute the cabin went on the market someone would snatch it right up. He'd hate to lose it but he'd need a significant down payment to qualify for a loan. He got his green drink and went back to the office.

TJ had cleared Win's schedule so he could audit equipment and prepare for Madison De Wolk's arrival the next day. Ordinarily, he hated doing inventory but because he and Darcy were doing it together he was actually looking forward to it.

The thing about him being her boyfriend had slipped out the other day. He didn't quite know how he felt about an actual bona fide relationship. But God she challenged him and he'd never been so hot for a woman in all his life. The truth was she kind of made him crazy . . . in a good way. And he couldn't remember a time when he'd ever been this happy. Singing in the shower and getting lost in the hours, daydreaming about a blond nymph with big blue eyes and deep dimples.

"I heard from Reggie," Win told TJ as he passed him in the hallway.

"Yeah?" TJ jerked his head at his office. "Come in and talk to me."

Win lay longways on TJ's leather sofa with his feet hanging off the end and his arms pillowed under his head. "He wants eight-fifty."

"Seems fair but that's a steep mortgage payment unless you've got a sizable down payment."

"Not that sizable." He sat up, got on his phone, and showed TJ the balance in his savings account.

TJ studied the number, got on the Internet, and made some notes on a yellow legal pad. "That would be your monthly payment, according to interest rates on a ten-year variable loan."

Win whistled. "No can do."

"Uh-uh. You need a bigger down."

"If we get FlashTag would my bonus cover it?"

TJ did a few more calculations on his yellow pad. "Yeah, maybe. But getting them is by no means a done deal. Apparently, they've scheduled a second trial with the Mammoth group as well."

Win leaned forward. "How do you know that?"

"Remember Joe Robalardi?"

Win drew a blank. "No."

"He worked for us a couple of summers ago as a guide. He's in Southern California doing freelance for Mountain Adventure. We still keep in touch and he let it slip that the FlashTag crew is coming back for a second round."

"Huh, well, that sucks. When were you planning to tell us?"

"I'm telling you now." TJ propped his feet up on the couch. "I'm hoping we have the advantage because of you and this Madison woman."

Win held up his arms. "Dude, I don't even remember her."

"Well, she remembers you. So turn on the Win Garner charm and bring home the prize."

Win pointed at the yellow pad. "You're supposed to be a financial genius. Figure out what I have to do to get Reggie's cabin. I want it. In the meantime, I talked to Lucky Rodriguez. He's in."

"What do you mean he's in? When did you talk to him?"

"Yesterday, over the phone. He's game to do business with us. We just have to work out the details. I told him you and I would go to his dude ranch and discuss ways we could cross-promote."

"Really?"

"No, I'm making it up." Win smacked TJ in the head with a throw pillow. "Oh ye of little faith, didn't you think I'd follow through?"

"Quite honestly, no."

"Well you were wrong, dickweed." He swung his feet onto the floor and went into the lobby to find Darcy. "You ready to do inventory?"

She'd worn jeans and a T-shirt because they'd be in the storage room most of the day. He liked the way the clothes clung to her curves. Hell, he liked everything about her.

"Let me just set things up to send calls to TJ." She fidgeted with the switchboard and he took a picture of her with his phone.

"I don't have any of you," he said, and studied the one he'd shot. "It's a good one of your dimples."

She gave him a look like he'd lost his mind. That was the thing about Darcy, she wasn't overly taken with him, like most women.

"I'm ready," she said, and together they walked to the big room in the back of the building where they kept the life preservers, the bike helmets, the personal flotation devices, and all the other gear they required their clients to use.

GA ran a strict shop when it came to safety. If any of the equipment wasn't up to snuff, they tossed it and got new. They'd had a few nasty situations, mostly involving avalanches in the backcountry, but that came with the territory. And then there was Stanley Royce, who because of his own carelessness had rolled down a mountainside in a portapotty and sued Garner Adventure. Otherwise, they had a good record.

"TJ just told me that FlashTag's also doing a second trial with Mountain Adventure. I had sort of hoped that De Wolk's coming was just a formality and that the account was ours."

"Me too." Darcy flipped open her tablet and started a spreadsheet. "I want my promotion."

"I want my house. Reggie called with the price and I can't swing it without a decent bonus."

"Should we go over the itinerary again?" She'd worked on it all night Tuesday while he'd worked on her.

"Darce, you ever think you might be wound a little tight?"

She laughed. "Maybe, but that's how I get stuff done.

Although in this case, I don't know why I bother, since you're just going to make your own last-minute plan."

"You've gotta admit that the impromptu hike, the bike ride, the picnic . . . it gave us an edge."

"You have an awful high opinion of yourself."

Instead of arguing, he pulled her in for kiss. She tasted like coffee, sugar, and something distinctly Darcy, a flavor that he constantly craved.

"We shouldn't do this in here," she said against his lips, but didn't try to pull away.

He wanted to tell her that he was falling for her but wasn't in the mood for one of her flippant remarks. Most women he'd dated would've given their right arm to hear those words, but not Darcy. She was a tough one to climb but he'd mastered some of the most difficult mountains in the world.

"No one can see us in here," he said. "Stop always trying to run the show."

For a second, she relaxed against him, tucking her head under his chin; then, just as suddenly, she grew restless. "We need to get this done."

He might not be the sharpest tool in the shed but he was starting to see a pattern. She wasn't so much of a control freak as she needed to feel useful. Organizing, setting up schedules, making busy work, Darcy could be like a machine sometimes.

There was nothing wrong with being productive. In fact, most people would see it as an asset. With Darcy, though, it was overcompensation. For her mother's digs or Lewis's neglect? Who could say? He certainly wasn't Sigmund Freud but she sure as shit didn't have to overcompensate with him.

"You want to work instead of making out, fine," he said. "But tonight, you're mine, baby."

"You might be a sex addict, you know that?"

"So far, you seem to be benefiting from my so-called addiction." He shot her a look, taking a slow visual slide down her body.

"I might need to stay home tonight. I don't like leaving Nana alone too often. Besides, we both need our rest for tomorrow."

Win sloughed off the rest bit. He could operate on very little sleep but Hilde was another story. "How is your grandmother?"

"She's doing much better. It seems the change in her medication made all the difference. But I want to keep an eye on her."

"I could come over to your place." He started sorting through the helmets.

"We'll see," she said coyly.

"Darce, it's not like we haven't been sleeping together for weeks." He backed her up against one of the shelving units and began kissing her all over again.

Darcy thought Madison De Wolk was ten times more beautiful than her bio photo on the FlashTag website. She was tall and slender with dark hair and blue eyes. Madison reminded Darcy a little of Delaney. At least lookswise. She deboarded a small plane in business attire—a pencil skirt, white blouse, and high heels—and Darcy assumed she'd come straight from the office.

The pilot loaded a small designer travel bag into the back of the van and Madison swung up into the passenger seat and nodded to Darcy as if to say *I'm ready to go now*.

Darcy suddenly got an attack of the shies but managed

to mutter, "Welcome to Glory Junction. I'm Darcy Wallace and I'll be—"

"Pleased to meet you, Darcy. The Four Seasons, right?" Madison turned away and began texting on her phone.

"Yes," Darcy sputtered. When she didn't immediately start the engine, Madison glanced up from her screen with impatience in her eyes.

Okay, right, she wanted to go. Darcy nosed out of the small airport parking lot and headed to the hotel. She'd hoped to talk a little bit about Saturday's schedule but Madison continued tapping away on her phone, not even bothering to look out the window at the passing view. Perhaps she was dealing with a work emergency. As Madison was the CEO of a burgeoning start-up, Darcy assumed she'd have to deal with crises.

As she drove, she snuck a few sideways peeks at Madison. Even Darcy's mother would've been impressed with how put together she was. Her blouse looked custom tailored, her shoes were Jimmy Choos, and her bag, Tory Burch. The long slit up the side of her skirt showed off a pair of tan, shapely legs that practically went up to her eyeballs. Win was always going on about Darcy's legs. Wait until he caught sight of Madison's. Maybe Darcy should tell her that tomorrow's activities would require long pants—and a super-baggy top.

She was almost relieved that his all-day white-water rafting tour had kept him from picking up Madison. Stupid, but Madison and Win were in the same league. The league of beautiful people.

Darcy pulled into the Four Seasons entrance and got out to open the back of the van so the bellhop could retrieve Madison's carry-on. She may have been in a rush to get to the hotel, but Madison stayed in the front seat with the door closed and continued to text.

Darcy went inside to make sure the reservation was in order and returned to the van where Madison was still typing away.

"Uh, everything is good to go," Darcy said awkwardly as she got back in the driver's seat.

Madison finally looked up. "Great." She reached into her handbag and handed Darcy a ten-dollar bill.

"Uh . . . oh . . . no, I work for Garner Adventure." Darcy didn't want to embarrass Madison but a tip. Really?

"That's okay," Madison said. "I know everything is all-inclusive, I won't tell if you don't." She sprang out of the van as graceful as a gazelle, leaving Darcy with the ten.

The next morning, Darcy tried to dress for anything Win might pull out of his bag of tricks. It wasn't easy finding something in her wardrobe that could serve double duty. Professional while being durable enough to climb Half Dome or whatever hell Win had in store. Friday evening, she'd been in a nice linen suit and Madison had still mistaken her for a limo driver. So perhaps she should worry more about comfort and flexibility.

She finally settled on a Colt and Delaney active skort and a Garner Adventure T-shirt. Sporty, yet it still said she was part of the team. Not a chauffeur. Like with the first FlashTag group, they were supposed to take Madison to breakfast at the Morning Glory and then for a tour of GA. Whether that would actually happen with Win at the wheel was up for debate.

She kissed Nana good-bye and took off for the Four Seasons. Win was meeting them at the restaurant. Madison was in the lobby when she got there and came out as soon as she spotted the van. Darcy would give her props for punctuality. Unlike yesterday, she was dressed in yoga pants, a sports tank, and tennis shoes. Her hair was tied back in a sleek ponytail and she was sans makeup. And even without it, she was still one of the most gorgeous women Darcy had ever seen outside of a fashion magazine.

"Hey, you're back," Madison said, and climbed into the front seat.

"I'm back." And I'm not the driver, she wanted to say, but decided it would be more prudent to let Madison save face by just pretending like there'd never been a misunderstanding. "Ready to go?"

"All set," she said, and began texting on her phone just as she had the night before. Not until they parked in front of the diner did she put away her cell.

Darcy had barely locked up the van when Madison disappeared inside the restaurant. She rushed to catch up and pushed her way to the hostess stand to claim their table. Win as usual was late. Felix waved her over to the table she'd reserved.

"Glad you could make it," he said being his usual surly self. Why he'd chosen to go into the hospitality industry was beyond Darcy. "Ricki is your server. I'll send her over to get your drink orders."

Darcy wanted a triple shot of espresso ASAP but decided to wait for Ricki, not wanting to upset Felix's apple cart. Madison started to say something, clearly confounded that the hired help was sitting down to break bread with her, but Win dashed in and all eyes fell on him. A few female diners did a double take, which was nothing new. Darcy had observed women falling all over themselves at the sight of Win. She wanted to shout, *Hands off, ladies, the man is mine.* But she knew better. He was just on loan until he moved on to his next conquest.

"Win Garner, look at you," Madison said as if they were long-lost buddies. "Last time I saw you, neither of us had showered in a week. You clean up well."

"So do you." He went in for a hug, which Darcy found peculiar since Win had claimed that he didn't remember her from his Alaska trip. "Seriously, Madison, you look fantastic."

Darcy suddenly felt like she was the odd person out here.

"You meet my partner in crime?" he asked after finally prying himself away from Madison and acknowledging Darcy with a nod.

Madison lightly touched Darcy's arm and grimaced. "I thought she was the van driver. I'm sorry, Darcy."

Darcy could feel her face burning. "No problem."

Apparently, Madison's apology was halfhearted because she immediately tuned out Darcy as if she were invisible and turned to Win. "We have so much catching up to do."

Again, with the bosom buddy thing. *Catch up on what?* Darcy wanted to ask. It was a freaking group trip. Seven days out of a lifetime. What news could they possibly have to share with each other?

"Yeah, so FlashTag, huh?" Win scooted next to her in the booth, leaving Darcy in the single chair on the aisle.

"I think I was still at Instagram back then."

"That's right." Win nodded his head and Darcy had to stifle an eye roll. She was pretty sure he was winging it. "And now you're the CEO. Way to go."

"What about you?" Madison turned in her seat so her head was only a few inches from Win's.

"I'm in charge of corporate accounts at Garner Adventure. I hope we'll be working together." He turned on the

signature Win smile and Darcy could've sworn she heard a
chorus of sighs echo through the restaurant.

"Me too." Madison put her hand on top of his.

And that's when Ricki came to the table to take their
orders. "What's everyone having today?" She smiled but it
looked forced.

Win got a waffle with everything on it. For a guy who
lived on kale drinks he sure had a sweet tooth. Darcy
needed to remind herself of that. Madison got fruit salad
and dry wheat toast. Big shocker there. Just to outdo her,
Darcy got coffee and plain yogurt with muesli. Not that
anyone noticed. Win and Madison were too busy reliving
their significant seven-day history.

Halfway through the meal, Darcy excused herself to
go to the bathroom. When she came back they were still
engaged in a conversation about their whale watching trip,
the one Win had gone on with another woman. Darcy felt
a little like an empty coatrack just taking up space in the
corner.

When the bill came Win paid it and they went to tour
GA. At least they were sticking to her agenda. At the office,
TJ, who'd shown up on a Saturday, introduced himself.
While they talked, Win pulled Darcy aside.

"I think it's going pretty well, don't you?"

Before she could get two words out Madison returned.
"It's a great building."

"We used to be in something smaller, off the beaten
track," Win said. "But we outgrew it with all the corporate
accounts we were getting."

She'd give Win credit. He was working it. Darcy just
wasn't sure if it was to get Madison's business, to get in her
yoga pants, or both. She supposed she should be thankful.
Her promotion relied on a grand slam and Win was pitching

them right down the middle of the strike zone. But instead of being thankful she was hurt—and jealous.

All morning long, she felt a stabbing pain in her chest. When Win decided they should do a bike ride by the lake like they'd done last time, Darcy used the excuse of paperwork to bow out. Win didn't even try to persuade her to come along.

Darcy could hear laughter drifting from the storage room as they gathered up helmets and water bottles. The pain moved down to her stomach and her eyes blurred as she pretended to stare at her computer monitor.

"How do you think it's going?" TJ stopped by her desk on his way out.

"Good, I guess. You know, the old Win charm." She tried to swallow but there was a lump in her throat.

TJ looked at her closely. "Why don't you go with them?"

Great. Now TJ was witnessing her humiliation. Either that or he thought she was shirking her responsibilities. Neither was good.

"The truth is I can't keep up." It wasn't a lie, she couldn't. "I don't think it's a particularly good image for GA to have me chugging behind them, out of breath." And heartbroken.

TJ tilted his head. "Suit yourself. But it seems to me that you're giving up without a fight. See you Monday."

She wasn't sure if he was talking about her lack of athletic prowess or something else entirely. And honestly, she didn't want to examine it too closely. She just wanted to spend the time sulking.

Three hours later, a sweaty Madison and a not-so-sweaty Win came back to the office in time for their lunch reservation. Darcy couldn't bag out of that too unless she wanted to come off as pathetic. So she tagged along, which is exactly how it felt. Darcy Wallace, the third wheel. Not surprising, Old Glory was full of tourists. More and more, the bar was attracting guests of the resorts, who came down from the mountain for some local flavor and to sample the many microbrews Boden had on tap.

"Hey." Boden waved from behind the bar. "I've got you set up in the back corner."

He led them to a table and for what seemed like the first time ever, Boden acknowledged Darcy's existence by casually draping his arm over her shoulder. She chalked it up to the fact that she'd made the reservation personally. Then he ruined the whole effect by ogling Madison. Even bedraggled from a bike ride, she still turned heads.

Darcy took the chair in the shadow of the restrooms, figuring it served as a metaphor for her crappy day. "How was the ride?"

"Fantastic," Madison said.

"Really good." Win smiled and Darcy was sure anyone in the bar with a good vantage point of that bright pearly grin of his melted. Women, men, small children, big dogs, it didn't matter.

"Sorry I missed it." About as sorry as she was for not having anal cancer.

A server hadn't come yet so Win got up to get them some drinks at the bar. Madison obviously thought it was a good time to check her messages because she whipped out her cell phone and started scrolling through the screen. That was fine, Darcy could just study the American flags on the wall.

Madison gazed past their table, presumably looking for Win, and spotted one of the oak barrels. "Ooh, peanuts. Darcy, would you mind? I'm kind of pinned in here."

There was a chair behind her. All she had to do was move it. But Darcy got up to get the silly peanuts. It was better than staring at red stripes and white stars all afternoon, not that she wasn't patriotic.

She returned with a basket. "So did Win tell you much about our corporate team building program?"

"He did." She tossed the phone back in her bag and snapped open one of the peanuts. "It sounds phenomenal. But as you know we're also talking to Mountain Adventure down south. We have a campus in Los Angeles so that might be more convenient and more cost-effective. But so far I'm partial to Garner Adventure." She turned her blue eyes on Win as he made his way to the table with three pints in his hand.

"The great thing about Glory Junction is it's super accessible." It really wasn't unless you had a private plane but pretty soon the only thing that would keep Darcy warm at night was her promotion.

Madison had already forgotten she was sitting there, now that the man of the hour had returned. Win handed Darcy her beer and winked. Then he completely ruined it by giving Madison a little shoulder rub. Darcy's heart sank and she spent the rest of the meal pushing her chicken Caesar salad around on the plate.

After lunch, they went to the river for a kayak cave tour. Before Darcy could stop it from happening, Madison claimed the second seat of Win's kayak, leaving Darcy to go it solo. The problem was she had never been in a kayak in her life, had no idea how she was supposed to paddle the thing, or steer it.

Win was so busy tending to the life jackets, the helmets, and the other details of their trip that he couldn't see she was panicking. She toyed with the idea of faking an illness—appendicitis, food poisoning, a torn rotator cuff—but she wasn't going to abandon the ship. She'd worked too hard to give up now. Besides, how hard could it be?

An hour later, she was seriously thinking of drowning herself.

"You okay there, Darce?" Win maneuvered his kayak and grabbed hold of hers to get it moving in the right direction. For the last fifteen minutes, she'd been paddling against the current and her arms felt like spaghetti.

She hissed at him and he gave her one of those hopeless looks as if to say, *What do you want me to do?*

I want you to kill Madison and throw her in the river so I can get in the back of your boat.

Madison turned around and waved, forcing Darcy to paste a phony smile on her face and say, "I'm having the time of my life."

"Ready to go inside?" Win pointed ahead at a series of limestone caves and Darcy had a sudden vision of thousands of bats roosting in the caverns and wondered whether it was painful to die from rabies.

She followed behind as fast as her limp arms would paddle. At least the water was fairly still in this part of the river. When they entered the mouth of the cave, instead of bats there were hundreds of stalactites dripping from the ceiling. According to the literature they gave to their clients, the icicle-shaped tubes were actually mineral formations and to Darcy looked straight out of a sci-fi movie. She found them oddly beautiful and creepy at the same time.

Madison oohed and aahed and took pictures with her phone, the phone she hadn't taken out once since she'd been with Win. The two of them took a selfie together underneath the stalactites and Darcy felt a tightening in her chest. They were gorgeous together. The kind of couple people whispered about as they passed by on the street. *"Can you imagine how beautiful their babies will be?"*

Darcy could imagine. And the band around her chest got snugger.

She took one last look at the mineral formations dangling like crystals in a futuristic fairy tale and paddled out of the cave. It and the day served as a wake-up call. It was time to stop playing before she got hurt.

Chapter Nineteen

Win took Madison to the hotel. All evening he'd counted the minutes until he could drop her off. Despite the day being an undeniable success, it had blown chunks. Madison had looked for every opportunity to hang on him and he'd looked for every opportunity to plug Garner Adventure, which had been exhausting.

And to think he had one more day of her incessant clinging. But his desire to prove himself, buy a house, and get Darcy her promotion overrode any impulse to flat-out tell her he wasn't interested.

"You want to come up?" Madison asked innocently enough but Win had been down this road enough times to not misinterpret what was going on here. Turning her down was going to take some finesse but no way in hell was he going back to her room.

"We've got an early morning, Madison."

She ran a finger down his shoulder. "One drink wouldn't keep us out past curfew."

One drink, his ass. But even more than not wanting to lose her business, he didn't want to hurt her feelings. She was a nice woman, extremely attractive, fun to be around, and at one time he would've been into her. But not now . . . not since Darcy. The revelation sort of knocked him for a loop. He'd had plenty of girlfriends over the years but *commitment* had always been an elusive term for him. Until now. The Britney fiasco had changed his consciousness and made him vow to be more responsible. But Darcy had changed his heart and made him want to be a better man. It was a shift he wasn't prepared to look at too closely because it scared him to death.

"Come on," Madison urged. "I'll make it worth your while."

Taking her chin in his hand and looking deeply into her eyes, he did what he did best and turned on the old Win Garner charm. "You're too tempting, Madison. One drink?" He made a get-real face and let the corner of his mouth slide up into a half grin. "That's some dangerous territory you're talking about. Don't you think we should keep this professional?" She was the CEO of a major company, she had to know what kind of minefield she was walking through here. It might be chickenshit but Win thought it would be better for everyone involved to let her be the one to walk away.

She arched one perfectly shaped brow. "We'd be good together. But, yeah, you're right. Let's get this deal done first. If things go as well tomorrow as they did today . . . well, let's just say I've been very impressed." Madison's eyes glided over him, leaving no ambiguity about how she wanted to celebrate.

"Good night." She leaned over and kissed him. But before it could get really started, he shut it down and walked her to the lobby.

"Get a good night's sleep. Today was strictly sightseeing. Tomorrow, I'm gonna show you what team building is all about." He intended to kick her ass so hard that by the time she limped to her hotel suite, she wouldn't have any energy left for him. Unfortunately, that would involve chucking Darcy's itinerary into the circular file.

She'd thank him for it later.

He drove to Darcy's house but all the lights were out so he sat in his Jeep for a while, staring up at her bedroom window. He was no authority on women but he knew when they were angry with him. And Darcy had been throwing some serious shade at his ass throughout the cave tour. He hated that he'd hurt her but he was only trying to get the account.

His cell phone sat in the console next to his seat and despite being the king of self-preservation, he dialed her number anyway.

"I'm in your driveway," he said. "Come sit in the car with me for a little while."

Her response was a loud click. She'd hung up on him.

Fifteen minutes ticked by while he contemplated his next move. He was just about to drive away when he saw her emerge from the shadows. All five-feet-whatever in pink fuzzy slippers and a nightshirt that said, SAVE THE CHUBBY UNICORN.

She opened the door, slid in, and said, "I don't want to hash this out now . . . or ever. Go home and go to sleep."

Yep, he was screwed.

Darcy started to get out of the Jeep when Win took her arm. "Don't," she warned.

"Bullshit! We're talking about this." He rested his back against the driver's door, his mile-wide chest heaving, his large, capable hands moving in the air. Sex on a stick.

"No, we're not." She was probably acting childish but she didn't care. "Where's Madison?"

"The hotel. I dropped her off after dinner. You should've come, Darcy, instead of leaving me holding the bag."

It had been a cruddy thing to do, especially because she wanted the promotion as badly as Win wanted his house, not to mention the acknowledgment of being able to land a big account. But she'd also wanted to save her dignity and watching Madison make a play for Win while she treated Darcy like the hired help . . . well, it was humiliating.

"She has no interest in doing business with me, only you." She glared at him. "And my gut tells me she wants to do a lot more than business. Unless you already took care of that?"

He drilled her with a look. "So, automatically you think the worst of me? That's just great, Darcy."

"Look, I really don't want to talk about this." She huffed out a breath. "It was a long day and we have to do it all over again tomorrow. Though I don't know why I'm even participating. You two are great all on your own."

"Give it a rest. This is business, nothing more. You're acting like a jealous high schooler so cut the crap." His bark took her aback. Win never shouted. In the year she'd known him, she'd never even seen him angry. It made her defensive.

"You didn't even act like you wanted me around."

"What are you talking about? The bike ride? I know you didn't like it last time and I didn't want to put you through it again. I was trying to be considerate. If you noticed I didn't change one of your damn plans. We kept right to the stupid schedule."

"Thanks for being so sensitive." She rolled her eyes because it was more civilized than punching him.

"You really think I wanted to be alone with Madison?"

She turned away from him and stared out the passenger window. "Not on purpose because I know you'd never intentionally hurt me. You're a good person, Win, just emotionally stunted. I knew that from the beginning and I don't blame you."

"Thanks, I appreciate that." His voice was thick with sarcasm. "It's really heroic of you."

They sat, filling the cab with silence until Win asked, "You can't truly believe anything happened between Madison and me?"

She hitched her shoulders, trying to appear indifferent. "Why not? Beautiful women are your thing. And you and I"—she waved her hand between them—"that was just sex, you helping out a friend. It was fun but I never expected . . . wanted . . . it to last."

"That's a shitty thing to say." He actually sounded wounded. She suspected it was a shock to his system to hear a woman say she didn't want him. "And for the record, I considered you a hell of a lot more than a friend. I've got plenty of those. You were . . . different."

Different. She'd always been different.

Darcy grabbed the handle on the door and started to open it. She couldn't deal with this now. She had too much on the line, including her self-respect. It was just supposed to have been sex. A good time. But somewhere along the way, the lines had blurred and this thing between them had become much more. Win had become too important. Her feelings for him too strong. And if she let him, he could break her heart.

"I'm leaving now and tomorrow we can go back to being coworkers. I'd say 'friends' but you already have *plenty* of those. You're free, so you and Madison can go crazy if you want. No hard feelings."

He got out and followed her up the path to her grandmother's house. "You are not breaking up with me."

She spun around, nearly tripping over her slippers.

"Don't worry, you can tell everyone it was you. No one would believe it's me anyway."

"Give me a break, Darcy. You're acting ridiculous."

No, she was doing what any sane woman would do: She was protecting herself.

"I'm letting you off the hook." She put her hands on her hips. "We had some good laughs, now it's time to get real. This thing between us was never meant to go anywhere. You, of all people, know that. Don't worry about it, Win, we're all good."

"Fine, Darcy." His voice was cold. "Whatever you say. Call me when you get over your insecurity trip, we'll do lunch." He walked away, jumped into his Jeep, and drove down the driveway without a second look.

She watched his exhaust plume in the breeze and waited for the sound of his engine to disappear in the distance. A part of her hung on to the hope that he'd hang a U-turn, hightail it back, and plead for her to be his. But just like the moon hiding behind the clouds, he was gone. And he'd taken a piece of her with him.

Her father would've called her little scene melodramatic, which she supposed it had been. Her mother would've called her a fool for ever thinking she could've held a man like Win. *Go back to Lewis, you were lucky to have him.*

She forced their voices out of her head, padded up the walkway into the house, and crawled in bed with Nana.

Instead of going home, Win swung by Old Glory. If he was lucky Dale would be there and could bust his head in. Then maybe he wouldn't feel so bad for being a douchebag. He'd screwed up with Darce and couldn't stomach the idea that he'd hurt her. Madison had basically treated her like a doormat and he'd tacitly gone along. He'd kept his mouth shut for a lousy business deal and he felt ashamed.

"Yo," Boden called from the bar. The place was packed. But what did Win expect for a Saturday night, even if it was past eleven? "Your brother's on fire tonight."

Uh-oh. He'd forgotten that Colt's band was playing. The last people he wanted to see were his brothers. But if he had to pick one it would've been Josh, who knew how to mind his own business.

Someone rammed him in the back and he reflexively swung around. Speak of the devil.

"It's about time you showed up," Colt said. "We only have one more set before we close this place down."

Win rubbed the back of his neck. "Darcy and I were showing that CEO around."

"How's that going?"

"Okay, I guess."

Colt watched him. "You okay? You look tired."

Win looked past him near the stage at the table the Garners usually commandeered whenever Colt played. "Where's the fam?"

"Mom and Dad were here earlier and left a little while ago, Josh and Hannah are around somewhere, and TJ and Deb had something else going tonight. Delaney's at the table. Go over and say hi."

"Uh, okay. Let me get a beer first."

Win turned to the bar and waved to get Boden's attention. "Give me whatever Colt's drinking." His brother was a craft beer snob. Win didn't much care as long as whatever he was drinking was cold and wet. But Boden would take all night giving a dissertation on every brew on tap—he had a lot—so it was easier to cut him off at the pass.

Boden drew him the beer as he eyed a couple of women

who'd just walked in. "If they're twenty-one, I'm Barry Bonds."

Win swiveled around to get a better look. He didn't recognize them. Probably tourists down from one of the resorts.

"Ingrid, take over for a sec," Boden called to one of the bartenders, and went off to check IDs.

Win snatched his pint from across the bar, left a ten, and strolled over to Delaney.

"Hey." She hopped up to hug him, then pulled out a chair. "Did you just get here? Keep me company."

He sat down. "A few minutes ago. We were wining and dining a prospective client."

"Colt told me. FlashTag, huh? That would be a coup."

"Yeah." He nodded.

She reached out and smoothed a wrinkle from his shirt. "You don't look too happy about it. Is it not going well?"

"It's going pretty well with the client." He didn't know why but he told her about Darcy. Even though the band was on break it was loud and she kept asking him to repeat things.

When he was finished telling her the story she said, "I had no idea you were seeing Darcy. Colt never said anything."

"I don't think he knows. We've been discreet about it since we work together."

"Probably a good idea, though it doesn't negate the fact that workplace romances are still a bad idea."

He was hoping for advice, not a lecture. "It worked for Deb and TJ."

"They were serious and in love."

"What makes you think we aren't . . . serious?" He

wasn't going to touch love. That was too much to think about.

Delaney was always diplomatic but Win could see her struggle with how to answer. It didn't take a genius to see what she was thinking.

"With all due respect, your track record at serious hasn't been that good." At least she had the decency to sound apologetic. "And I would hate to see Darcy get hurt."

Funny how no one ever worried about his feelings. Darcy had just dumped him, crushed him like a friggin' tin can. But hey, she was the injured party.

"That's bullshit, Delaney. When I thought Britney was pregnant with my kid, I stepped up, fully prepared to be a husband and a father."

"You did," she acknowledged. "But . . ."

Colt and his band took the stage and the crowd started to hoot and holler, making it impossible to hear Delaney. Honestly, Win welcomed the noise. He didn't need to be picked apart.

He sat through three songs and used having to get up early as an excuse to leave. On his way out, he ran into Josh and Hannah, who were playing a game of darts. He made the obligatory greetings, told them he had to go, and headed to the door.

A gust of fresh air hit him and for a fleeting second it lightened his mood. Then he caught sight of Rita on the side of the building, smoking a cigarette. She looked straight at him. Terrific.

"Mayor." He tipped an imaginary hat and hoped to make a clean getaway. But apparently, the day hadn't gone shitty enough.

Her gravel voice called after him. "Well, have you made up your mind about the calendar?"

"Sure. Whatever. I'll do it." If it would get her off his back and he could go home, it was worth it.

"Too late." She cackled. "I got that new fellow from search and rescue. His pecs are twice the size of yours."

He stopped walking and turned to face her. "You're kicking me out of the calendar?" What kind of bullshit was that? Women lined up for the amateur piece of crap because of him.

She blew a smoke ring, let out a hacking cough, and stabbed her finger in the air. "You think you're the only talent in this town? That's what you get for trying to jack me up."

Jack her up? It was voluntary. Free. "Expect a call from my lawyer and my agent."

He swung himself up into his Jeep and took off. The cat was waiting on his open windowsill, swishing its tail under the porch light when he got home. He went to pick it up and it hissed at him and ran away.

Even the damned kitty was mad at him.

At six the next morning, Win pulled into the turnaround at the Four Seasons. He was early so he checked his phone and opened an e-mail from Reggie.

"I've been in touch with Jenny, who's hot for the listing. She says June and July are prime time to sell real estate. I'd rather save the commission and not deal with the hassle of having strangers traipse through my house. So let me know if you're still interested."

Win dashed off a quick response. "I'm very interested and am trying to raise the money for a solid down payment. The truth is I wasn't planning to spend that much but your place rocks the house. I should know in the next couple of days. Can you hang on until then?"

He scrolled down to see if there was anything from Darcy. Nothing. Just in case, he checked his texts. He took her radio silence to mean she was still planning to show up for breakfast. Today, they were going to Tart Me Up so they could get an early start and because Darcy wanted to spread their business around town, especially since Rachel had come through the way she had for the picnic lunch.

He hadn't realized until now what a good business-woman Darcy was. If they got this account it would be largely due to her organizational skills and planning. No matter what happened with FlashTag he was going to see that she got a raise and promotion, even if he had to take a pay cut.

Madison emerged from the hotel. She'd dressed in shorts, a light-weight hoodie, and hiking boots. A back-pack was slung over her shoulder, which Win assumed held water sandals, a bathing suit, and any other inciden-tals she might need. Darcy had sent her a list. Even though Win planned to change the schedule up to include more intensive activities, the clothes she had on should suffice. If not, they'd raid supplies from GA's online store. Like with the others, Deb had made Madison a swag bag of gear to take home.

He tapped his horn to get her attention and girded him-self for another day of fending off her flirtations. She jogged up to the Jeep and opened the door.

"Good morning. It's chillier than I thought it would be." She got in and fastened her seat belt.

"By ten, the clouds should burn off and it'll get warmer. You hungry?"

"A little bit but I definitely need coffee." She turned in her seat and put her hand on his knee. "How are you? Did you get a good night's sleep?"

Her innuendo was clear. But his lack of sleep had nothing

to do with Madison. Nope, he'd tossed and turned because of a certain small blonde with cornflower blue eyes.

"I did." He took off down the mountain and found a parking space in front of the bakery.

When they got inside Darcy had already reserved a table and ordered a large bread and pastry basket with jams and butters, a fruit bowl, homemade granola, and a carafe of coffee. The woman got shit done. She gave him a tight smile and got up to welcome Madison. Like the rest of them, Darcy had on shorts and he took a moment to surreptitiously stare at her legs.

"How was dinner last night?" Darcy asked, and Win gave her points for professionalism. No one would've guessed that they'd had it out after he'd left Madison at the hotel.

"Fantastic," Madison said, and brushed Win's shoulder way too familiarly. No question today was heading toward a suckfest. "I'm sorry you weren't able to join us."

Win nearly laughed. The hell she was.

Darcy gave another one of her tight smiles. "Your company—if you choose us—will primarily be working with Win. I thought it was a good idea for you two to get to know each other better."

Win nudged Darcy's knee under the table. *Stop it.* The little witch.

"Win's been great." Madison grabbed two turnovers from the basket and put one of them on his plate.

The gesture was far too intimate and Win saw Darcy observe it with a frown.

"Win doesn't eat sweets," she told Madison, and Win had to bite a grin. Witch, indeed. "But I'll take it." Darcy snatched the pastry off his plate and licked some cherry filling off the side. He watched her with fascination and something moved in his chest.

Delaney was wrong.

"*With all due respect, your track record at serious hasn't been that good. And I would hate to see Darcy get hurt.*"

He was the one hurting.

Rachel came to the table with some warm-out-of-the-oven buns and introduced herself. Since Darcy had taken his turnover, he grabbed one of the buns, tore off a piece, and chewed. Boden didn't know what he was talking about. Rachel's buns were out of this world.

"These are fantastic," he said around a mouthful, and buttered the rest of the roll.

"Thanks. I just wanted to come over and say hello."

"Everything is wonderful, Rachel." Darcy got up and gave her a hug.

A few months ago, Little Bo Peep could barely string two words together without turning the color of a tomato. Now she was GA's freaking ambassador of goodwill. That was his job.

"Oprah's crazy about Tart Me Up," Win announced.

"Oprah Winfrey?" Madison suddenly appeared interested.

Was there any other Oprah? "Yeah. She mentioned Rachel and her bakery in one of her . . ." He looked from Darcy to Rachel because he honestly didn't know how the whole "Oprah loves Tart Me Up" rumor had started. But everyone in town said it like it was fact.

"Her list of favorite things," Darcy said.

"Wow." Madison seemed duly impressed.

As they finished breakfast Win said, "Ready to do some zip-lining and white-water rafting." If they had time he wanted to get in some paddleboarding, too.

Darcy shot him a look and when Madison went to the bathroom she said, "Zip-lining is not on the agenda. I suppose you read your tea leaves this morning and they said sliding down a rope would win you the account." She all but rolled her eyes.

She could make fun of his unorthodox methods all she wanted but they worked. "Nope. I'm kicking shit up a notch. Deal with it."

"I'm not dressed for zip-lining."

He wasn't aware there was a dress code. Eyeing her khaki shorts and polo shirt, he said, "You're afraid to do it, aren't you?"

"No . . . yes."

"I'm not going to let anything happen to you, Darce." He'd take care of her, even though for all intents and purposes she'd dumped his ass.

"Maybe it's a better idea for me to go back to the office and print up materials with all the programs we offer."

He glanced at the bathroom and back at her. "Do. Not. Leave. Me. Alone. With. Her."

She had the nerve to snicker. "Since when are you afraid of horny women."

"Since I met you." He went outside and waited by his Jeep.

A few minutes later Darcy and Madison followed.

"I left my car at GA," Darcy said. "I'll walk over and get it and meet you at the zip-line park."

"Nah." He opened the back door for her. "We'll all go together and reduce our carbon footprint."

She sneered at him when she thought Madison wasn't looking but climbed in. Madison, who seemed completely oblivious to his and Darcy's pissing match, got in next to Win and away they went.

The zip line—there were actually seven of them—was part of a private park near the lake and went through a forest of trees with peekaboo views of the water. It was about 250 feet above the forest floor, moved at forty miles per hour, and was a total of fifteen-hundred-feet long. GA had a contract with the owners to use it whenever they wanted, which was pretty righteous.

He found parking in the shade and they hiked up to the staging platform where they harnessed up. Darcy's face turned green as they climbed a circular stairway up to the tops of the trees.

"You scared of heights?" he said in her ear.

She gave him the finger. Real mature.

Madison, on the other hand, didn't know where to look first. She wore a gooey smile on her face like she'd just discovered the world wasn't concrete. "Wow. This is something."

He gazed across the horizon, trying to see it through the eyes of a person who hadn't grown up here. Yeah, it was pretty freaking amazing. He wished Darcy wasn't petrified so she could take it in. It was like flying through the trees. Win lightly touched the back of her neck and she squeezed her eyes shut.

"I don't think I can do this." It came out like a whisper.

He stopped and turned to face her, settling both hands on her shoulders. "You don't have to do anything you don't feel comfortable doing." He hated jack-off guides who pushed people into shit they didn't want to do. Parachuting out of planes, bungee-jumping, riding bulls, or any other sport. You let people go at their own pace and they have a good time. Otherwise you ruin it for them.

Madison had gone ahead of them, once again unaware of anything outside of her own personal sphere.

"You really don't want to be alone with her?" Darcy asked, trying not to look down.

"I can probably hold her off for a couple of hours. After that, who knows?"

She pinned him with a glare. "Because you're so irresistible."

Tired of the word sparring, he wasn't going to do this with her. He'd made it abundantly clear he wasn't interested in Madison De Wolk. Only Darcy. If she couldn't believe that she was no better than the rest of them.

He searched around for a staff member to take Darcy down. If he couldn't find one, he'd do it himself. Madison could wait.

She saw what he was doing and said, "I can get down myself. Being up is the problem."

"You sure?"

"Yes. Go. I want my promotion!" She turned around and began the long stairway down, calling to him that she would meet them on the other end.

But when he got there she was gone.

Chapter Twenty

Darcy had just finished hiking to the other end of the zip line when her cell phone rang. The reception was bad but she could still make out Nana's voice, just not the words.

"Nana? Nana? Hello?" She'd lost the call.

Pacing the forest, searching for a better spot, she was finally able to get through. But her grandmother's phone just rang and rang. Darcy's incoming call log showed it was the same number from which Nana had called. Her heart started to race as she tried several more times.

Pick up.

Panicking, she dialed Colt's number. She'd never called him before unless it was for work and her hands shook as she held the phone. It was probably his day off.

"Darce? Everything okay?" He sounded out of breath—and worried.

"It has nothing to do with GA," she stammered. "It's my grandmother. She tried to call me a few minutes ago and now I can't reach her. Her health hasn't been too good and . . ."

"Where are you?"

"I'm at the zip line place. Win took Madison De Wolk

up. I'm waiting for them but don't have a car and Win's got the keys to his."

"Okay, hang tight. I'll have someone do a welfare check or I'll go myself."

"You'll call me, right?"

"As soon as I know something. Cell reception there is shoddy. So stay where you are." He hung up.

She couldn't wait. There were a couple of zip-line employees waiting to help customers rappel down after their flight. One she recognized as a part-time guide at GA. A lot of college kids came for the summer for seasonal work and to enjoy the Sierra and patched together enough hours from various jobs to support themselves.

"Hey, Darcy." He waved.

She walked over to him. "Jamal, do you know anyone who could give me a ride to town? Win's got the keys and he's up there." She pointed at the line. "It's an emergency."

"I've got lunch in twenty minutes. Can you wait that long?"

"I can't. You think there's anyone else?"

"I'll check." He got on his walkie-talkie and had a conversation with a lot of static in the background. Jamal signed off and said, "Billy can take you. He's waiting up at the office."

Thank God. She didn't think she could stand here a minute longer and hiked back the way she came. Billy had an old Honda Civic with more dents than a crushed soda can. She got in and prayed it made it the eight miles to Garner Adventure.

"I really appreciate this," she said.

Billy was about Jamal's age, twenty, twenty-one, with a hipster beard and red bandana tied around his head. "Sure thing. Where do you want me to drop you?"

"Garner Adventure on Main Street. Do you know where it is?"

"The big log lodge near the Morning Glory?" His car hiccupped on an incline and she crossed her fingers that they didn't stall on the mountain.

"That's it."

Billy seemed unfazed by the Honda's sluggish performance, easing some of her concern. She spent most of the ride firing off a text to Colt that she was on her way home. As soon as Garner Adventure came into sight, she rushed out of the car before Billy even came to a complete stop. Thanking him again, she ran behind the building to GA's small lot, got in her car, and took off. Colt still hadn't called and a million images flashed through her head.

There were so many damned cars on the road, tourists up for the weekend, that it took Darcy twice as long to get home. When she saw an ambulance, a fire truck, and Colt's pickup in the driveway her heart dropped. She wedged her Volkswagen next to her grandmother's car and rushed to the house.

Colt met her halfway, his face grim. "They're taking her to Sierra General. She's unresponsive."

What does that mean? "She's not—" Darcy couldn't say it.

"No. But it's not good, Darce." He rested his hands on her shoulders.

"She has hypertension." She pulled away. "I have to tell the paramedics."

"They know. Her meds were in the kitchen."

"I want to go with her." For Nana's sake she was desperately trying to hold it together.

"Jake?" Colt called. "Can Darcy ride in the ambulance with Mrs. Wallace?"

"Yep. We're leaving right now."

Colt hurried Darcy to the back of the truck and helped her get in. Nana was lying on a gurney with an oxygen mask over her face, hooked up to an IV.

"Nana." Darcy touched her hand and it was cold. It was eighty degrees out but Nana was cold. And her pale skin, blue. "Nana, can you hear me?"

Other than a slight flutter of Hilde's right eye, which could've been Darcy's imagination, her grandmother didn't respond.

"She said she got up this morning, short of breath, opened the windows for fresh air, and still couldn't breathe," a paramedic . . . Sean, according to his name tag . . . said. "She called nine-one-one and by the time we got here she was barely able to talk."

"She has high blood pressure. Her medication just needs to be adjusted. That's all."

Sean didn't say anything and Darcy sat next to Nana and held her hand. Someone closed the back doors and the ambulance started to move and the siren blared. Sean stayed in the back with them. For a large man, he was good at maneuvering in the tight space and constantly monitored Nana's vital signs.

It was the longest trip of Darcy's life. When they finally arrived, there were medical staff waiting to take her grandmother inside. Someone, an orderly maybe, guided Darcy to the intensive care unit, where she was shunted to a waiting room.

"A nurse will come out soon and take you back."

"Thank you." That must've been when the shock hit her because she began to cry. She sobbed her eyes out, feeling alone and afraid.

Her parents. She needed to notify them but couldn't seem to make her hands dial the phone. She decided to wait for a status update and would call them when she had good news. At least she hoped it would be good. But after a solid thirty minutes passed she started to get antsy. What was taking so long? She tried to occupy herself by thumbing through a pile of old magazines, dog-eared from use. And when that didn't hold her attention, she cleaned out her handbag, dumping the flotsam that had floated to the bottom in the trash. Then, finally, she heard footsteps in the hall. But it wasn't the nurse or doctor who came to find her, it was Win.

"Colt called me." He walked straight at her and pulled her into his arms. "I'm sorry, I'm so, so sorry. Any word yet?"

She shook her head. "I keep hoping that it's just her blood-pressure medication, that they'll tweak it, and everything will be fine." She started crying again. "It's bad, Win, it's really bad."

"Shush." He rocked her back and forth like he'd done the time she told him about her parents' separation. "Hilde's strong."

She hung on to him, taking comfort in his embrace, taking comfort in his arms. The fact that he'd come here meant the world to her but what about . . . ? "Where's Madison? What about the itinerary?"

"I told her it was an emergency and we'd have to do it another time."

She stepped back. "GA could lose the account. You realize that, right?"

"You think I care? I didn't want you to have to go through this alone."

Before she could tell him to go and salvage the rest of the day, a man in green scrubs and a stethoscope came into the room.

"Ms. Wallace? I'm Dr. Gerard."

"Is my grandmother okay?"

He motioned for them all to take a seat. Win moved next to her and held her hand.

"Your grandmother is suffering from acute congestive heart failure. She needs emergency surgery to replace her aortic valve."

At first, Darcy had trouble absorbing the diagnosis. Acute congestive heart failure. Was that like a heart attack? "If you replace it will it save her?"

Dr. Gerard leaned in closer. "We hope so."

Darcy could feel a "but" coming on. To her, the doctor looked grim, almost hopeless but perhaps that was his everyday standing face. The face of doom and gloom.

"There's a minimally invasive procedure available, which I recommend for someone your grandmother's age," he continued. "It involves threading the new valve through the vascular system, instead of having to open her chest. As you can imagine, it's much less stressful on a person's system, especially an elderly person's. I've seen some patients go home in a day after TAVR." Darcy didn't know what that was and it must've shown in her expression because Dr. Gerard clarified. "Transcatheter aortic valve replacement."

"Okay, let's do that, then." It sounded like the answer to her prayers.

He made the face again. "Unfortunately, the closest hospitals that offer transcatheter aortic valve replacement are located in Sacramento or the Bay Area. In Mrs. Wallace's condition it would be extremely risky to transport her."

Dr. Gerard paused to make sure she was taking in everything he'd told her. Win stroked her palm with his thumb, the gesture a reminder that she wasn't alone in this.

"Why can't you just do something here, at Sierra General?" she asked.

"We can do open-heart surgery here but, frankly, at your grandmother's age that's also risky."

Open-heart surgery, jeez. Darcy took a deep breath. Lost in the gravity of the situation, she didn't know what to say. It was as if her tongue wouldn't move and there was a giant lump in her throat.

"Which one in your opinion holds the most risk?" Win came to the rescue. Yes, that's exactly what she wanted to know.

Dr. Gerard seemed to be contemplating the answer. "I'd say they're both equally risky. If she were stable, I'd like her chances better with TAVR."

Darcy finally found her voice. "Can we wait to see if she stabilizes?"

"I wouldn't advise it. We're looking at a short window of time here."

She rubbed her hand down her face. How was she supposed to make a decision like this? She'd always been decisive but she was in over her head. She'd always been the responsible one but just once she wished she had someone who could help bear the weight. This was too important to take it on herself. If she chose the wrong option Nana would die.

"Should you call your dad?" Win touched her arm, seeing her face strain with indecision. "He's Hilde's son." The implication was he should make the decision.

But Darcy wasn't willing to relinquish it to someone who didn't care as much as she did. Max loved his mother but Darcy couldn't live without her, that was the difference.

"I'll call him," she said, and turned to the doctor. "But you need to know right now, right?"

"As soon as possible. Does your grandmother have a conservator?"

Darcy wasn't sure but she didn't think so. More than

likely her grandmother would've put Darcy in charge of
something like that. She shook her head no.

"My grandmother has always been in relatively good
health." Until now.

"Would you like to try your father?" the doctor asked.

She looked at Win and he nodded.

"Why don't you go ahead and make a few phone calls.
I'll ask a social worker to come out and talk with you." Dr.
Gerard got up and disappeared behind the intensive care's
double doors.

Darcy dug her phone out of her purse and called her
father. When she got voice mail, she left a message for him
to call as soon as possible. Then she repeated the same
message on his office answering service. She had the same
luck with her mother. In the day of cell phones, you'd think
one of them would be reachable.

Win got up and filled a small paper cup with water from
the cooler and brought it to her. "No answer, huh?"

She shook her head. "They'll just make things worse
anyway." Her father was a practical man. But Darcy knew
sometimes you had to lead with your heart, not your head.
And Geneva . . . well, Geneva was all about Geneva. "What
do you think I should do?"

He gazed down at her, his eyes a darker blue than her
own. "Hilde's tough." He paused. "I think she should go to
Sacramento and do the procedure with the one-day recovery. Life's too short to spend it in a hospital bed. That's my
two cents. But the decision has to be yours."

As somber as she felt, his two cents made her laugh. It
was so Win. So elemental. So impulsive. And then it struck
her that he wasn't as impulsive as he seemed. With FlashTag
he'd taken the pulse of the group, read the signs, and made
decisions based on a quick analysis. He was in fact more

thoughtful than the fly-by-the-seat-of-his-pants person he let everyone see.

"I'm going to see if they'll let me sit with her for a little while," she said. Maybe if Nana woke up, she'd tell Darcy what to do.

"I'll be out here if you need me."

She stopped. "Uh, you don't have to stay. You could meet up with Madison. She doesn't leave until tomorrow, the two of you could have dinner."

His expression turned dark, darker than she'd ever seen it. "You think I'd leave you now? Jesus, for a smart woman, you're awfully dense. Go sit with your grandmother," he snapped.

She walked away feeling more confused than ever.

Win sent TJ a quick text. His brother wasn't going to be happy about the way he'd left things with Madison. Win had unceremoniously dumped her at the hotel and told her he had to go. If she was a decent human being she'd understand; Win had no reason to think she wasn't. He just hoped she wouldn't think GA was unreliable and choose Mountain Adventure instead. But really, in the scheme of things, getting the account wasn't all that important anymore. Not while Hilde was lying at death's door.

A reply from TJ came in and Win glanced at it.

Keep us apprised and tell Darcy we're thinking about her. I'll handle Madison.

His whole family would rally around Darcy when the time was right. He watched the clock, then got on his phone and searched *transcatheter aortic valve replacement*. Reading was never easy for him, especially something as complicated as medical terminology. But he forced himself to study the pros and cons. Thirty minutes later, Darcy returned to the waiting room looking more fragile than when she had left. He immediately rose and pulled her into his arms. There hadn't been a code blue or whatever they announced over the loudspeaker when a patient was in trouble.

"Anything new?"

"She's still unresponsive, though she opened her eyes for a few seconds. I haven't heard from my dad and the social worker, Dr. Gerard, and the duty nurse say I have to make a decision."

"What are you going to do?"

She braced herself against his shoulders and let out a breath. "You really think I should risk the transport?"

If Darcy made the choice and Hilde didn't pull through she'd never forgive herself. Let it fall on him, he'd take the hit because he wanted to be that man for her. Her man.

"Yeah, that's the way I would go." From everything he'd read online the procedure was revolutionary. The death risk of the procedure was only in the three-percent range and they didn't even have to remove the old valve, they could just push it aside with the new one. To him it seemed like a no-brainer, except for the part of getting her to the hospital and getting her stable enough to perform the replacement. "I think it's what Hilde would want if she could tell us."

She sagged into him, using his weight to hold her up. "I should tell the doctor that's my decision but I . . . can't. I can't even move."

"I'll do it for you if that's what you want."

"You're sure about this?" she asked.

He'd never seen her so irresolute. She might be bashful and self-deprecating, even insecure, but she was usually the biggest know-it-all on the face of the earth.

"No, honey, I'm not sure. No one is, not even the doctors.

We can only follow our guts and mine tells me this is the best option."

"Okay." For better or worse, she seemed to be resigned. "Will you come with me to tell them?"

"You've got it." He put his hand at the small of her back and nudged her forward. They'd do this together.

Four hours later, Win sat in the waiting room at Dignity Health Hospital in Sacramento. He made the two-hour drive in ninety minutes, which was saying something for a Sunday when half of Northern California was driving home from the mountains. Darcy had come on the flight with Hilde, who was barely hanging on and hooked up to so many breathing apparatuses that you could hardly recognize her.

If, by the grace of God, she stabilized, Dignity's medical team would perform the procedure. Otherwise, they were afraid she'd stroke out on the table. Darcy had finally reached her parents and they were on their way.

For now, it was a waiting game.

"All they had were these. Sorry." Darcy handed him some kind of a premade juice smoothie, which was fine by him, and snagged a seat. "Thanks for sitting watch. I needed a walk to clear my head."

Win took her by the hand and gazed into her eyes. "I'm here for you."

He'd never said that to a woman before and the knowledge socked him in the gut like a sledgehammer. Yet, she'd told him she was done. Done with him, done with what they could be. As far as he was concerned they hadn't even gotten started.

"You don't have to stay with me," she said. "My parents are coming and I know you have better things to do."

"Better things to do?" He cocked his brows. "Is it that difficult for you to understand that I want to be here with you?" *That I want you to need me*? *That I need you*?

Her eyes held him as if she were trying to grasp that he actually wanted to do something for her without expecting anything in return. He wasn't fucking Lewis. Or Geneva. He didn't want her to organize his files, suck in her stomach, or jump through crazy hoops to make him happy. He just wanted her to be. Just be.

She swallowed hard. Her eyes filled and she rested her head on his shoulder. "I'm not really good at taking help."

"Ya think?"

Chapter Twenty-One

Geneva was driving Darcy crazy, bossing around the nurses, asking every five seconds if she'd called Lewis, and generally being a pain in the ass. Darcy didn't know what was taking her father so long to get to the hospital but maybe it wasn't so terrible. Geneva was already on a tear about "your cheating father" and his "tramp girlfriend." It was probably better to keep them apart for as long as possible.

Win had gone home to get her clothes, figuring she'd be in Sacramento for a while. In her wildest dreams, she never would've expected him to be the person she'd lean on in a crisis.

Win was the guy you called for fun, not to make life-or-death decisions. Yet, that had been exactly what he'd done. When she'd been paralyzed with fear over Nana's care, he'd come to the rescue. *Reliable*, *empathetic*, *thoughtful* were not usually the words that people used to describe Win but he'd been all those things for her.

"Let's go to the cafeteria," Geneva said. "It's not like we're doing any good here."

The nurse had brought in a few chairs and Darcy had

been sitting next to Nana like a mother hen, waiting for her vital signs to improve.

"All right." It was late and the food service was probably closed but they could get a cup of coffee.

They went down the elevator and found a mostly empty cafeteria with only one person at the cash register and as she'd predicted the kitchen was closed. Darcy grabbed a cup of coffee and perused the cases of prepackaged foods, grabbing a bag of Oreos.

"You really don't need that, Darcy." Geneva took the package of cookies out of her hand.

Normally passive when it came to Geneva's demands, Darcy lost it. "I haven't eaten since breakfast, Mother. And if I want to stuff my face with cookies it's my damned right."

"You don't have to get testy about it." Geneva eyed Darcy's shorts and polo shirt. "I'm only trying to look out for you . . . for your figure."

"I don't need anyone to look out for my figure, my figure is just fine. Better than fine. Nana could well be dying. The last thing I care about right now is how I look." She snatched the cookies back, tore open a package of crumb cakes, and shoved one in her mouth just to be spiteful. The only thing Geneva hated more than Darcy eating junk food was people who ate their groceries in the store without paying for them first. She thought it was *uncouth*.

Well, Darcy thought Geneva was uncouth.

"I'm sorry."

The apology took Darcy aback. She hadn't even known the words existed in Geneva's vocabulary.

"We're both under stress," Darcy said, though Geneva's criticism was standard operating procedure.

"Yes. But I shouldn't tell you how to eat. It's awful."

Another shock for the ages. Her first impulse was to tell

Geneva it was fine, that Darcy wasn't insulted, but she was sick to death of being passive-aggressive. "You're right, it is. It's also hurtful and has given me a life-long complex."

Geneva looked away but not before Darcy saw tears in her eyes. "I'm sorry for that as well. Apparently, my preoccupation with perfection lost me a family."

Darcy wasn't sure if her mother was playing martyr. "You haven't lost me, Mother."

"I've lost your father."

Darcy started to say this wasn't the time for Geneva to whine about her pending divorce. Nana was hanging on by a thread and today wasn't about Geneva. But Darcy noticed a shadow of desolation pass over her mother's face that was so poignant it made her stop.

She wiped an empty table with a handful of napkins and told her mother to sit. "Are you okay?"

There was a long pause, then Geneva cleared her throat. "I should've been better to you . . . to Max . . . to Hilde. And now it's too late."

"It's not too late for me, Mother," Darcy whispered because she was having trouble finding her voice. "I'm still here . . . I'm still with you."

Geneva teared up. "I was the last person you called when Hilde had to be rushed to the hospital. I'm your mother and yet I was the last person you called."

"You were second because Dad's her son," Darcy argued. But her mother was right. She'd called Geneva out of obligation, not because she thought her mother would lend her moral support or a shoulder to cry on.

"That's not what I mean and you know it. You love me, Darcy, because I'm your mother. But you don't like me. And I can't say I blame you. Since Max left I've been taking a hard look at myself and there's not a lot to like."

Her mother spoke the truth so Darcy did too. "There

could be, you just need to stop being so critical. Do you know what it's like to never be able to live up to your mother's expectations? To never be good enough? To never be beautiful enough or smart enough, or successful enough?" Darcy closed her eyes. "It's crushing. It's scarring. It's . . . heartbreaking." She turned away so her mother wouldn't see the stream of tears running down her face.

Geneva reached across the table and touched her arm. "I just wanted you to reach your full potential. Don't you see, I only had your best interests in mind?"

She said it like Darcy had been a slacker. Someone who sat around all day, cramming her face with Doritos, and failing school. But she'd been a good student, a good employee, a good wife, and where had it gotten her? "Maybe I'd already reached it, maybe I was all I was going to be. Why couldn't that be good enough? Why?"

"You were good enough, Darcy. You're a wonderful daughter, more than any mother could hope for. The problem's with me, not you. In my eyes, I couldn't be a perfect mother unless I cured you of all my insecurities."

"As a result, you made them mine, Mother."

"I'm just starting to become aware of that." Geneva's voice sounded so sad that Darcy wanted to reach out and touch her. But the past had made that difficult, her mother had always been untouchable. "Do you think we could ever have a relationship? A real relationship."

"I don't know," Darcy said honestly. She wanted to. She'd always envied mother-daughters who were close, who actually enjoyed shopping or eating at restaurants together. But her resentment for Geneva ran deep. "I'd like to try. But first you have to understand that I'm not always going to be who you want me to be or do what you want me to do. Lewis, for instance. We're never getting back together, Mother. Never."

Geneva started to open her mouth and stopped herself. "I realize that. I suppose it took me long enough but I've come to terms with the fact that it's over. That man, the handsome one with the funny name, the one who lied to me, does he mean something to you, Darcy?"

She wanted to say no, that he was just a friend and a colleague, but she'd never been a good liar. "Yes." It didn't matter, though. Win was a great many things. Friend, lover, coworker. But a committed partner he was not.

Geneva didn't say anything. Darcy got the impression she didn't like Win and was pretty sure the feeling was mutual.

"We should probably get up there and see how Nana is doing," she said.

Geneva rose slowly. For the first time, Darcy noticed the crow's-feet around her mother's eyes and the wilting flesh around her lower jaw. Geneva Wallace had always been the picture of youth and beauty. Not so much anymore. It suddenly made Darcy sad. They'd lost so much time together. So much precious time.

"I love you, Mother."

Geneva came around the table and hugged her. "I love you, too, Darcy. I have always loved you."

Three days later, Nana rallied enough to have the procedure, though it was touch and go. Despite being awake and lucid, Darcy had never seen her grandmother this frail. She seemed to have dropped ten pounds and her color was chalky. Fearing a stroke, her doctors decided to keep her in the hospital a few extra days for observation.

By the fifth day, Darcy was climbing the walls and decided to return to Glory Junction long enough to sleep in her own bed and retrieve a fresh nightgown and clothes for

Nana to come home in. Max and Geneva had both gotten hotel rooms so they could be there round-the-clock and their constant bickering was driving Darcy nuts. A short reprieve was exactly what she needed.

Although TJ had threatened her with bodily injury if she stepped one foot in GA, she went to the office anyway. Just for an hour or two to catch up and find out what was going on with the FlashTag account, she told herself.

Win had come to the hospital a couple of times and had sat with her and her parents throughout the entire three-hour procedure. But summers at GA were busy and there were tours on the books that he couldn't reschedule and not enough experienced guides to pick up the slack. Considering all that—and the fact that he wasn't really her boyfriend—he'd gone above and beyond.

She was more appreciative than he would ever know. For the first time in her adult life, someone other than Nana had been there for her when she needed it most. The fact that it was Win was the biggest surprise of all.

"Hey." He met her at the door, sweaty and dirty and better looking than any man had a right to be. He went in for a hug and stopped himself. "I just climbed Sawtooth and am pretty ripe. How's Hilde?"

"Improving . . . I think. What's going on here?"

"Same old. No word from Madison. TJ said she's not returning his calls."

Darcy let out a breath. "She's angry that you two didn't have an affair for the ages."

Win squinted at her. "Very funny. That was never on the table."

She believed him. But a woman could dream and there were no shortages of the Madison De Wolks of the world. Beautiful, accomplished women, setting their caps for Win. It would always be like that.

"What do we do now?"

"Wait. Let TJ do some world-class sucking up." He shrugged. "Want to have lunch? I need to shower first but it shouldn't take long."

"All right." She was hungry and looking forward to something other than hospital cafeteria food. Chicken wings from Old Glory, maybe.

"You going back to Sacramento tonight?"

"First thing tomorrow."

"Good." He grinned. "Should we stay at Hilde's place or mine?"

Darcy darted a look around the lobby. "Shush. We're done with that, remember?"

"Nope. Can't say I do." He sauntered toward the men's locker room, arrogance in every step.

She went to her desk and sifted through time cards, making sure no one had screwed up her payroll system. TJ used to do it but as soon as he'd figured out that she could accomplish the work in half the time, he'd shunted the duty to her. Even after a promotion, she suspected she'd still be doing it, which was fine because she liked it. Darcy listened to voice mail and jotted down messages. Potential clients calling with questions about GA's programs and packages. Most of the pertinent information was already on the website but some wanted to talk to a human. She could understand that.

Twenty minutes later, Win stood by her desk, impatiently tapping his toe. His hair was damp and he had on fresh clothes. He smelled good, like soap and sunshine. "You don't need to do that."

"Five more minutes." She blew out a breath. Only a few days since she'd been gone and everything was already in disarray.

She managed to get the mess into some semblance of

order, grabbed her purse, and walked with Win over to Old Glory. They were approaching July but it felt more like August, hotter than a furnace. As soon as they got a table, Darcy checked her phone to see if there were any updates on Nana. Her parents promised to call if she took a turn for the worse.

"Anything?" Win asked.

"Nope. No news is good news." She would call after lunch just to make sure. "How's it been here?"

"Busy. And I missed the hell out of you." He leaned across the table and pecked her on the lips.

"What was that for?"

"Nothing." He sat back with a self-satisfying grin. "I'd kiss you for real but we're in public."

She arched a brow. "We talked about this, remember? No more kissing."

"Because of Madison? That's just bullshit and you know it."

It wasn't because of Madison. Win had dropped Madison to rush to Darcy's side when Nana went to the hospital, probably losing a lucrative account for his family's business in the process. He'd been the only person in her life besides Nana to ever put her first. If she hadn't already fallen for him that would've clinched it. "I told you from the beginning that you and I were strictly temporary."

"Yeah, that was stupid so I overruled it. We're still doing this."

"You don't get to decide," she said.

"But you do?"

A server came to the table and they ordered. Darcy scanned the restaurant to see if anyone had overheard them. The other diners seemed oblivious to the conversation, immersed in their own or their eyes pinned to the two flat screens in the bar.

When the waiter left Win persisted. "I like you, you like me, what's the problem?"

The problem was she liked him too much. And according to the physics of love, one person always got the short end of the stick and that person was always her. "It takes more than like to sustain a relationship."

He held her gaze. "The truth is I'm crazy about you and I think you're crazy about me."

He got the last part of that right. She wasn't buying the first part. Win was bored and she was his new playmate. "Right." She folded her arms over her chest, defying him to prove it.

"You don't believe me?"

"It's not that I don't believe you. I just don't think it'll last, given your revolving door policy. Besides, I'm not your type. Britney is, even though she was Looney Tunes. And she and I don't exactly truck in the same circle. You're larger than life, while most of the time no one knows I exist. You dazzle while I fade into the background, which is fine. I don't need to be the center of attention." Though she wanted to be recognized for her accomplishments. But that was enough, she didn't have to be the star of her own reality show. Whereas a spotlight followed Win wherever he went. "Women vie for your attention while I . . . Let's put it this way, no one is banging down my door to pose in a cheesecake calendar."

Win rolled his eyes. "Emphasis on cheese. Wow, I'm that shallow to you, huh?"

"Pretty much," she lied, because he was much deeper than anyone knew. But he was a sportsman who loved a challenge. An impossible mountain to climb, an extreme backcountry slope to ski, a big wave to ride, and an unwilling woman to conquer. But after laying herself bare she wanted to save a little face so she accused him of being superficial.

Their food came and they ate in stony silence. He picked up the check after a brief tug-of-war over the bill and they shuffled out, still not talking to each other. They got to GA and she was about to go inside when he steered her to his Jeep.

"What are you doing, kidnapping me?"

"We're going somewhere private where I can talk some sense into you."

"I've got stuff to do, Win. I have to check in with my grandmother."

"Go ahead. No one's stopping you." He opened the passenger side and hoisted her into the cab as if she weighed nothing, his hands drifting down her backside. The man was all hands. There was no sense fighting him so she decided to hear him out.

While he took the main road out of town she called the hospital. Nana answered and sounded better than she had in days but a nurse came in and she had to go.

"Mom and Dad are still there, right?"

"Yes, dear, and they're driving me nuts." But Darcy got the impression it was a good nuts. Hilde was happy to be surrounded by family . . . and to be alive.

"I'll see you bright and early tomorrow, Nana. Anything you want me to bring?"

"Bring Mr. December. I could use a little eye candy."

"I heard that, Mrs. Wallace," Win shouted into the phone. "I'm glad you're feeling better."

She chuckled and hung up.

"Now there's a woman with taste, unlike her granddaughter." He pulled into Reggie Brown's driveway.

"What are we doing here?"

"Looking. Reggie's out of town for two days. He's giving a tomato talk at UC Davis."

Darcy didn't ask how he knew that, figuring they'd been in touch over the cabin. "Are you getting it?"

"Not unless the deal with FlashTag goes through, which isn't looking too good."

She let out a breath. "I'm sorry, Win. You should've stuck with Madison." She turned in her seat to face him. "But what you did for me . . . I think you saved Nana's life. If it wasn't for you pushing me to transport her I think she would've . . . Thank you."

"Don't thank me, be with me." His blue eyes held hers like he was staring into her soul. "All that shit you said at Old Glory isn't who I am, Darcy. Maybe it once was but it isn't anymore. And all that stuff you said about yourself, it's crap. You're the one who's bigger than life. Anyone who doesn't see it is blind. I've never felt the things I feel for you with any other woman." He turned away and gazed out over the property. "I was hoping you'd be a part of this with me, even move in at some point."

"You're asking me to live with you?" Except for saying the *L* word, he was pulling out all the stops, she'd give him that. But how soon until he found someone or something else to entertain him?

"Yeah. If it's not this house I'll find another. Just say yes, that you'll give us a chance."

She was quiet for a long time. "You'll get bored and where will that leave me?"

"That's the thing Darcy, I won't. Every day with you is a crazy adventure, whether you're sneaking into my bed or making me follow one of your strict schedules, or popping off with your smart mouth. God, you make me laugh. And the sex is epic. You light me up, baby."

She stared across the cab at him, stunned. Could he

really mean it? A dozen thoughts filtered through her head and when she added them all up it came down to one thing. Fear. She was scared out of her mind. Divorcing Lewis had been painful and had made her feel like a fool and a failure. But she'd survived. She wasn't sure she could with Win. He had the power to destroy her.

His hand slid across the console and clasped hers. "Take a risk on me. You won't be sorry."

"I can't move in with you," she blurted. "Nana needs me now more than ever."

He nodded. "Okay. We can work that out in the future." Future? As long as she'd known Win he'd never looked past tomorrow. "But be with me, be my girlfriend. The rest of it is just details to be figured out later. You're good at that kind of stuff. Come on, Darce, just say yes."

She wanted to, she really did. But it felt like she was back at the zip line, staring 250 feet below.

"What would this girlfriend thing entail?" She was stalling.

He smirked like he knew he was about to seal the deal. "Lots of sex for one. Your Nana's pie and us being a team."

"I don't like sports." That was the other thing. He better not expect her to suddenly become a hiker or a biker. There was zero chance of her skiing anytime soon and she was allergic to kayaks.

"I don't mean that kind of team. Leave the adventure sports to me. I'm talking about an emotional partnership."

"You're laying it on a little thick, don't you think?"

He pulled her over the center of the Jeep into his lap and kissed her silly. "This is a better use of that smart mouth of yours. This settles it. We're together now."

She hadn't committed to anything but that was Win for you. Presumptuous and infuriating and . . . Mm. He was kissing her and she couldn't think. Her body was too busy responding to his with a throbbing ache that set her on fire. They were fogging up the windshield when his cell rang. He glanced at the caller ID on his dashboard phone holder. They both recognized the number.

"What?" Win answered, trying to catch his breath.

Darcy couldn't make out the other end of the conversation. Win listened while TJ rattled on. She pulled her shirt down and flipped open the visor mirror to check her hair, her pulse still pounding. Darcy loved Win Garner. There it was, pure and simple. Like a million women before her, she loved him.

And against her better judgment she was going to take the leap and put her faith in him not to make mincemeat of her heart.

"Madison called." Win put the phone back on the dash. "She wants me to come to Santa Clara and close the deal."

"What—what about me?" She wanted to be part of winning the FlashTag account as much as anyone else.

He didn't say anything for a few minutes, leaving her hanging. "She just wants me."

She let out a mirthless laugh. "Of course she does. She wants in your pants and once again I'm getting edged out . . . of getting the account." Edged out of getting Win.

He sat up straight. "What do you mean 'once again'? I've never edged you out of anything. We're equal on this."

She noted that he wasn't denying the fact that Madison was hot for him.

"I'll be the guide in charge," he continued. "Corporate team building is my specialty. She wants me to meet the staff. It seems pretty reasonable that I should visit the company, get a sense of the culture and the employees. But if you don't want me to go, I won't."

"No—no, that would be ridiculous." GA needed the account as badly as she wanted her promotion. They'd just been offered a second chance and she'd be insane, not to mention selfish, to put the kibosh on it. "You should go."

"And you should trust me."

"I do." At least she wanted to. With all her heart.

Chapter Twenty-Two

Win had pretty much all he could take of Madison De Wolk and FlashTag. Everyone at the company was great. Friendly—Madison too friendly—accommodating, and down-to-earth. But Win had never been a city or a suburban dweller and Silicon Valley was a lot of sprawl and smog. And he missed Darcy. He'd only been gone two days and he missed her like crazy, which was a million kinds of weird.

Never before had he been that hooked on a woman. Sure, he'd had his fair share of cravings that kept him seeing the same woman for a while but not anything like this. This was a bone-deep yearning. Not just for sex, but to hear her voice, her laugh, just to be near her.

The good news was it appeared that GA was going to get the account and tomorrow, after a good night's sleep, he'd be going home.

TJ had called a dozen times to check up on him, which was par for the course for his big brother, the king of control freaks. Darcy had been caught up with getting her grandmother settled in at home and hadn't had time to talk much. Hilde was weak but the prognosis for a full recovery, promising. Thank God. When he got home he was planning to go over to the house and grill them dinner to celebrate.

"Is your lobster good?" Madison picked at hers, making Win wonder if she even liked seafood.

"It's great." Though the dim lighting was driving him berserk. He liked to see what he was eating but he assumed the votive candles were supposed to be romantic. Probably Madison's idea.

The restaurant was owned by a big-deal chef, had high, open-beam ceilings and interesting structural objects on the wall, a sort of abstract interpretation of the sea floor. At the entrance, there was a huge built-in fish tank. Everything was "farm-to-table" and they served two kinds of butter—goat and cow—in handcrafted dishes with warm, crusty bread. It had a prix fixe menu with a price tag as big as California. And yet, people made reservations a year in advance. Madison apparently knew one of the investors who still had to pull strings to get them in. He would've been happy with the Vietnamese place down the street from his hotel.

At least FlashTag was footing the bill. And Madison wasn't sparing any expense, including a bottle of Screaming Eagle, Second Flight for seven hundred bucks. He checked the menu to make sure it wasn't a typo. Nope.

"Sorry, our angel investors would look askance at me dropping a few grand on the actual Cabernet," Madison said.

"What's this?" It was red, that much he knew.

"It's a combination of grapes. Merlot and Cabernet Franc, I think. The original Screaming Eagle is just Cab and it's thousands of dollars."

Insane. He'd rather spend the money on a vacation.

"Taste it." She made sure to touch his hand as she pushed his stemware closer.

All night, she'd started in again with the flirting and overt touching. A few times, she'd posed with him for selfies.

She just didn't get that this . . . them . . . wasn't happening.

It seemed pretty unprofessional for the CEO of a major company to continue to persist. Then again, social media start-ups weren't like the rest of corporate America. He'd read somewhere that the executives of a lot of these outfits sat around all day, smoking pot. Not your normal breed of suits. In fact, the dudes mostly wore jeans and hoodies and never seemed to shave. Except for the shaving part, the women dressed pretty much the same way. Some wore T-shirts under blazers. Almost everyone had an Apple watch or a Fitbit and a messenger bag strapped across their chest. It was a little like a clone bank.

Not Madison so much, though. He noticed she had a penchant for designer clothes. Tonight, she wore a fitted dress and stilettos. She looked great, very sexy. But Win simply wasn't interested.

He'd just be happy when dinner was over and he could go back to his room to get a good night's sleep. First thing in the morning, he was heading back to Glory Junction.

"What do you think?" she asked as he took a sip.

He didn't want to seem ungrateful but it tasted like wine. "Wow, it's something else."

"Right?" The toe of her shoe brushed his calf and he moved his leg away, trying to be subtle.

"You eat rich foods like this all the time?" Win had noticed that FlashTag brought food in for its employees every day. Pasta, sandwiches, soups, everything you could imagine. One day there was even a taco bar, beer, and margaritas. Right in the middle of the day. They were pretty laid-back in the adventure business but nothing like Silicon Valley. The place was off the hook with perks.

"Are you kidding? I mostly grab food on the run. But I wanted to do something nice for you because you drove all this way and you've been so great." She leaned across the table, giving him a generous peek down her cleavage.

Win felt as if he was on a slippery slope. "Not necessary, but much appreciated. GA is looking forward to some serious team building with FlashTag." *That's right, keep it strictly business.*

"I like the way you think." She made it sound like he'd been talking about sex. "Now that we've got this thing sown up, I think we should celebrate."

He held up his hundred-dollar glass of wine. "Isn't that what we're doing?"

"We can do better than this." She twirled the red liquid, her eyes never leaving his. "I think we should go back to your room after dinner?"

Whoa, talk about being direct. Win was used to being propositioned on a fairly regular basis but she just came right out with it, no beating around the bush. He liked her style. You want something, go after it. But he still wasn't interested.

"Ah, Madison, we talked about this. Besides the fact that it's unprofessional, I'm involved with Darcy." Was he? She'd never actually said yes to his proposal. The truth was he didn't know where he stood with her.

"I'd wondered about that," she said. "The way you took off when her grandmother got sick . . . well, it was very commendable. I convinced myself that you were just really good friends because she doesn't seem like your type at all."

Win thought it was presumptuous of her. She barely knew him; how would she know what his type was?

"No offense to Darcy," she continued. "But she seems . . . just not what I would expect for someone like you."

Yeah, what was that? The implication pissed him off.

"It's funny because I never thought I had a type until I fell in love with Darcy." Love. Whoa, that's what this was. He loved Darcy Wallace. The knowledge roared through his head like a freight train. For the first time maybe ever, he was in love. No one had ever made him feel the way Darcy did. From the night she'd crawled into his bed, he hadn't been the same. She tested him, captivated him, turned him on to the point where he couldn't keep his hands off her. But most of all, she got him and he got her. No artifice, just a hundred-percent real.

"That must be why I never fell in love before." He put down his glass. "Because Darcy's my only type. She's the one, the only one." He smiled because the revelation made him ridiculously happy.

He was in love. Crazy in love with Darcy Wallace.

"Why didn't you just tell me from the get-go, instead of letting me make a fool of myself?" she asked, but didn't sound angry, just curious.

"You didn't make a fool of yourself, Madison. Darcy and I are pretty new and you and I . . ." he said, winking. "We'll always have Alaska."

They laughed like two old friends.

"Do you have any single brothers?" she asked. "I take it TJ's off the market."

Win grinned because not too long ago they'd all been single and miserable. "I'm afraid we're all taken."

"All the good ones always are."

She paid the bill and took him back to the hotel, a big high-rise with an indoor pool, decent gym, and a couple of bars and restaurants. Instead of going straight to his room, he wandered into the lounge in the lobby and ordered a beer. He found a spot near one of the flat screens to watch the baseball game, hoping that by the time he went up to bed, Darcy would be available to talk on the phone. He just wanted to hear her voice.

Halfway through his beer, a group of women invaded his space and tried to chat him up. He wanted quiet so he took the elevator up to the ninth floor. In the room, he stripped out of his clothes, turned on the game, took a quick shower, and sank into the bed. It was the first chance he had to check his messages so he propped a few pillows behind his head and scrolled through e-mail on his phone. Nothing that couldn't wait until he got home. He noticed there were a couple of alerts on his FlashTag app. Darcy had downloaded the damned thing on his cell to make a good impression.

For shits and giggles, he tapped on the logo and waited for the site to come up. And uh-oh . . . there were two pictures of Madison sitting in his lap. He remembered her taking the photo at the restaurant. An innocent pose for an innocent selfie. But the snapshots, with the lighting of the restaurant and the placement of Madison's hands, looked anything but innocent. It looked more like a spread in *Maxim* magazine.

"Shit, shit, shit," Win chanted as he jumped out of bed, found a clean pair of pants, and shoved them on. This was exactly the kind of crap Darcy expected of him. He grabbed his discarded phone and dialed her number. But she didn't answer. He called Hilde and nothing. Where the hell was she? She was supposed to be bedridden. "Shit," he yelled again.

Darcy had also downloaded the app on her phone and while she wasn't a huge social media user, this stuff had a tendency to spread. Screw it. He decided to make the 220-mile drive tonight. Nip this shit in the bud.

He called down to the valet to get his Jeep and raced down the stairs with his duffel. Silicon Valley traffic was legendary and he was going to be right in the thick of it. But he didn't give a damn. He had to get home and explain to Darcy that the pictures were nothing and there was a better than good chance she wouldn't believe him.

As he sat on I-680 in a parking lot of automobiles, he had a come-to-Jesus moment. Darcy wasn't the only insecure partner in this relationship. All his life, he'd used his charm and good looks to worm his way into people's lives. He'd collected them like baseball cards and discarded them just as easily. It was never his intention to hurt anyone but it had always been his way of fitting in, of being more than he thought he was.

He should've told Madison from the beginning that he was in love with Darcy. And that he was a one-woman man.

By the time he got to Sacramento, he tried her cell and home phone at least twenty more times, leaving more than a dozen messages. He was almost tempted to call Colt to do a welfare check and was starting to fear that Hilde had wound up in the hospital again.

Win pulled off at one of the exits to get gas and a cup of coffee to make the rest of the drive home. While he sat at the pump, he dialed TJ.

"How'd it go?" his brother asked by way of greeting. Always the freaking businessman.

"Good. Madison said she'll call you Monday to work out the details but she's gonna sign. Hey, you wouldn't happen to know where Darcy is, would you?"

"She was at work today. Why?"

Win didn't want to get into the photos. TJ would chalk it up to Win being up to his usual tricks. "I've been trying to call her to tell her I'm on my way home but she hasn't been answering. I'm concerned about Hilde."

"Haven't heard anything. You want me to cruise by Mrs. Wallace's house and check up on them?"

He did but what good would it do? He already knew they weren't home or someone would've answered the goddamn phone. And if an ambulance had been called TJ would know. That kind of an emergency spread through Glory Junction faster than a brush fire in summer. "Nah, I'll be home in a couple of hours." No need pulling TJ into his soap opera. There was a good chance Darcy already knew about the photos and was ignoring his calls.

He hit more traffic outside of Sacramento, folks driving to the mountains for the weekend. At this rate, it would take him forever to get home. At ten, he finally pulled up to Hilde's house. Darcy's Volkswagen was nowhere to be seen and his stomach lurched. She'd either gotten the hell out of Dodge as soon as she'd seen those pictures or Hilde had taken a turn for the worse.

It was too late to knock on the door but he wasn't going to wait for a decent hour. He got out of his Jeep and rang the bell. All the lights were out and no one answered. He pressed the heel of his hand against his eyes and broke down and called Colt.

"Everything okay?"

He heard a TV on in the background. "I don't know. I just rolled in and Darcy and her grandmother aren't home. I've been trying to call her all night."

Win heard Colt shuffling around. He was probably turning off the television or moving to a different room.

"As far as I know there was no emergency response to the house but it's Jack's night. You could call Sierra General but with HIPAA law they won't be able to tell you anything. All you can do is wait and keep trying to call her. What about her parents? You have their phone number?"

He didn't. "No. I'll just hang out here and keep trying her. Sorry I called so late. I hope I didn't wake up Delaney."

"It's only ten. Call me when you know something. I don't care what time it is."

Win smiled to himself. He had a good family. A damned good family. "Roger that."

An hour later and still nothing. Tired of waiting in his Jeep, he got out to stretch his legs. A pair of lights came up the drive and he sighed with relief until he saw the car. It was an Audi. He didn't know anyone who owned an Audi.

A tall, older dude got out of the vehicle. It was hard to tell with only the porch light on, but he didn't look particularly menacing. "Can I help you?"

Win approached him. "I guess I could ask the same. This is my girlfriend's grandmother's house. They're not home right now."

The man opened the passenger door and there was Hilde. "Win?" she shielded her eyes from the glare of the porch light. "Is that you? This is my son, Max."

Darcy's dad. "Pleased to meet you." He stuck out his hand and Max shook it. "Where's Darce, Mrs. Wallace?"

"She's not home?"

"Nope. Not answering her phone either."

"I'm sure she just went out with friends after work. I was supposed to stay overnight with Max in Reno and realized I forgot my medication."

Win thought she looked good, not at all like someone who'd just gone under the knife.

"Come in the house," she told Win.

Max carried a floral overnight bag, which Win assumed was Hilde's, and put it in her bedroom. "I'm heading home, Mom."

"Don't be silly. I dragged you all the way here in the middle of the night. Stay over."

Max gave Win a cool assessment and apparently determined he wasn't a threat. "It's best that I go now. I have a tee time at eight."

"All right, dear, drive carefully." She kissed him goodbye and as soon as he left the house said, "He couldn't wait to get back to that girlfriend of his."

"Darcy told me about that." And now she was going to

look at him the same way. As a cheater. "So you have no idea where she is, huh?"

"My guess is she used the opportunity of not having to babysit me to get out on a Friday night. It's only eleven. I wouldn't worry. You're welcome to wait for her here, watch TV, whatever you like. But I'm going to turn in. I still don't have all my energy back and frankly my son is exhausting."

He winked at her. "You're looking pretty spry to me, Mrs. Wallace. Next week we're going rock climbing."

She chuckled and headed off to bed. He wandered around the house for a bit. It was small and there wasn't much to see but he'd always liked the cottage. It felt like a place that hugged you when you came home. If Darcy was still talking to him he hoped they could make their house together feel the same way.

He checked his phone again but it was useless. This time he'd screwed up for good.

It was after midnight when Darcy got home. Her mother had wanted her to stay the night but she'd rushed back to Glory Junction from Reno as soon as she'd learned that her grandmother was there alone. Her phone had lost its charge earlier in the day and she'd been keeping tabs on Hilde, using her mother's cell.

She carried her packages up the stairs. Geneva had insisted on buying Darcy some new summer clothes and for the first time in her life, she hadn't resented her mother's choices. After a rather lovely shopping spree, they'd had dinner at a new, trendy restaurant, and had caught a movie. Then she'd made the thirty-five-minute trip home.

She turned on the light in her bedroom and found a naked Win in her bed. He jolted upright and rubbed his eyes.

"You weren't supposed to be home until tomorrow," she said.

"Surprise!" He seemed a bit tentative, like he was checking her reaction to him being in her bedroom in her grandmother's house with that amazing body of his on display.

It reminded her of her own visit to his studio apartment and she giggled. A God's honest girly giggle.

"You haven't seen them, have you?"

"Seen what?" She put her bags down.

He crooked his finger. "Come to bed and I'll show you."

"Does my grandmother know you're here?" She let her eyes roam over him. All of him and he was pretty sure she purred like a cat.

"Yep. She's good with it."

Darcy didn't doubt it. Hilde was no prude, that was for sure. She kicked off her shoes and started to join Win on the bed.

"Take off your clothes first."

"Did we get the account?" She pulled her blouse over her head and watched Win's eyes heat as he took in her lacy bra. Since they'd been seeing each other, she'd invested in much better lingerie.

"Yep. But I've got to talk to you."

It sounded serious but for some reason she wasn't alarmed. She finished undressing and crawled under the covers next to him. "Tell me."

He rolled her under him and came up on both elbows so he wouldn't crush her. "I love you. I know I told you I was crazy about you, that I wanted to be with you, but while I was gone I had time to think. And the realization hit me like a twenty-foot wave. I'm so freaking in love with you, Darcy, that I'm crazy with it. I think about you constantly, always want to be with you, and . . . you're the best thing that's ever happened to me and I'd never do anything to screw that up." He slid off her and hung over the floor, searching for his pants. After fishing his phone out of the pocket, he tapped the FlashTag app on his screen and handed it to her. "It's not what it looks like. It was just Madison being Madison. I told her I'm with you, that I love you. You believe me, right?"

He flopped onto his back and shielded his eyes with his hand.

She pushed a couple of pillows behind her head and inspected the pictures for a good long time. "What's up with your hair in this one?"

"Huh?" He scooted up so he could have a better look. "I think it's just the lighting. Well, are you pissed?"

She kept studying them. Madison definitely looked like she'd had one too many and Win was wearing his slightly bored look. Darcy had seen it more times than she could count at GA's morning meetings while TJ prattled on about profits and losses.

"Say something, dammit."

She blew a lock of hair out of her eyes. "There's not much to say other than I've seen you take better pictures."

"Nothing happened. I swear."

She tossed the phone onto his side of the bed. "I believe you."

"You do?"

It was mean but she sort of enjoyed the look of shock on his face. "Why would you lie to me? If you wanted to be with Madison, you'd just dump me. You've always been a player, not a cheater. No one has ever said that about you. And for as much as this town talks, especially about you, the word would be out by now."

She picked the phone back up and pointed at the photograph. "What is that?"

Win squinted at the screen. "Some kind of raviolis in cream sauce."

"It looks good. Really rich, though."

"They were . . . and why the hell are we talking about food? Come here." He pulled her on top of him. "I love you. Do you love me?"

"Yes."

"That's all you're going to say? Just yes?"

"Did you want poetry?"

Win seemed to contemplate the question. "Yeah, I sort of do. Tell me why you love me."

She looked down into his face and melted into his blue, blue eyes. "Because you're really good-looking?"

"Ah, come on, that's bullshit," he huffed, and she laughed.

"It's simple: You make me blindingly happy, Win Garner." He was the first thing she thought of in the morning and the last person she wanted to see at night. He was her everything. "At first, I was afraid to love you, afraid that you'd let me down. But I've also had time to think and something my mother told me made an impression. She said she'd felt as if she couldn't be a perfect mother unless she cured me of all her insecurities. In a way, I was doing the same thing with you. I'd convinced myself that you were a bad bet, totally unreliable, because I was really insecure about myself. The truth is you're the most reliable man I've ever known and you know what proved it to me?"

"What?"

"When Nana got sick. You were willing to make the call on her care so if things went south I wouldn't blame myself." Her eyes teared up and she wiped them with the back of her hand. "You did that for me. It was a selfless gift and I'll never forget it. I love you, Win Garner. And I'm not afraid anymore."

He jiggled his hand from side to side. "That's not bad but I would've liked more. Maybe something about how the birds sing whenever I'm near."

"Are you actually quoting a Carpenters song? I hate the Carpenters."

"But you love me." He waggled his brows, then peeled off her really good lingerie, and pulled her beneath him.

She found the light switch and in the darkness, they found each other. Their hands, their mouths, their bodies melded in the sweet summer heat. And somewhere in the distance she heard birds chirp and a cricket sing, and her heart soared.

Epilogue

There was enough food to feed an army—or the Garner family. Darcy kept adding dishes to the long picnic table Reggie Brown had left at the log cabin. Some kind of tortilla surprise Deb made, which kind of looked scary, to tell the truth. Pies from Nana and Hannah. A case of craft beer from Colt and Delaney. Mary and Gray had brought a big bowl of fruit salad. Besides a beautiful floral arrangement, Foster came with fresh bread. Boden a huge tub of chicken wings and Rachel brought cupcakes—the cute ones with the GA logo.

They were off in a corner, fighting about something. Darcy had no idea what had set them off but it appeared that the baker and bartender didn't like each other too much. She was staying out of it, going for a drama-free afternoon if that was at all possible.

Josh grabbed a couple more folding chairs from the deck and put them around the table. And Geneva helped Darcy put out more settings as the guests arrived. Her father and his new girlfriend sat on the dock with their feet in the river. It was more than a little awkward to have both her parents and Max's concubine (Geneva's word, not

Darcy's) under the same roof but they'd all promised to
behave.

Lucy and Ricky had jumped out of Gray's truck and had
hit the water, running. Darcy couldn't blame them. Late
August had brought record-high heat but it was shady
under the trees.

If the bugs didn't bite them to death, they planned to eat
alfresco. Win had strung twinkly lights in the trees so when
it got dark they could keep the party going. He'd piled
wood by the fire pit for s'mores later. And Darcy suspected
that by the end of the day, half of them would wind up in
the river like the dogs.

The place needed a lot of work but with Win's dad and
brothers they could do much of the rehab on their own.
Nana was trying to talk Win into adding a hummingbird
garden to the yard. Darcy said they should just hire a gardener before they killed everything. But Nana promised to
help. Every day she was looking stronger. Even her doctors
were impressed with how quickly she was recovering.

As Darcy gazed around the property her throat clogged.
It was such a happy home, a house she knew would hold a
lot of memories.

Next month, she was moving in with Win and though
there'd been no official proposal, they'd knocked around
the idea of a spring wedding. In the meantime, Geneva was
planning to stay at Nana's house until she found something
of her own. Max had bought her out of the mausoleum and
Geneva was thinking of starting her own mortgage brokerage firm in Glory Junction. Darcy still didn't know how
she felt about that. But she and her mother were slowly
mending fences and taking the time to get to know each
other.

As for Win, Geneva still wasn't a fan. She appeared to
be the only woman in the Western world, besides Ricki,

that is, who wasn't bowled over by Win Garner's charm. But Darcy had no doubt that she would eventually come around. The good news is that she'd given up on Darcy ever reconciling with Lewis. And for his part, Lewis had stopped calling. Last Darcy heard, he'd hired a really good IT person and someone to keep the books.

"Hey, VP, nice spread you've got here." TJ draped his arm over her shoulder. Ever since he'd promoted her to GA's vice president of operations he'd been calling her VP. As obnoxious as it was, she liked the ring of it.

"Thanks. It's a good home, isn't it?"

"Hell yeah, and for the price, this thing will appreciate tenfold." He launched into a lecture about the worth of California real estate. Darcy listened politely, even though she'd heard this spiel at least a dozen times. Finally, she saw Deb in the distance and used needing to talk to her as an excuse to leave the conversation.

"Is he talking about real estate again?" Deb rolled her eyes, then gazed at the river. "It's a sweet piece of property, though. And the house is perfect. You guys will get it all fixed up, put your own personal touch on it, especially now with the extra income."

Darcy had gotten a nice raise and now that Win was taking on more responsibility at GA, he'd be making more money, too.

"It looks like we'll be teaming up with Lucky Rodriguez on a few projects," Darcy said. Win had made that happen and she thought the cowboy camp would be a great option to offer their clients. "I think it'll really round out our portfolio to have the dude ranch at our disposal, don't you?"

"Oh God, not you, too." Deb laughed. "For a minute I thought you were my husband."

"Great place." Colt strolled over with a plate in his hand. Darcy had never seen a person eat so much or so often. He watched the dogs drag a stick from the river. "I think we should work on the dock first. There's still enough time this summer to use it."

That was a Garner for you. "Don't you think the roof should come first?"

"Nah." Colt looked up at the sky. "We've got time before the rainy season."

Darcy shook her head. "Whatever Win wants to do." But she knew he would side with Colt. He was champing at the bit to make the rickety old thing functional so he could launch his boats and kayaks from it.

"Hey, good-looking." Win grabbed her around the waist and swung her in the air. "I've got the grill going and the wood chips soaking. How 'bout you and I disappear for a few minutes?" He didn't wait, just tugged her away from Colt and Deb without caring that it was rude.

She looked at him suspiciously. "You're not going to do something crazy like propose in front of all our family and friends?"

"Nah, I've got that worked out. It'll be private, just the two of us. I promise."

"Thank you." She looped her arms around his neck and he lifted her and carried her away with her legs wrapped around his hips. "Where we going?"

"Somewhere where we can be alone, even if it's just for a few minutes." He took her around the side of the house and they sat on a log. "What's the deal with your parents?"

Darcy shrugged. "They've promised to be good. So far, no plates have been broken and no curse words have been hurled. Mother was even cordial to the 'concubine.'"

Win laughed. "As long as you're okay with them being here. Because this is all about celebrating your promotion." He waved his hand at the house and the property. "And about us. Our future. The future of our kids."

She liked the sound of that. "We haven't really talked about that."

"Between us getting the FlashTag account, me buying the house, and you getting promoted to vice president, there hasn't been much time to talk about anything. Let's go on a vacation. We've earned it."

"Will you make me hike and bike and climb mountains?"

"Not if you don't want to. We could just hole up in a hotel in the wilderness and have sex twenty-four-seven."

"Works for me." She crawled into his lap and he wrapped his arms around her.

"Kiss me now and then we'll go back and entertain our guests. Colt's probably eating all the pie."

He pressed his lips against hers and the warm pull of his mouth made her hot. His taste intoxicated her.

"Mm." She closed her eyes, pressing against him.

"Give me your phone."

"Huh?"

He grabbed it out of her shorts pocket and kissed her again. This time, long and slow, making her toes curl. And as they stopped to take a breather, he snapped a picture.

"Check it out." He handed the cell to Darcy and she examined the snapshot.

As usual, Win looked like every woman's fantasy. All blue-eyed and golden-tanned. His lips curved into that half smile that never failed to stir her blood. But it was the image of her that was surprising. Her face positively glowed and she was . . . beautiful. Radiant to the point of being unrecognizable. She stared at herself and smiled.

"Let me see that." Win took the phone from her and tapped on the FlashTag app.

"What are you doing?" She tried to grab it away but he was typing.

"Showing off my hot girlfriend." He hit the post button and handed her back the phone.

The caption read, *Love you. Win.*

"Love you right back," she said, and threw her arms around him.

They kissed some more and returned to the party, arm in arm, through the trees, under a big orange Glory Junction sun.

Connect with Us

Visit us online at
KensingtonBooks.com
to read more from your favorite authors, see books
by series, view reading group guides, and more.

for sneak peeks, chances to win books and prize packs,
and to share your thoughts with other readers.

facebook.com/kensingtonpublishing
twitter.com/kensingtonbooks

Tell us what you think!

To share your thoughts, submit a review,
or sign up for our eNewsletters, please visit:
KensingtonBooks.com/TellUs.

Books by Bestselling Author
Fern Michaels

___**The Jury**	0-8217-7878-1	$6.99US/$9.99CAN
___**Sweet Revenge**	0-8217-7879-X	$6.99US/$9.99CAN
___**Lethal Justice**	0-8217-7880-3	$6.99US/$9.99CAN
___**Free Fall**	0-8217-7881-1	$6.99US/$9.99CAN
___**Fool Me Once**	0-8217-8071-9	$7.99US/$10.99CAN
___**Vegas Rich**	0-8217-8112-X	$7.99US/$10.99CAN
___**Hide and Seek**	1-4201-0184-6	$6.99US/$9.99CAN
___**Hokus Pokus**	1-4201-0185-4	$6.99US/$9.99CAN
___**Fast Track**	1-4201-0186-2	$6.99US/$9.99CAN
___**Collateral Damage**	1-4201-0187-0	$6.99US/$9.99CAN
___**Final Justice**	1-4201-0188-9	$6.99US/$9.99CAN
___**Up Close and Personal**	0-8217-7956-7	$7.99US/$9.99CAN
___**Under the Radar**	1-4201-0683-X	$6.99US/$9.99CAN
___**Razor Sharp**	1-4201-0684-8	$7.99US/$10.99CAN
___**Yesterday**	1-4201-1494-8	$5.99US/$6.99CAN
___**Vanishing Act**	1-4201-0685-6	$7.99US/$10.99CAN
___**Sara's Song**	1-4201-1493-X	$5.99US/$6.99CAN
___**Deadly Deals**	1-4201-0686-4	$7.99US/$10.99CAN
___**Game Over**	1-4201-0687-2	$7.99US/$10.99CAN
___**Sins of Omission**	1-4201-1153-1	$7.99US/$10.99CAN
___**Sins of the Flesh**	1-4201-1154-X	$7.99US/$10.99CAN
___**Cross Roads**	1-4201-1192-2	$7.99US/$10.99CAN

Available Wherever Books Are Sold!
Check out our website at **www.kensingtonbooks.com**